AN APPARITION FROM THE PAST

Lenoir knelt over the body and moved the man's collar to take a look at his neck. He had expected to find rope burns, but what he saw there instead caused him to cry out and stumble backward onto his rump.

Impossible!

He scrambled to his feet, but then his body failed him, refusing to obey his command to flee. Instead he stood rooted to the spot, staring. His mind buzzed uselessly. He could not be sure how long he stood there. A minute? An hour? Whatever the case, he was thoroughly lost in his own world when he heard the voice.

"What's this?"

Lenoir jolted so badly that his knees nearly gave way. Even so, he had never been so glad to see Kody. The sergeant, for his part, appeared not to notice Lenoir's state of shock, his gaze fixed instead on the corpse lying broken among the roots. He knelt before the body for a closer look. "Neck snapped, looks like, as though he fell out of the tree. . . ."

Lenoir scarcely heard him. There was a strange roaring in his ears, a sound distantly and unpleasantly familiar, like a bad dream. A dream about a night spent huddled in the shadows, listening to the blood rushing through his veins and praying for daylight. Nowhere to hide, no one to come to his aid . . . and then the burning on his arm, the burning and the chill, the horrible sense that the warmth of his life was being sucked out through his flesh. . . .

"That's odd," Kody said. He pulled back the man's collar just as Lenoir had done. "Have you ever seen marks like this, Ins

Lenoir could n   response; when non   and
turned back to th   has

d . . .

been . . . I don't know. The skin is gray, as if he's been dead for days, but the rest of him looks . . . Well, I'd say he's only been dead a few hours."

Lenoir understood the sergeant's confusion. He understood that it should not be possible for some of the body's flesh to be necrotic while the rest was not. Not unless the man had had some sort of terrible infection. . . . Lenoir experienced a brief twinge of hope at this thought, but it disappeared immediately. There was no infection, he knew. There was only one possibility.

Like judgment, like death, the green-eyed man had caught up with him at last. . . .

DARKWALKER

A NICOLAS LENOIR NOVEL

E. L. Tettensor

A ROC BOOK

ROC
Published by the Penguin Group
Penguin Group (USA) LLC, 375 Hudson Street,
New York, New York 10014

USA | Canada } UK } Ireland | Australia | New Zealand | India | South Africa | China
penguin.com
A Penguin Random House Company

First published by Roc, an imprint of New American Library,
a division of Penguin Group (USA) LLC

First Printing, December 2013

 REGISTERED TRADEMARK — MARCA REGISTRADA

ISBN 978-0-451-41998-9

Printed in the United States of America
10 9 8 7 6 5 4 3 2 1

To Don, for his support;
Joshua, for his guidance;
Jessie, for her enthusiasm;
My family and friends, for their encouragement;
and Reuben, for Zach.

This book is a gift of

**THE FRIENDS
OF THE
MORAGA LIBRARY**

Moraga Branch, Contra Costa County Library

CHAPTER 1

*I*n the dark hours of a frostbitten morning, someone is
digging. He is alone, unobserved, the sounds of his
toil smothered by the mist that clings like a death shroud
to the headstones. An icicle moon hangs in the sky, its
cold light partially obscured by the naked branches of
oak trees. Below, veins of shadow thicken and throb
over the uneven ground. It is here that he attacks, plung-
ing the point of the spade into the breast of the earth,
twisting, steam leaking from the wound as he gouges his
way deeper.

He mutters to himself as he digs. He resents being
here, surrounded by cold and damp and death. He cannot fathom why he has been asked to do this, to unearth
what has already been buried, to revisit what has already been decided. He shudders as he thinks on it. It is
truly sickening, what he has been sent here to do. Ex-
huming the body of a child is gruesome enough to dis-
turb even him, a man who has known more of death
than of life. But he keeps digging all the same. He has
been well paid, and besides, he is not the sort of man

who believes in Judgment. He cannot imagine what it means to be damned.

Sergeant Bran Kody blew into his hands, rubbing them briskly together in the morning chill. He should've brought gloves. It was always damp in this bloody swamp. Surrounded by marshlands and bisected by the Charan River, Brackensvale suffered from a perpetual plague of mist, especially on a late-autumn day like this. The fog had nowhere to go, trapped within the close dark wood that encroached on the town, choking out light and suffocating sound. Through the haze, it was just possible to make out tiny dwellings of soggy timber that hunched between the trees, their sagging rooftops furred with moss and freckled with mildew. So disfigured, they practically disappeared into the surrounding forest, misshapen heaps of brown and sickly yellow that seemed to hide among the trees as though ashamed to be seen. The eye refused to linger on these decaying shacks, instead passing quickly over them, as over a cripple in the street. The air smelled of rotting leaves, wood smoke, and the subtly cloying odor of the swamp. Not for the first time, Kody wondered why anyone lived here.

"Nothing like this has ever happened before," the priest was saying, his breath blooming in the cold. "This village is a quiet place. We are pious people. I cannot believe that anyone in Brackensvale would commit such an evil as this."

Kody didn't have to glance at his superior; he knew

well enough the expression that would be on Lenoir's face. A sardonic smile twisting the thin lips, smug eyes narrowing above the long nose. Kody had seen it dozens of times before. At every crime scene, there was always someone—usually a priest—who insisted that the perpetrator couldn't possibly be from the local area. The truth almost always proved otherwise, the vast majority of crimes being committed by someone known to the victim. But civilians couldn't be expected to know that, and besides, these people were in a state of shock. They deserved a little indulgence, in Kody's opinion. Inspector Lenoir, though, rarely bothered to mask his contempt.

"Oh no?" said Lenoir lightly. "We should not bother to question anyone in the village, then?" His throaty accent somehow heightened the sarcasm.

The priest flushed slightly. "I only meant that none of my parishioners would have disturbed the child's rest. Why, the entire village attended his burial!"

The inspector ignored that. Turning to the father, he said, "Do you have enemies, sir? Anyone who would want to hurt you?"

The father shook his head stiffly. His hands were on his wife's shoulders, steadying her. The woman had stopped weeping, but she still looked as though she might swoon. Kody studied her carefully, searching for . . . *What, exactly, Sergeant?* he chided himself inwardly. *The parents have no reason to lie. If they'd wanted their kid's body dug up, they needn't have done it in secret.* Besides, the woman's anguish was obviously genuine: her face was pale, drawn tightly over high cheekbones and a sharp nose, and her eyes were faded and dull.

"Maybe it was a mistake?" ventured the priest. "Some kind of accident?"

Lenoir snorted softly. Lowering himself to his haunches, he asked, "When was the grave dug?" He eyed the shallow pit, then braced his palm against the edge and dropped down inside. The earth sounded with a dull thud, like a single heartbeat.

"Two days ago," the priest said. "The child had only just passed."

"He will have started to decompose," said Lenoir, "but it is probably too soon for him to be giving off much of an odor."

The mother choked out a sob, and the father's knuckles went white as he gripped her shoulders more tightly. Kody fired his superior a withering look. Sometimes he wondered whether Nicolas Lenoir had an ounce of human feeling at all.

"These wagon ruts are fresh, Inspector," Kody said, more to banish the silence than anything else. "Maybe they'll tell us—"

"That the perpetrator drove a wagon?" Lenoir said blandly.

"Yes, sir, and also maybe where he went."

The inspector shrugged. "By all means, Sergeant, if you wish to follow the wagon ruts you may do so, but it will not get you anywhere." He hauled himself up out of the grave, a graceless maneuver that left the front of his coat covered in mud. Kody didn't offer a hand. If the man chose to let himself go like that, then he deserved to deal with the consequences on his own.

Once he had righted himself, Lenoir continued. "Even if the thief was foolish enough to have left so obvious a trail, the only way to pass through these trees with a wagon is to take the path to the west of the village where it meets the road to Kennian. A dozen or more horses and wagons will have passed down that road since yesterday, including our own. You will lose the trail before you have even begun."

The priest coughed politely to cover the embarrassment he presumed Kody was feeling. He needn't have bothered. Kody was well accustomed to being humbled by Lenoir. Besides, the inspector had a point. That was the trouble with working alongside Nicolas Lenoir. The man was impossible: arrogant, apathetic, and with a sour disposition that suggested he would rather be doing just about anything other than police work. But he was also damn good—when he could be bothered.

"If you wanted to track something, Sergeant, you would get further with the boots," Lenoir said, pointing at his feet.

Kody's gaze dropped to the footprints dimpling the freshly turned earth. *At least four sizes of them,* he noted, *maybe more. And two days' worth of coming and going around the grave. How are we supposed to know which prints are the corpse thief's?*

Lenoir answered the unspoken question. "These are the ones we are looking for." He squatted beside a print that had been partially covered by another and slowly traced his finger around the heel. "You see, Sergeant, how deep is the tread here. This is a man, large, and he is wearing heavy work boots, not everyday footwear like you or I."

Kody waited for Lenoir to flesh out the thought. It was one thing to identify what type of boots the perpetrator had been wearing. It was quite another to find the owner of the boots.

"How many people live in Brackensvale, Sergeant?" Lenoir asked, seeing Kody's skepticism.

Kody considered. "I don't know, maybe two hundred?"

"At most. This is the smallest hamlet in the Five Villages. Two hundred, of which how many are women and children?"

The priest supplied the answer: "About two-thirds, Inspector."

"Perhaps seventy men," concluded Lenoir, "and in a village of this size, no more than one or two shoemakers."

"Just the one," the priest confirmed.

"There we are. And do you suppose he could name which men in the village come to him for work boots of approximately this size?"

Kody felt the familiar flush of excitement as he realized Lenoir was right. It wasn't much, but it was certainly a start, a way to narrow down the field of possible suspects to a manageable size. "Should we measure the boot print, Inspector, or bring the shoemaker here to see it for himself?" His limbs had already begun to tingle with the thrill of the hunt.

But no sooner had he picked up the scent than Lenoir hauled back on his lead. "There is no point, Sergeant," the inspector said languidly, and he began to pull his gloves on, as though readying to leave.

Kody was momentarily too surprised to speak. The father, though, reacted immediately: he lurched forward, his hands balling into fists. "What do you mean, no point?" His voice trembled with anger, and Kody feared for a moment that he might hit the inspector.

But Lenoir faced him coolly, his expression without pity or shame. "Alas, sir, we cannot find the man who stole your son's body. It is a fruitless endeavor."

The father spoke through clenched teeth. "Didn't you just say you would be able to track the boots?"

"I said you would get further tracking the boots. But not far enough, I am afraid. These boot prints are not of an unusual size, so at least a dozen or so men in the village might fit them. And that assumes that the thief even lives here, which your good priest has insisted is not possible."

The mother started to weep again, half burying her face in her handkerchief. The father stood rooted before Lenoir, shaking with impotent rage. The priest, seemingly lost for what to do, just stared at the ground.

"But, sir," said Kody, "maybe—"

"There is nothing we can do, Sergeant." Lenoir's eyes bored into him, demanding his silence, and Kody held his tongue. Anger smoldered inside him, but he didn't dare let it show, not in front of others. That would be unprofessional.

Turning back to the father, Lenoir said, "I am truly

sorry, sir, but unless you have some idea of why someone would want to steal the body of your child, we
have no hope of finding out who did it. No hope at all."
To the priest, he said, "If you learn anything new, you
know where to find me."

With that, he walked past the still-shaking father
and across the churchyard. Kody could do nothing but
follow.

Their horses were tethered on the far side of the
church, a good distance away from the graveyard. Satisfied that they could no longer be overheard, Kody
dared a protest. "Inspector, I don't feel right about just
dropping the whole thing. Couldn't we make some inquiries in the village?"

"It is a waste of time, as I have told you." Lenoir
tightened the cinch on his saddle; his horse exhaled
sharply, expelling a frigid cloud.

"But, sir—"

Lenoir whipped around. "Enough, Sergeant! Use
your head! What good is it to chase a dozen suspects
without so much as a hint of motive? Would you have
me engage the entire Metropolitan Police on the case?
Assign one man to every suspect, trace their movements for weeks on end? Who will then patrol the
streets of Kennian? You alone, perhaps?"

"Of course not. It's just that—"

"It is just that you are using your emotions rather
than your brain. Of course it is disturbing, what has
happened. But it is also an insignificant crime. It is a
theft, and a small one at that. It is upsetting to the parents, but what they truly grieve for is their child's life,

which we cannot restore. I will not waste the resources of the Metropolitan Police in what would almost certainly prove a futile effort to recover something that is fundamentally without value."

So saying, he slung himself into the saddle and turned away, heedless of the cold glare Kody fixed against his back.

CHAPTER 2

Nicolas Lenoir strolled the main thoroughfare of Kennian, hands in the pockets of his long coat, moving at the leisurely pace of a man without purpose. This was not the same as not having a destination, for he had one: the Courtier, a rather grandly titled eating house that he frequented at least five times a week. It was not an overly convenient location; Lenoir lived more than two dozen blocks to the east, in a cramped and disordered apartment that he avoided as often as possible. But the portly cook who presided over the Courtier's bustling kitchen was the only man in all of the Five Villages who could do a passable impression of steak *serlois*. Asking for still-bloody beef anywhere else was as good as putting oneself at the mercy of the superstitious butchers that passed for physicians in this city. And though characterizing the Courtier's meat as filet was perhaps stretching the limits of credulity, at least one did not require a handsaw to cut through it.

Though Lenoir's step bent to the Courtier, he was in no hurry to arrive there. In truth, he seldom moved with much urgency—had not for years—but especially not in the evening. Though he knew it was irrational, Lenoir could not help feeling that the sooner he arrived at the eating house and took his supper, the sooner his evening would be over, whereupon he would be required to sleep. And sleep was something Nicolas Lenoir avoided for as long as possible.

For one thing, there was nothing more depressing than the morning, and one was never more conscious of the morning than when one woke to it. At least when he did not sleep, Lenoir could imagine that one day bled seamlessly into another, an endless monotony he could plod through without really marking the passage of time. But when he slept, the day ended and thus began anew. And to wake without purpose, without desire or direction, was almost enough to drive a man mad.

On top of this, Lenoir had recently developed an even more pressing reason to avoid sleep. His dreams had become strange and vivid, and though he could rarely recall them in much detail, the quickening of his heartbeat and the moistness of his brow upon waking were evidence enough of their darkness.

When he could remember, Lenoir knew he dreamed of Serles. He would wake to lingering images of her elegant galleries and cobbled plazas, of stylish ladies with billowing silken sleeves and wide bonnets trimmed with lace. Sometimes he would recall a moment in time: his steps haunting the halls of the Prefecture of Police, or passing the grim facade of Fort Sennin. Once he even woke with the tantalizing scent of glazed strawberry tarts in his nose.

Those were the hardest mornings, when Lenoir was confronted rudely by his past. Usually it invaded subtly: the smell of lavender, perhaps, or a sauce that reminded him of *caroule*. These intrusions he could cope with, for they were fleeting and faded quickly. But when he dreamed, the past barged roughly into his mind and usurped his thoughts, and he would spend weeks in agony, struggling to cast out memories of the city of his birth. It pained him to remember Serles. He shrank from it almost as much as he shrank from remembering the man he had been when he lived there. Her beauty and his youth were lost to him both, and he had no desire to think on either of them.

Nor was Lenoir greatly more enthusiastic about contemplating the present. Kennian was an amiable sort of city, large enough to contain varied society and ample diversions, yet not so large as to overwhelm. But the surrounding hamlets that made up the remainder of the Five Villages were so backwater, so provincial, as to evoke the darkest days of the Cassiterian Empire. Lenoir thought it unaccountably bizarre that the villagers of Brackensvale, Denouth, North Haven, and Berryvine should exist so near the cosmopolitan capital, yet still retain the insular ways of small communities in the middle of nowhere. So when Lenoir grew weary of Kennian, as anyone must, he had nowhere to fly to for a change of scenery. There was simply no other city in Braeland worthy of the journey. He longed to leave this country behind, with its harsh accents and crude tastes, and return to his homeland. But he dared not.

"A copper for your thoughts, mister?" said a voice, breaking into Lenoir's musings. He turned at the sound, but could not immediately locate its source. Then he saw a shadow moving in a doorway, barely discernible in the failing light of evening. He glanced at the sign hanging crookedly above the doorframe and was surprised to see that he had already reached the orphanage. He must have been walking faster than he realized.

He addressed his reply to the gloom of the doorway. "If you have a copper, Zach, I shall have to arrest you for theft."

"Fair enough," said the boy brightly, stepping out into the thoroughfare. "How 'bout you give me a copper, and I'll pretend to be interested in your thoughts?"

Lenoir eyed the scruffy creature before him. Skinny, unkempt, and unwashed, Zach probably appeared pathetic to those who did not look closely enough. The careful observer, though, noting the keenness of his gaze and the impish curl of his mouth, would know him at once for the quick-witted, street-savvy survivor that he was.

"I suppose you are looking for dinner," Lenoir said.

Zach grinned. "Always."

"All right, but if you steal any purses, you are on your own. I cannot have trouble with the Courtier or I will starve." He crooked his neck sharply. "Come."

The boy fell in step beside him, tugging his faded hat over the tips of his ears. He had outgrown the hat by at least one winter, Lenoir judged, and it no longer covered him as it should. As he fussed with it, Lenoir was struck once again by the boy's height—or rather its lack. Though nearly ten, Zach barely came past Lenoir's elbow. A lifetime of poor diet had stunted the boy's growth such that he was the size of a healthy child of six or seven.

"Anything exciting today?" the boy asked.

Lenoir shrugged. "No. A small crime, no motive. A waste of a day."

"You always say that," Zach said, disappointed.

It was true, Lenoir supposed—he could not recall the last time he had found a case interesting. "All right, I will humor you. It was a theft, but nothing valuable. Someone stole a body."

"You mean a *dead* body?" Zach's eyes rounded; then his nose wrinkled in disgust. "Why?"

"You tell me."

Zach looked up at him. "This game again? I'm not very good at it."

"You are better than you think. Proceed."

He was quiet for a moment, chewing his lip in thought. "Whose body was it?"

"A boy, about your age, in fact. He lived in Brackensvale."

"How did he die?"

The question brought Lenoir up short. "I don't know," he admitted. "I should have asked, perhaps. That's good, Zach—you are doing well. Now, for the purposes of our game, let us assume the cause of death is not important."

"Was he rich?"

"Rich?"

"Well, maybe they buried him with some jewels or something." Zach's eyes lit up in childish delight at the idea.

Lenoir chuckled. "You have heard too many tales of the ancient Cassiterians, I think. The parents were poor. They would not have buried the boy with anything valuable."

Zach's brow puckered as he thought. He fell silent, and neither of them spoke again until they reached the Courtier. Lenoir hauled on the door, golden warmth spilling forth into the flat light of evening. Rough laughter and the clink of crockery tumbled after, and finally the smell of sawdust and roasting meat. Zach passed under Lenoir's arm as he held the door open, and soon the boy's small form disappeared within a sea of patrons, only to bob to the surface a moment later behind an empty table. By the time Lenoir sat down, Zach was ready with his next question.

"Do they have witches in Brackensvale?"

Lenoir blinked. "What does it mean, 'witches'?" It still happened occasionally that someone would use a word Lenoir had not heard before.

"You know," the boy said impatiently, "like Adali doctors who use magic to cure the sick. I've heard they sometimes use dead bodies in their spells."

Lenoir laughed. Sometimes he allowed himself to forget that Zach was, after all, only a child. "Perhaps you are young enough yet to believe in magic."

The boy scowled at this. "Adali doctors can heal mortal wounds with berries and spit and ground-up bones. Everybody knows that."

Lenoir twisted in his chair and waved for the barmaid. Over his shoulder, he said, "The Adali have a special gift for healing, it is true. But they are an ancient race, and they wander all over the land. It is only natural that they have learned a few tricks."

Zach was unconvinced. "They can talk with their animals."

"They are a herding people, Zach. It is instinct, such as you may find even among beasts. It is mysterious, yes, but hardly magic."

He ordered wine. He knew Zach preferred ale, but the boy would have to settle for what his host was offering. Beer was simply not something Lenoir could ever seriously consider consuming.

Zach let the matter drop and they waited in silence for the barmaid to return with the wine. When she did, Lenoir said, "Stew for the boy." Zach pulled a face, and Lenoir smiled. "You will thank me when you grow tall." There was no need to tell the barmaid what he wanted for himself; it had been years since he had ordered anything else.

When the food arrived, Zach plunged into his bowl as though expecting to find treasure at the bottom. He ate with alarming speed, his spoon scarcely escaping his mouth before it was captured again. It seemed impossible that he could chew in the brief intervals between mouthfuls; it was a marvel the boy did not choke himself. Lenoir watched with grim fascination, his own meat barely touched by the time Zach was through.

"Since you have finished your supper," said Lenoir, eying Zach's empty bowl in mild disbelief, "and I have scarcely begun mine, we shall have to find something to occupy you while I eat. Suppose you tell me about the people in this room?"

"What about them?" Zach's gaze was fixed on Lenoir's steak. "I don't know anybody here, if that's what you mean."

Lenoir took a bite of his meat. It was overdone, but still edible. "That is the point, Zach. You do not know them, so you must look closely in order to decide what they are like. You must form an idea of who they are based on their clothes, their expressions, what they are saying and doing."

"You mean I should make up stories about them?"

"In a manner of speaking. You want to be an inspector someday, yes? Solve puzzles and defeat evildoers?" When he was met with silence, Lenoir looked up from his meal to find Zach sulking.

"Why do you always do that?"

"Do what?"

"Make fun of me about wanting to be a hound. You make it sound like I'm a stupid kid who wants to go out and save princesses or something."

Lenoir paused, his fork and knife hovering on either side of his plate. What the boy said was true, he supposed; he routinely teased Zach about his desire to become an inspector. Lenoir knew he should be flattered that the boy looked up to him. Instead he found himself irritated by Zach's naive notion of police work, mostly because it reminded him of his own illusions so long ago, illusions that had been cruelly and painfully shattered. Still, he did the boy an ill turn by constantly throwing cold water on his ambitions. It was only natural Zach would aspire to something greater than his station in life. *Do not begrudge the boy his dreams, Lenoir. They will be taken from him soon enough.*

"You are right, Zach," he said, diving back into his meat. "I apologize. Now, back to our task. A good inspector must be aware of his surroundings, down to the last detail. He must be able to tell certain things about a person just by looking—what he does for a living, for example, or something else about his life that may be important."

Zach cocked his head. "How?"

Pausing again, Lenoir scanned the room until his eyes came to rest on a couple huddled together in a back corner. They were almost shielded from sight by a beam supporting the ceiling, but even so they stood out, at least to him.

"Do you see the man and woman near the back of the room?"

Zach followed his gaze and nodded. "I see them."

"She is his mistress. They are having an affair."

The boy looked at him skeptically. "Says who?"

Lenoir skewered a piece of meat and dragged it through the juices pooled on his plate. "See where they have chosen to sit? It is the worst table in the room. It is too dark, and far enough from the hearth that it is no doubt cold as well. It is difficult to see them behind the beam, so they will probably have trouble getting the barmaid's attention. And see also how they are dressed?"

"They look rich," Zach said thoughtfully. This obser-

vation, at least, fell squarely within his area of exper-
tise. A street urchin such as he could spot wealth as
easily as a hawk finds a snake in short grass. "Too rich
to be in a place like this," he added.

"Exactly," Lenoir smiled. "They are here because
there is little chance of being seen by anyone they
know. They are obviously hiding, and from the way
they sit so closely together, they are obviously lovers.
Yet they are not equals. She looks rich, yes, but that is
only because of her gloves and the fur she wears
around her neck. Her dress is not up to the same standard. The fur and the gloves are most likely gifts from
her lover. A man of his station would never marry so
far beneath him, and he is too old to be a bachelor.
So . . . an affair." He popped the forkful of meat into his
mouth and waggled his eyebrows at Zach.

The boy laughed, delighted. "Do it again!"

"I think not. It is your turn now."

Zach looked doubtful, but he sat up, peering over
Lenoir's shoulder at the Courtier's patrons. His gaze
skipped from person to person like a stone skimming
the surface of a lake, unable to find anyone he was confident enough to describe. At last, his eyes came to rest
on a young man hunched over a bowl of stew. "Him,"
Zach said firmly.

When Lenoir merely raised his eyebrows expectantly, Zach said, "He's got no money, you can tell by
his clothes. He's hungry too—see how fast he eats?"
Here he hesitated, waiting for the inspector to pass
judgment on his performance so far.

"Go on," said Lenoir.

Zach was quiet for a moment, watching. Lenoir watched too. The youth was indeed a pathetic sight. He had no cloak, but only a threadbare shirt, surely unequal to the cold outside. His hair was greasy and matted, and every so often he paused from shoveling stew into his mouth to scratch, betraying the lice in his scalp. More than anything, however, it was the look in his eye that gave him away: hunted, darting around the room as though searching for threat or opportunity. Zach had chosen well. He might not know his subject personally, but all the same, the youth was all too familiar.

"He's going to make a dash for it," Zach said confidently.

"A dash?"

"He can't pay, I'd bet a copper on it. When he's finished eating, he's going to run."

As though sensing someone's eyes on him, the youth looked up from his bowl. It was empty, Lenoir saw. The youth's gaze flitted around, then locked with Lenoir's. They stared at each other for a heartbeat, and in that moment, Lenoir knew Zach was right. An instant later, just as Zach had predicted, the youth shoved his chair back and bolted.

He had not chosen his table well. The room was too crowded and he was too far from the door. He never made it. By the time he reached the entrance to the Courtier, the barman had vaulted over the bar and was blocking the doorway, meaty fists raised. The youth hesitated, panic etched onto his thin face. He backed away between the tables, but found no comfort there: one of the patrons planted a boot in his backside and propelled him forward, straight into the arms of the barman.

The barman grinned, his great paws seizing the youth by his upper arms. "You picked the wrong place to steal a meal, lad," he growled. Then, his face contorting with malice, he hurled his captive headfirst into the door. There was a sickening crunch, and the youth collapsed in a heap of rags. But the barman was not finished with him: he grabbed the youth by the top of his britches, hefting him easily, and used his body like a battering ram to open the front door. They disappeared out into the street.

Some of the patrons followed, eager to see the excitement outside. Most continued about their business, as though nothing had happened that they had not seen many times before. Lenoir, for his part, returned to his steak. When he had finished, however, and the barman still had not returned, Lenoir sighed and rose.

"Stay here," he told Zach, and headed out the front door.

The scene was gruesome. The youth was on his hands and knees, a long, sticky string of blood dangling from his lip to the dirt. His face was split open in several places, and one eye was swelling shut. His drooping eyelids showed him to be moments away from losing consciousness. The barman stood over him, sleeves rolled up, shouting.

"Get up, you piece of filth! We're not done here!" The small crowd of onlookers jeered their approval.

"All right," called Lenoir, "that's enough. You have made your point, Barclay."

The barman looked up, scowling at the interruption. When he saw Lenoir, the scowl turned from anger to disappointment. "Come on, Inspector—he's getting his due!"

"You don't need to kill him. He will not be back."

"He's a bloody thief," Barclay said indignantly, "and if I don't make an example of him, there'll be more where he came from! Can't you at least arrest him or something?"

Lenoir shrugged. "I could, but what would be the point? The man is obviously starving. I can throw him in jail every other day, but he will still steal to survive. So why waste the time and money? It will do no good. The best you can hope for is that he steals from someone else."

"Then let me finish, Inspector. I'll see to it you eat for free for the rest of the month."

Lenoir sighed again, tilting his head to survey the pathetic form hunched in the dirt. The youth might lose consciousness, but he did not appear to be close to death. "All right. Five minutes. But be careful, Barclay—if you kill him, I will have to arrest you."

The barman grinned. He grabbed the youth's clothes two-fisted, hauling him up. Lenoir did not wait to see the rest; he turned and went back inside the Courtier. He had no desire to see what had been purchased for a month's worth of steak.

Stars drift overhead like a slow cascade of sparks. He watches, transfixed. Long has it been since he has seen such beauty. He remembers little of beauty from his life, but he remembers the stars. Like him, they are eternal. They have been with him since the beginning.

The wagon plods along. He is not sure how long the journey has been—he no longer measures time as mortals do—but he knows they have gone far. Wherever the gravedigger is taking his burden, it is a long way from the place the boy was buried. The soil clinging to the body, once black and moist, has dried out; specks of it cling to the left eye. It is like looking through a dirty window. The right eye is still closed, but one is enough. He cannot feel, cannot hear or taste or smell, but he can see. He has seen the gravedigger, through that dirty left eye, and condemned the man to death. He might have struck already, but he knows instinctively there are others involved, and he would see them too.

The wagon shudders to a halt. After a pause, the sky above jerks and shifts as the body is pulled roughly from the wagon. It falls and lands in a tumble. For a moment, all he can see is the ground; then the body is rolled over, and he is looking into a new face. The newcomer scans the corpse with obvious concern, as though looking for injury, even though the child is long dead. Over his shoulder, a third man is talking to the gravedigger, gesturing angrily at the body. The gravedigger looks confused and afraid.

He takes in all three faces—the gravedigger and the two newcomers—memorizing every feature so he will know them when the time comes. For now, he waits. There may be others still.

The third man hands the gravedigger a purse and

sends him on his way. The man kneeling over the body brushes loose soil from the boy's hair. Slowly, gently, he closes the left eye.

It does not matter. He has already seen them. They are already marked.

CHAPTER 3

Lenoir was in a foul mood by the time he reached Lady Zera's. He could not banish the sight of the starving youth from his mind. It had spoiled his enjoyment of the wine, and he dreaded the effect it might have on his dreams. He needed diversion, entertainment, something to take his mind off what had happened. And so he had headed for Zera's, as he had done so many nights before.

"Darling!" she called gaily as Lenoir was ushered into the room by a neatly trimmed servant. She swept through the crowd, silken sleeves billowing, to embrace Lenoir, kissing him twice on each cheek. She smelled faintly of jasmine, as she always did.

"So wonderful to see you this evening, Inspector." She smiled, taking his elbow.

"How could I not come? To miss an evening at the most celebrated salon in Kennian would be foolish indeed."

Lady Zera's laughter tinkled like crystal. "You do flatter me, Nicolas. Come, meet some of my guests.

Lord Keefe is here this evening, which is a first, and here is Mr. Jolen, whose treatise on the natural flaws of man is making quite a splash these days—is it not so, Mr. Jolen?"

Lenoir allowed himself to be shown through the room, smiling, exchanging kisses and handshakes and cordial greetings. Many of the guests he already knew, for much of Kennian's elite could be found in this room at least once a week. The city's most luminous personages, from artists to philosophers to noblemen, regularly adorned the plush sofas and settees, waxing eloquent about big ideas or simply trading gossip. Zera kept her cellar well stocked and her servants well trained, and was herself a captivatingly exotic woman of such charm and eloquence that she kept the conversation flowing as effortlessly as the wine. Lenoir felt himself relaxing even as he accepted his first glass. For a man such as he who had spent his entire adult life observing people, Lady Zera's salon was a glut of stimulation.

After he had made the rounds, Lenoir found himself a seat near the exquisite bay window that looked out over the high street. The dark panes cast his image back at him, haloed by the glow of the lamps inside. He looked haggard in this light, pale and poorly rested. And so he was. Anyone would be who had not slept a moment in almost a week.

He sank onto the embroidered cushions of the window seat and raised his glass to his lips, his eyes systematically surveying all that was before him. Much of the room was steeped in shadow, owing to Zera's preference for low, moody lighting. It showed her apartments to best advantage: the flickering lamplight flamed on the baroque details of the decor, casting portrait frames and velvet curtains in mysterious relief. Her fine furnishings stood out like jewels, sumptuous ruby and sapphire upholstery clasped within elaborate gilt whorls.

Yet all this was a happy coincidence. The real reason the light was kept low was to allow nooks of gloom to gather in the corners, cloaking their depths from prying eyes. It was in these spaces that the most interesting guests lingered, that they might pursue their vices undisturbed. Sweet-smelling smoke from long pipes drifted lazily toward the ceiling, gathering and roiling like storm clouds above prostrate smokers whose glazed eyes stared vacantly into the shadows. Scholars held heated debates in twos and threes, their hands moving animatedly, the occasional raised voice punctuating their sibilant whispers. Plotting revolution, no doubt, Lenoir thought wryly. If only they knew, as he did, what revolution was like to live through. Then of course there were the lovers, illicit and shameless, who flirted and teased with impunity in the absence of their spouses. All these vices were so very fashionable at the moment, in this time and place where to live to excess was to celebrate life to the fullest.

A voice drifted across the room, and it was as though Jolen had heard Lenoir's thoughts. "Man's weaknesses are nothing to be ashamed of," the philosopher was saying from his position at the center of a large group of guests. Zera, to whom his words were apparently addressed, was stretched spectacularly on a daybed, fanning herself with a hand-painted silk fan.

"They are flaws, yes," Jolen continued, "but flaws that were designed by God, and are therefore as natural as our bodies. They *belong* to us."

"But, Mr. Jolen, I thought God did not make mistakes," Lady Zera said. There were murmurs of assent from the other guests gathered around to listen.

"That is just my point!" Jolen said earnestly. "Our flaws are not mistakes. They were absolutely intentional. They are what make us mortal, what separate us from the perfection of the divine!"

"And so," said Zera, "to explore them fully is to explore what it means to be human." More noises of agreement from the crowd, even a smattering of applause. Lenoir could not help but smile at how adoring Lady Zera's guests could be. The irony of it—that an Adali woman, and no Lady at that, could hold such sway over Kennian's "polite society"—never failed to amuse him.

"Precisely!" cried Jolen triumphantly. "You are a keen student, Lady Zera. In embracing our flaws, we celebrate the gifts God gave us! Conversely, to hide from these weaknesses, to deny them, is to deny God's will."

"A dangerous philosophy, sir," Lenoir cut in. All eyes turned to him, including Zera's. "By this logic, no one should ever show self-restraint."

Jolen was unruffled by the challenge. "Not at all. One must always show restraint. My point is that the boundaries of what society deems acceptable will shift once we acknowledge the natural flaws of man. We need only show restraint within those boundaries."

"Society's boundaries may certainly shift," said Lenoir. "Indeed, they have already shifted—or perhaps one might say *drifted*—considerably. But what about God's boundaries? What about the great balance of fate?"

Jolen frowned. "I do not take your meaning, sir," he said stiffly.

"I speak of consequence. Of judgment. Not the judgment of mankind, but of something higher, more powerful. We are all called to account for our actions, called to pay for what we have done. You cannot escape it—fate will have its vengeance." As he spoke, Lenoir felt the familiar darkness pooling inside him, and he suppressed a shudder.

Jolen, meanwhile, appeared to be suppressing a sneer. "I am sorry, Inspector, but I'm afraid I don't believe in fate. I believe in science." And with that, he turned his attention back to the more appreciative members of his audience.

Feeling suddenly gloomy again, Lenoir twisted in his seat to look out the window. There was little activity in the street; it must be getting late. As he turned back, his gaze drifted over the angled window to his right and a reflection flashed in the glass: a pale face with fierce green eyes.

Lenoir's heart seized, and he gripped the arms of his chair in momentary terror. But the image vanished as suddenly as it had come, and he saw that it was only the reflection of two small glasses of absinthe. He turned to find Zera holding the liquor out to him, a knowing smile on her lips.

"You have dark thoughts this evening, Inspector." She handed him a glass.

Lenoir did not hesitate: he tossed the absinthe into the back of his throat, its fiery bite bringing tears to his eyes.

"One is generally meant to sip absinthe," Zera observed dryly.

"Is that so? Bring me another and I will be sure to do it properly."

Still smiling, the hostess waved to one of her servants and another glass was brought. Zera sat on the window seat, nestling herself between Lenoir and the wall. She looked at him through golden eyes, her face angled playfully to his. "Always looking at the dark side of things, Nicolas," she purred, swirling her own absinthe in its tiny crystal glass. She had added sugar and water to hers, giving it a cloudy appearance. Such was the fashion, but Lenoir preferred his straight. He did not want to dilute the color. Swallowing its blazing green felt like confronting a fear.

"Jolen's ideas are all the rage, you know," Zera said. "Many young scholars think as he does."

Lenoir snorted. "Of course his ideas are popular. They offer the perfect excuse for indulgent behavior, and that is the order of the day, is it not?" He gestured meaningfully with his glass, then took a sip, savoring the taste: sweet, licorice, scorching.

"You are in a contrary mood, Nicolas. Have you had a difficult day?" Without waiting for an answer, she slipped her arm under his. "Tell me about it."

"Not much to tell. A boy's body was exhumed illegally in the Brackensvale Cemetery. No one knows where the body was taken or why."

Zera shivered. "Horrible!" she whispered, her fine eyebrows coming together. "Whoever heard of such a thing?"

"I have, actually," said a voice. Lenoir and Zera turned to its source, a tall, angular gentleman sitting nearby. He had a severe face and a sour expression, which Lenoir recognized as his habitual aspect. "My apologies for eavesdropping, Lady Zera," the gentleman said, turning a pipe over in his hands. "It was quite inadvertent."

"Not at all, Lord Feine," said Zera graciously.

Feine removed a small leather pouch from his pocket and set about filling the pipe with tobacco. He had an unhurried air, as though he savored the curiosity his words had aroused. Lenoir watched detachedly as he fiddled with the pipe. It was an ostentatious thing, with a family crest etched into the bowl.

"There was a similar incident a few weeks ago," Feine said at length. "I am rather surprised you hadn't heard, Inspector."

Lenoir shrugged. "Probably no one told the police. Many crimes go unreported."

Feine grunted, still absorbed in preparing his pipe. "In any case, a boy's body was stolen from North Haven. No one has the faintest idea why. My valet is from there, and he says the whole village is in shock."

"I do not doubt it," Zera said. "What a monstrous thing to do! Some people are simply mad."

"Indeed," said Lenoir. As they spoke, other guests were congregating around them, taking seats near the bay window. Zera was seldom without her admiring retinue for long.

"Speaking of mad"—Zera raised her voice for the benefit of the others—"Mrs. Hynd here has heard a delicious rumor about our dear Duke of Warrick. Won't you tell us, Mrs. Hynd?"

Lenoir was impressed by how seamlessly Zera changed the subject. Understandably, she was not keen on regaling the other guests with gruesome tales of children's corpses.

A plump woman with improbably perfect curls burst into giggles. "Well," she began breathlessly, "apparently, the duke is in search of a new wife! I'm told he has his people making a list of all the unmarried women in the Five Villages!" She dissolved into giggles again, covering her lips with her fingers as though trying to contain them.

There was much appreciative laughter at this. Zera, for her part, was shaking her head incredulously. "Can you imagine his looking beyond Kennian," she asked the room in general, "as though he'll find a proper wife among the milkmaids?"

"I can well imagine it, Lady Zera," said a nobleman whose name Lenoir had forgotten. "He may be the most powerful man in the Five Villages, but even so, what sane, respectable woman could possibly want him for a husband? I suspect he will be obliged to find someone who is neither!"

More laughter. Lenoir supposed His Lordship (what

was his name? Lenoir could not think through the growing haze of liquor) had a point. Only the greediest, most foolish sort of woman would rush to take the place of the duke's last wife, whose death, along with her son's, had been brutal and suspicious.

"Well, I for one hope he manages it," said one woman. "He needs to start a family again. It's just awful how he pines after his dead loved ones, so many years later."

"Probably shouldn't have murdered them, then," someone retorted, provoking scandalized laughter and cries of "Shocking, shocking!"

With the salon's guests chatting so briskly now, Zera could relax again. She leaned conspiratorially toward Lenoir. "The power of rumor," she murmured. "Is it not the axle grease of society?"

"It is, though I suspect the objects of rumor do not always think that a good thing. But perhaps you can speak to that yourself—there have certainly been enough rumors about you lately."

A shadow of anger flickered across Zera's lovely features, but it was gone almost immediately. "So it would seem," she said coolly. "Apparently, I am running a brothel and an opium den full of revolutionaries and freaks."

Lenoir gave her a wry smile. "The price of success, my dear. Consider it a compliment to be worthy of such notoriety."

"Compliment or no, I would be grateful indeed to know who is behind it. Can you find out?" Lenoir laughed quietly, but Zera would not be deterred. "I am serious, Nicolas. I have worked too hard and sacrificed too much to allow my place in society to be compromised by vicious lies. I am . . . vulnerable."

"Zera, no one thinks of you as Adali anymore."

She tossed her head proudly. "For the moment, perhaps, but that can change. People are fickle, as you well know. These rumors have only to take root, and I will be Adali once more, a savage putting on airs in the big city, little better than a trained monkey. I cannot let my guard down, not even for a moment. I *must* put a stop to these rumors." She paused. "What about that boy you are always telling me about—the one who is so good at picking up stray bits of information? Could he find out who is spreading this poison?"

"Possibly. I will ask him."

"Good," Zera said silkily, rising. "Now if you will forgive me, I am neglecting my guests." She disappeared into the crowd.

Shaking his head, Lenoir took another long pull of liquor. His vision was already growing blurred, but it would be many hours before he stopped. Only when the absinthe in his glass seemed to take the shape of a pair of cold green eyes did he finally rise, weave his way unsteadily home, and give himself over to sleep.

CHAPTER 4

"I still don't understand why they wouldn't have reported it to the constable," said Kody, his gaze drifting over the gallery of skeletal white poplars flanking the road to North Haven. The trees offered little protection from the cold gusts blowing down from the hills; icy blades of wind sliced through the ribs of the forest, whistling eerily. The horses bowed their heads against the chill, their progress watched hungrily by a murder of crows that sheltered in the branches above, flapping and cackling. *Must be carrion nearby,* Kody thought.

Lenoir still hadn't said anything, so Kody continued. "If my son's body was stolen, I'd want to find out who did it and why."

"Perhaps there are circumstances surrounding the incident that the victims do not want known," said Lenoir. "Or perhaps they did tell the constable, but he did not trust the Metropolitan Police with the information."

I can't imagine why. Maybe it's because half the force

is corrupt, and the other half is incompetent. Kody sighed inwardly, pushing the bitter thought aside. It wasn't *that* bad. But it was getting harder and harder to be optimistic about the Kennian Metropolitan Police, and working with Lenoir wasn't exactly a morale booster.

"Whatever the reason, Sergeant, I do not want a repeat of yesterday's incident. Unless someone can provide us a motive, or at least a solid lead, it is virtually certain that we will never find this child's body. The crime scene is far too old, and the trail will have gone cold long since. So do not be too hopeful."

God forbid anyone should be hopeful, Inspector.

Their horses crested a hill in the road, and the shambling outline of North Haven rose from the earth like a corpse from its grave. It slumped and careened at all angles, its crude construction slowly yielding to the ravages of the relentless Braelish winters. As they got closer, the impression of decay and neglect only grew stronger. Crumbling, desiccated mud walls propped up thatch roofs scabbed over with moss, the dwellings separated from one another by desultory little fences of woven sticks. The main road remained dry and hard-packed beneath their horses' hooves, a sign that it rarely saw wagon traffic. That didn't surprise Kody. North Haven was barely larger than Brackensvale, and every bit as provincial.

Maybe that explained the mistrustful stares of the townspeople they came across. As they rode down the main street, people turned to gaze up at them, their expressions dark and forbidding. Crowds stopped talking as they passed. A mangy-looking dog scampered out from a nearby yard and followed them for a while, barking loudly and nipping at the heels of the horses until Kody threw a crab apple at it, sending it slinking off into the trees. In all, it wasn't the warmest of welcomes.

"This is why city folk never leave Kennian," Kody said under his breath. "You'd think we were an occupying army, the way these people act. What's their problem, anyway?"

"You have answered your own question, Sergeant. City folk almost never set foot in the villages, and when they do, it does not tend to be good news."

"Bit of a chicken-and-egg thing, isn't it?" Kody said, eying a blacksmith warily. The man had stopped working as they drew near, and there was something vaguely threatening in the way he held his heavy iron hammer.

Lenoir smirked. "Perhaps you should explain that to them. I'm sure they would appreciate your insight."

The constable met them in the village green. He looked nervous. *And so he should,* Kody thought disapprovingly. A felony had gone unreported, which meant that the constable was derelict in his duty. He was supposed to report weekly to the Metropolitan Police—or immediately, if the crime was serious. Lenoir had said that a few weeks had already gone by since the local boy's body was stolen. Either the constable hadn't known about it, or he had failed to report it. Neither possibility reflected well on him.

"Good morning, Inspector," Constable Brier said wanly, taking the bridle of Lenoir's horse. "Your message was cryptic, and a bit sudden too. The messenger left not two hours ago—I haven't had time to learn much."

"The message contained all the relevant information, Constable," said Lenoir. "We are here to investigate a crime that should have been reported—when? How long since the boy's body was stolen?"

Brier's barely restrained nervousness tumbled out of him now. "I heard nothing of it, Inspector! Your message took me completely by surprise!"

Lenoir raised his eyebrows. "Indeed? That is disturbing, Constable, since I am told the entire village talks of the matter."

Brier turned a deep crimson. He opened his mouth, but apparently he didn't know what to say, because he closed it again.

"Let us get started, then," said Lenoir, and Brier nodded numbly. Fetching his own horse, he led the way back onto the main street.

There were three churches in town, and the first they visited wasn't the right one, as its priest was quick to inform them. When they got to the second, larger church, they could tell right away they were in the right place. Where the first had been busy, with several market stalls out front and a steady stream of parishioners through the main doors, this church was all but deserted. With its crude stone construction—blocky and impersonal, overgrown with ivy—it looked like a neglected tombstone.

The priest came out into the courtyard to meet them. "I heard your hoofbeats on the flagstones. I have been expecting you, after a fashion." He wore a weary expression, but his manner was friendly enough as he showed the officers where to tether their horses.

"What do you mean, you have been expecting us?" asked Lenoir when they had dismounted.

The priest sighed. "I knew this matter could not long escape the attention of the Metropolitan Police. It is simply too horrible."

"Why didn't you report it, then?" Brier snapped. "We could have raised the hue and cry!"

The priest eyed Kody and Lenoir apprehensively; he was probably wondering whether they would arrest him. "Can you imagine what it is like to have something like this happen at your church? My parishioners should think this a holy place, not a place of evil. I wanted to keep word of the incident to myself and the parents, not have it become known throughout the Five Villages."

Brier pointed an accusing finger at the priest's chest. "That was not your decision to make!" He would have said more, but Lenoir raised a hand, and the constable subsided.

"You must have known that would be impossible, Brother," said Lenoir.

"Apparently so, as you see. Since news of the theft became known, not a single family has come to lay their loved ones to rest. They think this place is defiled."

Lenoir frowned. "Defiled?" Either he didn't know the word, or he was simply astonished at how provincial these people were.

In case it was the former, Kody explained, "The outer villages are superstitious. People out here favor supernatural explanations instead of reason."

The priest's expression hardened. "Ah, yes, of course. Well, I trust your reason will provide a ready explanation for what has happened here. Mr. and Mrs. Jymes will no doubt be comforted that the superior minds of Kennian are involved in locating their son's body." Kody felt himself flush as the priest turned away, heading for the cemetery.

"Somehow, Sergeant, I do not think you have struck a blow for intervillage relations," said Lenoir.

The priest showed them the plot where the boy's body had been. "It was stolen in the night, of course. Only one day after the burial."

"How old was he?" asked Lenoir.

"Called to God at nine years," the priest intoned gravely.

Kody felt a jolt. Could it be a coincidence? "The boy in Brackensvale was also nine, Inspector."

Lenoir didn't seem to hear. He gazed at the grave site, visibly annoyed. "The evidence has been destroyed."

The priest was unapologetic. "You would not have found anything, Inspector. Footprints and the work of a spade—nothing more."

"How did the boy die?" Lenoir asked.

"Fever."

"And his parents, where are they?"

"Not far from here," Brier said, eager to help. "I can take you there, if you like."

*   *   *

They remained in North Haven until late afternoon, but they didn't learn anything useful. So Lenoir said, anyway, but Kody thought they were overlooking an important detail.

"The two boys were the same age," he pointed out as they rode back to Kennian. "That must be significant."

"Why must it?" Lenoir asked indifferently.

"Well, it can't be coincidence."

"Of course it can, Sergeant. The corpse thief is obviously interested in fresh bodies, ones that have not yet decomposed. My guess is that we are dealing with a philosopher of some kind, someone who is using the bodies for research purposes. He looks for a dead child, and then he digs it up. Two children aged nine died recently, so he dug up two children aged nine. It is not significant."

As a rule, Kody didn't see much point in arguing with people who'd already made up their minds—and that went double for Lenoir. But he wasn't willing to let this one pass, not without a fight. "With all due respect, Inspector, wasn't it you who taught me that every detail is significant?"

"I also taught you not to allow yourself to be distracted by them. You must consider the motive, Sergeant. If you cannot explain *why* the crime has been committed, you will never solve it. You must focus on the whole of the thing, find the story behind it."

"That's exactly what I'm trying to do. Maybe there is no pattern here, but maybe there is, and we have to *want* to see it. Whether it's a constellation or just stars depends on who's looking."

Lenoir sneered. "Such affection you have for that

hackneyed saying of yours. You do realize it makes you sound like a romantic fool?"

They fell into a cold silence. *If I'm a romantic fool,* Kody thought bitterly, *you're a lazy bastard.* Lenoir didn't want to acknowledge a pattern because that would mean they had a lead, and they would be obliged to follow it. If Kody was right, they could bide their time until another nine-year-old boy died, and then watch the grave until the thief appeared. But as usual, Lenoir seemed perfectly uninterested in solving this case.

Kody didn't know how much longer he could cope without his frustration boiling over. He'd specifically requested to serve under Nicolas Lenoir, since the man was something of a legend. Lenoir had done a lot to professionalize the city's police force—in fact, he'd practically founded the Metropolitan Police ten years before, remodeling it after the renowned Prefecture of Police in his native city of Serles. That done, he'd gone on a brief but spectacularly successful rampage against Kennian's complex criminal networks. He and Sergeant Crears (now *Constable* Crears) had broken up the largest thieving ring in Kennian's history, recovering almost a million crowns' worth of goods and arresting the city's most notorious crime lord. Crears was promoted, and Lenoir received a commendation from the lord mayor.

But those days were long gone. Having secured his place as the top inspector on the force, Lenoir no longer felt the need to exert himself. He still hauled in the occasional big fish, but mostly he just went through the motions. He was a brilliant detective; Kody had seen flashes of his genius on plenty of occasions. But mostly he was cynical and indifferent, and Kody had a hunch that wasn't the worst of it. Instead of propelling his career forward, working as Lenoir's deputy had frozen his progress, ensuring that he never had the chance to break a major case. Quite simply, Lenoir was holding him back.

No more.

He broke the silence. "I understand this case probably isn't worth your attention," he said coolly, "but if it's all the same to you, I'd like to look into it a little further."

Lenoir glanced at him out of the corner of his eye, his expression unreadable. "As you like, Sergeant, but it is a waste of your time. You will not find anything."

Maybe not, Kody conceded inwardly, *but at least I'm willing to look.*

CHAPTER 5

Darkness already held sway over Kennian by the time Lenoir quit the headquarters of the Metropolitan Police. A cold, damp fog was seeping into the streets like a slow poison through the veins of the city; Lenoir had to turn the collar of his coat up to shield his neck from the chill. He was in an ill temper as usual, rankled by Kody's thinly veiled contempt. How sick he was of the sergeant's judgment! As though a whelp such as he had anything to say to Lenoir, who had been catching criminals since before Kody had seen his first winter. The man's treacly affection for the law was sickening, and his ambition would have been laughable, were it not so pathetic. Kody genuinely believed he would fix the force someday. Catch the criminals. Save the world. Lenoir snorted contemptuously, sending a plume of mist into the air. One day, the sergeant would learn what the world was really like, and Lenoir could only hope he was there to see it.

Anger drove his step as he headed for the poor district. He needed to find Zach before the boy turned in for the night. It was not difficult; Zach had a few reliable haunts, and Lenoir found him at the second tavern he checked. He did not even need to go inside; as he rounded the corner of the inn, he spied Zach tumbling into the street, the wrathful innkeeper towering above him. Lenoir was reminded forcibly of the incident at the Courtier the night before, and his mood soured still further.

"If I catch you in here again, you little mongrel, I'll cut your throat for you!" The man's shoulders heaved with rage, and he cocked his leg back, as though he were preparing to kick the pile of rags in the dirt.

"Will you, sir?" Lenoir said mildly, stepping into the glow of a streetlamp. "And who will run your establishment while you are in jail?"

The innkeeper squinted into the light. "Who are you?"

"I am Inspector Nicolas Lenoir of the Metropolitan Police, which you know perfectly well, since you have seen me in your tavern a dozen times or more."

The innkeeper's lip curled. "So I have, with this little thief in tow." He pointed a thick finger at Zach, who had righted himself and now stood defiantly before his accuser. "You keep bad company for a policeman."

"The company I keep is not your concern. And besides, what proof have you that the boy is a thief? Did you see him take anything?"

"One of my customers was pickpocketed, and I've seen that boy around enough to know what he's about."

Lenoir approached Zach. "Turn out your pockets." The boy searched his face for a moment, but when he saw that Lenoir was serious, he did as he was told, reaching inside his trousers and turning out his pockets. They dangled like a pair of hound's ears, empty.

"There. You have no evidence with which to accuse the boy. Do not let me hear of you mistreating him again."

The innkeeper responded through a tightly clenched jaw, "He has no reason to be in my place. He's not a paying customer. It's my right to put him out if he can't pay."

"So it is." Lenoir dropped some coins into Zach's palm. "Go inside and buy yourself a meat pie." To the tavern owner, he said, "Now he is a paying customer."

The man could do no more than stand there shaking with anger as Zach walked triumphantly past, trailed by Lenoir. He did not dare challenge an inspector of the Metropolitan Police.

Zach was grinning from ear to ear when they sat. "That was brilliant! It was just like the first time we met. Do you remember?"

"Indeed I do, though I hardly think it something to be proud of." Lenoir was never sure whether Zach fully appreciated how close he had come to his demise. Had Lenoir not happened upon the Firkin at the exact moment Zach was being hauled outside for a beating, the boy would almost certainly have met his end. To this day, Lenoir was not entirely certain why he had intervened, or at least why he had not dragged the boy off to face the magistrate. He told himself that it was simply too much effort to arrest and process a child who would only wind up at the end of a rope one day.

And in truth, Lenoir did not begrudge Zach his thieving ways—not then, and not now. Zach had been dealt a poor hand, poorer than most in this city of ill fortune, yet he never let that grind him down. He could have done as the others did, rattling aimlessly about the orphanage all day, taking whatever life and the overworked nuns saw fit to dish out. Instead he took his fate into his own hands, day after day, at not inconsiderable risk to life and limb. If he was crafty enough to make his own way, why should Lenoir interfere? On the contrary, he was impressed with the boy's grit and adaptability. As long as Zach confined himself to petty crimes, Lenoir was content enough to let him alone, especially since he had proven himself a valuable resource.

That did not, however, mean that he would allow himself to be duped by the boy. He eyed Zach shrewdly. "Where is it?"

At first Zach's expression was all innocence, but when it became clear that Lenoir was not going to fall for it, he grinned again. "Under my hat."

Lenoir sighed. "You should be more careful, Zach. There are many in this neighborhood who would dash your skull to pieces without a second thought."

"Lucky I have you to protect me."

"What makes you think I will protect you next time?"

"Because if you don't, you'll have to find someone else who can get you the information I do, and that won't be easy."

Lenoir laughed in spite of himself. The boy knew his

own worth. That was good. "Earn your keep, then. I have a job for you." He waved the barmaid over and they ordered dinner. While they waited for it to arrive, Lenoir got down to business. "Tell me, Zach, have you ever heard of Lady Zera?"

"I think so. Doesn't she own a brothel?"

Lenoir grunted thoughtfully. Zera's fears about her reputation seemed to be well founded. "She does not. In fact, she runs quite a reputable salon on the high street."

"What's a salon?"

"It's a gathering of people, hosted by someone of renowned taste."

"Like a party?"

"Of sorts, a party for the wealthy and the elegant, where they can show off their knowledge of literature and philosophy."

"Sounds boring."

Lenoir smiled. "Sometimes. But a talented host will ensure that there is enough fine liquor and other indulgences to make up for the rarified conversation. It is also a place for the fashionable to be seen."

"Are you fashionable?" the boy asked guilelessly.

Lenoir almost choked on his wine. "Certainly not," he said, dabbing at his shirt, "but Lady Zera is, exceedingly so. She is one of the most admired hostesses in the city. That is no small thing, because she also happens to be Adali."

Zach's eyes widened. "Really? Does she know magic?"

"Come, now, Zach, not this again. You know better than to believe such superstitious nonsense. Your neighborhood is full of Adali. How many of them are witches?"

The boy considered. "They're thieves, mostly."

Lenoir winced at the generalization, widely held though it was. "On the contrary, most Adali are ordinary, law-abiding folk. But it is true that many fall to crime. Life is hard for them here. An Adal living in the city is cut off from his clan. He is poor and despised, so he makes his way as best he can."

"Then why do they come here?"

Lenoir paused. For one so young, the boy asked insightful questions. *Perhaps he would make a good inspector after all.* Aloud, he said, "I suppose they come to make their fortune. Perhaps some of them do not want to raise cattle for the rest of their lives." Just as many were prostitutes and other forms of trafficked slaves, but Lenoir saw no point in troubling Zach with the darker realities of Adali life. The boy knew all too well what it meant to be poor, desperate, and preyed upon. "In any case, Lady Zera has gone to great pains to dissociate herself from her people."

"Why?"

"Because she does not want to be stained by association. Kennians do not like the Adali, Zach."

"Because they steal?"

"Among other complaints. Few people take time to consider what it must be like to live in the city's slums, what it takes to survive. If they did, they would find much to admire. Instead they see only what is alien and frightening, and they judge the whole race by its worst examples. Lady Zera does not want to be judged alongside the rest. She wants to fit in here in the city, and so far she has succeeded admirably. She is elegant and refined, and it helps that she is very beautiful. People are prepared to overlook the fact that she is Adali. Otherwise, she would have no place in fashionable society. And that brings me to the point, Zach. Where did you hear that Lady Zera runs a brothel?"

Zach shook his head. "I don't remember."

"I need you to put your ear to the ground. Someone is spreading rumors about Zera, and I want to know who is behind it."

Zach scowled. "*Boring*. Who cares about gossip?"

"Zera does. In her business, reputation is everything. She has made a good name for herself, but she is still Adali. It would not take much of a scandal to ruin her."

"How am I supposed to find out who started a rumor?"

"Start with the other salon hostesses," Lenoir suggested. "Such rumors are usually invented by those who are envious or competitive. Seek these ladies out, or their servants. Failing that, see if you can find out who is actually doing the talking. Whoever is behind it may have paid someone to provide grist for the mill."

Their food arrived. It was half cold, and the venison loin on Lenoir's plate looked like a giant rusted nail. His nostrils flared in disapproval, but his belly could not wait for a better option. He glanced at the table for a fork and knife; seeing none, he stopped the barmaid.

"What for?" she asked, visibly bewildered.

"For eating like a civilized human being, madam."

She rolled her eyes. "Bloody Arrènais snob," she muttered as she flounced away.

"Bloody Braelish barbarian," he retorted under his breath.

"So when do I get to meet Lady Zera?" Zach did not wait for cutlery, but plunged his fingers straight into his pie.

Lenoir snorted. "Why would Lady Zera want to meet you?"

"Because I'm irresistible," the boy deadpanned.

Lenoir burst out laughing. "Zach, one day you will be a man, and a man must learn his place in the world. Take no offense, but believe me when I tell you that Lady Zera will never in her life come within ten miles of the likes of you."

The noise of the alehouse was beginning to bother him. He was accustomed to the silence of the cemetery, the airy nothingness that settled like fine ash over a place of death. This place was too alive. The light seared his eyes, the laughter jangled his nerves. He felt too warm sitting here in the glow of the hearth. All around him, folk were talking and drinking and milling about. He wished they would go away, all of them. His drunkenness only heightened his irritability, and he knew that if he did not leave soon, he would find himself in a brawl.

He had been tense ever since leaving Brackensvale. Everywhere he went, people felt hostile. He knew he must be imagining it, yet he could not shake the feeling that his guilt was as obvious as the beard on his face.

People stared at him accusingly, as if they knew. Children especially—they looked frightened whenever he came near, as though they expected him to do them harm. He could not long linger in a crowded place such as this before he began to sweat, sure that at any moment the Metropolitan Police would descend upon him. If they caught him, he would swing for what he had done—or worse.

The gravedigger stood up abruptly, his chair scraping along the floor loudly enough to draw looks from the other patrons. Slamming a few coins on the table, he grabbed his cloak and headed for the door. Outside, it was cool and quiet, and he took deep, grateful breaths. His head seemed to clear some. He pulled his cloak over his shoulders, his gaze moving briefly over a man standing in the shadow of a doorframe. He felt a moment's annoyance that his solitude should be interrupted again so soon, but when he looked up from fastening his cloak, the man was gone. Good.

He weaved a little as he made his way down the street, but there was no one to see. It was late, and the windows that faced the street were dark. The streetlamps struggled against a moonless night, doing little to illuminate his way. That was just as well too. He had always preferred to abide in darkness.

As he walked, he became dimly aware that the sound of his own footsteps was echoed by those of another somewhere behind. He turned, angry words on his lips, but there was no one there. Strange—he was sure he had heard something.

He turned into a narrow alley. His footing was uncertain, obliging him to keep his gaze trained on the ground as he walked. Suddenly, a shadow spilled across the stones in front of him, liquid black, flitting from right to left. He looked up at the rooftops in time to see movement.

He froze, and there was a moment of stillness. Then the air exploded in whirring and flapping as a clutch of pigeons burst forth from the eaves. The gravedigger's cry of shock dissolved into a string of curses at the filthy creatures.

Just ahead, the end of the alley was marked by a shaft of pale light from a nearby streetlamp. But the way was not free: standing silhouetted against the glow was a man. It was the same man, the gravedigger realized, that he had seen in the doorway near the alehouse. Little of his face was distinguishable in the darkness, but his eyes were clearly visible, shining as though lit from within. They were an uncanny shade of green, vivid like those of a cat, only brighter.

There was something in those eyes, something that caused a cold sliver of fear to slide itself like a blade into the gravedigger's ribs. He checked his stride and turned, retracing his steps up the alleyway. He moved as quietly as he could, straining to listen to the darkness behind him. Footsteps sounded, echoing closely in the narrow confines of the alley. The gravedigger quickened his step, listening carefully. Sure enough, the footsteps behind increased their pace.

A sob of terror clutched at the gravedigger's throat, and he burst into a run.

He made for the river, taking random turns in an

effort to break his pursuer's line of sight. But he did not know the city well, and soon the street disgorged him onto a bridge. It was horribly exposed, but he had no choice: he pounded on, his head bent low as he sprinted. Only when he reached the far edge of the bridge did he look up, and what he saw stopped his heart. There, waiting for him at the other end, was the man with the flashing green eyes.

It was impossible, unnatural. The gravedigger's knees buckled, and he sank slowly to the ground. "Please," he sobbed quietly as the green-eyed man approached. "Please."

The man stood over him now, expressionless. The gravedigger's last thought was that he looked like an avenging angel.

So beautiful.

CHAPTER 6

"Brier and I canvassed most of the town," Kody was saying, "and nobody could recall seeing a stranger around before we arrived. But then, just as I was getting ready to give up, a laundry girl told us that she had seen an Adali man ride in the night before. She couldn't tell us much about him—apparently, she didn't see his face—but she did say he was wearing a purple riding cloak, the traditional embroidered kind. Pretty distinctive, wouldn't you say? Anyway, she said it was almost dark when he arrived, so he would have had to find a place to bed down for the night."

Lenoir was only half listening to the sergeant's babbling. The other half of his attention, the more interested half, was devoted to spinning a copper coin on the surface of his desk. He let it whirl until it began to wobble, whereupon he slapped it flat and took it up again, flicking it between his thumb and forefinger to set it off anew. He was not normally given to such fidgeting, but this routine of Kody's had been going on for days, and Lenoir was at his wits' end. He had reminded the sergeant how many times—a dozen?—that a crime unsolved after the first two days was likely to remained unsolved forever. But still Kody was undaunted, riding out to Brackensvale or North Haven day after day in a fruitless attempt to turn over some useful clue in his hunt for the corpse thief.

"The innkeeper denied seeing any Adali, but of course he would. Bad for business if word got out that he let such folk sleep in his beds."

"That is one explanation," said Lenoir. "Another might be that he had not in fact seen your Adal." The coin set forth again.

Kody frowned as he watched its progress across the desk. "Yes, well . . . So that's the latest from North Haven. The bit from Brackensvale is even more interesting: apparently, the gravedigger from the boy's cemetery is missing. Nobody can be sure exactly how long he's been gone—guess he wasn't missed—but even the priest can't recall seeing him since the boy's body went missing."

He paused, seemingly waiting for his listener to comment. Lenoir merely slapped the wavering copper piece down. Kody flinched; Lenoir could see the muscles in the sergeant's jaw twitch.

"Am I keeping you from more important matters, Inspector?"

Lenoir met his eye for the first time since the conversation began. "Yes, Sergeant, you are. And keeping yourself from them as well."

Kody nodded slowly, his jaw still taut. "Really. So nothing I've just told you has any value, then?"

"The value of a piece of information lies in our ability to make sense of it, to determine its significance. Otherwise it is just a distraction." Lenoir leaned over the desk, arms crossed. "So, tell me, Sergeant, what is the significance of what you have just told me? Your Adali stranger in North Haven, your missing gravedigger in Brackensvale—what do they mean? What has one to do with the other? We do not know the fate of either, so how will they help us find the corpses?"

"I don't . . . I haven't . . ." He floundered. "I just need more time—"

"Would you search the Five Villages for a man in a purple cloak, Kody? Would you abandon your search for the bodies to look instead for the missing gravedigger? Begin a new investigation that may or may not be related to the one you are supposedly pursuing?"

Kody's face flushed, and his hands balled into fists. Lenoir knew the sergeant wanted to hit him, was a heartbeat away from leaping across the desk. But as always, Kody's discipline won out and he merely took a long, shaking breath.

Lenoir rose from the desk and fetched his coat. "You have not got a constellation here, Sergeant Kody," he said, heading for the door, "and it's time for you to grow up and quit stargazing." He did not wait for a reply, but left Kody sitting alone in his office.

His step was brisk as he headed down the stairs to ground level, where the bulk of the Metropolitan Police went about its business. The second floor was reserved for men of rank such as Lenoir; the rest of the men shared a single open space on the ground floor, an area affectionately known as "the kennel." Today, as always, it was a hive of activity, for a city as large as Kennian had more than enough crime to keep its six-hundred-odd hounds busy. Most of the sergeants, watchmen, scribes, and others who milled about the kennel were occupied with petty crimes, for more serious affairs were reserved for the inspectors. Even so, Lenoir occasionally envied the lower ranks the simplicity of their work. He remembered fondly his days on the streets of Serles, how the citizenry looked to him as a symbol of justice, a chivalric figure to whom they could run when they were in distress. Chasing down thieves, breaking up duels—so satisfying, so uncomplicated. The life of an inspector was not so. Not in Serles, and not in Kennian.

"Inspector," said a voice, breaking into Lenoir's thoughts. A young watchman approached him at the foot of the stairs. "Sergeant Innes sent me to find you, sir. He's at Merriton's place."

"Merriton?" Lenoir frowned, riffling through his memory for the name. "The surgeon?"

"Yes, sir. He's with some nobleman—I think he said his name was Arleas? Anyway, he's been beaten pretty bad. Unconscious, face like a heap of plum preserve."

Sighing, Lenoir nodded. Visiting a surgery was reliably unpleasant. At best it was a place of pain; at worst it offered up some of the most gruesome sights ever beheld. Lenoir would rather watch an autopsy than the work of a barber or surgeon. At least with an autopsy, the poor soul having bits of him sawn off was already dead. Still, he should be grateful for something to do that did not involve listening to Kody drone on about the corpse thief, so he thanked the watchman and headed out.

He arrived at Merriton's to find the situation just as the watchman had described it. On a slab in the middle of the room lay a finely dressed man of middle age, or so Lenoir judged; in truth it was difficult to tell, for he had been beaten to the point of being virtually unrecognizable. His face was grotesquely swollen: thick fleshy eyelids the size of a child's fist, cracked lips, skin a palette of vivid purples and blues. The surgeon, Merriton, hovered above him, whistling softly to himself as he draped leeches across the unconscious man's bruises. A short distance away, Sergeant Innes loomed over the scene like a gargoyle.

Innes inclined his head in acknowledgment as Lenoir approached. "Morning, Inspector. Thought you'd better see this, seeing as this fella's a nobleman and all."

"Arleas is his name," Merriton supplied cheerfully. "I told you that already. I know his chambermaid quite well." He resumed his whistling.

Tempted as he was to comment on that detail, Lenoir focused on the task at hand. "Why didn't you take him to a proper physician?" he asked Innes. Merriton glanced up sharply, but decided to hold his tongue.

Innes, a great ogre of a man, shrugged his massive shoulders. "Dunno, Inspector. Only I found him not far from here, and he looked in pretty bad shape, so I just figured I'd better get him seen to quick."

"And quite right too," said Merriton. "These wounds need bleeding right away, or the dark blood will infect him."

Lenoir suppressed a shudder. He had grown accustomed to living in Braeland over the past decade or so, even if it was considerably less advanced than Arrènes and the other civilized nations to the south. But occasionally he was reminded that this little country was scarcely more than a land bridge to the savage lands beyond, and nothing called that to mind quite so forcibly as medical matters. Situations such as these made it seem as though he had stepped back through time to the dark days before the Age of Awakening.

The surgery looked more like a torture chamber than a place of healing. The tools of Merriton's trade were laid out on a long table like an exhibit in a museum of the macabre: saws, carving knives, rasps, and even more sinister-looking devices whose purposes Lenoir could not even begin to guess at. A putrid smell hung in the air, vaguely reminiscent of a butcher's on a hot day, as though the reek of rotting flesh had somehow seeped into the very floorboards. Or perhaps the smell came from the bloodstained rushes strewn beneath the patient's slab. The thought caused Lenoir's stomach to twist over itself.

He turned to Innes, who was idly swatting at the flies buzzing near his ear. "Has he been unconscious since you found him, Sergeant, or did he say anything?"

"Nothing, sir, but I found this on him." Innes held out a letter, unsealed, which Lenoir took. It read simply, *This afternoon, tea time.* Lenoir turned it over and examined the seal. He recognized the family crest immediately, even though he had been half-drunk the last time he saw it.

"Very well, Sergeant, stay with him. If he wakes within the next two hours, find out who did this to him. If he doesn't, fetch a goddamn physician, will you?"

Innes grunted again as Lenoir shouldered past the surgeon, who was admiring his handiwork with a disturbingly satisfied grin.

Lord Feine kept Lenoir waiting for nearly an hour. It was possible he knew why the inspector had come and sought to avoid the interview altogether, but Lenoir thought it equally likely that Feine simply took pleasure in reminding his guests of his superior rank. In any case, his expression when he finally arrived showed neither nervousness nor smugness, but merely the sour look he always wore, as though nothing around him were quite to his liking.

"How good to see you, Inspector," said Feine, his inflection utterly flat. He strode across the room to a handsome wingback chair near the hearth, his hand fluttering at Lenoir in an anemic invitation to sit. "Can I offer you some lunch?"

"Very kind, sir, but no, thank you. I'm afraid that I am not paying a social call."

Feine arched a single finely trimmed eyebrow. "Indeed? Official business, then? How disturbing." Lenoir judged that His Lordship would sound more disturbed if he had just located a hangnail. Feine produced his pipe, and Lenoir found himself staring for the second time at the family crest that ostentatiously adorned the bowl.

"There was a man beaten in the streets this morning, savagely so," said Lenoir, studying Feine's expression carefully.

The eyebrow leapt again. "Awful."

"I believe you know the victim, since if I am not mistaken, he is a fellow parliamentarian. Arleas is his name."

"Ah, yes," said Feine, as though Lenoir had just correctly identified a species of plant. "I know him well. Splendid fellow." He held Lenoir's eye and said nothing more.

Lenoir knew already where all this would lead. Feine had not even bothered to inquire what any of this had to do with him, the way an innocent man, or a man inclined to pretend innocence, would do. Such confidence in a suspect could mean only one thing: he considered himself untouchable. Sometimes this was because the suspect believed there was no evidence to condemn him. More often, however, when it came to the nobility, it was because they were simply not afraid of whatever evidence there might be.

"I would like to show you something, Lord Feine," said Lenoir, rising. "May I?" He took Feine's silence for permission and approached. "This letter was found on the victim. It bears your seal, but I think it must have been written by someone else in the household. The handwriting is quite . . . feminine, wouldn't you agree?"

Feine looked over the letter, and for the first time, his expression cracked. It was subtle—lips slightly pursed, nostrils flared almost imperceptibly—and it was gone in an instant. But it was enough for Lenoir. "I wonder, sir, if you are the sort of man to allow himself to be humiliated. I must say you do not seem to me such a man."

Feine had mastered himself once again, and he smiled as he handed the letter back. "And you do not strike me as the sort of man whose lifestyle can be supported on the salary of an inspector. Men of such modest means do not often find themselves frequenting Lady Zera's salon."

There it was. Lenoir had seen it coming; Feine's demeanor had told him to expect it.

A long silence followed, filled only with the wordless exchange of two men staring at each other. At length, Lenoir said, "Lady Zera's is indeed a place of extravagance. One struggles to fit in."

"I can imagine," said Lord Feine with mock sympathy. "But one needn't."

Another stretch of silence. Finally, Lenoir turned and headed for the door. "I will consider the matter, Lord Feine. Until then, keep your men away from Arleas. I daresay even you would be hard-pressed to afford a murder charge."

The shutters of the boy's eyelids fly open, letting sunlight stream in. The abruptness of the change would have been blinding, if such a thing were possible. But the boy is dead, and as for him, he cannot be blinded, because he does not truly see, not in the sense of the living. Instead of blinding him, the light reveals a bounty of new clues, and he studies them meticulously. He sees the same two men who came to collect the body. There are new faces too. They are speaking, all of them at the same time, their lips moving as one. Singing? Chanting? Without sound to guide him, it is impossible to tell. He knows every language of mortal men, but he cannot read lips.

Some of the room's occupants are just outside his field of vision. He can see their hands moving. If they shifted only a little—

Wait. Something is wrong. Only now does it occur to him to wonder how the corpse's eyelids come to be open.

He senses another presence. Not out there, but in here, where there should be nothing but an empty husk. He reaches out into the void, and he feels it brush against him. He is not alone.

It lasts only a moment. The presence lingers just long enough to recognize the death here, the wrongness. It departs, but not before he senses its confusion and sadness. It did not come of its own volition. It was summoned.

It has been centuries since he felt rage, but he feels it now, thick and hot and writhing. This should not be. This is a sin far greater than that which called him here. He longs to loose his wrath upon them now, but there is too much light; he is powerless. No matter, he tells himself. They cannot escape him.

He will have his vengeance.

CHAPTER 7

The day had started out badly and seemed determined to grow worse. Lenoir had awoken with a terrible headache and a bitter taste in his mouth, thanks to another long evening at Zera's. There had been nothing edible in his apartment—the cheese had gone off and the bread was stale—so he had made his way to the station without breakfast. There he had been forced to endure an hour of Kody's inane speculations, followed by the stomach-turning scene of a man subjected to bleeding by leech (on second thought, perhaps the lack of breakfast was a blessing.) To cap it off, the nobleman responsible for the crime assumed that Lenoir's silence could be bought, which assumption, to his immense annoyance, was not entirely unwarranted.

By the time evening threw its dark cloth over the rooftops, Lenoir had worked himself into a veritable froth of ill humor. Feine had not even waited for him to produce real evidence before deciding that it would be easier to bribe his way out. A vindictive sort would take that as a sign the deal could be sweetened.

Lenoir was feeling awfully vindictive.

If Feine thought silence came cheaply, he would soon learn otherwise. But first, Lenoir needed leverage. The lover's letter alone was not enough to convince the magistrate. At most, it suggested an affair between Lady Feine and Arleas, but in itself that proved nothing. He needed something concrete, something that tied Feine directly to the beating. Fortunately, he had an idea how to get it.

He found Zach at the Firkin, the same shabby inn where the two of them had first become acquainted. The boy was lounging near the hearth, a flagon of ale in hand (where in the flaming below had he gotten *that*?), scanning the room for likely prey. When he spied Lenoir, his face split into a wide grin, and he waved enthusiastically. Lenoir could not deny that it felt good to receive such a welcome, even if it came from a sorry little street mongrel. God knew there were few enough who took any joy in Lenoir's presence.

"What are you doing here, Zach?"

The boy scowled. "Well, now, here's a fine greeting."

"Infringed dignity sits oddly on you," Lenoir said wryly. "I thought you were supposed to be looking into something for me."

"And so I am! You can't blame a fellow for taking a break now and then. It's cold as Durian's grave out there."

Lenoir could not disagree. Even this close to the hearth, the frequent comings and goings at the tavern door kept the room steeped in a perpetual chill. Not that the patrons took any notice; most were too far into their cups to heed much of anything. The Firkin was one of Kennian's more raucous taverns, which was one of the reasons Zach could so often be found here. Drunkards took little notice of their purses being lifted.

"Anyway," said Zach, "I don't know why you're acting all surprised. You came here looking for me."

"Is that so? And how do you reckon that?"

"You never come in here unless you're looking for me."

Lenoir grunted. "Very well, I concede the point. The fact remains, however, that you have an unfinished task."

"Don't I know it. I'm not getting anywhere." Zach looked darkly at the flagon in his hand, as though it were responsible.

"It is not an easy thing I have asked you to do," Lenoir admitted. "But do not allow yourself to become discouraged. I have great faith in your talents."

Zach sniffed, his petulant expression disappearing under the rim of his flagon.

Lenoir would have dearly liked to know which of these tavern rats thought it appropriate to give a full flagon of ale to a boy of nine, but he did not have time to worry about that now. "In the meantime, I have another task for you."

"All right," Zach said warily, licking his lips.

"I need you to put me in touch with some hired muscle."

"Hired muscle?"

"A thug, Zach. The sort of man who hires himself out for his fists."

"Ah." Zach grinned. "Now, that's more like it. I don't know about high street gossip, but cutthroats and mercenaries are my specialty. Let's go."

Lenoir drew up short when he recognized the alley. The narrow, twisting path ended at a small courtyard hemmed in by two- and three-story buildings, their dark frames leaning haphazardly in a semicircle like a cluster of drunks huddled over a game of bones. It was a dead end, meaning Zach had only one possible destination: the Hobbled Hound.

"You come to this place?" Lenoir asked in mild amazement.

Zach turned, his features barely discernible in the shadows. The alley was dark save for the washed amber glow of the braziers in the courtyard up ahead. The wavering firelight sketched eerie shapes on the plaster and beams of the shop faces, long since closed for the night.

"Sometimes," Zach said. "It's not as bad as you might think."

"I'm relieved to hear it," Lenoir muttered, resuming his stride.

The alley deposited them in the cramped square that formed the boundaries of the Hound's domain. The inn itself sat nestled at the far end, flanked between two larger buildings and gazing out at the courtyard like a crime lord who knows better than to turn his back to the door. A pair of braziers burned on either side of the entrance, throwing their light over tightly closed shutters and a heavy door. A faded sign bearing a likeness of a three-legged dog hung from a post just above the doorframe, but the crest was a bitter joke. The name of the inn had nothing to do with hunting dogs. Rather, it derived from a particularly nasty incident that had taken place on the premises many years ago, involving a sergeant of the Metropolitan Police, an ax, and a very ugly crowd.

A pair of hard-bitten fellows huddled together near one of the braziers, ostensibly warming their hands. Lenoir knew them for lookouts, keeping an eye peeled for someone just like him.

"I hope you know what you're doing, Zach," he growled as he followed the boy across the courtyard and through the door, the lookouts tracking him every step of the way.

The place was not busy, at least not compared to neighborhood stalwarts like the Firkin. About a dozen tables dotted the floor, most of them occupied by rough-hewn men at assorted games of chance—bones, cards, and what looked like a variation of madman's mirth, only with a stiletto. Lenoir's gaze lit upon daggers and swords, pistols and crossbows. Every man in the room was armed with something, and many carried more than one, the weapons ostentatiously displayed as though they were some sort of status symbol—which, Lenoir supposed, was exactly what they were.

Zach paused, scanning the room. He flashed Lenoir a confident smile, but Lenoir did not miss the way his fists clenched and unclenched at his sides. His bluster notwithstanding, the boy was nervous. That simply proved he was not a fool.

"This is the place to come if you want to hire a cut-throat," Zach said in a low voice. "These fellows all know each other. Some of them come from the streets. Some used to be soldiers. Be careful, though—lots of them are drunks, and they're not much fond of hounds."

"You don't say." Lenoir was acutely aware of the eyes on him, and they were not friendly.

"How long is this gonna take?" Zach's eyes were still darting around the room. He seemed to be looking for something. Or someone.

"I don't know," Lenoir said. He made his way over to the bar.

The barman made no move toward him. He just stood there, wiping out a mug with a filthy rag and ey-ing Lenoir balefully. "You shouldn't be here, hound. Get yourself killed, you will."

"Whatever gave you the idea I was a hound?" Le-noir asked sarcastically. He gazed down at his dark coat, his neat if modest trousers, his leather shoes. He might as well have worn a sign that read *Kennian Met-ropolitan Police* around his neck.

The barman seemed to appreciate that. He grinned and snorted through his nose.

"I have not come here to make trouble," Lenoir said. "On the contrary, I am offering a business propo-sition."

"That so?" The barman put his mug aside and tossed the rag over his shoulder. "Let's have it, then."

"I have been offered a substantial amount of money to overlook a certain instance of wrongdoing." Lenoir was getting a little ahead of himself, but this cretin had no way of knowing that. "If I can turn up the heat, I have no doubt I will be offered an even more attractive sum. I am prepared to part with a percentage, in return for incriminating evidence."

The barman's laugh crackled in his throat. "You must think I'm right stupid, mate. You think you're the first hound to come up with that one?" He shook his head, still smiling.

Lenoir was considering how to respond when Zach suddenly appeared at his elbow, tucking his body up against the bar as though shielding himself from view. The boy was pale and sweating, and his gaze had taken on a hunted look. All signs of his earlier bravado were gone. Zach was not just nervous, Lenoir realized; he was *terrified*.

Lenoir glanced around the room, trying to pin down what had spooked the boy. There were plenty of candidates: the whole tavern seemed to be staring at them, each grisly face more menacing than the last. But then one of them started across the room, and Zach whimpered like the small child he was.

The man must have weighed two hundred pounds, and though he wore only a single dagger at his hip, Lenoir had the distinct impression that was because he required nothing else. His nose had obviously been broken more than once, and a nasty scar carved a pink trench through his left cheek. He glared at Zach as he weaved between the tables, fists balled at his sides.

"Who is that man?" Lenoir hissed.

Zach swallowed hard. "My uncle. Please, we have to leave now. Right now, Inspector."

"Your uncle? I thought—"

"Please!" Zach squeaked, and there was such dread in his eyes that Lenoir could not deny him. He grabbed the boy's arm and made for the door. As soon as they were outside, he broke into a jog, hustling Zach along through the alley until he judged they were far enough away. Thankfully, no one seemed to be following them.

Lenoir stopped to catch his breath. "What was *that* all about?"

Zach's face was turned away, and he dragged his sleeve across his eyes. "Nothing," he said sullenly.

Lenoir regarded him with a sigh. This was not the wisecracking, wily creature he was accustomed to. *Sometimes I forget you are a child, Zach.* Aloud, he said gently, "It was obviously something. You said he was your uncle?"

Zach nodded. "Not by blood, though. He was married to my mum's sister. When they got sick—my mum and my auntie—I went to live with him for a while. It wasn't . . . he . . ." Zach fell silent, shuddering.

"He beat you." Lenoir could see it in the hang of the boy's shoulders, in the twitch of his fingers. He knew the signs as well as if he were looking into a mirror.

Zach did not answer directly, but he did not have to. "When they died, he threw me out. And that was fine, really, but . . . then I got in trouble, and the hounds came around to his place. They caught him with some stuff he shouldn't have. He was in jail for a while."

"I see," Lenoir said, and he did. He saw it all too clearly. "And did you know he would be in there tonight?"

Zach shrugged disconsolately. "Maybe. He's there sometimes. I hoped he wouldn't be."

"But you knew it was possible. And you came anyway."

He shrugged again. "You needed to go there." He still avoided Lenoir's gaze, as though he were ashamed.

Nine years old, and already afraid to show weakness. Lenoir felt a stab of pity. "Will he try to come after you?"

"Nah. He just told me to stay away from him, is all. Said he'd sort me out right good if he caught me within a mile of him." He scowled. "Like I'd *want* to be around the likes of him, anyway!"

Lenoir passed a hand over his eyes. He suddenly felt very tired. "It's late, Zach. Go home."

"What about your hired muscle?"

"Never mind that. I will see you tomorrow night, and we can work on Zera's problem."

"Okay," Zach said. "See you later."

Lenoir watched the boy slink off like a whipped dog. Guilt tugged at his belly. Zach had deliberately put himself in danger, without even asking why. He had probably assumed Lenoir was trying to solve a crime. Would he still have done it if he knew the truth? Lenoir had to admit he was touched by the boy's loyalty.

He would have to make it up to Zach tomorrow.

"Here it is, Inspector," the scribe said, laying a sheaf of parchment on Lenoir's desk.

"At last," Lenoir said coolly. It had taken the scribe all morning and the better part of the afternoon to find it.

"Sorry, Inspector," the youth said, flushing. "But without a name . . . I had to go to the city clerk's office to look through the marriage records, and—"

"That will be all," Lenoir said. The scribe swallowed, nodded, and vanished.

Lenoir pulled the dusty pile of papers toward him. It was a healthy stack, nearly half an inch thick, bound together with twine. Zach's uncle was obviously no stranger to the Kennian Metropolitan Police. Lenoir loosened the twine and scanned the writing at the top of the uppermost page. "Thad Eccle," he murmured aloud. Thirty-two years of age, six foot two, approximately two hundred ten pounds. Scar on the left cheek. *Definitely our man,* Lenoir thought. The scribe had done his job well.

Second-degree theft, the charge on the topmost page read. Approximately two hundred crowns' worth of goods recovered from Eccle's premises, including forty pounds of silverware, two pewter door knockers, sundry items of jewelry, and a gilt mirror. *Sentence: not less than two years to be served in Fort Hald.* A comparatively light sentence. Too light, in Lenoir's view. The incident was dated three years ago. That meant Zach had been living on the streets since the age of six. Lenoir had more or less known that, but his mouth still took a sour twist.

He thumbed through several random places in the pile. *First-degree theft. Battery. Attempted battery.* Each one carried a prison term. Thad Eccle seemed to have spent as much of his life in prison as out, going back to . . . Lenoir pulled out the bottom page. *Battery*, the charge read. Eccle had been eight years old. A lifelong criminal, irredeemable. He was fortunate to have escaped the hangman's noose. Perhaps he had a patron, someone who paid off the magistrate for a more lenient sentence. The more talented thieves often had such protection, provided they turned a consistent profit for the crime lord they served. The moment they became too inconvenient, they were cut loose, or worse. Judging from Eccle's record, he was one charge away from the gallows. *He should remember that,* Lenoir thought. *And if he does not, I shall have to remind him.*

Lenoir ate an early supper before heading for the orphanage. He wanted to get a head start on the evening, for Zera's patience was wearing thin. She had pressed him terribly last time, demanding an update on Zach's progress. The rumors had only gained momentum in the intervening days, growing not only more frequent, but more outrageous as well. Zera was now said to have a den of misfits that she kept as slaves to serve at the pleasure of her salon guests. Talk would have it that she kept them caged until evening, subjecting them to opium and other mind-numbing substances to keep them docile. Lenoir could not imagine how anyone could believe such nonsense. He would have found it amusing were it not for Zera's outrage.

The sun had just sunk behind the tiled rooftops when Lenoir arrived at the orphanage. He knocked, and when the door swung open, he found himself looking down at a tiny nun of vaguely shrewlike appearance, her beady eyes and upturned nose contriving to give her a mistrustful look.

"What has he done this time?" she snapped.

Lenoir blinked, taken aback. "I am sorry, Sister— you misunderstand. I am looking for Zach."

"I know who you're looking for. What's he done?"

Lenoir could not suppress a smile. "Any number of things, perhaps, but I am not here to take him away. I would just like to speak with him, if you please. He . . . owes me a favor."

"I'll bet he does," she said sourly. "But he's not here. Haven't seen him since this morning."

Lenoir frowned. "Is that normal?"

"I'm lucky if I see some of these kids three times a week. Zach's usually around, though, at least at mealtimes."

"Do you know where he might be?"

"You're an inspector, Inspector. Why don't you go and find Zach, and when you do, you can tell him that the next time he skips out on his chores, there'll be a licking waiting for him when he gets back!" And with that, she slammed the door in Lenoir's face.

He stood on the threshold for a moment, staring at

the closed door in astonishment. Then he turned to go. He was halfway down the street when he heard the door open again, followed by the patter of bare feet against stone. He turned to find a small boy scampering after him wearing nothing but a nightshirt.

"Go back inside, boy. You will catch your death of cold."

The child seemed not to hear. "Mister," he said breathlessly, "are you looking for Zach?"

"Yes."

"If you find him, can you ask him if I can come too?"

Lenoir looked pityingly at the boy. "Why do you want to go with him? You are well taken care of in the orphanage, no? Whatever Zach is doing, I am sure it is not as much fun as you think."

"But I want to go with the rich people," the boy whined. He gave an exasperated little stamp of his foot, wringing a corner of his nightshirt in his hands.

Lenoir narrowed his eyes. "The rich people?"

"The ones Zach went away with. I want them to take me too."

"What do you mean? Who did Zach go away with?"

"I don't know, but they had a carriage, the big fancy kind. He got into the carriage and they took him away."

A strange feeling was creeping up Lenoir's neck, the prickling sense he always got when something was wrong. "Did Zach know these people?"

The little boy shrugged his thin shoulders. Lenoir could see he was shivering. "Tell Zach I want to come too," he said again, then turned and ran back to the orphanage.

A hand shot out of the open door and grabbed the little boy by the sleeve, dragging him inside, and the door slammed shut on stern words. Lenoir watched without really seeing. A cold weight had settled in his stomach. He could think of a hundred reasons why Zach would want to ride in a carriage with strangers. He could not, however, think of a single reason why anyone would want Zach in their carriage.

CHAPTER 8

By the next morning, Lenoir was convinced that something terrible had befallen Zach. He had passed a sleepless night thinking about the boy, turning the possibilities over and over in his mind. The rational part of him said this was paranoia, that drink and nightmares and sleeplessness were a potent elixir for fevered imaginings. But that same part of him, the part that had guided him through more than twenty years of police work, also told him that he would be foolish to ignore his instincts.

It was the carriage that sealed it. Few could afford such a luxurious mode of transport, and people like that did not go around picking up stray orphans—at least not with good intentions. Unlikely as it seemed, therefore, Lenoir had to treat Zach's disappearance as a kidnapping.

The uncle was an obvious place to start. Thad Eccle had not even troubled to mask his ill intentions the other night; he had gone after the boy in full view of everyone at the Hobbled Hound, including an inspec-

tor of the Metropolitan Police. He could easily have
followed Lenoir and Zach out of the tavern and trailed
the boy back to the orphanage. Admittedly, the carriage was harder to explain. A man of Eccle's means
could not afford a horse, let alone a carriage. He could
have stolen it, Lenoir supposed. Or perhaps, if Lenoir's
hunch was right, and Eccle was under the patronage of
a wealthy crime lord, he might have access to a carriage that way. But why bother? If Eccle was tailing the
boy, he could easily have snatched Zach without subterfuge. Why go to the trouble of procuring a carriage?
For that matter, why snatch the boy at all? He could
have dealt with Zach right there in the street.

Troublesome questions all, but Lenoir had always
believed that motive trumped everything else when it
came to solving a crime. Thad Eccle certainly had a
motive; he had made that clear at the Hobbled Hound.
So Lenoir grabbed his coat and a loaded flintlock and
headed for Eccle's last known address.

The poor district was a bustle of activity, even at this
ungodly hour of the morning. Carts selling bread and
hot pies were already doing a brisk trade, and butchers
and greengrocers and fishmongers were busy laying
out their wares in the predawn gloom. Lenoir kept to
the center of the street, in spite of the mud. It was easier than jockeying for position with broomsticks and
wheelbarrows and apple crates, and a little muck on his
trousers was preferable to running the risk of being
doused with a pail of slops from a window. He wended
his way between slow-moving wagons, choosing his
steps carefully to avoid horse shit and the occasional

trickle of privy runoff. Odors both tempting and foul clashed for dominion over his nose. He threw an arm over his face to block them all.

He turned west onto Eccle's street, a narrow canyon cutting a perfectly straight path between the sheer cliff faces of the tenement buildings. Washing lines formed a sagging canopy from one side of the street to the other, looking like bedraggled pennants at a fair. Lenoir passed beneath them, scanning the numbers at the top of each stoop until he came to number 56, a four-story rookery with a simple facade of gray stone. He climbed the steps and tried the door. Unlocked. Lenoir grunted in satisfaction and slipped inside.

Peeling paint lined the walls of a long, shadowy corridor stained with soot. The hallway was empty but for a jumble of sound and smells: pots clanging, bacon sizzling, babies crying, and the dry, stiff toll of bootheels crossing the floor. Snatches of conversation floated, disembodied, in the air, scarcely muffled by the thin doors of the flats. Somewhere on the second floor, a dog barked. Lenoir counted eighteen doors as he passed. Eighteen doors, but how many windows? Few, judging by the thickness of the air. *Packed in like rats in the hull of a ship*. Suddenly, his own flat did not seem so cramped.

He was out of breath by the time he reached Thad Eccle's flat on the third floor. He paused to collect himself, positioning his flintlock so that its handle protruded obviously from his coat pocket. Then he rapped on the door and waited.

Nothing. After a long pause, he knocked again. This

time, something shuffled on the far side of the door, and the floorboards beneath Lenoir's boots creaked. A rough voice barked, *"What?"*

"Thad Eccle."

"Who wants to know?"

"I am Inspector Lenoir of the Metropolitan Police. Do not make me force the door. It would not be fair to your landlord." That was pure bluster. Forcing doors was Kody's job; Lenoir had not attempted it in years.

Fortunately, Eccle could not see him through the door, or he might have called Lenoir's bluff. Instead there was a muttered oath, and the sound of a bolt sliding out. The door opened a crack. An unshaven face loomed over Lenoir, bleary-eyed from sleep. "You," Eccle said.

"Indeed."

"What do you want?"

Lenoir considered the carved gargoyle before him. There was no point in trying to intimidate Eccle physically—that much was obvious. The man outweighed him by at least fifty pounds, all of it muscle, and the knuckles grasping the door were scarred from use. Lenoir could draw his gun, but that would only make him look fearful. He would not get anything from Eccle that way. Instead he adopted an air of supreme boredom. It was easily done, for Lenoir wore that expression more often than not. "I am here for the boy," he said.

The uncle did some appraising of his own before he replied. His gaze swept over Lenoir's shoulder, noting the lack of backup, before taking in the flint-lock slouching conspicuously in Lenoir's coat pocket. "What boy?"

"Do not waste my time, sir. I am a busy man."

"If you mean that little piece of rat filth I saw you with the other night, I haven't seen him since."

"Oh?" Lenoir arched an eyebrow. "You seemed to have some rather urgent business with him."

The scar on Eccle's left cheek was a deep pink trough, shaped like the f-hole of a violin. A bottle to the face, Lenoir judged, probably in the man's youth. When he smiled, as he was doing now, the scar coiled like a serpent about to strike. "You could put it that way. He owes me."

"He owes you, or you owe him?"

Eccle's smile widened unsettlingly. "Both."

"Have you collected?"

"Not yet, but I will."

"You are remarkably frank for a man under suspicion. Has it occurred to you that I could arrest you on the spot?"

Eccle snorted. "For what? He's my nephew—I got every right to discipline the little bugger. But as it happens, I haven't seen him."

"And if I were to search your flat right now?"

"You're welcome to try, hound, but I'd ask myself if it was worth the bother." He sagged through the door-frame, giving Lenoir a better look at his massive frame.

Lenoir debated drawing his pistol. To stall for time, he said, "I want you to understand something. The boy may have information on a case I'm working. Therefore, he has value to me. I would be very put out if he were . . . indisposed."

"What's that to me?"

Lenoir gave a thin smile. It would not be as threatening as Eccle's gargoyle grin, but he hoped it would do the job. "I'm sure you are aware that I have the ability to make your life extremely inconvenient, if not a good deal shorter. You are on thin ice with the Metropolitan Police, Eccle. And I carry a great deal of weight."

Eccle's eyes darkened. "I told you, I haven't seen him since that night. If I'd wanted to do for him, I'd have done it by now. I know the orphanage where he lives. I told him to stay away from me, and he didn't listen. Looked to me like I needed to make my point again, so I did."

Lenoir eyed Thad Eccle's brutish face carefully. He found much to dislike, but no evidence of deceit. More importantly, what Eccle said was true—he could have gone after Zach at any time since his release from prison a year ago. Why do it now, especially when he knew a hound had seen him chase the boy out of a tavern the night before? Eccle would have to be incredibly stupid to risk it, and he did not come across that way. And then there was the matter of the carriage. . . .

It doesn't fit, Lenoir concluded unhappily. He could not discount the possibility altogether, but it seemed unlikely that Eccle was involved. It was time to pursue a different thread. "Stay away from Zach," Lenoir said in parting, "or you will wish you had."

Eccle stabbed a finger at him. "Keep him away from me, or you'll wish you had." So saying, he slammed the door.

Lenoir's next port of call was the orphanage. It was only a little after dawn, so he was not surprised when the nun he had spoken to the previous night answered the door in her nightgown. She squinted up at Lenoir with sleep-crusted eyes and a thoroughly disapproving expression. "This had better be important, Inspector. You're waking the children."

Lenoir was in no mood for chiding. "I trust you consider it important, madam, that a child in your care has gone missing. Unless you have seen Zach since yesterday?"

"I haven't, but you obviously don't know much about running an orphanage. These kids go missing all the time. Sometimes they come back, sometimes they don't. I'm not running a prison here. If they want to run away, I can't stop them."

"And it has not occurred to you to suspect foul play?"

She passed a hand over her face in a gesture that was more weary than tired, and when she spoke, her voice was gentler. "These children lead difficult lives, Inspector. They mostly do all right until they're about Zach's age. That's when they start getting into trouble. They fall in with thugs, get to stealing and such. And then one day they walk out my door and never come back. Usually it's because they fancy themselves all grown up. They resent the rules around here, having to account for where they've been and what they've done, and they figure it's time to make their own way. But sometimes it's worse. They get into something they can't handle, or end up in the wrong place at the wrong time. I've buried more than a few of those children. So when a boy like Zach goes missing, all I can do is pray to the good Lord that he's one of the ones who decided it was time to make his own way."

"Alas, I doubt that very much. Zach has his schemes, to be sure, but he is too smart to give up a warm bed and a guaranteed meal to go off and live in a ditch somewhere."

She grunted. "I'll give you that."

"I need to speak with the little boy from last night, the one who came outside to talk to me. He may have an idea where Zach went."

The nun was shaking her head before he even finished speaking. "He's asleep, at long last. Come back later."

"Every hour is precious, madam," Lenoir said coldly. "I need to speak with the boy now."

"He's four years old, and a teller of tales besides. What could he possibly—"

"Now."

She flushed angrily, and for a moment Lenoir thought she was going to slam the door in his face again. But she spun and disappeared inside, returning a few moments later leading a whimpering little boy, the same child Lenoir had spoken to the night before.

"Well, Adam, I know you're sleepy and confused, but the inspector here is *very important*, and he needs to speak with you *right now*." She tugged the boy's hand and dragged him into the sunlight. The child whimpered again, digging his small fist into his eyes, and the nun gave Lenoir a look that was both smug and scathing.

Lenoir squatted so that he was eye level with the boy. "Adam, do you remember me from last night?"

He shook his head.

"You told me you wanted to go with Zach, remember?"

"Yeah."

"Do you still want to go?"

Adam perked up a little at that. He nodded solemnly.

"I need you to tell me about the rich people you saw. What did they look like?"

The boy shrugged. "I don't know."

"Try to remember, Adam."

"I can't," he whined, his face collapsing into a scowl. The boy was cranky and tired; Lenoir sensed he was on the verge of tears. He tried a different tack.

"What about the carriage? Was it nice?"

Adam nodded.

"What did it look like?"

"Golden," said the little boy, with something more like the enthusiasm he had shown the night before.

Lenoir eyed the child skeptically. *A teller of tales,* the nun had said. He did not need to look up; he could sense the smirk she was directing his way. "Are you sure it was golden, Adam?"

"Yep, and blue."

"He means green," the nun interjected. "He gets them mixed up. Don't you, Adam? You mean green like your blanket?"

Adam furrowed his brow in thought. "Yeah," he said doubtfully, "green."

"Can you remember anything else about the carriage?"

"It had angels on it."

"That's good, Adam. What else?"

He shook his head. "I'm sleepy."

The nun took the boy's hand again. "I think that will do, Inspector," she said sternly. "A gold and green carriage with angels on it. That ought to be enough for you."

Reluctantly, Lenoir rose. He did not even have a chance to thank the boy before the nun had dragged him inside and closed the door.

His next stop was the local wheelwright, and it proved to be an excellent move. Lenoir had not gone far in his description of the carriage before the wheelwright began to nod knowingly. "That's one of them for-hire jobs, Inspector, the kind folks get for special events and the like. I've done a lot of work for that company—it's not far from here, actually." He walked Lenoir out of the work yard to point him in the right direction.

"And you're certain that's where the carriage is from?"

The man nodded again. "They paint all of their carriages that same green and gold, so as they're easy to recognize. Sort of like advertising, I guess."

When Lenoir arrived at the company's front shop, he saw immediately what the wheelwright had meant. A green and gold carriage sat idle in the street, its coachman slouched casually on his perch. It was a distinctive enough contraption, for aside from the garish green of its hood, its faux-gilt frame was so elaborate—with great swooping wings and frescoed door panels—that it was clearly designed to be noticed. From a distance it might pass for something grand, and certainly it was enough to impress a small boy. But up close it was tired-looking and shabby; the cherubim on the panels were badly drawn, and the paint was peeling. The seat cushions looked old and worn. According to the wheelwright, this was the less expensive of the two carriage-for-hire firms in town, and Lenoir could readily see why.

As he approached, a couple was exiting the shop, accompanied by a man wearing the same livery as the coachman. The footman, for so he appeared to be, assisted the lady to climb into the carriage; Lenoir quickened his step to reach them before they departed.

"Hold a moment, please," he called. The lady leaned out of the window with a quizzical expression, and the three men turned their heads to look at Lenoir.

"What can we do for you, Inspector?" said the footman after Lenoir had introduced himself.

"Actually, it is your coachman I wish to speak with." Lenoir looked up at the man on the perch. "Sir, were you driving this carriage yesterday afternoon?"

"I was," said the coachman warily. He looked uncomfortable in his tacky green tunic.

"Did you pick up a young boy in the poor district, sometime in the afternoon?"

The man shook his head. "No children, sir, not yesterday. But you might try the other coachman, Marrick." His yellow glove gestured in the direction of the shop. "Out back, washing the other carriage, I think."

Lenoir followed the coachman's directions through the shop and out to the back, where a man in breeches and an undershirt was mopping the running gear of an identical green and gold carriage. He swore under his breath as he worked, and did not seem to notice Lenoir's presence until the inspector cleared his throat.

"Oh, excuse me, sir," Marrick said sheepishly, rising. "It's only that the paint keeps flaking off when I wash it. Frustrating, you know?"

Lenoir was supremely uninterested in the tribulations of carriage washing, and he hoped his expression conveyed as much. "I am here from the Metropolitan Police, and I would like to ask you a few questions."

A worried look crossed the coachman's face. "The police? Is there something wrong?"

"I wonder if you can think back to yesterday, to the people you drove in your carriage. Do you remember a boy, about ten years old? Name of Zach?"

"Oh yeah, yeah," Marrick said enthusiastically, clearly relieved. "I remember the kid. Filthy little beggar, he was. . . ." He paused, flushing slightly. "Excuse me again. No disrespect intended. . . ."

"Not at all. That is quite helpful, actually. It means we are almost certainly talking about the same child. Was this yesterday afternoon?"

The coachman nodded. "Picked him up over on Barrow Street, about two hours before sunset, I think."

"Was there anyone else in the carriage?"

"Course! The boy couldn't very well have paid for it, now, could he?" Marrick gave a timid laugh.

Lenoir did not so much as hint at a smile. "Perhaps you would indulge me, sir, by telling me who else was in the carriage."

The coachman scratched the back of his neck nervously. "Oh, right. Well . . . he didn't give his name, actually. I mean he hadn't booked or anything, he just flagged me down. We're not supposed to do that, if you want the truth—my boss would box me around the ears if he knew. Doesn't conform to the image, he says, picking up folks as though they were common hitchhikers. . . ."

Lenoir listened to the man's drivel without comment, his face expressionless. But this seemed only to intimidate Marrick further, and he began to wander so far off topic that for a brief moment Lenoir considered cuffing him into silence. In the event, he merely said, "Stop. Try to focus, please. Short answers. Now, where did you pick this man up?"

"Warrick Avenue," the coachman gulped.

"And where did you drop him off?"

"Berryvine."

Lenoir blinked in surprise. Berryvine was almost two hours west of Kennian. "He must have paid you well."

Marrick only nodded mutely.

"Was the boy with him when you dropped him off?"

Again, Marrick nodded.

"And did you have the impression he knew the boy?" Zach's uncle flashed briefly through his mind.

Marrick considered this. "Well, I couldn't hear their conversation from up front. But now you mention it, I guess not." He hesitated, then shook his head firmly. "No, I reckon he couldn't have known the boy, because he seemed to just sort of happen upon it. See, at first he just said he wanted to ride around town for a bit, but when he saw the boy, he asked me to stop. I don't know what he said to the lad, but he looked happy enough to get in the carriage. And then the customer just asked me to take them to Berryvine, and that's it. I dropped them on the main street, and he didn't say where they were headed." Marrick paused guiltily. "Guess I should've known something wasn't right, him picking up a strange child like that."

Lenoir ignored this, a knot tightening in his stomach. Any lingering doubt that Zach had met with foul play had now dissolved; the coachman's description sounded like a classic case of a predator luring a child. Such things were not uncommon in Kennian, and orphans were especially vulnerable. Few people thought to wonder about the disappearance of a street urchin, and those that did tended to dismiss it as nothing out of the ordinary, just as the nun at Zach's orphanage had done. All too often, the first sign of foul play was the discovery of a corpse.

Lenoir had only one question left. "What did he look like, this man? Would you know him if you saw him again?"

Marrick glanced skyward as he thought. "Well, let me see . . . He was tall, I suppose." This seemed the limit of his powers of observation, for he was silent a long moment. Lenoir was on the verge of giving him a solid shake when the coachman added, "Oh, and his skin had a darkish hue. Might have been Adali."

It was not much, but at least it was something to go on. If the man really was Adali, that would certainly narrow the field. Lenoir was skeptical, however, as he always was when a witness identified a suspect as Adali. As a race, the Adali were so distrusted that many witnesses either lied outright, preferring to see an Adal in jail rather than no one at all, or merely remembered the suspect as an Adal, when in fact that was not the case. The mere presence of an Adali camp near one of the outer villages was often enough to provoke a surge in the number of reported crimes.

He needed to return to headquarters and see if he could find Kody, for he would need help if he was to interview residents of Berryvine quickly. He only hoped the sergeant was there and not out chasing his phantom corpse thief.

Kody was in the middle of dictating a report when Lenoir found him. He was taking his time, waiting patiently while the scribe scratched his words out in full. You never knew when the smallest detail could be important, and Kody wanted to make sure that the scribe got everything down. He'd made it clear that he wouldn't tolerate shorthand or paraphrasing, so he paused often and for as long as it took for the quill to stop moving. He'd just started up again when Lenoir stalked up to the scribe's desk. The inspector didn't even offer a greeting before cutting into Kody's recitation.

"Get your riding cloak, Sergeant. We have work to do."

The scribe looked up from his notebook, his quill poised in midair. He glanced uncertainly between Kody and Lenoir.

Because I'm not doing any work here? Kody thought irritably. Aloud, he said, "I'm in the middle of a report, Inspector. I spent the morning talking to some of the other sergeants, and I found out some interesting things."

Lenoir's lip curled. "Excellent. I can see you are on the verge of solving the crime of the century. But if you can delay your historic triumph for a few hours, I require your assistance to find a real, live child."

Kody felt heat rise to his face, but he bit back the caustic reply that was on his lips. There was no point in antagonizing Lenoir. The man was his superior and had every right to divert him to another case. In truth, Kody was surprised Lenoir hadn't already done just that. Still, if he didn't finish his report now, there was a good chance he might forget some detail that could prove pivotal later on.

"If you could just give me five minutes, sir," he said as evenly as possible, "and I'll be finished here. I want to get this down while it's fresh in my mind."

A moment of indecision flashed across Lenoir's face. Then, to Kody's relief, he said, "Be quick about it."

Kody cleared his throat, then hesitated uncertainly.

"An Adali male was spotted," the scribe supplied helpfully.

"Right. An Adali male was spotted in Brackensvale some days ago by the blacksmith, who lodged a complaint with the constabulary claiming that this Adal had stolen a horse and most of his tools. Constable Sownes visited the village, but was unable to locate the suspect, and no one else in town reported seeing anyone matching the suspect's description. Referring to Constable Sownes's own report on the matter, quote, 'It is possible that an Adali male was in fact in Brackensvale. However, there is no evidence that the individual was involved in the theft of Mr. Estes's horse or his tools,' end quote."

Kody glanced at Lenoir to see if the inspector had caught the significance of this. But it didn't look as though Lenoir was even listening; he stared fixedly at the floor, his eyebrows knotted as though he was deep in thought.

Pursing his lips in irritation, Kody waited until the scribe's quill stopped bobbing. Then he raised his voice a little and said, "I would like to refer here to my previous report, in which I noted that a witness in North Haven claimed to have seen a strange Adal in town on or about the night the Jymes boy's corpse disappeared. To have a witness in Brackensvale also claim to have seen a strange Adal on or about the day the Habberd boy disappeared is quite a coincidence."

Still Lenoir didn't look up. Was the man stone deaf? Or was he feigning indifference purely out of spite? *To the below with him,* Kody thought sourly; if the inspector could ignore him, he could ignore the inspector.

"Lastly, I was informed that Constable Crears of Berryvine reported a boy missing yesterday. A live one, that is. His parents haven't seen him in two days."

It was as though Lenoir had been startled from slumber. His head shot up. "What did you say?"

At last. "A boy has gone missing in Berryvine, Inspector," Kody repeated gravely. "A *nine-year-old boy*."

Lenoir swore quietly in Arrènais, his gaze abstracted. Then he said, "Get up, Sergeant. You have finished your report. We must ride to Berryvine immediately."

Kody was momentarily stunned. He'd never seen Lenoir react so vigorously, not even for a murder. Wary but hopeful, he grabbed his cloak and followed Lenoir to the police livery.

As the stable boy fetched their mounts, Lenoir said, "The boy I am looking for is also in Berryvine. But he was taken there from Kennian."

Of course. Kody should have known better than to think Lenoir gave a damn about some merchant's boy in Berryvine. "Whose son is it?"

Lenoir frowned. "Pardon?"

"I assume he's a nobleman's son? Or did his family offer money to find him?"

He knew he'd gone too far as soon as he said it. Lenoir turned to him slowly, his face a cold mask, and when he spoke, his voice was low and dangerous. "That is the last time I will tolerate your impudence, Kody. If there were another sergeant I could count on to assist me, I would relieve you of your duty here and now.

Fortunately for you, your colleagues are buffoons and imbeciles. But if I hear so much as a single word out of your mouth between here and Berryvine, I will have you thrown in Fort Hald for insubordination. I do hope I have been clear."

He snatched his horse's lead out of the hands of the startled stable boy and heaved himself into the saddle. Kody followed suit, his face burning. Lenoir had never spoken to him like that before, but he didn't doubt for a moment that the inspector would follow through on his threat. Whatever questions Kody had, he'd have to swallow them. It would be a long ride to Berryvine.

CHAPTER 9

The rag in his mouth was sour with someone's sweat. Zach would have gagged, but his tongue was immobilized. His lips were raw and chapped, and he was desperate for water. But he hadn't seen anyone in a long time. Hours, probably. It was almost as if they'd forgotten about him—which was weird, considering how much trouble they'd gone to in bringing him here. They had actually been pretty careful with him up until now, almost as if they were afraid of hurting him. But they weren't taking any chances either; his wrists were bound so tightly that his arms had gone numb behind his back. He'd long since given up trying to work at the knot. It was too tight, and anyway he had only his fingertips for leverage. He had dragged himself along the floor of the room, heels to bottom, in search of a loose nail or something else he could use to cut himself free, but that hadn't worked either. It was too dark to see, and groping along the floorboards with the flats of his hands turned up nothing.

Zach didn't know what they wanted from him. He

hadn't asked, and no one had volunteered the information. The Adal who brought him here had said he needed help on his berry farm, a few extra hands to pick the remaining fruit before the first frost. He'd offered money, but not too much—not enough to make Zach suspicious. It had sounded like easy work, and it wasn't as though Zach had other commitments. There was Lenoir, of course, but the only payment the inspector ever offered was food. That wasn't a bad deal, but it wasn't the same as money. Zach could spend coin of his own on the food and drink he liked, not the greasy, tasteless stew Lenoir insisted he should eat, or the sour wine the inspector insisted he should drink.

Still, Zach was angry with himself for not realizing it was a trap. The Adal hadn't been the first to try to lure him somewhere, after all. Besides, he should have known that an Adal wouldn't own a berry farm. The Adali never stayed in one place long enough to till fields, and anyway, the townsfolk wouldn't have stood for it, not when there were so many local people without land of their own. But none of this had occurred to Zach yesterday when he had climbed aboard that ugly carriage. Then he'd thought only of the coin he would earn and what he would spend it on. A new hat, first of all, and then some shoes. And after that he would take his friend Kev to an eating house—the Courtier, maybe. And Kev would see that Zach really did know a bigshot inspector, and Lenoir could tell Kev about how important Zach was to his work. Then Lenoir and Zach would teach Kev how to make up stories about people, stories that were true and that you could tell just by looking. And then maybe Kev would want to be a hound too, and they could be partners someday.

Zach's throat started to close a little, and his eyes misted. He swallowed hard, determined not to cry. There wasn't anyone to see him, but still.

A loud bang sounded, startling him. A door had been slammed shut in the room next door. Muffled voices came through the wall, and the creak of some-one's weight traveled along the floorboards to where Zach was sitting. Turning his back to the sounds in the next room, Zach inched along the floor toward the wall until his shoulders were up against it. The voices came through more clearly now, and thin blades of light flickered in and out of view as shapes moved about in the other room.

Zach's heart sank as he realized the voices were speaking Adali. There were at least three of them, he judged, and maybe more. They sounded excited, but maybe a little nervous too. Zach strained to hear every word, even though he didn't understand any of it. Then there was a new voice, a boy's voice. That was strange. Zach tilted his head so his ear was against the wall, closing his eyes and concentrating on the boy's voice. He didn't seem to be speaking words, and his voice sounded strangely stifled. He was probably gagged too. Not with the others, then—a captive like himself. So he wasn't alone here.

He listened for a long time, but he couldn't make out what was going on. Then after a while something strange happened to the voices. The men—they all sounded like men—started chanting, or so it seemed to

Zach. Their voices dropped into a low monotone, and they all uttered the same unfamiliar words. This went on for a minute or so, and Zach wondered if they might be praying. And then the boy cried out, a single word that Zach understood perfectly even through the gag.

"No!"

The boy started screaming. The chanting grew louder, and there came a strange, frantic thumping noise, maybe from the boy trying to escape. Then more screaming, the boy's voice ripped open by terror. Somehow it was even scarier for being muted by the gag, as though it trapped the horror in the boy's throat.

Zach wanted to cover his ears, but he couldn't move his hands. He hunched up his shoulders, but it didn't help. The screaming went on and on, it wouldn't stop, and now sobbing, and Zach was sobbing too because he couldn't shut it out. It filled him up, drowning his insides; it was all he could hear, he could even taste it in his mouth. And when finally the boy's voice died away and the house fell silent, Zach was still sobbing, his body trembling like an aftershock.

CHAPTER 10

Lenoir was still stewing when they arrived in Berryvine. He could not afford to let his anger get in the way of the investigation, however, so when Kody cleared his throat uncertainly, Lenoir said, "Speak, Sergeant."

"Will we be checking in with the constabulary, sir?"

"Naturally. Crears might have information we need. Why—is there a problem?"

"No, sir, of course not. I only ask because we don't usually involve the constables."

"And why should we? Most of them are incompetent fools. Crears is different."

"I have nothing but respect for Constable Crears, sir," Kody said stiffly.

"As well you should. He is the best officer I have ever worked with, present company included."

Kody held his tongue.

They found Crears just outside his office, apparently organizing a search party. There were about twenty people gathered, most of them wearing uniforms. The constable was handing out maps and giving instructions. When he spotted Lenoir, he paused as though slightly taken aback. Then he cocked his head toward the hitching post in a gesture that said, *I'll be with you in a minute*.

Crears was a small man with flaming red hair and keen blue eyes. He had aged since Lenoir had seen him last; gray had started to overtake his beard, and his face was lined and worn. But he remained fit as ever, striding toward them with the lively gait of a man half his age.

"Inspector," he said, shaking Lenoir's hand. He and Kody exchanged handshakes as well, Crears seeming almost as a child next to the burly sergeant.

"Surprised to see you two. Wouldn't have thought a case like this would earn a visit from the Metropolitan Police. Not yet, anyway."

Not until the child turned up dead, was what he meant.

"Normally not, perhaps," admitted Lenoir, "but there are two boys missing in this village, it would seem." When Crears raised his eyebrows, Lenoir said, "Another boy was taken from the poor district of Kennian last night, an orphan called Zach."

The astonishment on Kody's face brought Lenoir's anger to a boil again, but he put a lid on it. "According to the coachman I questioned this morning, Zach was brought here last night, in a green and gold carriage. Has anyone mentioned it?"

Crears shook his head. "But I haven't been asking. Maybe someone saw a carriage like that. I can have some watchmen ask around if you like."

"If you can spare the men." Lenoir glanced around at the small crowd. "And it seems as though you can. How many watchmen do you have working for you?"

"A little less than fifty."

Kody whistled softly, impressed. "How do you afford it?"

"They're volunteers, mostly, although they get a small stipend. Trained them myself. Semiprofessional, I guess you'd call it."

Innovative, Lenoir thought approvingly. But he would not have expected any less from Crears; it was that sort of creativity and good sense that had landed him the plum constabulary in the Five Villages. Crears would have made inspector if he had stayed in Kennian, but he preferred Berryvine. Lenoir did not blame him. Berryvine was the second largest of the Five Villages, and like Kennian, it was a "village" by tradition only, having long since outgrown the name. Berryvine was a proper town, and out here, Crears was lord of his own fief. If he acquitted himself well, he could be chief of the Metropolitan Police one day—if he wanted it. Lenoir was not sure he would.

"In any case," said Lenoir, "it is worth looking into the carriage. We can assume that both boys were taken by the same person, so whatever helps me to find Zach should also turn up your boy."

Crears looked over his shoulder and waved, summoning a wiry youth, who came trotting over. The constable said something quiet to him, and the young man nodded and loped off again. Then Crears said, "I questioned the boy's parents yesterday, but since you're here, Inspector, maybe you'd like to have a go as well. Good chance of turning up something I missed."

Lenoir and Kody followed Crears across town to a row of handsome stone town houses just off the main street. The buildings were neat and orderly, each one built right up against the next such that there was no space between them. Stone steps led up from street level to wrought-iron fringed landings in front of elaborately carved doors.

"Granne is a merchant," Crears told them. "Dyes, mainly, from the berry farms. He trades them for all kinds of things—cloth, cattle, coin. He does well, as you can see. I assume his boy is being held for ransom."

"A reasonable assumption," said Lenoir, "but in this case I am doubtful."

"Oh?" The constable's clear blue eyes searched Lenoir as he gestured toward a set of stone steps.

"Whoever took Zach obviously was not interested in money, since the boy has no family."

"And you're sure it's the same person who took the Granne boy?"

"It would seem a strange coincidence, particularly since the boys are the same age."

"Zach is nine?" Kody cut in excitedly. "I *knew* it!" When Crears looked at him quizzically, Kody added, "Someone has been stealing the corpses of nine-year-old boys. I haven't—that is, *we* haven't—been able to figure out why. And now this."

They had reached the doorstep of the town house,

for which Lenoir was eminently grateful. He could not decide what was worse—that the sergeant had every reason to gloat, or that he was not doing so.

A girl of about fifteen answered the door. At the sight of Crears, her expression lit up with hope. "Did you find him, sir? Did you find our Mik?"

Her face fell as Crears shook his head. "Not yet. But we will."

The girl ushered them inside and bade them sit, then went to fetch her father. The three officers sat in silence, each lost in his own thoughts, until Granne returned with his daughter and his wife.

"This is Inspector Lenoir and Sergeant Kody of the Metropolitan Police," said Crears. "I wanted them to talk to you, see if they could turn up anything I didn't." Lenoir noticed that Crears did not mention what brought them to Berryvine. He supposed the constable did not want word to spread that they might have a serial offender on their hands. Besides, these people would not want to hear that their son was not Lenoir's only concern.

"Constable Crears tells me your son disappeared two days ago," said Lenoir, "sometime in the afternoon." Granne only nodded mutely, so Lenoir continued. "When was the last time you saw him?"

It was the mother who answered. "At the midday meal. He went out to play after. Said he was going to find his friend Bean." She smiled wanly, her hands twisting unconsciously in her lap. "That's not his real name—Bean—but Mika has always called him that. I don't suppose I know what his real name is, actually. . . ." She trailed off, her gaze dropping to the floor.

"The friend didn't see him," Crears put in quietly. "Says Mika never showed up."

"No one saw him come out of the house?" Lenoir asked. Crears shook his head.

Kody cleared his throat discreetly. Lenoir gave him leave with a wave of his hand, and Kody asked, "Did Mika ever mention feeling like he was being watched? Or maybe you noticed someone hanging around the house?" Again, heads shook.

This was not going anywhere. Lenoir rose, his fellow officers following suit. "Thank you for your time, and I am very sorry for your troubles. We will do our best to find your son."

Outside, Crears asked, "What next, Inspector?"

Lenoir gazed down the length of the street. They were in the merchant district near the heart of the town, yet still very close to where the farmlands began. This unusual layout owed to the particular history of Berryvine, which, as its name suggested, revolved entirely around berry farming. No one wanted his business too far away from his customers, and thus, in spite of its size and prosperity, the town of Berryvine was built more or less in a long, straight line, several miles north to south, but less than two miles east to west.

"Where does the friend live?" Lenoir asked Crears.

"Bean? That way." The constable pointed west down the length of the street. It ended only a few hundred paces away, emptying into a nearby field.

"So the boy would presumably have been taken somewhere en route."

"If he was taken at all," Crears said. "It's possible he just ran away."

"No," said Lenoir firmly, starting up the street. "He was taken."

They made their way toward the field in silence. Lenoir scanned the rows of town houses as they went, searching for an alleyway or some other hidden route by which a kidnapped boy might be secreted away without being seen by passersby. It was a quiet street; only the muted trill of pigeons accompanied their footsteps. From behind them the fading babble of the main avenue sounded like a distant creek. Ahead, a wagon trail ran perpendicular to the street, and beyond it the field opened out before them, revealing the long, ordered rows of a raspberry farm.

"Does this wagon road run the length of town?" Lenoir asked.

"More or less," said Crears. They had reached the edge of the field now, and they turned their backs to the rows of raspberry bushes. The breeze sweeping across the field was cold on the back of Lenoir's neck; winter was coming.

"And the gardens of this last row of houses overlook the length of it?"

"They do."

Lenoir knelt, scrutinizing the wagon road. The grass grew long between the wheel ruts, and the earth was packed hard where the weight of the fruit-laden wagons came to bear. Lenoir despaired of finding any trace of what he was looking for, but then he got lucky. As he moved a little southward along the road, he spied a scar on the edge of one of the wagon ruts, as though a horse crossing over the road had tripped when its hoof failed to clear the hump of grass between the deep ruts. Lenoir tried to suppress the flutter in his stomach. It was too early to get excited. Far too early . . .

Crears had seen it now too. He turned ninety degrees to his right, following the line of the hoof marks toward the field. Sure enough, there was evidence here too, even more plain than the track on the road. The spaces between the raspberry rows were only just wide enough to permit a man to comfortably pick the fruit. A horse could pass through, but not without damaging the bushes. The trail could not have been more obvious: the dark soil was littered with sprigs of heart-shaped raspberry leaves, some trodden beneath the crescent moon of a horseshoe.

"But wait," Kody said as Crears and Lenoir started into the field. "How do we know this is our kidnapper? That could be anyone's trail!"

Lenoir bit back a harsh reply. He did not have time to explain every little thing to Kody, and anyway, was it not obvious? But he could not afford to alienate the sergeant any more today. He needed Kody to be sharp, not brooding after yet another row. So instead he answered, as patiently as possible, "It could be someone else's trail, yes. But probably not. Think about it, Sergeant. You are a kidnapper. You have just seized a child in broad daylight, in his own neighborhood where everyone knows him. Now you must make your escape. Where do you go? The street has no alleyways, no hidden routes to take between the town houses. You can either go east, back to the main avenue full of people, or west, out to the fields. Of course you go west, and now you are on the wagon road. Do you take it, in full view of every back garden on the west side of town? Or do you take the boy into the fields where no one can see you?"

"Folks around here don't take kindly to people riding through the berry fields," Crears added. "More than likely this is our man. But even if it isn't, we'll still be headed in the right direction."

They moved single file through the canyon of foliage, their footsteps muted by the closeness of their surroundings. It was the ideal getaway route, Lenoir realized. The bushes were thriving here, growing so densely that very little light filtered between the leaves. And they were high, almost to the top of Lenoir's head. They would not completely conceal a man on horseback, but if he hunched over, no one would be able to tell who he was or what he was carrying. He would not even have to stain his clothing, for the fruit had long since been picked.

Lenoir called ahead to Crears, "Do you know whose farm this is?"

"Can't remember his name, but yeah, I know him. He's got kids of his own. Can't imagine he'd have anything to do with it."

"How much land has he got?"

"Not that much. A couple of hides, maybe."

"And then someone else's land."

"Right, and then it gets to—"

Crears stopped so suddenly that Lenoir walked into him. "What is it?" Kody called from behind.

Crears turned around, his expression set. "Let's go back for the horses, Inspector. I know where we're going."

CHAPTER 11

"The place has been abandoned for years," Crears explained, twisting in his saddle to speak over his shoulder. "The crop came up blighted one season, and the owner just left it. The fields have lain fallow ever since. It's a sore point with the local farmers."

Understandably so, Lenoir thought as they approached along the wagon road that separated one property from another. It was as though the road were a boundary between two worlds, one bright and young and alive, the other dull and overcome with decay. To their left, emerald green fields were lined with bushes as neatly ordered as military ranks. Yet only a few feet away, the neighboring property was overgrown with thistles and clover. A wide, ugly trench had been dug between the road and the abandoned farm, a crude attempt by the neighbors to keep the weeds from invading their land.

It only grew worse the closer they got to the farm buildings. A pair of old fruit wagons sat at the head of the drive, one of them pitched forward like a wounded animal on its knees. It had been stripped of its front wheels, some opportunistic neighbor having salvaged them.

Crears was right to bring them here. It was the perfect place to keep someone against his will. No one would happen upon the site, and there was nothing within earshot. Even if the boy managed to escape, he would probably be too disoriented to get far. Lenoir only hoped that the three of them would be able to manage whomever they found here. Crears had sent one of his watchmen to round up as many others as he could, but that would take time, and they dared not wait. Every minute that passed was another risk taken, for there was no telling what the kidnapper intended.

They dismounted about halfway up the drive, tying their horses to a fence post that did not look up to the task. Lenoir had brought a sword, plus a brace of flint-locks that Crears had loaned him. The sergeant and the constable were similarly armed, though Kody pre-ferred a crossbow to a pistol. He insisted that he could load it faster and that it aimed truer, and Lenoir did not argue, for he had never seen Kody miss a shot.

There was no evidence of the place being occupied. They could not see any horses, and there was no sign of life from the barn. The farmhouse itself was in ruins. The western half of it had collapsed, leaving a wreck-age of rotting wood overgrown with ivy, and what was left standing had a precipitous lean, as though it could go at any moment. It appeared to consist of two rooms, probably the main room and a single remaining bed-room. Someone had boarded up one side of the larger room where the wall had caved in, but it was shoddily done and probably offered only the barest protection from the elements.

Lenoir, Kody, and Crears circled around the house. A path led from the back down to the river. It looked to have been recently trod. Lenoir made a mental note of it, but first they needed to investigate the house. Crears stationed himself at the back door and drew his pistols, while Kody and Lenoir made their way around to the front. They paused before the door. It had been painted once, but that was clearly long ago; only a few chips of white still speckled the shaggy gray wood, and shadows were visible between the shrunken slats. Lenoir could probably have shouldered his way past the door, but there was no telling what awaited them on the other side. They readied their weapons. Kody towered behind Lenoir, leveling his crossbow just above the inspector's shoulder. Lenoir raised his pistol. Then he gave a short nod, and Kody pivoted and kicked the door off its hinges.

There was a flurry of movement in front of Lenoir's face. He leapt back and bumped into Kody, but the burly sergeant held his ground as he fired the crossbow. The spring snapped to and a loud thud sounded against the far wall, and then all was silent. As their eyes adjusted to the gloomy interior, Lenoir spied a small shape pinned against the wall at eye height. A quail twitched in its death throes, its breast blasted through by Kody's bolt.

"Nice shot," said Lenoir.

They stepped over the threshold, the shadows of the

interior parting to reveal their contents. Dust swarmed angrily in the beam of light streaming through the open doorway. It lit upon a rotting wooden floor and naked walls, and for a moment Lenoir thought the room was empty. Then he saw the boy—gagged and blindfolded, bound to a chair. He knew immediately it was the wrong boy, for his hair was yellow like his mother's. His head sagged, and for a moment Lenoir feared he was dead. But as Lenoir moved toward him, the boy's head rose. There was something strange about the way he moved, an eerie calm that drew Lenoir up short.

Kody elbowed past and knelt before the child. He removed the blindfold first. He reached for the boy's bonds next, then changed his mind and pulled the gag from his mouth. The boy said nothing. He made no move, not even to wet his cracking lips. He simply watched Kody, his face impassive, as though he were not interested in what the sergeant was doing.

Crears was just coming around the front when Lenoir found the bedroom door. It was off to the right, closed. His heart surging with hope, Lenoir burst through.

The room was barren. At least, it appeared to be. "Get out of the doorway, Crears! You're blocking the light!"

The constable complied, but Lenoir already knew it was useless. Zach was not there. Lenoir got down on his hands and knees, searching for anything that might be a clue. There was a dark stain on the floor next to the door, and Lenoir sniffed at it, fearing the scent of blood. What he smelled was not blood, however, but urine.

"He was here," Lenoir said as Crears entered the room. "I think he—"

Lenoir was drowned out by a scream. There was a crashing sound from the room next door, and Kody swore loudly. Lenoir and Crears rushed back into the main room to find a bizarre sight: Kody was tussling with the boy, who was shouting and tearing at the sergeant with all his strength.

"What are you doing, Kody?" Crears cried. "You're hurting him!"

"What do you want me to do, let him claw my eyes out?" Kody was trying to restrain the boy's wrists. "Calm down! It's all right, you're safe now! *Stop it!*"

Despite his size, he was having trouble keeping the boy in check. The attack was so vicious, so frenzied, that for a brief moment Lenoir even thought the sergeant might be overcome. Then Kody seized the boy by the shoulders and spun him around, clasping him in a bear hug that pinned his arms at his sides. The boy continued to struggle, spitting and shrieking like a fiend, but the sergeant held him fast.

"What's the matter with him?" Kody growled. He had a gash on his right cheek, shallow but bleeding.

Crears knelt before the boy, just out of range of his flailing legs. "Mika! Mika, it's me, Constable Crears! You remember me, don't you?"

But Mika did not seem to remember the constable. His eyes rolled back and he screamed again, as though something before him were too horrible to look at.

"They must have done something to scare the wits out of him," Crears said.

"I think it is worse than that, Constable," said Lenoir grimly. "Look at him—the boy is mad." Mika had begun to tear at the bottom of his shirt, as though he would rip it from his body.

"Take him outside, Sergeant," Lenoir ordered. "Try to keep him calm until the watchmen arrive. We can't bring him with us like this."

Crears looked disturbed as he watched Kody drag the boy out of the farmhouse, and when he spoke again, his voice was distracted. "There's a path out back. Looks to have been used recently."

"I saw it."

"I'll stay here and help with Mika." Lenoir started to protest, but changed his mind and merely nodded. As constable of Berryvine, Crears would consider the boy his responsibility. Lenoir did not envy him that, nor did he envy him the task of delivering the news of Mika's condition to the family.

The path behind the house led between a jumble of rosebushes that might once have been beautiful, but were now little more than a thicket of thorns. They had obviously been pruned at one time, and still retained some hint of their former shapes. The riot of growth that had since burst forth gave them the look of cages that could barely contain the wild creatures within, stray limbs reaching out between bars to claw at Lenoir's cloak as he passed.

The sound of the river wandered up the path to meet him. He could already smell the clay that lined its banks, and the damp air grew chilly as he made his way toward the water. A tentative chorus of frogs had just begun, only to fall silent as Lenoir drew near. Here the path descended steeply before disappearing behind the trunk of an enormous willow tree. Beyond it, the river was slowly disgorging a ribbon of mist that retained its shape, as though a great snake were sloughing its silvery skin. The opposite bank was all but obscured. Lenoir could sense the trees looming behind the veil, but the only evidence of their presence was the occasional disembodied branch materializing and then dissolving in the roiling fog. Their unseen closeness made him feel as though he were being watched.

At the foot of the path, the tracks Lenoir was following turned over themselves, creating a muddy mess. They drew right up to the river's edge: dimpled boot-heels filled with water pointing in different directions. He had to squat to examine them, for the willow tree at the river's edge cast a thick cloak of shadow over the ground. Now that he was closer, he saw that the prints had not been made as recently as he thought, for the peaks of the tracks were rounded, not sharp-edged as they would have been if the footprints were fresh. It looked as though someone had come down to the river to draw water, or perhaps to wash something. Lenoir spied a mark that might have been someone setting a jug down in the mud.

Beside him, the willow tree leaned far out over the water, the shaggy tips of its bottommost branches grazing the surface. It looked as though the tree might eventually topple over; so acute was its angle that the roots farthest from the river had begun to tear up through the ground. They were thick, as big around as a man's thigh, and knotted over one another like a nest of vipers.

That was why it took Lenoir so long to notice the body.

He started back up the path and might have walked right by had he not spied a flash of metal out of the corner of his eye. Peering through the gloom, he saw what had caught his eye: a buckle, attached to a boot. What he had taken for one of the roots was actually a man's leg, crooked at the knee so that the rest of the body lay concealed behind the mound.

Drawing a flintlock, Lenoir approached cautiously. The leg made no movement, and from the angle of it Lenoir was quite sure that its owner was not merely resting in the lee of the willow tree. His suspicions were confirmed when he walked around the mound of roots and found the wide, vacant eyes of a corpse staring back at him.

The particulars of the scene rushed into his brain, registering themselves one at a time: male; Adal; twenty-five to thirty years old; dead less than twenty-four hours. Lenoir holstered his pistol and approached, cocking his head to reconcile his view with the crumpled form before him. The man was on his back, his body draped across the tangle of roots so that his feet were higher than his head. One leg dangled over the top of the roots—the leg Lenoir had spotted from the path—and the other was splayed at an unnatural angle. The corpse's head lolled back, openmouthed, hanging over the edge of a root. Neck broken, Lenoir gauged, almost as though the victim had fallen from the tree.

He gazed up at the branches above and immediately spied a green scar where the bark had been worn away. It looked as though someone had tried to hang the man. A lynching, perhaps?

Lenoir knelt over the body and moved the man's collar to take a look at his neck. He had expected to find rope burns, but what he saw there instead caused him to cry out and stumble backward onto his rump.

Impossible!

He scrambled to his feet, but then his body failed him, refusing to obey his command to flee. Instead he stood rooted to the spot, staring. His mind buzzed uselessly. He could not be sure how long he stood there. A minute? An hour? Whatever the case, he was thoroughly lost in his own world when he heard the voice.

"What's this?"

Lenoir jolted so badly that his knees nearly gave way. Even so, he had never been so glad to see Kody. The sergeant, for his part, appeared not to notice Lenoir's state of shock, his gaze fixed instead on the corpse lying broken among the roots. He knelt before the body for a closer look. "Neck snapped, looks like, as though he fell out of the tree. . . ."

Lenoir scarcely heard him. There was a strange roaring in his ears, a sound distantly and unpleasantly familiar, like a bad dream. A dream about a night spent huddled in the shadows, listening to the blood rushing through his veins, praying for daylight. Nowhere to hide, no one to come to his aid . . . and then the burning on his arm, the burning and the chill, the horrible sense that the warmth of his life was being sucked out through his flesh. . . .

"That's odd," Kody said. He pulled back the man's collar just as Lenoir had done. "Have you ever seen marks like this, Inspector?"

Lenoir could not answer him. Kody waited for a response; when none was forthcoming, he frowned and turned back to the corpse. "It looks like his neck has been . . . I don't know. The skin is gray, as if he's been dead for weeks, but the rest of him looks . . . Well, I'd say he's only been dead a few hours."

Lenoir understood the sergeant's confusion. He understood that it should not be possible for some of the body's flesh to be necrotic while the rest was not. Not unless the man had had some sort of terrible infection. . . . Lenoir experienced a brief twinge of hope at this thought, but it disappeared immediately. There was no infection, he knew. There was only one possibility.

Like judgment, like death, the green-eyed man had caught up with him at last.

CHAPTER 12

*H*e couldn't breathe. He had been running for too long; every part of his body protested. His thighs trembled as he doubled over to catch his breath, and his heart thundered so that he could feel it in his temples. He glanced up at the sky, but it was obscured by a cataract of cloud, making it impossible to tell the hour. How long did he have until sunrise? Unless it came soon, there was no chance of him escaping. Not this time.

Mustering what strength he could, Lenoir loped to the end of the alley, but was dismayed to find that it opened into a courtyard. A dead end. The alley was short—perhaps he could retrace his steps in time to find another way. But when he turned he saw them again: eyes in the darkness, eyes that flashed like a cat's, yet stood too far off the ground to be anything but a man's.

He whirled back to the courtyard, praying to find an escape route that he had missed before. Perhaps he could climb a balcony, or find a place to hide? But he knew better: he was not a climber, and there was no hid-

ing from his pursuer. Those green eyes could pierce stone.

He ran to a doorway at the far end of the courtyard and pounded on the heavy wood, the blows reverberating within the enclosed space. But the door did not open. No lamp was lit; no one was coming to Lenoir's aid. And now the green-eyed man had stepped into the courtyard. He moved with uncanny grace, his step liquid. Raven black hair framed a youthful face so pale and beautiful it could have been shaped from marble. And like a sculpture, his expression was fixed, showing no pity, nor any hint of human feeling. His eyes were the color of absinthe, burning with a light that was unmistakably fey.

The green-eyed man loosed the scourge from his belt, that many-tongued whip that sought Lenoir's flesh. And with a flourish of his wrist that seemed no effort at all, he sent its barbed lashes forth.

The scourge gripped Lenoir's forearm near the elbow, jerking him to his knees. At first his terror was such that he could make no sound. When finally he screamed, it was with a violence that seemed to tear the inside of his throat. The barbs pierced his arm, but the pain was nothing, nothing compared to the sickening sensation of his flesh dying. There was something wrong with the whip, something terrible, a malevolence so potent that it made him nauseous. A chill rushed up his arm, filled his chest. . . . Now he could feel his consciousness ebbing, as though the barbs piercing his flesh were tiny vampiric fangs, draining his lifeblood. . . .

Lenoir woke to the sound of his own screaming. His

frantic gaze took in the room around him, and at first he was wildly disoriented. After a moment his mind sparked to life and he knew he was in his own apartment. Yet the nightmare had been so real, so visceral, that he clutched at his arm, his fingers seeking proof that the scourge was no longer constricted around him like a snake. He felt the familiar numbness below his elbow, cold skin stretched over dead flesh that his blood never warmed. He was used to the morbid sensation by now, but for the first time in ten years, he half fancied that his flesh prickled somehow, like a limb gone to sleep that was slowly regaining circulation.

Lenoir heaved himself out of bed and went to the washbasin to splash water on his face. It was cold and bracing, for he had left his window ajar the previous afternoon and had been too out of sorts to bother closing it when he returned home from Berryvine. He stared at his reflection in the looking glass, willing himself to gain some mastery over his still-fluttering heart. It would do no good to panic, he told himself. If the green-eyed man was really here in the Five Villages, there would be no escaping him. Luck had saved Lenoir the last time, such luck as never visited the same man twice. The nightmare had been vividly accurate in every detail save one: it had been early morning when Lenoir found himself cornered in that courtyard ten years ago—not night as it had been in the dream. Dawn had broken at the far end of the alley, sending a lance of sunlight into the courtyard, and somehow that had saved Lenoir's life. He could not remember what happened, for he had been virtually unconscious by that time. But he remembered seeing the light, remembered wondering if it was a sliver of Eternity peeking through as the door to Heaven closed, barring his entry. And when he woke, the green-eyed man was gone, along with the terrible scourge he wielded. The only sign that he had ever been there was the scar on Lenoir's arm, that hideous patch of gray skin that would never again feel warmth, nor any other sensation at all. Forevermore it would feel as though someone else's flesh had been grafted onto his own, thick and foreign. Forevermore Lenoir would carry that reminder of his brush with death, of his cheating the avenging angel that hunted him.

Yes, an angel, or a demon, perhaps. Either way, Lenoir knew with absolute certainty that although he thought of his attacker as "the green-eyed man," he was nothing of the kind. Men did not carry cursed weapons that sap human life with a mere touch. Men did not vanish from one shadow only to reappear in another. And no man alive had ever had such eyes—that violent, uncanny green that glimmered as though lit from within. Not a man, but a spirit—a vengeful spirit that sought Lenoir's blood in payment for his sins.

That morning in the courtyard had been Lenoir's last in Serles. He had boarded a stagecoach that afternoon, away from his city, away from his country and everything he had ever known. He had gone north to Braeland, that mist-cloaked isthmus stretching like a bridge across the veil to the underworld, the last outpost of civilization before reaching the savage shores beyond. He never saw his pursuer again. He thought he had escaped forever.

But I was wrong. He has come. How could he possibly have found me? But he had, and what was worse, he seemed somehow to be connected to Zach's disappearance. It must be so, for though there had been many murders in the Five Villages since Lenoir had been here, none had borne the telltale marks of the scourge.

He would drive himself mad thinking about it. He had to get out of the apartment, had to find company. Lenoir grabbed his coat and headed out, making for his destination by instinct more than conscious thought. He needed someplace crowded, someplace familiar and comforting. And he needed a drink. He could only think of only one place that would do.

Zera herself met him at the door. To his inquiring glance, she said, "I had to fire my doorman. You just cannot imagine what he's been up to." She raised her eyebrows significantly, but she did not elaborate, and Lenoir did not ask. "Besides," she continued, looping her arm through Lenoir's as she led him up the stairs, "there is a certain country charm in welcoming one's own guests, don't you think? I believe I shall declare it a fashion."

"As you say, madam," Lenoir replied distractedly. His eyes had fixed on a pale green light that came into view as they reached the top of the stairs: a panel of the stained-glass screen that separated the main part of the salon from one of its more notorious corners. When lit from behind, it gave off a glimmer the color of absinthe. This bit of glass often caught Lenoir's attention as he entered the room, particularly if his mind was preoccupied. Tonight, it positively mesmerized him.

He realized belatedly that Zera was still talking to him. "Nicolas," she said coolly, "I sense I do not have your undivided attention."

Lenoir blinked and tore his gaze away from the screen. "I'm sorry. What were you saying?"

She regarded him with a severe look, her dark eyebrows stitched together. She rarely permitted herself to express such raw displeasure, and it made Lenoir acutely aware of her imposing height. The Adali were an unusually tall race, but Zera's height so suited her, rendered her so exquisitely statuesque, that Lenoir had ceased to notice it. "I was asking whether you had any news from your informant," she said.

"My informant?" Lenoir echoed vaguely.

Zera's mouth tightened. "My word, Inspector, are you quite well? The *boy*, Nicolas. What's his name?"

"Zach." The name brought Lenoir's whirring mind to a sudden halt. He blinked once, and Zera seemed to come into sharper focus. "His name is Zach, and no—I have not had any news from him. None at all. You see, Zach has been kidnapped."

Zera's lips parted, but no sound came. Now it was she who blinked, her customary poise perturbed. "Kidnapped?" She seized Lenoir's arm and steered him away from the other guests, her head bent conspiratorially. "Nicolas, are you quite *sure*?"

"I am quite sure," he said, unsettled by the finality in

his own voice. "Zach and another boy were both taken yesterday. We found the house where they were being kept, but only one of the boys was still there. And he was . . . unwell."

Zera shuddered. "What has the world come to? First children's corpses and now this. . . ." She frowned suddenly. "Actually . . . Nicolas, do you think they might be related?"

Lenoir had seen this question coming. Zera was uncommonly clever, and she loved to speculate about his work. He supposed it gave her a sense of intrigue. "Kody certainly thinks so."

"Who is Kody?"

"One of my sergeants. He is a competent investigator, but he is given to elaborate notions of conspiracy. He sees connections everywhere."

Zera's long fingers covered her lips, her golden eyes round with wonder. "But in this case, he could be right."

"It is certainly difficult to dismiss it as coincidence," Lenoir admitted. "If it had only been Zach . . . So many orphans meet ugly fates in this city. But two children, both nine-year-old boys, just like the corpses . . ." He shook his head, frustrated. "Yet I can think of no logical explanation for it. *How* are they connected? It makes no sense."

Zera regarded him for a moment, then looked over her shoulder and waved at a servant. "Here, Nicolas." Her voice was honeyed with concern. "Come and sit. We will get you some wine, and you will feel better."

She seated them on a pair of sumptuous chairs near

the hearth. Ordinarily, this was a popular spot for patrons of the salon to gather, but Lenoir noticed out of the corner of his eye that one of the servants was whispering to nearby guests, shepherding them to a discreet remove. Zera had mastered the art of catering to the needs of her guests, even those of modest stature such as Lenoir. She seemed to know exactly what they wanted without having to be told. Sometimes she even knew what Lenoir wanted before he knew it himself. And there was something so natural about the way she managed her staff, communicating wordlessly with them so that things seemed simply to unfold according to her unspoken will. Truly, she was a natural-born hostess.

The wine arrived and Lenoir gratefully took a glass. Zera took one too, though she did not raise it to her lips. She waited for Lenoir to speak, perched on the edge of her seat with her long legs crossed daintily at the ankles. Her expression was warm and open, inviting him to confess his troubles. And so he did.

"It has been a long time since I loved my work, Zera. I think you know that."

She gave him a sad smile. "You do not often seem happy, it's true."

"I used to be happy. Or if not happy, at least I was satisfied. At least I had purpose. I was very good at my job. I was the best."

"You are still the best, Nicolas," Zera said, leaning forward to put a hand on his knee. "Everyone says so. They say you are a marvel, that you can find out anything you want to know."

Lenoir snorted softly and sipped his wine. "Perhaps that is so, but that is precisely the problem, you see. I do not *want* to find out anything—not unless it gets me something. Or gets you something." He raised an eyebrow, reminding her silently of the many times he had used his investigative skills to pass valuable information to Zera. She was a born hostess to begin with; tipped off about the closet vices of her guests, she was a wonder. Armed with the right information, Zera could coax even the naturally cautious into revealing their sins to her. Thus the powerful and the highborn frequently found themselves beholden to Lady Zera in one way or another. She catered to their whims, indulged their desires, and guarded their secrets. In so doing, she ensured her stature among the influential of Kennian, an elite circle no Adal before her had ever infiltrated.

"This business with Zach—it is the first time in so long that I have actually felt . . . I don't know . . ." He trailed off, unable to find the words.

"You are too hard on yourself."

"Am I? Kody does not think so. He despises me and I cannot blame him. I used to see the world through his eyes; I know only too well what I must look like."

"What do you mean?"

"Kody sees himself as a champion of justice." Lenoir could not help smirking as he said it. "He wants to subdue the evildoers of the world."

"That sounds a little childish," Zera observed coolly. Lenoir was not sure if she really meant it, but he was grateful to her for saying it.

"Maybe it is, but I cannot fault him for his ambitions. I used to share them, more or less. There was a time when I was obsessed with my career, to the point where I virtually forgot what it was to lead a life outside the Prefecture of Police." He paused. It seemed like another life, long dead and largely unmourned. "I too questioned my superiors when they claimed a case was unsolvable. Back then, there was no such thing—not to me, at least. But that was before."

"Before what?"

Lenoir was silent for a moment. How could he explain it? Before the betrayal. Before the broken promises, the shattered hopes, the incompetence and outright treachery of those who claimed to shepherd the New Order. "Before I saw justice for what it truly is," he said finally.

"And what is that?"

"An artificial construct of the powerful, venal and infinitely elastic."

Zera puffed out a breath. "That's quite a dark view for a man in your profession, Inspector."

"It is the truth, though I had to grow up a little before I saw it. I was in love with the law, back when I was young. I was in love with the idea that the law made everyone the same, no matter where they were born or whose blood was in their veins. I wanted to believe in the revolution. I wanted to believe that there was punishment for those who did wrong, no matter how much money they had or how many titles."

"I think I see what you mean. Even I know that isn't true."

Lenoir drank his wine. It was not true, not in Serles and not in the Five Villages. No one thanked you for arresting a man like Lord Feine. It would embarrass too many powerful people—the lord mayor, whose wife was a particular friend of Lady Feine; the speaker of Parliament, Feine's sometime hunting companion; the myriad of titled relatives who presided over the handsomer properties of the Five Villages. It would shock the sensibilities of the foolish commoners who thought there was something inherently *better* in the character of a nobleman. Besides, Feine would never remain imprisoned, not when he could buy off the magistrate, the jailer, the local news pamphlets. And once he was out, if he was bloody-minded (which the nobility so often were) he would come after Lenoir, looking for the satisfaction of squashing the insignificant police inspector who dared to smear his precious name. No, justice was not blind. She was a prostitute, for sale to the highest bidder.

"Once I realized the law could be bought," he continued, "everything changed. I saw what a farce it was, a lot of playacting, everyone just going through the motions, especially where the rich and powerful were concerned. Gradually, I began to understand why. These ridiculous crimes of passion—it was not as though they were serial killers, after all. And you cannot bring back the dead, so what is the point of it, anyway? You will never bring such people to justice, and you cannot undo what they have done."

Zera nodded sympathetically. "It's true, unfortunately. There isn't a punishment in the world that will bring back the dead."

"And so . . ." Lenoir trailed off. He could not quite bring himself to say it, but he did not have to. Once again, he felt the coins in his hand, cold and heavy. *The price of silence.*

"And so you let the dead rest," Zera said firmly, "and kept their secrets to yourself, and if you stayed quiet about what you couldn't change, and did well by it, that is only human nature. You can't torture yourself over it, Nicolas. You just grew up and saw the world for what it really is, that's all."

So Lenoir had told himself for years. When he woke in the morning and felt no sense of purpose, when he touched the dead flesh on his arm, as numb as his soul, when he drank himself into oblivion and saw the faces of the dead he had betrayed—every day of his life, Lenoir told himself that it was just the way of things, that no sensible man would have done other than he did. But he knew better.

And so did the green-eyed man.

CHAPTER 13

The ravens showed them the way to the camp. They circled and wheeled in the pallid sky, rustled and cawed from the branches that lined the road. By the time Kody and Lenoir were near enough to see the wood smoke rising from the clearing, the chorus of ravens was so loud that it drowned out the sound of their hoofbeats on the road. *The choir of death*, as they were known in scripture. Kody wasn't much of a religious man, but it made him shudder all the same. Ravens could often be found in large numbers near Adali camps, since there was always a bounty of food to be had. The Adali weren't accustomed to staying in one place for long, so sanitation wasn't their strong suit. They let their refuse pile high near the campsite, attracting all sorts of scavengers. The presence of ravens near Adali camps was so common that the two had become inextricably associated with each other in folklore. *And they wonder why everyone thinks of them as heathens and witches.* Kody's nose wrinkled at the smell that wandered out from the camp to meet them.

It was a pungent blend of cooking fires, cattle, and rotting vegetables. No doubt there were other perfumes mixed in there too, but he didn't care to think about them.

Reds and yellows began to appear through the trees off to their left, the first sign of the colorful Adali tents. Their bright hues blended into the surrounding woods surprisingly well during autumn and summer, but now that the leaves had fallen, they stood out like wildflowers after a forest fire. They were as out of place as the Adali themselves, who should long since have headed north for the winter in search of warmer climes. As the trees gave way to a clearing, the rest of the settlement came into view. It wasn't especially large, probably home to no more than a hundred or so individuals. And they seemed to have only modest possessions, even by Adali standards. Aside from a clutch of about thirty skinny cattle grazing near a single wagon, the only livestock Kody could see was a handful of goats that competed with the ravens for the choicest pieces of garbage. The tents looked old and weather-beaten, and the children that emerged from them to watch the horsemen approach were scrawny.

Kody scanned the trees for signs that more cattle were about, but he couldn't see any. No horses, no bleating of sheep. Could this really be all the livestock they had? If so, this clan would be awfully low down the food chain of Adali society. They'd be isolated, marginalized, even preyed upon. It was a depressing fact of Adali life that the weaker clans were at constant risk of attack, raided for cattle and slaves. Sometimes the raiders came from the south, from Braeland and beyond, but more often, they were Adali from rival clans. Young women and children were especially vulnerable, since they could be kept for wives and workers, or sold as prostitutes in the south. This clan should have moved back north weeks ago, but they obviously felt too exposed to roam among their own kind. Kody wondered if that would make them more likely to talk, or less.

A pair of dogs came bounding out of the camp to meet them, their excited barking announcing the arrival of visitors. "Do you think we'll get anything out of them?" Kody asked quietly. The Adali were a secretive lot, especially when it came to police investigations.

"Hard to know." Lenoir eyed the dogs warily as they loped alongside the horses. His stallion's ears were pinned back, warning the dogs to keep their distance. "Sometimes they cooperate if they think it will avert suspicion from their kind. But in this case, since the dead man is Adali, I doubt they will be very helpful. The Adali are fiercely loyal to one another, and protective of their ways. If there is justice to be meted out, they prefer to do it themselves."

Kody doubted the wrongdoers shared that preference. Adali justice was uncompromising, sometimes downright brutal. It was also undeniably effective. The clan elders kept a tight rein on things; contrary to popular belief, crime rates were lower among Adali who remained with their clan than amongst the general population of Kennian. It was the city-dwellers, those who were cut off from their traditions and society, who were responsible for a disproportionate number of crimes in the Five Villages.

They dismounted at the edge of the camp. Already, half a dozen people were staring at them, looking even less welcoming than the North Haveners had been. Understandable, maybe. There weren't many reasons for outsiders to enter Adali camps, and none of them were good news. People came bearing accusations, threats, and demands. No one wanted an Adali community nearby. They were bandits; they trespassed on farmlands; they attracted wild animals. If a plague broke out in one of the Five Villages, the Adali were blamed for that too. They'd learned to expect hostility from anyone who came looking for them. Especially hounds.

Kody pulled the rolled-up parchment out of his saddlebag and unfurled the sketch. It was crudely done—the nose wasn't quite right and the charcoal had smudged in a couple of places—but considering that Lenoir had given the scribe only ten minutes to produce the drawing, the man had done a decent job of it. It certainly looked enough like the dead man that anybody who knew him should be able to recognize him.

Lenoir headed for the center of the camp, where a group was coming together to meet him. As poor as they were, Kody couldn't deny they were impressive. Tall, sharp-edged, with skin the color of strong tea with a jot of milk. Their amber-eyed gazes were fathomless, unfathomable. Elaborately carved jewelry of bone and horn adorned long fingers and graceful necks, and their robes, though worn and faded, were still strikingly colorful in comparison with the drab browns and grays favored by the Braelish.

The elder, who looked to be about sixty, was a classic specimen: small mouth, high cheekbones, and keen, wide-spaced eyes. She wore a severe expression, her thick eyebrows drawn together and her mouth pursed in a thin line.

"We are Inspector Lenoir and Sergeant Kody of the Kennian Metropolitan Police," said Lenoir, his voice slightly raised for the benefit of the crowd. "We are here to ask a few questions regarding an incident in Berryvine."

A few of the onlookers sneered, as if to say, *Of course you are.*

"What kind of incident, Inspector?" asked the imposing woman. Her accent was thick, but she spoke the words clearly.

"We have found a body—an Adali man—and we would like you to identify him, if you can."

Kody took his cue to hold up the sketch, showing it around at the small crowd. A few more had gathered near to listen, but for the most part the community seemed to be going about its business, pointedly ignoring the presence of the outsiders. It seemed to Kody like an act of defiance, a subtle message that they wouldn't let their lives be disrupted every time someone showed up at their camp to accuse them of something.

As the Adali studied the drawing, Kody studied the Adali. For the most part they didn't react, but here and there Kody picked up small cues. A young woman's eyes flared slightly before going cold. A boy in the center of the crowd stirred before someone shifted in front of him, blocking him from view. A man with his arms folded spat on the ground. Lenoir, meanwhile, was involved in some sort of staring match with the elder. They held each other's gaze, both of their faces impassive, taking the measure of each other. She had not even glanced at the drawing.

"We do not know him," the woman said.

Lenoir arched an eyebrow. "Oh? Surprising, considering that he was found dead just outside Berryvine. No more than a fifteen-minute ride away, in fact."

"And why should that be surprising, Inspector? Are we meant to know every Adal in the Five Villages?"

Lenoir looked over his shoulder at Kody and smiled. "You see, Sergeant—I am not so clever as I sometimes claim. I would not have thought that an Adal who was not a member of this clan would be welcome so nearby."

Kody responded with a theatrical shrug. "Me neither, sir. Only friends and family of this clan allowed, or so I thought."

"Obviously we still have much to learn about Adali ways, Sergeant." Lenoir turned back to the leader, still smiling.

She just stared at him.

"I assume you are aware that withholding evidence is a crime," said Lenoir.

"I assume you are aware that we do not recognize your jurisdiction over us," said the elder. *She speaks Braelish pretty well for a foreigner,* Kody thought dryly.

I'll bet she's had occasion to use that phrase once or twice before.

Lenoir gave a slow nod, his head bent. Kody could tell he was thinking about bringing her in, wondering if it would be worth making the threat. They couldn't do it themselves, of course—they'd need all of Crears's men to help. The clan would never willingly allow one of their own, especially their elder, to be taken by the police; there would be bloodshed if they tried. Lenoir must have concluded that it wasn't worth it, because he turned and walked away from the group, saying, "Come, Sergeant," as though Kody were a bloody dog.

Lenoir was right, though—it wasn't worth it. Kody knew that, but it still burned his blood. These people knew the dead man—it was as plain as the sun in the sky. But they had no intention of remanding him to the law. It would take all day to bring the elder in, and for what? She probably wouldn't say anything anyway, not without Parliament signing a writ giving them leave to use some of the harsher interrogation techniques. By then, the boy would probably be dead.

"What now?" Kody growled as they mounted their horses. The Adali were still clustered around their leader, staring with their inscrutable amber eyes.

"If we cannot get information out of the Adali themselves, we must try the next best thing."

"And what's that?"

"There is an apothecary near the northern boundary of Berryvine. We passed it on the way here."

Clever, Kody thought grudgingly. The Adali were renowned for their use of potions, poultices, and the like.

In bygone days, they wouldn't have stooped to trading medicinal herbs with townsfolk, but modern Adali were less discriminating. They'd had a taste of the conveniences of civilization, and they liked it. A good apothecary, especially one located at the edge of town, would have almost as many Adali clients as villagers. Maybe the apothecary would recognize the dead man. At the very least, he should be able to tell them something useful about the clans that passed through the area.

Kody drew a deep, satisfied breath as they regained the road. *This* was how an investigation was supposed to be run. For the first time, he could sense Lenoir's commitment to the case, and though he had no idea what made this one special, he was grateful for it. He only hoped that they found this Zach boy alive. If they didn't, there was no telling when—or if—Lenoir would take an investigation this seriously again.

The apothecary was just opening his shop when the two policemen arrived. It looked as though he'd been fetching supplies; each arm was burdened with something. Over his left shoulder was slung a small sack that gave off a spicy scent when he shifted its weight to fumble for his keys. Under his other arm, he carried a bushel of some type of herb that Kody didn't recognize. It sure wasn't one of the ones used for cooking, and that was about all the thinking Kody cared to do on that subject.

"Please come in," the apothecary said, shifting his bundles again as he pried his key free from the door.

Ordinarily, Kody would have offered to help, but for some reason he was reluctant to handle whatever the man was carrying.

The shop was small and disordered, and it was dark, even after the man lit a lantern. There were no windows, and the door faced to the west so that little sunlight entered. "It's better for the fungus," the apothecary explained as his guests blinked in the gloom.

The mixture of smells was almost dizzying. Some spicy, some sweet, some earthy—and beneath it all, the unmistakable scent of decay. Kody had visited an apothecary before, but this particular shop obviously catered to a different clientele. Instead of remedies for cuts, bruises, and headaches, this apothecary stocked ingredients for less everyday purposes. *Not going to think about that either,* he resolved grimly.

"What can I do for you chaps?" the man asked once he was snugly behind the counter. He was tall, and regarded them with large amber eyes. *Do you maybe have some Adali blood in you, friend?* If so, he might not be any more cooperative than the rest of them.

"We are trying to identify this man," said Lenoir, gesturing at Kody to produce the drawing. "Have you seen him?"

The apothecary frowned thoughtfully and took the drawing, holding it near the lantern. "Hmm, I don't think so. Have you checked with the Asis clan?"

"Is that the camp just outside town?" Kody asked. "We've just come from there. They claim not to know him, but we think they're lying."

"Why is that?" the apothecary asked coolly. "Because they're Adali?"

His amber eyes were vaguely challenging now, but before Kody could reply, Lenoir said, "Because they were lying. We could tell from their faces that they had seen the man before. Even one of the children knew him." So Lenoir had noticed that too. Of course he had.

The apothecary shrugged. "That could be. I suppose they might have assumed he had done something wrong and wanted to look into it themselves. The Adali prefer to do their own punishing."

"The man is dead," Kody told him.

"Is he, now? Well, in that case, maybe they wanted to protect themselves. The Adali are very familiar with guilt by association." He smiled thinly.

"That is a plausible explanation," Lenoir said, "but I think there is more to it. One of the clan members spat on the ground when he saw the sketch."

Kody snorted softly, amazed. Lenoir had been busy staring down the old woman, but he still hadn't missed a thing. The spitter had been silent and far enough to Lenoir's left that Kody would have assumed he was beyond the reach of the inspector's peripheral vision.

"An outcast, maybe," the apothecary suggested. "When an Adal is exiled from his people, they repudiate him altogether. They don't even acknowledge his existence anymore."

"And what would get a man exiled from the clan?"

"Oh, lots of things." The apothecary heaved the sack he had been carrying up onto the counter and started untying its cord. Kody watched with morbid fascination, half afraid to see what was inside. "Winding up in a Braelish jail is usually enough, since the crimes that put you there would have been punished even more severely by the clan. They also banish those who are seen to disrespect Adali values. Usually the offense is spiritual or religious in some way. Knowing the Asis clan, I'd bet it was *khekra*."

"What did you say?" Lenoir frowned. "Hek-rah?"

The man smiled. "Close enough. Adali magic. Or rather, a particularly dark brand of Adali magic. The Asis clan had a couple of witchdoctors who were famous for it once upon a time, but they renounced *khekra* years ago. They say it's brought them nothing but grief, and they're probably right. The elders have always frowned upon it, but these days, anybody caught meddling with dark magic is banished, or worse."

Kody and Lenoir exchanged glances. They'd heard of such magic, of course—everyone had. In the more backwater villages, especially, all sorts of bad luck, from weather to disease to accidents, was said to be the work of Adali sorcery. But the more educated folk of the Five Villages dismissed that as superstitious nonsense.

The apothecary inverted the sack onto the counter, causing Kody to take an involuntary step back. To his relief, however, he saw that it was only a bundle of dried flowers. "You chaps look a little skeptical," the apothecary said. "I suppose you don't believe in magic."

"Do you?" Lenoir asked.

The other man shrugged, fetching a large earthenware pot from somewhere behind the counter. He started to separate the flowers from one another and drop them into the pot. "I've been dealing with Adali for more than twenty-five years, and in that time I've seen a lot that I can't explain. Their gift for medicine is undeniable. On top of that, when you come across an Adal who's had a string of uncannily bad luck, you almost always find that he's offended someone recently. The Adali live in constant fear of hexes."

Kody snorted. "A man who believes he's cursed has a way of making his own bad luck."

"Maybe," the apothecary said, "but in that case, it doesn't really matter if the curse is real or not, does it? It works just the same."

"Do any of these spells involve using children?" Lenoir asked bluntly.

He was trying to shock the apothecary, and it worked. The man's hands froze momentarily. "Why do you want to know?" he asked in an icy whisper.

Kody opened his mouth to reply, but Lenoir cut him off. "Never mind that. Answer the question. Have you heard of any form of *khekra* that requires the use of children?"

The apothecary's gaze dropped back to the dried flowers, his now-trembling fingers clumsy in their progress. "God help me, I have," he murmured, "and it's robbed me of many a night's sleep."

Kody stared, feeling suddenly ill.

"Who told you of it?" Lenoir asked. "You said the Asis clan had witchdoctors who were famed for *khekra.*"

"I said they *used* to. Their elders forbid it now."

"Why?"

"You've noticed how poor they are? About ten years ago, their herds fell prey to some sort of plague. They were completely wiped out, down to the last animal. Then the witchdoctors started turning up dead. The elders were convinced the clan was being punished for something, something to do with *khekra*. They outlawed it, gave it up completely. After that, anybody who was caught performing *khekra* was banished or executed. The damage was done, though. The clan's place in Adali society is compromised. They're no longer able to negotiate for the choicer migration routes. They don't even bother showing up at the annual gathering of the clans. There's just no point. They have no leverage, can't pay any tribute to the powerful clans. That's why they're still hanging around Berryvine so close to winter—they have no place else to go. And without proper grazing lands, they can't rebuild their herd. They're so poor that they hardly even get raided anymore. There's nothing left to take."

Except maybe their women and children, Kody thought darkly. It certainly sounded like the Asis were in desperate straits. Desperate people did desperate things. *We're on the right track.* Still, he couldn't quite manage to feel happy about it. This was going somewhere terrible; he knew it in his guts.

Lenoir tapped the charcoal sketch. "Let us suppose that you are right, and this man was exiled for sorcery. What use could he make of a child? What would be his purpose?"

The apothecary lowered his voice and spoke quickly, as though he wanted the conversation to be over. "*Khekra* makes use of anything you can name—herbs, minerals, animal parts."

"And human parts," supplied Lenoir.

Kody felt his lip curl in revulsion. *Savages.*

"Sometimes. Usually it's nothing sinister—fingernails, or hair, or a drop of blood. But it matters where you get the material from. *Who* you get it from. The younger the source, the purer it is, and pure components make for more powerful spells."

"So they use children," Kody said disgustedly.

The apothecary was sweating now. He lowered his voice even further, until it was barely above a whisper. "The Adali believe that children make for powerful medicine, strong enough to cure even a mortal wound. But I've never heard of them really hurting a child, only taking a little blood."

"Only?" Kody snapped, barely able to suppress his outrage.

The apothecary swiped his arm across his dampened brow. "Look, I'm only . . . I'm just telling you what I know, Sergeant. I'm just trying to help."

Lenoir's countenance was stone. "What about dead bodies? Can they be used in medicine?"

The poor apothecary was turning green. He shook his head weakly. "No. Dead flesh is polluted; it would never be used for medicine. A curse, maybe, but I doubt any Adal would risk it. They believe that sins against the dead are punished from beyond. The Adali always treat the dead with great respect."

Lenoir's gaze became abstracted, his brow furrowed in thought. Then light returned to his eye, and he asked, "What kind of spell would call for a child *and* a corpse?"

The other man shook his head, apparently at a loss. "I don't . . . I've never heard of anything like that." He put a hand over his belly, as though he felt sick. "What's going on, Inspector? My God, has someone—"

"Who could tell us more?" Kody interrupted.

"Any Adal *could*, but I doubt anyone *would*. You must understand, Sergeant, these things just aren't discussed—not even among the Adali. I should never have been told about any of this. God knows I wish I hadn't been."

There was a long pause. Then Lenoir said, "That will be all, thank you."

The sunlight was fierce when they stepped out of the shop, and for a moment, all Kody could do was squint. When his eyes began to adjust, he realized that a pair of Adali women was waiting for them by the horses. "Inspector," one of them said as Lenoir approached. Kody recognized the younger of the two; she'd been gathered with the others when they had questioned the elder.

"The man you are looking for," the older woman said in a thick accent, "he is dead?"

Kody held up the sketch and showed it to them. "Did you know him?"

The older woman scanned the parchment sadly. "Yes. He was . . . he used to be my brother." The younger woman reached for her hand and squeezed it.

"What was his name?" Lenoir asked.

"I cannot say," the sister said. "It is forbidden to speak the name he once had. He is not . . ." She paused, frowning, as though searching for the right words.

"He did not exist," the younger woman supplied.

"What do you mean, *didn't exist*?" Kody asked incredulously.

Lenoir understood. "He was exiled."

Ah. The apothecary had said that when someone was banished, the clan no longer acknowledged his existence. Kody hadn't realized he meant it quite so literally.

"Why do you ask of him?" the sister wanted to know. "When he died . . . he was doing wrong?"

Lenoir considered her with narrowed eyes. "I think you know the answer to that."

The sister shook her head; the horn beads of her earrings clacked with the movement. "No. He has been gone a long time, living in the city. The shame he made here, when he existed . . . that would not concern you."

"It might," Lenoir said. "Tell me about it."

"It is forbidden," the sister said.

"Did he practice . . ." Kody caught himself before he used the word; he sensed it would only upset them. "Did he make medicine?"

The sister's eyes filled with tears, and she dropped her head. "Medicine," she whispered tremulously. "Yes. He helped many people."

"*Many* people," the younger woman said fiercely. She and the sister exchanged a look.

"Was that why the elders sent him away?" Kody asked.

The sister looked away, her lips pressed into a thin line. It was the younger woman who answered, "It was not for the medicine. The elders knew about that, though they pretended they did not. It was for the . . . for the rain."

Lenoir frowned. "The rain?"

"Not the rain. The . . ." She hesitated, her fingers twitching as though to grasp the unfamiliar words. "When it does not rain," she finished helplessly.

"Drought?" Kody hazarded.

"Yes, drought. For three seasons, it did not rain. The herd was dying. We were already so poor . . . the people were sick and suffering."

"My brother tried to help," the sister said quietly. "He made a spell. He was caught."

"And they banished him," Lenoir finished. "Have you seen or spoken to him since?"

The sister stiffened. "No."

"He did not exist," the younger woman reminded them.

"How long ago did he cease to exist?" To Kody's surprise, there was not a trace of sarcasm in the inspector's voice. As absurd as the conversation sounded to Braelish ears, it was all too serious for the Adali, and for once, Lenoir was being respectful.

"Four seasons," the younger woman said. "Perhaps five." That meant about two years, Kody knew. The Adali measured seasons by their migration patterns. A season began when they quit Kigiri to head south to Braeland, and ended when the arrival of autumn turned them home again. *Except now the Asis don't go back north. That must throw everything off for them.* For the first time, it occurred to Kody that the Adali didn't really have any experience of winter until they came to Braeland. *How do they manage? They must drop like flies,* he thought grimly.

"You say he was living in the city," Lenoir said. "Do you know what he was doing there? Where he lived, who his associates were?"

The sister shook her head, her beads clacking. Her amber eyes were sad, but resigned. Kody decided he believed her.

"You must tell me his name," Lenoir said.

"It is forbid—"

"I know," Lenoir interrupted, "but a boy's life is at stake, and I do not have much time."

"A boy's life?" The woman paled. "My brother would not hurt a child."

"You sure about that?" Kody challenged. "He got himself exiled, didn't he?"

She threw him a sharp look. "His shame . . . He made those spells to help people, not to hurt them. He made bad things, yes, but he was only trying to help us. If he was still making bad things when he died, it must have been for the people. For the clan."

Kody felt his lip twist, but he managed to bite down on a sarcastic reply. As for Lenoir, he merely said, "That may be, but the fact remains that a child is missing, and your brother was involved somehow. What can you tell me about his magic? Can you think of any reason why your brother might take a child?"

"He would not hurt a child," she insisted, her voice rising in pitch. "I have already said what I should not. Do not speak more of this. It is *forbidden*." Her amber eyes were wide with fear.

We're pushing too hard. We're going to lose her. Lenoir saw it too; he raised his hands in a mollifying gesture. "Forgive me. I will not ask any more about magic. But I must have your brother's name. If what you say is true, your brother would not want the child to be hurt, but if I do not find him, the boy could die. Please."

The women looked at each other. The younger one said something in Adali, shaking her head. The sister sighed. They conversed for a moment, and then the sister turned back to Lenoir. "What I do could make *me* banished," she said. "But if a boy is in danger, and this can help you, I must. In return, I ask that you see that my brother's body is burned, in the Adali way. Do not let them put him in the ground." Her eyes welled up again, and she swallowed hard.

"I will see to it," Lenoir promised.

"His name . . ." Her voice quavered, and she swallowed again. "His name was Raiyen."

"Thank you," Lenoir said.

"You've done the right thing," Kody added.

The woman nodded. Then she said something to her companion in Adali, and they turned and headed back up the road toward the Asis camp, the younger woman wrapping her arm around the sister's shoulder as they walked.

Excitement churned in Kody's guts. They were really getting somewhere now. "Where to next, Inspector? Back to the city?"

"To the station. When we get there, we will split up. You will head out to the slums, Fort Hald, anywhere there is likely to be a concentration of Adali. Now that we have a name to go with your sketch, you may be able to find someone who knew this Raiyen."

Kody nodded. "And you?"

"I will be with the scribes, looking for any record of him or any other known members of the Asis clan living in the Five Villages. It may be that Raiyen sought out his own kin."

"Makes sense."

"If we are lucky, we may also be able to find someone to tell us more about *khekra*. We still do not understand the motive, and that is the most important clue."

They mounted up and headed back for the city, riding at a brisk pace. They'd barely hit the outskirts of Berryvine when they heard galloping hoofbeats behind them. Kody twisted in his saddle and recognized Constable Crears and two of his men riding hard toward them.

When they had caught up, Crears said, "I'm glad we found you so quickly. There's another body, sir, and we think it's only an hour or two old. Adal man, midtwenties."

Lenoir and Kody exchanged a look. "Go, Sergeant.

Start your inquiries in the city. I'll stay with Crears and attend to this. We'll meet up tomorrow."

"Yes, sir." Kody nodded crisply to Crears, then turned and rode off, leaving Lenoir to deal with the corpse.

As he rode, Kody's mind started to race. He'd learned more about Adali culture in the last twenty minutes than he had in the past twenty years, and he wasn't sure what to make of it. But he knew one thing for certain: whatever was going on, it was much bigger than the boy—and it was getting out of hand.

CHAPTER 14

Lenoir followed Crears into a narrow alley on the eastern side of town, where a group of the constable's men were gathered around the body. They were muttering to one another and there was some laughter, but they fell silent when they saw Crears approach. The constable would not approve of disrespectful banter, regardless of whom the victim was.

There was nothing remarkable about the way the body was situated. It lay near the intersection of two alleyways, angled in such a way as to suggest that the victim was attempting to flee around the corner of one alley into another as he fell. The man lay on his side, one knee drawn up toward his chest and both elbows tucked into his body, a little like a stabbing victim. But there was no blood anywhere, and no obvious wounds.

As though reading Lenoir's thoughts, Crears said, "We haven't figured out what killed him yet. I gave him a quick once-over, but I didn't find anything."

Lenoir grunted and glanced around. There were five watchmen standing over the body, including the two that had accompanied Crears to fetch Lenoir. "Which one of you found him?" Lenoir asked, and the tallest of the watchmen raised his hand. "The rest of you can go. This alley is too small for all of you to be here—you'll contaminate the scene."

The watchmen exchanged glances, but they did not move, looking instead to their commanding officer.

Crears colored slightly. "You heard the inspector! Go!" He turned apologetically to Lenoir. "I'm sorry, sir. . . ."

Lenoir waved his hand dismissively. "Do not concern yourself. It is only proper that your men should show such loyalty." In fact, Lenoir was envious; he had a hard time believing Kody would demur over the orders of a superior. Not that Lenoir had done anything to earn the sergeant's loyalty.

The alley was now empty save for Lenoir, Crears, and the watchman who had found the body, and Lenoir suddenly became conscious of the darkness of the place. The buildings that flanked the alley were three stories high, shading the body so that the skin appeared dark gray, as though the man had already begun to decompose.

"When did you come upon it?" Lenoir asked the watchman.

"Just over an hour ago. She showed me." The man pointed to the far end of the alley, where a young woman with a flower cart stood pale-faced and trembling in the sunshine. "She's been there the whole time," the watchman added, his voice lowered. "I think she's in shock."

"And did you question her?"

"I did," said Crears. "She says she didn't see anything. Just walked past and saw him lying there. She could tell from his position that something wasn't right, so she called the watch."

Lenoir looked down at the corpse again. A feeling of dread was oozing from the center of his body into his extremities, like bile leaking out of his stomach. He did not want to examine the body, especially not in front of Crears.

"Did anyone else in the area see anything?" he asked, floundering for excuses to delay. "Did you question the passersby?"

Crears regarded him curiously. "Some of my men are doing it now. You might have seen them out in the street? I got them started on it before I came to find you."

Of course he did. Damn him.

There was a stretch of silence. Crears looked uncomfortable. He started to speak, then glanced at the watchman and fell silent, scratching his beard. At length, however, when Lenoir still made no move, Crears chose duty over decorum and said, "Inspector, aren't you going to take a look at the body?"

Lenoir nodded numbly and squatted. There was no getting around it.

The man's shirt was already open, presumably from Crears's initial inspection. There was no blood on the clothing, no bruising or cuts on the flesh. The skull appeared to be intact. Lenoir rolled the body onto its back. The corpse had not yet begun to stiffen, but the skin on one side was vaguely purple, in sharp contrast to the pallor of the rest of the body. The discoloration suggested that the body had been lying on its side for at least an hour. Crears had been right about the approximate time of death.

"Two hours at most," Lenoir said.

"He was still warm when I found him," said the watchman, "and no discoloration. Can't be sure, but I think most of that two hours started from the time I went to get the constable."

"But you did not see anyone suspicious?"

Lenoir did not have to look up to know the watchman was annoyed; it came through clearly in his voice. "I would have said so, Inspector."

It was a stupid question, but Lenoir was just talking, his eyes skimming over the corpse as he tried not to notice the tear in the man's trousers just below the knee. But the pale flesh peeking through the cloth snagged at the corners of his vision, holding his gaze. He could not bring himself to look directly at it, but neither could he look away. How he wished Crears and the watchman would leave.

"Constable!" someone called from the street, as if on cue. "I think you'd better come and hear this," and to Lenoir's tremendous relief, Crears turned and headed down the alley.

Seizing upon the opportunity, Lenoir looked up at the watchman. "Go with him." The watchman frowned and opened his mouth to speak, but seeing Lenoir's expression, he thought better of it and obeyed.

Lenoir reached for the corpse's leg, but then he hesitated, his hand trembling as it hovered over the body. The trouser leg was torn in three places, leaving ribbons of cloth than ran more or less from the ankle to the knee. Steeling himself, Lenoir pushed it aside to expose the flesh.

The puncture marks were deep and angled, as though a great fanged beast had seized the limb in its jaws and tried to drag its victim away. Yet there was no blood—at least not fresh. The scratches that led into the puncture marks should have been livid and red, but instead they were a deep blue against flesh the color of slate. The capillaries were visible, a delicate inky web that crawled over the exposed part of the leg. It looked as though the blood was frozen beneath the skin, and suddenly Lenoir felt frozen too. The dread that had been leaking out of his stomach had seeped through his entire body; he was numb with it.

One of the corpse's arms was now draped over its chest, having shifted position when Lenoir rolled the body onto its back. He saw that the fingertips were torn and bloodied, and he glanced instinctively at the flagstones near the head. He could picture it all so vividly: the man clawing at the stones in a vain attempt to drag himself away from his attacker, his leg clasped in the deadly embrace of the scourge. Lenoir's chest tightened as he imagined the man's panic, his inability to understand how all the strength had suddenly fled from his limbs. Lenoir's own arms felt leaden, and the metallic taste of fear was in his mouth. His gaze fell to the corpse's eyes, wide and staring at the sky. He saw himself reflected there, a pale face in a golden mirror.

The sight transfixed him. It was as though he watched himself through the dead man's eyes. He looked like a man marked for death. *And so you are. Death has found you. It sees you. It will have you at last.*

It felt like a dream, slow and surreal, so when Lenoir turned and saw the absinthe eyes glinting from the branching alleyway, he thought it was all in his mind. But then the dead flesh on his arm suddenly began to burn as though blood flowed through it for the first time in a decade, and Lenoir knew instantly that he did not dream.

The green-eyed man was there.

The spirit did not move at first. He merely regarded Lenoir silently, his pale face impassive. Lenoir did not move either, frozen in place by a terror more paralyzing than any he had ever felt. He was like a startled rabbit, hoping to go unnoticed, not daring to flee lest he provoke the predator. Perhaps the spirit would not recognize him; perhaps it had been too long, and there had been too many others marked for death for his face still to be familiar.

An eternity passed, a stretch of such profound stillness that time itself seemed to have stopped flowing. Lenoir held his breath until he felt his lungs must burst. When he could stand it no longer, he hauled himself up and tried to run.

He had not even got to his feet when the leather tongues of the scourge struck out, glancing off his boot and sending him tumbling to the flagstones. Lenoir braced himself for the killing blow that must surely follow—but it did not come. Instead the spirit approached, head tilted, curious. Like a cat toying with unfamiliar prey, the spirit had only used enough force to subdue his victim so that he might consider it more carefully. He seemed unresolved, as though he could not decide whether to attack—and for a brief, wonderful moment, Lenoir experienced a rush of hope.

But then the absinthe eyes narrowed a fraction. It was barely perceptible, yet it was the most expressive Lenoir had ever seen that face, and like a dam bursting, his breast flooded with fresh panic. The spirit knew him.

Again Lenoir scrambled to his feet, his gaze locked on the sunlit street ahead. But the spirit anticipated him; the scourge snapped around the corner, aimed for his head. Lenoir ducked, the cursed weapon missing him so narrowly that his hair was ruffled. When the whip struck the wall, the masonry was blasted apart as though hit by cannon fire. It was impossible that stone should yield to leather, but Lenoir had no time to ponder it; he pushed off the ground with all fours and sprinted in the opposite direction along the alley—away from the scourge, but also from the safety of the sunlight.

The part of Lenoir's brain that was still capable of rational thought told him that it was pointless, that he could never outrun the green-eyed man. He had aged ten years since last he had fled this hunter, a decade of growing tired, of putting on weight. The spirit, however, had not changed, remaining eternally young—as though youth was a concept that mattered to the supernatural. The green-eyed man would never run out of breath; his limbs would never tire. Lenoir could hear his attacker giving chase, and he almost wanted to give up, to give himself over to the judgment he knew he deserved. But the instinct for survival was too powerful, and he ran with all the strength he had.

He reached the far end of the alley and shot a fleeting glance in either direction. He almost sobbed in despair at what he found: another alleyway ran perpendicular, the length of it cast in shadow by the looming buildings. Both directions led to still more alleyways—not to the street, not to the sunlight. Lenoir had the fleeting impression of a rat in a maze finding only dead ends, but for him the dead ends would be literal. After a moment's hesitation, he lunged to the right, for the way seemed slightly shorter. He only realized how close the green-eyed man was when he heard the wall blast apart behind him. A stone glanced off the back of his skull. His vision flashed and he staggered forward, but he kept his feet and continued to run. He had to reach the sunlight. He was not even sure whether that would be enough to save him, but he had always believed that it had been the sunrise that delivered him from the green-eyed man ten years ago, and it was the only hope he had.

Pausing to wield the scourge had cost the spirit time, but he was closing in again. Lenoir did not dare look back. He kept pounding forward in spite of his lungs, in spite of his legs, in spite of his brain. He made it almost to the next T-intersection when someone came around the corner ahead of him, a man carrying firewood over his shoulder. Lenoir saw him in time to twist out of the way, nearly blundering into the wall in front of him before banking left and making for the street. A crash sounded behind him, followed by a string of oaths, and he knew the green-eyed man had collided with the villager. Some part of his mind registered that the spirit must be solid after all. Another, more basic, part of his mind told him that the collision would cost the spirit another few precious seconds. Perhaps it would be enough.

The street was just ahead. The sunshine that spilled across its flagstones looked to Lenoir like the very rays of Heaven. He could not move fast enough; he felt as though he were running through some sort of invisible, viscous fluid that impeded his movements, making his limbs maddeningly slow. He strained against it, pushing forward as every joint ached with the effort.

If he had not seen the sunlight ahead, had he not been so close to it, he would never have fought back when the scourge tripped him up again. He would have resigned himself to the inevitable, allowed the life to be sapped from him with only a twinge of regret. But the sun-drenched street gave him hope, and when the cobbled stone beneath his feet exploded and he was pitched onto his face, he wanted only to survive. He scrabbled forward on his knees and elbows like some wriggling lizard trying to escape a hawk. His upper body was in the street when he felt the flare of pain in his ankle. He was jerked backward, but he grabbed the corner of the nearest building just in time to prevent himself being pulled all the way into the alley. He braced his elbows against the side of the building, straining to keep the upper half of his body in the street. He could feel the barbs tugging and tearing at his flesh as the whip was drawn back like a fishing pole with a catch on the line. He hauled himself forward with all his might, but already he could feel his strength flagging. The burning chill began to seep out of his ankle. His veins bristled with frost, and a wave of nausea washed over him, though whether from pure terror or the sensation of his flesh dying he could not tell. An image flashed, unbidden, in his mind: the corpse lying in the alley nearby, his lower leg shredded, his fingertips torn and bloodied from his vain attempt to drag himself forward . . .

There was an angry shout from above, and Lenoir looked up to find a fast-moving carriage bearing down on him. For a moment he thought he had traded one death for another, but the driver managed to swerve the horses just enough to avoid running him over, the hooves of the nearest animal treading no more than a hand-span from Lenoir's skull. As the carriage rattled past, the traces came within reach, and Lenoir seized on to the dangling leather, first with one hand, then with both.

He lurched forward. The pain was instant and intolerable; the flesh in his ankle tore more deeply and his arms felt as though they would be ripped from their sockets. He was forced to let go of the carriage. But the sudden, unexpected jolt of momentum had been enough to wrench the spirit forward into the street. Lenoir felt the scourge go slack. He wriggled free. Then he heard a scream, and he looked back, despite himself.

The spirit was on hands and knees in the street, a curtain of shining black hair covering his face. A woman on the opposite side of the street was pointing at him and shrieking, drawing looks from other passersby. Hands flew to mouths; people cursed and shouted. The woman was the first to flee, and others soon followed.

At first Lenoir thought he was imagining it: smoke appeared to be rising from the spirit's body, from his hands and from the face Lenoir could not see. Then he realized that it was not his imagination. The spirit's flesh was burning. The skin on the pale hands withered like thin paper put to flame, great holes opening up to reveal the tendon and bone beneath. The spirit staggered to his feet and turned to face Lenoir.

When he raised his head, Lenoir saw the most gruesome sight he would ever behold. The beautiful, marble-chiseled face was melting. The flesh of one cheek had dissolved entirely, leaving corded muscle the color of raw meat. The lips were gone; teeth shone through in a grisly mockery of a grin. The eyelids on one side were oozing away, uncovering a single white orb with an absinthe pupil. That pupil was fixed on Lenoir, and it carried a simple, unmistakable message:

This is not over.

The spirit stared at Lenoir for a long moment, seemingly oblivious to the screaming and crying that surrounded him. Then he turned dispassionately away and strode back into the alley.

Lenoir could not help himself. He got shakily to his feet and moved toward the alley. The street was virtually empty now, and Lenoir stood in the center of it, keeping well out of reach of the shadows. When the alley came into view, Lenoir was somehow not surprised by what he saw there.

The green-eyed man stood in the gloom near the entrance to the street. His face was virtually whole again, save for a patch of his cheek that was closing up even as Lenoir watched. His searing gaze bored into Lenoir, but he did not venture back into the light.

Any doubts Lenoir had harbored about this creature's immortality vanished in that moment, along with any remaining hope that he could survive for long. He had manufactured no fewer than three escapes from the green-eyed man, miraculous escapes that he scarcely understood. No man deserved that kind of providence. Certainly Lenoir did not.

He turned away from the alley and headed back up the street to find Crears and the others. His limbs were shaking terribly, and his pant leg was shredded at the hem. His clothing was streaked with dirt from the street. He would need to think of an excuse to explain his disheveled appearance to Crears, but he had plenty of time to come up with something plausible. After all, he would be taking the long way round.

CHAPTER 15

It had been a long time since Kody last visited Fort Hald, Kennian's main prison, and now he remembered why. It was the sort of thing that could make a man seriously question his career choice. No sooner had he plunged into the echoing gloom than he felt his whole body tense, as though every fiber of his being were counting off the seconds until he could leave. Despair saturated the place, assaulting his senses. The sounds of it clamored in his ears: the cold rattle of chains against stone, the low mutterings of the insane, the skittering of vermin in the shadows. His nostrils flared at the smell of it, a fetid cocktail of iron, mold, stale urine, and pestilence. Its chill, clammy touch issued forth like a phantom breath from the bowels of the dungeons. Its taste was the bile rising in his throat. But nothing was worse than what met the eye.

The hollow, cadaverous faces that peered between the bars held no emotion. Few showed any interest in Kody; many didn't even seem to register his presence. Some sat motionless, mouths open, staring at nothing.

Others paced their cells as much as their shackles would allow, shambling noisily back and forth in mindless monotony. Sickness was everywhere—open sores, rattling breath, clouded eyes. Kody had the unsettling impression of being surrounded by an army of animated corpses.

He'd always considered it ironic that those found guilty of capital crimes were put to death, while those convicted of more minor offenses were incarcerated here. Given the choice, Kody would rather be hanged twice over than spend even a month in this cage of the damned. He couldn't help feeling a little guilty about his own role in condemning people to rot away in this place.

He shook off such thoughts and tried to focus on the task at hand. He had reason to hope this visit would be fruitful, at least. Instead of flashing Raiyen's sketch around the Camp in the faint hope that someone would recognize him, Kody had decided to follow Lenoir's logic and start with known members of the Asis clan. He'd been told that the woman he'd come here to see, Marani, was an exile, just as Raiyen had been. She almost certainly knew the dead man, and he might have contacted her when he moved to the city. Kody also hoped to learn more about *khekra*. If the Asis clan had once been renowned for its witchdoctors, as the apothecary had said, Marani might know something of their arts.

He found her with some difficulty, since the majority of the female prisoners were Adali (as were a disproportionate number of the men), and none of them were eager to own their identities. Eventually, a middle-aged woman separated herself from the others and moved toward the bars, albeit reluctantly. She regarded Kody suspiciously through occluded eyes. She would be blind soon, he guessed, opaque masses overtaking her amber pupils like ice thickening over a lake.

She stopped a few paces back from the bars, as though she feared Kody might reach through and try to grab her. "What do you want?" she demanded, her voice croaking from disuse.

"I need to ask you a few questions." Kody held up his sketch. "Do you know this man?"

She gave it a cursory glance. "Nope."

"Come on," Kody scoffed. "He's a member of your clan."

Marani shrugged. "So? I don't know him."

"Let me help you. His name is Raiyen."

She frowned, peering more closely at the sketch. "Ha! So it is. Didn't recognize him. He was just a boy last time I saw him."

"A boy?" Kody was taken aback. "How long has it been since you lived with the clan?"

"Going on fifteen years now." She said it as though it were something to be proud of.

"And how long have you been in here?"

"Five years, or thereabouts. Got you hounds to thank for that, don't I?"

Damn. So much for that line of questioning. Marani had been in prison the entire time Raiyen had been in the city. She couldn't possibly help Kody track down his last known associates. *I should have thought of that.*

It hadn't even occurred to him to ask about her sentence. *All right, time for plan B.* "In that case, maybe you can help me with a little research I'm doing."

"Research?" She scowled suspiciously.

"That's right. About the Adali. About some of your . . . cultural practices."

She let out a short, incredulous laugh. "Our 'cultural practices,' is it? And what in the Dark Flame is that supposed to mean? What are you bothering me for, hound? Who sent you?"

"I'm sure you remember Sergeant Izar?" She should—he was the officer who put her here.

"That traitor?" Marani spat emphatically on the ground. "To the below with him! No true Adal, that one—turning his back on his own kind!"

Kody had expected this reaction, but it still brought heat to his cheeks. "You'll speak with respect! Izar is a fine officer."

"Bah! Zaid clan—liars and bullies, the lot." She looked meaningfully over her shoulder at her fellow prisoners, as though daring anyone to disagree.

"Maybe," said Kody coolly, "but they're a lot more respected than the Asis clan, aren't they?"

A cold smile stole over Marani's face, but she made no reply.

"I hear your clan has had a bad bit of luck."

"What would you know of it? Not a hound in the Metropolitan Police knows a thing about the Adali. None but that mutt Izar."

"Maybe so, but I'm a quick learner. You'd be surprised how much a determined hound can pick up. For example, I know that the Asis clan used to be known for its witchdoctors."

Marani's expression darkened. "I don't belong with them anymore." She backed away from the bars a little. "Whatever they did, it's nothing to do with me."

"I know that. They banished you, didn't they? Izar didn't tell me what for. Come to think of it, he didn't tell me what you're doing in here."

"Murder," someone called from the back of the cell. Marani shot a scathing look behind her, but with her poor eyesight she couldn't tell who had made the remark. She settled for another volley of spittle.

To Kody, she said mockingly, "I'm innocent."

He shrugged. "I don't care."

"Then what do you want?" she shrieked, lunging suddenly at the bars. "Why are you *here*, hound?"

Kody was momentarily taken aback by the outburst, his hand straying reflexively to the sword at his hip. Marani stared at him, wild-eyed, her shoulders heaving. The woman was half-mad, he realized. If he wanted to get anywhere with her, he'd have to be more direct. "I want to know what kind of *khekra* your kin are meddling with, and why."

Marani backed away again, her fear unmistakable. A strange silence descended on the cell. The mention of *khekra* was like a pistol shot in the air, stunning everyone.

"What do you know about *khekra*?" Marani whispered.

"I know it exists. I know it uses human blood and suchlike to make medicine."

Marani barked out a tense laugh. "That ought to be the least of your worries, hound."

Finally, we're getting somewhere! Kody was careful to keep his voice neutral. "What else should I be worried about?"

"Marani," one of the women called warningly, "this is Adali business."

Marani ignored her. "Whatever bits they take for medicine, it's only a small amount. A few drops of blood, or a bit of hair. No one gets hurt, not for medicine. But *khekra* can do other things besides healing."

"Like curses." Kody tried to keep the disbelief out of his voice, but he obviously failed, because Marani sneered at him.

"Don't believe in curses, hound? Why get me to tell you about *khekra*, then?"

"Because it doesn't matter what I believe. Whoever is kidnapping children obviously believes, and that's what counts."

"Kidnapping, is it?" Marani grunted thoughtfully. "And what makes you think it's got something to do with *khekra*?"

Kody left that alone. "Are there curses that involve using children?"

She made a rude hand gesture. "Bah! How should I know? I'm no witchdoctor."

"What about other kinds of magic?" Kody asked, trying a different angle. "Are there spells that can do the opposite of curses?"

Marani's eyes narrowed shrewdly. "Looking for a

favor, are we? Make you better looking, maybe, or smarter?" She cackled, pleased with herself.

Kody didn't take the bait. "Let's say I was looking for a favor. Could a witchdoctor help me?"

"If you made it worthwhile, maybe. But you wouldn't get no favors from the Asis, not after everything they've been through on account of *khekra*. Not unless you had something real, real good to trade for it."

"Money is always popular," Kody said dryly.

Marani snorted. "For little favors, sure. Kidnapping is a pretty big favor. Even if you found someone willing, he'd be a fool to risk it. Get himself banished, or hanged, or worse. Like to bring down the whole clan while he was at it."

She had a point. If an Adal were caught kidnapping Braelish children, Adali all over the Five Villages would pay the price. Lynch mobs would sprout up from Kennian to Brackensvale, and the Asis clan would be their first target. Their camp would be burned to the ground, the people driven off. And the Asis had nowhere else to go. If there was one thing Kody admired about the Adali, it was their loyalty to their kin; even if Raiyen wasn't the benevolent soul his sister claimed, he wasn't likely to risk those consequences lightly. Besides, the sister and her friend had said that Raiyen got himself exiled trying to help his people. He must have known that the elders were onto him, turning a blind eye to his medicine, but he drew their wrath anyway, trying to do something about the drought. For him to turn around and knowingly put his clan in danger . . . it didn't fit, not without a major incentive.

There has to be something big on the table, Kody thought, *something worth the risk.* "What would it take to get you to do something like that, Marani?"

She gave a sneering smile. "Oh, that's easy, hound. Get me out of here, and I'm all yours."

Kody didn't get anything useful out of her after that, and none of the other prisoners would talk to him, not about *khekra.* The word itself was like a spell, a hex of silence. The interview had been fruitful, though. Kody felt sure he was narrowing in on a possible motive, and Lenoir always said that understanding the motive was the most important part of solving a crime. *"Do not let yourself be distracted by the details,"* Lenoir had told him, time and again. *"They are important, but you must understand how they fit together, how they tell a story. Understand* why *the crime has been committed, and the rest is simply a question of* how.*"*

Kody chewed on that as he made his way back to the kennel. *Suppose the sister was right, and whatever Raiyen was up to was supposed to be for the benefit of the clan. Maybe he was even trying to earn himself a pardon, a way back into the elders' good graces. So what could the clan possibly get out of all this? What is it they need?*

An idea was forming in his head, but he needed to knock it around with someone. Fortunately, he knew just the right sparring partner.

"Izar!" he called as he stalked purposefully across the kennel.

Sergeant Izar was hunched over his desk, scribbling something on a sheet of parchment. He looked awkward, his bowed posture and splayed knees making the desk seem like children's furniture. Not for the first time, Kody marveled at the man's height. Being well over six foot himself, Kody figured Izar had to be just under seven.

The Adal glanced up as Kody approached. "What is it? I have a lot to get done by the end of the day."

Kody was not deterred by Izar's abruptness; it was simply his way. "This won't take long. I just have a couple of questions."

With a reluctant grunt, Izar gestured for Kody to grab a chair. "Five minutes."

Kody didn't waste a single second. "Is it true that the Adali don't use currency?"

Izar's expression darkened immediately. Like most Adali, he was suspicious of any line of questioning linked to his race. "What's this about, Kody?"

Kody spread his hands in a mollifying gesture. "Izar, you know I respect you. Just humor me, all right?"

Izar considered him for a moment, his amber eyes scanning Kody's face for—what? Hostility? Disdain? Kody was a little hurt that Izar wasn't prepared to give him the benefit of the doubt. Granted, his question was sensitive, but they'd known each other for years.

"The Adali use currency," Izar said eventually. "Every culture uses currency, Kody. It's what sets us apart from beasts." Kody did not miss the subtle irony in Izar's tone. There were plenty in the Five Villages who wouldn't set the Adali apart from beasts.

"What I mean is, they don't use gold or paper money, or anything like that," Kody said.

"Not traditionally, no, although that is changing. In Adali culture, wealth is measured in cattle. To a lesser extent, in goats or sheep."

"That's what I thought. So the Asis clan—that group camped near Berryvine—they're about as poor as it gets."

Izar didn't respond. He was waiting for Kody to explain where he was going with this.

"Here's what I don't understand. Wealth is power, right? Influence. But it seems to me that if a clan's wealth is measured in cattle, there's a certain degree of luck involved. If you have a bad year—boom! You're at the bottom of the heap. And the reverse is also true, presumably."

Izar smiled faintly. "And what would be wrong with that? Do you think that a society where status is based on an accident of birth makes more sense than a system where those who are most skilled at husbandry—or agriculture, or industry, or whatever—earn a privileged place?"

"I had no idea you were such a philosopher," Kody said dryly.

"You brought it up."

"I'm just trying to figure out what it takes for a clan that's going through a bad patch—the Asis clan, say—to get out of it. Sounds like it could be pretty easy, in principle. Couldn't someone just buy them a bunch of cows?"

"That might work. The Kennian Ladies' Society of Benefactors, maybe."

Kody rolled his eyes. "Very funny. Seriously, would that be enough to change their fortunes for a while?"

"I doubt it. Cows are a currency, so their value comes when they're traded—as tribute to the more powerful clans, or as a bride price, that sort of thing. A clan that had its cows given to them for a single season might be able to move a little ways up the social ladder, but without a way of sustaining the herd size, it would not last."

It made sense; a one-off gift could never replace a steady income. "So how does one sustain the herd size?"

"Skill, but mostly access to water and plentiful grazing. And that is bitterly contested."

"The clans fight over it?"

"Sometimes, though not as much as they used to. A couple of hundred years ago, just about every conflict the Adali fought was over grazing land. Fortunately, the elders eventually came up with a more civilized way of carving up the beast."

"And that is?"

"Every spring, there is a conference of all the major clans in Kigiri. It's called the *Orom*. The migration routes for the season are decided there."

"The *Orom*," Kody repeated thoughtfully. The apothecary had mentioned something about an annual meeting of the clans. "How does it work?"

"It's sort of like an auction. Clans buy the right to

pass through the prime grazing lands. They pay in cattle, of course."

"Who do they buy the rights from?"

"Each other."

Kody frowned. "I don't get it."

"It's a different concept of land ownership than we have in Braeland. Land is a collective good, owned by the people. So it isn't bought and sold, exactly. It's more like leasing, with the rights going to the highest bidder. In theory, title is only held for a single season. But the richest and most powerful clans always buy the rights to the best migration routes, those with fertile land and plentiful water. The same clans tend to buy the same routes year after year, because no one can outbid them. Every so often, though, a lower-ranking clan has a really good year, and a route changes hands. It's an investment, because access to good grazing land strengthens the herd."

"But if everybody owns the land, then who gets paid? I mean, say I give a thousand cows for a tract of land. Who gets the cows?"

"The people," Izar said, as though it were obvious. "The payment is put into a pool, and at the end of the auction, the pool is divided amongst the poorest clans. That's how we make sure that no one is completely destitute. It doesn't end up being much once it's split between a handful of clans, but it is enough to prevent the people from starving."

"So . . . the cows that are paid for access to grazing routes go to *charity*?"

Izar shrugged. "That's one way of thinking about it."

"Huh." *Not a bad system,* Kody thought. "Imagine if the rich folks of Kennian had to pay into a pot for the poor every year. Life would sure be different."

"The Adali take care of their own, Kody. The people are a herd, and a herd must stay together to survive."

"Then what happened to the Asis clan?"

Izar winced. "Like I said, the payment they get from the *Orom* isn't much, and sometimes it is not enough. Things are hard for Adali everywhere, especially with the droughts these last couple of years. Even the richer clans are losing animals, which means they have less to pay into the pot, so there is less to go around. I guess the Asis have decided that staying put, even where they are not welcome, is better than taking their chances heading north."

"But if somebody were to give the Asis enough cattle, they could trade for a good route next season."

"Maybe, but what then? If they had to trade away most of their herd to get access to the land, what good would the land be? They would just be in the same place all over again the next season. It takes years to build up a herd."

"Maybe the system isn't so great after all," Kody said sourly. "Seems to me that it all but guarantees that the powerful clans stay powerful, and the poor stay poor."

Izar shrugged again. "I didn't say it was fair. Besides, change does happen. There is always the chance that a clan has an especially good year. Plus, the poor clans sometimes broker alliances with the more powerful ones, through tribute and marriages. That earns them a measure of protection."

Kody pondered that. It seemed to him that while some limited mobility might be possible, by and large the clans occupied the same rung in the social ladder year after year. Especially a clan like the Asis, who obviously had no means to buy the support of a more powerful clan. It was a vicious cycle: fewer cattle meant limited access to grazing lands, and that in turn meant weaker herds. A poor clan without alliances was easy prey, subject to cattle rustling, slave raids, and worse. In spite of what Izar had said about the people being a herd, the Adali were not immune to the baser instincts of human nature. "A clan like the Asis is past the point of no return," he said, more to himself than to Izar.

"Definitely. I doubt they will ever go home. However tough it is for an Adal to make his way down here, it's a lot better than putting your children and your herds at risk back home. Over time, the clan will probably just dissolve into the Five Villages. They would not be the first."

They sat in silence for a moment. Kody tried to think of another question, but he couldn't. He rapped the desk in frustration. He was so close, but there was something he just wasn't seeing. "I guess my five minutes are up. Thanks, Izar."

Izar's amber gaze held him. "Are you going to tell me what this is about?"

"I think a couple of Asis are up to some bad business." Kody didn't elaborate; he had no desire to test Izar's patience with talk of *khekra*. "But I'm convinced they're just foot soldiers. I need to find their paymaster, but to do that, I need to figure out how they're being paid. . . ."

He paused. His heart beat faster. "Wait."

Izar smirked. "I know that look. Take a deep breath, Kody."

"I've got an idea."

"You don't say."

Kody stood abruptly. "I've got to go. Thanks again." He weaved between the desks toward the back of the kennel. "Hey, Hardin," he called.

A portly officer with a ruddy complexion looked up from his desk. "Hiya, Kody."

"How'd you like to come with me on an interview?" Hardin was not exactly a pedigree hound, but he was at least trustworthy, and Kody knew better than to charge off without backup. That kind of amateur mistake could get you killed. He would have preferred to bring Izar—the Adal was the better hound by far—but it wouldn't be fair to drag him into a case like this. Izar had been forced to put enough of his people behind bars.

"Where's Lenoir?" Hardin asked.

"Busy."

"I don't know. . . ." Hardin gazed at the pile of parchment on his desk. "I got all these reports to deal with. . . ."

Kody suppressed an impatient growl. "Look, you're always complaining about being stuck behind that desk. Here's your chance to get out there and get your hands dirty. Now, do you want to come or not?"

"All right," Hardin said unenthusiastically.

Ingrate, Kody thought. But even that was not enough to dampen his excitement. "Wait here a second." He charged up the stairs, taking them two at a time. He scrawled out a hasty note and left it on Lenoir's desk. Then he rounded up Hardin, grabbed a meat pie from the vendor across the street, and headed out to chase his lead.

CHAPTER 16

L enoir drifted down the high street of Kennian in a daze, his eyes fixed upon the darkening sky. The haze from thousands of cooking fires smothered the setting sun, staining it bloodred. The streetlamps were already being lit, flame-eyed sentries that stood guard against the intrusion of the gloom. Where their glowing gaze could not reach, shadows crept slowly out into the street with the unobtrusive stealth of a predator stalking its prey. Lenoir could feel the crawling darkness like a physical presence closing in around him. Every foot the shadows gained was another bit of territory conquered for the green-eyed man. The invasion would not cease until Lenoir was surrounded, besieged by the darkness with no hope of escape.

He could have tried to explain his predicament to Crears, but what would be the point? Even if Crears believed such an outlandish tale, it was no use putting him in danger. The Berryvine Watch could do nothing to help. There would be no place to hide once night had fallen. Lenoir did not know whether the light of a streetlamp would be enough to keep the spirit at bay, but it did not matter—the scourge would be able to reach inside a protective circle of light. Walls would not shield him, not if the cursed whip could shatter stone. And there was no use in running, for there was nowhere the darkness did not rule. Daylight would not come for many hours.

The street was all but deserted at the dinner hour. The shops had closed, leaving the faces of the buildings blank. To Lenoir they seemed almost as alive as the shadows, pitiless observers of his plight, spectators of some gruesome rite of sacrifice. He was alone and exposed at the center of a great arena, waiting for his death to issue forth from one of the many tunnels that flanked him.

He heard footsteps to his right. They were coming from a side street, a thin canal of gloom that concealed the source of the sound. The glow of a nearby streetlamp crowded his vision, blinding him to all but his immediate surroundings. The shadows had reached the far side of the high street.

He could sense the presence now as it drew near, and he hurried under the umbrella of the streetlamp, knowing as he did so that it could not possibly protect him. His pulse stuttered, his breath came in shallow gasps. He felt strangely light-headed, almost giddy, and suddenly he knew he did not want to run. This time he would not fight back. This time he would let the green-eyed man take him.

"Why, Nicolas—how lovely to see you!"

Lenoir did not recognize the voice through the roaring in his ears, and when Zera drew into the light, he felt the air leave his body. For a moment the dizziness intensified, and he feared he might faint. Then a great weariness settled over him. Was it relief or disappointment?

"Nicolas, are you well?" She came closer, her features etched with concern. She did not wait for Lenoir to reply. "You look awful! How pale you are . . . there isn't a drop of blood in your lips! Come with me and we'll make you some tea."

Lenoir felt numb. It was a struggle to form words. "I would not want to trouble you. I'm fine."

"Don't be silly," Zera said dismissively, taking his arm, "it's just up the road. And I'm not having a salon tonight. It will just be the two of us."

Lenoir allowed himself to be drawn forward, but he felt no desire to go with her. He felt nothing at all. "You are not safe with me," he told her. "You should let me be."

She seemed to think he was teasing her. "Oh my, how dramatic! Police work must be picking up these days!"

"I am not joking, Zera," he said dully.

She stopped and gave him a long, hard look. "Are you trying to frighten me or impress me?" Before he could answer, she continued. "If you really are in trouble, then you should come inside with me at once. You're safer there than standing in the street."

Lenoir made no further attempt to dissuade her, but followed mechanically as she led him up the street to her apartments. He allowed her to take his coat, ig-

nored her question about the dust and the ragged tear
in the right armpit. Her expression grew increasingly
worried as she fussed about him, giving brusque orders
to a servant to brew a pot of tea.

"And fetch some brandy," she called. "I fear the inspector may need it." To Lenoir, she said, "Sit here."

He did as he was told. They were in the winged
chairs near the hearth again. Lenoir found himself
wondering idly whether firelight could banish the
green-eyed man.

"Is it Feine?" Zera asked him.

"What?" Lenoir gazed at her stupidly. The name
meant nothing to him.

"Lord Feine. Surely you don't think you're the only
one who worked out what happened to Arleas? His
affair with Lady Feine was hardly a secret, at least not
within these walls."

Lenoir almost laughed. The idea of Lord Feine being dangerous to him seemed ridiculous. What could
he have to fear from Feine, or any other mortal, when
he was being hunted by something supernatural, something that could sap his life with a single touch? To
Zera, he merely said, "No. It is not Lord Feine."

A strange look came over her. "This doesn't have
something to do with that missing boy, does it?" She
sounded tense, as though she feared the answer.

Lenoir massaged his temples. Nothing could be
gained by telling her the truth. She would think him
mad. Perhaps he *was* mad. Then again, she was Adali,
and even though she had left the ways of her kin behind, she would have grown up surrounded by tales of

the strange and the supernatural. Perhaps she did not share the rest of society's skepticism toward the existence of ghosts and demons. Perhaps she would think it only natural that judgment could be sent from another plane.

He did not decide to tell her, precisely. He simply spoke. "I am hunted, Zera."

She nodded slowly and stared into the hearth, the flames reflecting in her golden eyes. "Who is it?"

"It is not a *who*. It is a *what*."

She frowned. "What do you mean?"

"A spirit, Zera. A vengeful spirit from beyond. He has followed me here from Serles. I thought I had escaped him, but I haven't. He is here, and he wants me dead." Lenoir was surprised by the calm in his own voice. Yet he knew that it was not courage that steadied him; it was resignation.

Zera's reaction was surprisingly measured. She had drawn back slightly in her chair, as though she suddenly found herself too close to him. Her brow was creased over hard eyes and tight lips. She seemed to hover between fear and anger, still unsure whether he teased. "A vengeful spirit from beyond." Her tone was not mocking, but matter-of-fact—she was making sure she understood.

"I am sure you will think me mad." Lenoir smiled ruefully. "I have no doubt I would think so in your place. But I promise you that what I say is the truth. I have been touched by the hand of death. Twice." He reached down and pulled up his torn pant leg.

Her cry was muffled by the hand that flew to her

mouth. She looked away sharply, but a moment later, her eyes were drawn irresistibly back to the mottled gray of Lenoir's shin. It was punctured and scored by the barbs, but there was no sign of blood.

Lenoir's own gaze lingered on this new scar, so very like the one he bore on his arm. The spirit was killing his body piece by piece. "It is cold to the touch," he observed blandly, his fingers gliding down into his boot. "The flesh has died." Zera had turned away again, her face in her hands, so Lenoir let his pant leg drop. She had seen enough. She could not disbelieve him now.

"What happened?" she whispered, and now her voice shook.

"I don't know. I have not seen him for ten years. I thought I had escaped. But then I saw the signs of his work, and I knew he had returned."

Zera shook her head mutely. She did not understand. How to explain it to her?

"There is an ancient myth in Arrènes, about avenging angels called *carnairs*. When mortals sinned gravely, the *carnairs* were sent forth by God to punish them. There was no escaping their wrath. They were immortal, inescapable. They tortured their victims and drove them mad."

"The Adali have such tales. But as you say, they are myths."

"Just so. But the spirit that hunts me is no myth. He is real. And like the *carnairs*, he has been sent to punish me."

"But how do you—"

"I just know. The first time I saw him, I knew. I looked into his eyes and I knew he wanted me dead. And I knew I deserved it."

He told her about that night in Serles, when dawn had broken and lanced through the green-eyed man like a spear from Heaven. He told her about his flight from the city of his birth, a permanent exile that he regretted more bitterly than anything before or since. And he told her about his afternoon in Berryvine, when the spirit's flesh had melted from his bones only to regenerate moments later. Lenoir was relentless in his telling of it, sparing no detail. By the time he finished, Zera was shaking so badly that she spilled brandy on herself when she tried to take a sip.

Lenoir, for his part, felt somehow calmer for having related the tale, as though speaking it aloud made it somehow more fathomable, more prosaic. He could approach the problem now, try to think it through.

"The ironic part is, I do not think the spirit came here for me," Lenoir said reflectively. "He is somehow connected to Zach's kidnapping."

Zera choked on her brandy for the second time. *"What?"*

"I know, it is an incredible coincidence. Or perhaps it is fate—I no longer know the difference. But when we found that boy in the farmhouse, we also found a body—an Adali man."

"You never told me that."

"No. I did not even want to think about it. When I saw him, I knew immediately how he died. I knew the spirit had killed him. And he killed another Adal today in Berryvine. He must have come here for them." He smiled bitterly. "Finding me was just serendipity."

There was a long silence. Zera stared into the flames. Lenoir could see that she was shaken to the core, and he felt a twinge of guilt. He should not have burdened her with this horror. It had nothing to do with her.

"What are you going to do?" she asked him eventually.

"I don't know."

"You should go to a soothsayer."

The suggestion surprised him. Zera was the last person he would expect to refer him to a fortune-teller. "What for?"

Zera's expression was severe. "You know how I feel about these things, Nicolas, but there are times when such considerations must be put aside. Your life is in terrible danger. This . . . *thing*, this green-eyed man, is not of this world. If you have any chance of escaping him, you need advice from someone who can see beyond this world."

"And if I have no chance of escaping him?"

"Then think of the boy!" she snapped. "I won't allow you to sit here feeling sorry for yourself and waiting to die, not when there's a chance you might learn something that could save you, and the boy too! Perhaps the spirit has a weakness other than sunlight. Or perhaps there's a way you can appease him."

"A soothsayer could tell me these things?" Lenoir asked skeptically.

Zera gave a frustrated sigh and slumped back in her chair. "Not just any street charlatan, obviously, but a real one might. Such practices are common amongst the Adali, and even I have seen things I cannot explain. You have nothing to lose by trying."

Lenoir supposed she was right. His life was forfeit; there was nothing left to lose. "I will do as you say. There is a sergeant I know who visits soothsayers now and again. Perhaps he can guide me. I will speak to him in the morning."

"Do it now. Tonight. If this thing is as dangerous as you say, you have no time to spare."

On that, at least, they agreed.

"A soothsayer?" Sergeant Cale leaned against the doorframe of his apartment, regarding Lenoir with a wary expression. "At this time of night?" It was a not so subtle dig. The sergeant had been startled to find Lenoir at his door, and gave no sign of making him welcome. Over Cale's shoulder, Lenoir spied a poorly lit space even more cramped and disorderly than his own. "Begging your pardon, Inspector, but I never took you for the type to believe in such things."

"I do not," Lenoir said flatly. "But my investigation requires that I speak to a soothsayer. An Adal."

"There's dozens of them in town, and they're almost all Adali. Surely you don't need my help to find one?" It was borderline insubordinate, but Cale obviously suspected he was being made fun of. It would not be the first time; his occasional patronage of soothsayers had earned him much ridicule at the hands of his fellow hounds.

"That is true, Sergeant," Lenoir said, putting just enough frost in his voice to warn the junior officer against further evasion, "but my requirements are more specific. I need a soothsayer with a strong reputation, and what is more, I need someone who is also practiced in black magic."

Cale looked startled. "Black magic? But, sir—"

"I am investigating a series of kidnappings, and I have reason to believe that Adali magic is involved. I need to speak with someone who is renowned for such things. You are known to frequent Adali soothsayers. You must have some idea by now of who they are and what they do. Now tell me what I want to know, Sergeant, or I'll have you written up." His impatience was only half-feigned. He gave little credit to the idea of psychic powers, still less to magic and spells, but he was at a dead end, both for himself and for Zach. He was not going to stumble blindly through the streets and settle for the first soothsayer he came across. If he was going to speak to a charlatan, he wanted to speak to the best.

"Merden," said Cale sullenly. "I'd go to Merden."

"Where is he?"

"The market district."

Lenoir frowned. It seemed unlikely that he would find what he was looking for in that part of town. The market district was a high-traffic area, and from what the apothecary had said, Lenoir would have assumed that anyone practicing *khekra* would wish to remain out of sight.

Seeing his expression, Cale gave a knowing smirk. "You wouldn't think a soothsayer could afford the rents in the market district, would you? But he has a steady clientele. He's the best, they say. He'd better be, for what he charges."

Lenoir nodded; this Merden sounded like his man. As he turned to go, Cale said, "Kody was looking for you at the kennel earlier."

"I will see him later," Lenoir called over his shoulder, and Cale shut his door.

"I'm sorry to call at such a late hour," said Kody, "but I'm afraid a boy's life is at stake, perhaps more than one."

"How distressing. Anything I can do to help, of course. Please have a seat, Officers."

"Thank you. To begin with, can you tell me whether you are acquainted with the Adali clan camped just outside Berryvine?"

"I am not. I rarely travel."

"I see. Well, I paid them a visit recently, and they seemed to be in very dire straits."

"The Adali are usually in dire straits, Sergeant, as you have undoubtedly noticed."

"Yes, but this clan looked to be especially hard up. Not much in the way of livestock, for one thing, and their kids didn't look very healthy."

"And?"

"And we have reason to believe they are involved in the kidnapping of at least two young boys."

"I see. For ransom, I suppose?"

"I don't think so. I think they have something bigger in mind."

"Oh?"

"Let me explain." Kody ran through his theory, patchy though it was, trying to ignore the increasingly incredulous look Sergeant Hardin was directing his way.

"That is . . . quite a theory. Forgive me for being blunt, Sergeant, but you seem to have made a number of logical leaps."

"I won't deny that, but it all fits, doesn't it?"

"Does it?"

"I guess it depends on how you want to see it. Whether it's a constellation or just stars depends on who's looking."

"And does your inspector see this . . . *constellation*?"

"I haven't discussed it with him, but I'm sure he will, once I connect the dots for him."

"Very well. That's all I need to know."

"I . . . pardon?"

"Kody—"

"Just a minute, Hardin. What do you mean, that's all *you* need to know? I'm the one asking the—"

"Kody!"

Pain exploded at the back of his head, so sudden and sickening that he nearly toppled out of his chair. He fumbled clumsily for his sword, but his movements were sluggish. Hardin cried out again, wordlessly this time.

Kody blinked furiously, trying to banish the dancing specks of light from his vision. He couldn't see his attackers clearly, but he could tell that there were three of them, all of them armed.

He never stood a chance.

CHAPTER 17

The shop was improbably located between a butcher and a tailor, though Lenoir would not have known it if Cale had not told him what to look for. The storefront was utterly anonymous, a blank door beneath a blank set of windows shrouded in curtains. There was no signage, nothing even to indicate the presence of a place of business. If Lenoir had not been seeking it out, his eye would have passed over the shop entirely, without even registering its existence. Obviously, Merden was not relying on spontaneous passersby for patronage.

Lenoir hesitated at the door, feeling a strange mixture of dread and embarrassment. He did not really believe this man could help him. Did he perhaps have something to lose after all, some remaining scrap of dignity that he would forfeit in this pathetic attempt? He hovered there for long moments, uncertain. What ultimately prompted him to knock was not hope—for he had none—but the undeniable hunger to *know*.

"It is open," came a muffled voice. Lenoir recognized the lilting Adali accent even through the door.

The shop was surprisingly bright inside, lit by dozens of wax tapers in neat rows on either side of the room. Lenoir's first impression was that of a church. Then his eyes adjusted to the light, and he found himself enclosed in a cave of the macabre. The shop was crowded with . . . wares? Spell components? Lenoir could not guess at the purpose of the items around him. Horns from all manner of beasts dangled from the ceiling like stalactites. Jars filled with mysterious dark shapes lined the walls like veins of ore, warping and bending the candlelight. Bushels of dried matter were clustered about the counter, behind which a tall, gaunt-faced man watched Lenoir with flickering eyes. He said nothing, seemingly waiting for the visitor to announce his purpose.

"You are Merden?" Lenoir called from the door. He had taken only a single step into the shop.

"Plainly."

"I am Inspector Nicolas Lenoir of the Kennian Metropolitan Police." The introduction sounded needlessly formal, even to his own ears.

Merden said nothing, waiting for Lenoir to continue. His silence was profoundly unnerving.

"You are a soothsayer?" Lenoir was still hovering in the doorway like a nervous child.

A look of irritation passed over Merden's face. "Is it your custom to pose questions to which you already know the answers?"

"Yes, actually," Lenoir sighed, stepping into the shop and closing the door. "I apologize, sir, if I am awkward. Matters of the occult are . . . unfamiliar . . . to me.

To be frank, only the greatest necessity compels me to be here."

Merden regarded him dispassionately. "And what necessity is that?"

Lenoir cast about for words. Even though he had related this tale once already, it still sounded ridiculous, even to him. "I am haunted by some sort of malign spirit," he said, choosing simplicity. "It seeks my death, and it has nearly succeeded. I need to know what it is, and whether I can be rid of it."

"Interesting." Merden spoke with the detached curiosity of a philosopher examining an intriguing specimen. He gestured to a small table. "Have a seat, Inspector, and tell me more."

Lenoir repeated much of what he had told Zera, though he spared the soothsayer the sight of his wounds. Strangely, he felt more emotion in the telling than he had at Zera's, as though he were confessing to a priest. Could this be hope after all, or was he merely relieved to tell someone who could truly understand?

When he had finished, Merden remained silent, considering him. The soothsayer's golden eyes were slightly narrowed, his lips pursed behind a steeple of long fingers. The prominent points of his cheekbones were brushed in candlelight, casting his angular features in stark relief. There was something strangely comforting about that face, calm and exotic and profoundly wise.

Merden stood. "This tale of yours sounds familiar," he said, returning to the counter to search for something.

Lenoir felt his mouth drop open in surprise. "You know of this creature?" He leaned forward eagerly, his skepticism temporarily forgotten.

"Perhaps. There are many spirits who have the power to haunt us from beyond the veil, and vengeance is a common motive for them to do so. No doubt a man in your profession has many enemies in the spirit world. Cases unsolved, perhaps, or justice undelivered."

Lenoir winced inwardly. It was painfully near the mark.

"I will prepare a tea for you. It should help us to see the truth of things."

"A tea?"

"You will sleep," the soothsayer explained, "and you will dream. When you are in the proper state, I can direct your inner eye. Together, we shall see who, or what, this spirit really is."

Merden put a pot of water on the hearth to boil. Then he made a brief tour of the shop, fetching various jars from the shelves and pinching off bits of dried . . . things. It reminded Lenoir that there was another purpose to this visit, a distraction for which he was profoundly grateful.

"I am told you are also skilled in *khekra*," Lenoir said in what he hoped was an offhanded way.

There was the faintest pause in Merden's movements. A less perceptive man than Lenoir would have missed it altogether. "I thought you were unfamiliar in the ways of the occult."

"As you see, I have been forced to learn quickly."

"And what have you learned, Inspector?" Merden fetched a mortar and pestle and began grinding something that looked like horn. Lenoir tried not to watch, but there was nowhere comforting to rest his gaze; everything his eye fell upon invited morbid speculation as to its origin and purpose. At one point he found himself staring at the stuffed corpse of a monkey. Decoration or ingredient? He supposed he did not want to know.

"Not much," he admitted. "I am investigating a series of crimes that I have come to believe involve *khekra*, but beyond that I have few leads. Whoever is behind these acts is using children, but I do not know for what purpose."

"How are they using children?" Merden's tone was businesslike, that of a physician diagnosing an ailment.

"I have no idea. We recovered one of the children that had been taken, and he was whole, but quite mad."

Merden paused in his work, his brow furrowing. "Odd. And disturbing. You say he was taken?"

"Kidnapped."

"What makes you think *khekra* is involved? I have never heard of it being associated with kidnapping. Why would anyone go to such extremes? Making medicine need not cause harm. Often as not, the child is a loved one. I helped my father make medicine as a boy. I was proud to serve my clan."

"At the outset, they were using dead bodies. But now they have progressed to kidnapping children."

Merden's frown deepened as he tipped the crushed horn onto a growing pile of ingredients. "That does not make sense. Children are used because they are pure, the dead because they are impure. You would not use them both; one cancels out the other."

This was better information than they had gotten from the apothecary. Lenoir sensed that so long as he did not imply Merden was a suspect, or press him into admitting outright that he practiced dark magic, the soothsayer would answer his questions. "Perhaps they are inexperienced?" he suggested.

"That is likely, for using the dead is deeply unwise. It invites retribution from beyond. Every Adal knows this." Merden glanced up and looked as though he might say more, but instead he pressed on with his work. He was chasing the pile of ingredients onto a small square of cheesecloth, which he tied into a bundle. The tea was nearly prepared.

"For what purpose might one use the dead?"

Merden fetched the boiling kettle. "Although dead flesh is a powerful ingredient, there are very few spells that are worth the risk, and all of them are difficult to accomplish. My guess is that your kidnappers began with one spell and have now moved on to another. Perhaps they failed in their first attempt. The madness of the child you recovered is an important clue, Inspector. I am not sure what to make of it, but all the signs point to some sort of necromancy."

"Necromancy? What does it mean?"

"Broadly speaking, it means meddling with the souls of the dead." Merden set a steaming mug in front of Lenoir and sat down. "Don't touch it yet, Inspector. It is steeping. Most necromancy is fairly innocuous—

communing with spirits, and so forth. It is a staple of what I do here, for example, and can be accomplished with or without magical means, depending on one's gifts. But more powerful spells are rumored to exist, including those that can animate the dead for a brief period, or even restore someone to life. I have never heard of anyone succeeding at such things, but the world is full of people foolhardy enough to try."

"I am not sure I follow. If someone were trying to restore the dead to life, what would he need a live child for?"

"That I cannot tell you," said Merden, indicating that Lenoir should take the mug, "and so it is time to drink, Inspector."

The odor emanating from the mug was so putrid that Lenoir's stomach turned over, but he did as he was told. He tried to ignore the grit in his teeth as he swallowed, and could only be thankful that the bulk of the ingredients had been strained through the cheesecloth. He would not have been able to swallow anything solid without vomiting. He emptied the mug, gratefully accepting a swallow of water afterward. It did little to cleanse his traumatized palate, but at least it chased away the grit.

While he waited for the tea to take effect, he thought aloud. "Let us assume that you have failed in your attempt to restore a dead child to life. You must now accomplish the same aim using different means. Your new strategy involves using a live child."

"You left out an important detail in your account,"

Merden chided. "You did not say the corpses were also children. Is it not obvious? Having failed in their attempt to resurrect dead children, your kidnappers are attempting to channel the departed souls into live hosts. That explains the madness of the child you found. The poor boy probably has a second soul, or a fragment of one, competing with his own for control of his body."

Lenoir stared, speechless with horror. It was easy enough to imagine someone attempting dark magic. Lenoir had encountered plenty of religious fanatics and superstitious fools in his day. It was another thing entirely to witness actual evidence of the magic working, albeit imperfectly. There could be some other explanation for the boy Mika's condition, of course—something infinitely more plausible—but Lenoir could not deny that Merden's speculation made sense. Nor could he deny the evidence of his own scars: some of the supernatural world, at least, was terribly real.

"Presumably it was not their design to crowd two souls into one body," Merden said reflectively. "That would achieve nothing. One assumes they were trying to resurrect a dead child entirely, and suppress the soul of the host. I have never heard of such a thing, but it is theoretically possible. If they were to succeed . . ." He shook his head. "Appalling and unethical, but impressive, in its way. Perhaps they are not so inexperienced after all."

Lenoir shuddered. "It does not make sense. As far as we know, the kidnappers are not known to the children.

They took three corpses, all unrelated, and the parents knew nothing of it. Why resurrect a stranger's child?"

"That is curious," Merden agreed. His face turned watery, and he had two heads.

The room tilted.

The floor gave way.

Lenoir slept.

Velvet. Rich and sumptuous and shining in the shifting firelight. Velvet and satin, porcelain and swirling dark ebony. Everything glitters, sight and sound colliding together in a dazzle of flashing jewels and tinkling laughter. Shadows dance on the wall, beautiful and vaguely threatening. The images flicker past too quickly to understand. They bleed together like dyes in a washbasin.

Where are we?

Confusion. Lenoir's thoughts trickle through his fingers. He is unable to grasp them.

I don't know.

Yes, you do. *The voice is thick and warm, like honey. It fills Lenoir's mind. He feels its gentle pressure against the inside of his skull.* Concentrate, *it commands.*

Blades of light ricochet off the facets of cut crystal glasses. Fragments of faces reflected in a shattered rainbow. Her eyes, golden, luminous.

Lady Zera's.

She hands him something. Absinthe. It glows in the bottom of the glass, the violent green of poison. Confusion gives way to fear.

Good. Focus on your fear. What is it?

Absinthe eyes. Porcelain skin. Ebony hair. The youth is

standing in the street, the night amassed behind him like an army. He is emotionless. Pitiless. Streetlamps throw shadows on the cobblestones. They coil and twist and resolve into a snake with many tongues, twining around the arm of the beautiful youth with the absinthe eyes.

Somewhere in the vast hollow of the sky, a voice is screaming.

When he woke, Lenoir found himself slumped against the wall near the hearth, shivering. Or was it shaking? He could not be sure. There was a foul taste in his mouth, and his head throbbed horribly.

Merden appeared with a mug in his hand. "Drink this." Lenoir hesitated, his blurred vision trying to make out the liquid inside. "It is only water," Merden assured him, and Lenoir took it.

Merden occupied himself in a back room somewhere while Lenoir recuperated. He had no idea how long he had been out, or whether Merden's efforts to see into his dreams had been successful. The last thing he remembered was discussing the case, and the details of that conversation were vague. They would return in time, he supposed, but right now his thoughts were jumbled and thick.

When Merden reappeared, he continued going about his business as though Lenoir were not there. Perhaps Lenoir should have been grateful to be given all the time he needed to recover, but instead he was irritated at the soothsayer's mysterious silence.

"Well?" he growled. "Did you succeed?"

"Yes." Merden did not elaborate.

Back to this, Lenoir thought sourly. "Perhaps you would be so kind as to tell me what happened?"

Merden regarded him impassively. "Are you much practiced at sarcasm? It is a most unbecoming habit."

"I have many unbecoming habits, sir, but it is the habit of being stalked by a spirit that concerns me most."

Merden's sigh was so grave that it struck fear into Lenoir's heart. "It is as I thought. The spirit that hunts you is familiar to me. He figures prominently in many Adali legends. He is the Darkwalker, the champion of the dead, and if he counts you among his prey, your time is short."

Lenoir huddled closer to the hearth, pressing his back against the warm stones. "I already knew that I was marked for death. The spirit made his intent perfectly clear."

"Most likely you also know *why* you are so marked." There was no judgment in Merden's tone; it was simply a statement of fact. "The spirit exacts vengeance for sins committed against the dead. That is why the Adali treat their departed with such respect, for to defile the dead is to invite the wrath of the spirit. He has been known to my people for as long as our traditions record."

"What can you tell me about him?" Lenoir spoke mechanically, guided more by habit than conscious thought. He did not really expect to learn anything useful, but he had come here to try.

"Very little, beyond what you have already seen for yourself. He abides in shadows, and is able to move almost instantaneously between them, provided the dark is deep enough. Sunlight is his enemy, but it cannot destroy him completely. He is immortal, though he was once a man."

That statement pierced the haze of numbness; Lenoir blinked in surprise. "What, an ordinary man?"

"Yes, though he died young. He was called Vincent. Legend tells us little else, except that his immortality is a curse, punishment for some terrible act he committed in life. It must have been terrible indeed, for he was damned to an eternity of slavery, sent forth to visit vengeance upon those who do wrong by the dead. It is said that he has no will of his own, at least none he can exert. He is controlled by an unknown force, compelled to go where he is sent, to kill those who have been marked."

"Perhaps it is God who compels him," Lenoir said, turning his gaze to the fire. His thoughts writhed like the flames.

"Would your God show such wrath? What manner of sin would merit such punishment, I wonder?"

"You sound as though you pity him."

Merden considered this. "Perhaps I do. Enslaved for all eternity, your only purpose to murder and terrorize? Is that not the foulest torture conceivable?"

Lenoir looked at him askance. "You will forgive me, sir, if I have difficulty summoning much sympathy. He has shown little enough for me."

"Do you deserve sympathy?" Merden asked bluntly.

Lenoir had a brief but vivid memory: a rain-slick street, a body, a shabby transaction of whispers and gold. Lenoir could feel the shape of the coins in his hand, cold as death, heavy as guilt. He had weighed them gently, thinking, *So this is the price of silence.* The price of murder unanswered, of justice denied. No, he did not deserve sympathy. "Can I be rid of him?" He knew the answer already, but he had to ask.

Sensing his resignation, Merden did not trouble with false comfort. "I am amazed you have avoided him for as long as you have."

"I was free of him," Lenoir murmured. "I escaped." And then the corpse thieves brought him back, led him straight to Lenoir. Fate would not be denied.

"For a time, perhaps, but he was bound to find you. The Darkwalker can see through the eyes of the dead. Their memories are his memories. Their lifeless eyes are his windows to the world. That is how he knows his victims—he *sees* them. In your line of work, Inspector, it is surprising that it took this long for you to cross his path again."

Lenoir stood on unsteady legs. He did not want to hear any more. None of it would help him. Nothing could help him.

He paid Merden's fee—a staggering amount—and lurched out into the street. It was just before dawn. One more day to face, one last chance to find Zach and deliver him from the dark arts that awaited him. One way or another, Zach's fate was all but decided.

Lenoir turned his steps toward the station. He was exhausted, but he could not afford to sleep. Besides, he had no wish to face the dreams that would await him. He needed to put the green-eyed man out of his mind.

He needed to focus all his energy on finding Zach. Kody was an early riser, and would be at the station soon. They would recruit others—Izar, perhaps, and any other sergeants worth their pay. There were few enough of them, but Lenoir would take all the help he could get.

The streets were quiet. In a few minutes, the lamps would be doused, and the market district would come alive for the day's trade. Lenoir told himself that these few minutes were safe, that the green-eyed man could not possibly find him in time to do him harm.

He was wrong.

Lenoir did not see where the attack came from, but the street behind him bucked and shattered. He shielded his head against a hail of cobblestones, peering between his arms for a glimpse of the spirit. He caught a flicker of movement, and he dove instinctively in the opposite direction. The air cracked like a pistol shot as the whip missed its target. Lenoir scrambled to his feet.

The spirit was standing directly in front of him, poised for another strike.

"Damn you, Vincent!" Lenoir screamed in impotent rage. Such was his fury at being cheated out of one last day that it momentarily eclipsed even his fear.

The spirit froze, arm suspended midmotion, and for the first time, Lenoir saw genuine emotion in those uncanny green eyes. It was surprise.

The spirit was stunned for only a moment, but it was long enough for Lenoir to break away, heading back the way he had come toward a labyrinth of back alleys.

He knew these streets well, and if he chose his route carefully, there was a chance he could lose his pursuer amidst the maze of twists and turns.

It soon became clear, however, that the Darkwalker knew these streets at least as well as Lenoir. How could he not, when he was older than the city itself?

Fool.

The spirit easily anticipated his path, for many of the alleys were dead ends. It took no more than a brief glance at each intersection to track his prey. All Lenoir had succeeded in doing was cornering himself in a series of shadowed canyons that would delay the touch of dawn. It was no longer dark enough for the spirit to leap ahead of him, but the height of the buildings would shelter him from the sun for a good while yet, far too long for Lenoir to keep up his frantic pace. The spirit would not tire, but Lenoir could already feel his lungs burning. It was hopeless. Still, he kept running, instinct driving him on.

Before long, he found himself back in the square where Merden's shop was located, and he made for open ground. Though dawn had broken, however, the sun's rays had yet to clear the tops of the buildings.

Merden was outside, closing up shop. Lenoir's frantic footfalls drew his attention, and when he looked up, he gasped and pinned himself against the door.

"Get inside!" Lenoir cried, making for the other side of the square.

Merden hesitated, transfixed in horror. Then he spun and unlocked the door, disappearing inside. Lenoir was relieved; he did not want the soothsayer's blood on his hands. They were stained enough already.

He was heading due east, he realized grimly. Continuing in this direction would only delay his exposure to sunlight. But what choice did he have? He could hear the spirit's footfalls behind him, so close. He could be no more than a hand-span outside the reach of the scourge.

"Vincent!" called a cool, clear voice.

The shock of it brought Lenoir up short. He whirled around.

So did the green-eyed man. Apparently, a thousand-odd years of immortality was not enough to erase the instinct to respond to one's own name.

Merden was standing in the middle of the square, a long wooden staff in his hand, and as Vincent turned, the soothsayer threw his arm high. The tip of the staff flared with a light so blinding that Lenoir had to shield his eyes.

He did not dare waste the opportunity. Turning his back on the square, Lenoir kept running. He was loath to leave Merden behind, but the soothsayer had seemed so calm, so in command of himself, that it was tempting to believe he was in no danger. Would the spirit kill someone not expressly marked for death? Lenoir had no way of knowing.

He ran until he could not take another step. His knees gave out, and he collapsed in the street, gasping for air. It was only then that he felt the warmth of the sunlight bathing the street. He had survived.

*   *   *

Lenoir found Merden back in his shop, sipping tea. The soothsayer looked rattled, much more so than he had in the square. He did not, however, seem surprised to see Lenoir.

"Lavender tea? Calms the nerves."

Lenoir scarcely registered the question. "How did you do it?" he whispered in awe. "What magic do you possess that you can summon sunlight at your will?"

Merden stared at him for a moment, then burst out laughing. "Is that what you think you saw?" He rose and moved behind the counter. He drew out the staff, showing it to Lenoir. There was an angled mirror lashed to the end. This was no magic; Merden had merely used the mirror to reflect the sun's rays down into the square.

"I use it to search for items on the top shelf," Merden explained, demonstrating. "Hardly arcane technique."

Lenoir fell into a chair, shaking his head in disbelief. "Incredible. You saved my life, Merden."

"You are endowed with an uncommon store of luck, Inspector," Merden said soberly. "My people believe that such gifts are not random."

Lenoir made a wry face. "And yet I do not feel so very lucky."

"That is understandable."

"Perhaps I will take some of that tea."

"That too is understandable," said Merden, and he fetched another mug.

CHAPTER 18

The station was still relatively deserted when Lenoir arrived, for the hour was yet early. Even so, the place was charged with a strange energy. Watchmen stood huddled in close groups of twos and threes, speaking in low tones. There were at least half a dozen sergeants in the kennel, unusual at this early hour, and they were all donning weapons and coats as though intending to hit the streets en masse. One of the scribes, a pretty young woman whose name Lenoir did not know, leaned against a nearby desk, weeping. Something was wrong.

He spotted the chief across the room, shaking his head and scowling as he listened to a report from Sergeant Innes. The chief was almost never seen down in the kennel, preferring the private space of his office. And he was certainly never at the station before breakfast.

Something was very wrong.

"Chief," Lenoir called.

The chief glanced up, his mouth tightening when he

saw Lenoir. He shook his head again and dismissed Innes. "Where have you been?" he asked gruffly as Lenoir approached.

"I worked through the night," Lenoir replied, an uneasy feeling creeping over him. "What has happened?"

Chief Lendon Reck paused, regarding Lenoir with tired eyes. His skin sagged around the deep lines of his face, and his thick eyebrows, drawn together in a characteristically severe line, were almost completely gray. He should have retired long ago, probably, but the chief seemed to think there was no one in Kennian capable of taking his place. In principle, Lenoir agreed, but he did not think he had ever seen the chief looking quite so worn as he did at this moment.

"What is it?" Lenoir repeated quietly.

"Sergeant Hardin is dead, and Kody is in a coma. They don't think he'll make it."

Lenoir stared.

"One of the watchmen found them about two hours ago. Innes has already been to the scene. Sword through the gut, both of them."

"They tried to make it look like a robbery," Innes put in, rejoining them. "Didn't do a very good job, though, Inspector."

"No blood in the alley," the chief said. "The bodies had obviously been moved. Plus, Kody took a nasty blow to the skull. Lucky, in a way—getting knocked out probably saved his life. The killer obviously didn't realize the sword hadn't done the job." He paused again. "I'm sorry, Lenoir. I know he's one of your best."

Lenoir swallowed, finally able to speak. "Not just

one of them, Chief. He is the best we have." *And a better man than any of us,* he added silently.

Innes nodded; none of the sergeants would disagree. "When we find the bastard who did this, we're going to hang him with his own guts." The big man left to join the others, grabbing a brace of pistols off a desk as he passed.

The chief sighed, watching the sergeants quit the building with purposeful strides. "I think they might do just that. I'm going to have a serious discipline problem on my hands." He looked back at Lenoir. "Any idea who might have done this?"

Lenoir sat heavily on a desk. "No. When I left him yesterday, we were riding back from Berryvine. We planned to question some of the local Adali community. If I were Kody, I would have started with Fort Hald."

"Not very helpful," the chief said, scratching the stubble on his chin. He had obviously been roused from sleep to attend matters at the station. "If they'd met with foul play at the prison, we would have heard about it from the guards. Besides, I saw Kody myself yesterday evening, coming out of your office. If you're right about the prison, he must already have been there and back."

"But if he found a lead . . ."

The chief nodded. "Sergeant Cale says he saw Kody talking to a couple of the other sergeants. Then he and Hardin left together. I'd wager he found something all right, and he decided to take Hardin with him to investigate. We're looking for Izar now. Hopefully he'll have some information."

Lenoir would not have picked Hardin, but he kept the thought to himself, for there was no need to speak ill of the dead.

The chief pointed at one of the watchmen. "You there! Round up the inspectors! Probably still asleep, the lazy bastards. Send one of them to the scene, the other two to the prison. In the meantime, I want to speak personally to every single one of you who saw Kody yesterday. I want to know every move he made. I want to know what he had for lunch and when he went to the privy, understood?"

Lenoir passed a hand over his eyes, feeling more exhausted than he had in months. "And me, Chief?"

Reck regarded him gravely. "If I could, Lenoir, I'd send you home. You look bloody awful, and you smell worse. God only knows how you spend your nights. But I can't spare you, even if you look like it's your last day in this world."

Lenoir snorted. *If you only knew, Chief.* "I will be fine. As much as I would like to find out what happened to Kody and Hardin, however, there are other lives at stake."

"Oh?"

"The case Kody was working on involves kidnapped children. I have reason to fear that the life of at least one child is at imminent risk. I must continue my work. If I find those responsible, I believe we will have Hardin's murderer."

"We'd better. Nobody kills one of my hounds and lives to gloat about it." He stalked away, raising his voice for the benefit of everyone in the kennel. "You hear me, people? I want this bastard dead by this time tomorrow, but it'll be at the end of a rope and not on the point of a sword. Got that? Now let's get moving!"

Lenoir headed up to his office. If Kody had been there, perhaps he had left a report of his findings that afternoon. It seemed unlikely that the sergeant could have found anything concrete from questioning random Adali, but the fact that he and Hardin had been attacked strongly suggested that he had found *something*, enough to set him on the path that ended in Hardin's murder.

Sure enough, Lenoir found a note on his desk, scrawled with Kody's crooked handwriting. He had not used a scribe, and he had not filed a full report. Kody was the most conscientious officer Lenoir had ever worked with, a fact Lenoir generally found irritating. If the sergeant had not filed a report, it meant that he had been in a hurry. Perhaps his lead had been time-sensitive. Or he might simply have been excited. As meticulous as the sergeant was, he was also overeager, another quality that annoyed Lenoir. Kody might have allowed his enthusiasm to get the better of his diligence.

The note did not shed much light. It confirmed that Kody had indeed visited the prison, and that he had found a lead he deemed worthy of follow-up. Beyond that, however, there were no details. *I will brief you as soon as I get back,* the note said, but it did not say where he was going, or what he had learned that had piqued his interest. Lenoir read it over twice. He crumpled it into a tight ball and threw it away.

He sat for a moment, twitching with fury. Then he leapt to his feet and swept his arm across the desk, knocking an inkpot and quill to the floor. His rage still unsatisfied, he grabbed his chair and threw it against the wall. That done, he leaned against the desk, feeling foolish and spent.

He cursed the sergeant for his impatience. The one time it really mattered, when his bureaucratic instincts might actually have been useful, Kody had gone off half-cocked. Instead of waiting for Lenoir, he had rounded up a bungling drunk of a sergeant who was utterly incapable of looking out for him if things went sour. His sloppiness had resulted in Hardin's death, and quite possibly his own.

And now there was no one to help find Zach. For the first time, Lenoir needed Kody, and the sergeant was not there. Nor was anyone else; the entire Metropolitan Police force was out looking for Hardin's murderer. Lenoir had no leads, and no support. He would never be able to convince the chief to spare any resources to help him, for there was nothing in this world more determined than a hound looking for a hound-killer. Nothing, perhaps, except the green-eyed man.

Lenoir paused.

The idea struck him with such force that he could not believe it had not occurred to him before. Perhaps some part of his mind, the part that looked to survival above all else, had blocked it out. Whatever the reason, Lenoir saw his path clearly now. It was not an easy one; it could only end in his death, even if he succeeded. But he had been staring death in the face for days now. Perhaps he was finally growing used to it. Kody might already have paid the ultimate price for trying to save Zach, and he had never even met the boy. Could Lenoir do any less?

He righted his chair and replaced the inkpot and quill on his desk, taking care not to step in the spatter of fresh ink on the floor. He closed the door to his office and headed down the stairs. The kennel was filling with watchmen and scribes, their faces angry or sorrowful. Some called to Lenoir, offering the condolences and expressions of hope they imagined he wanted to hear. He ignored them and made for the street.

He was famished. No longer pressed for time, he decided to head to the Courtier. He hoped they stocked the kitchen early; he was in the mood for a steak. There was a good chance this would be his last meal, and he wanted to enjoy it.

Zach shivered against the cold. It was damp in this room, and smothered in constant darkness. The musty smell of rotting vegetables clung to the air, an odor that reminded him of the kitchen at the orphanage. The association wasn't comforting. His movements sounded muted against the earthen floor, suggesting a tightly enclosed space. He was in a cellar of some sort. He'd been here for more than a day, he guessed, though it was impossible to measure the passage of time in the dark.

He'd been alone for a very long time. He could hear his captors coming and going, their footfalls sounding above his head, loosing cascades of dirt that fell into his eyes. He couldn't even wipe away the grit, since his hands were still bound. At least they had removed the gag. Apparently, they didn't mind if he screamed, so Zach didn't bother trying. He was braver than that, anyway.

He had mapped out the room as best he could. It was about five leg spans by ten, with a set of stairs leading up to a door. He'd counted fifteen stairs, for all the good it did him. There were a couple of crooked shelves on one wall, which Zach had explored in detail, searching for a nail or anything else he could use to cut through his bonds. No such luck; the shelves were bare, and whatever hardware affixed them to the wall, he couldn't find it.

He slept a lot. There wasn't much else to do. When he wasn't sleeping, he spent a lot of time thinking about Lenoir. He was sure the inspector was looking for him. Lenoir had always said that Zach was valuable, and Zach took him at his word. Lenoir wouldn't want anything to happen to him. Still, Zach wondered what was taking so long. Lenoir was the best inspector in the Five Villages—everyone said so. He could find anything and anyone. So why wasn't he here yet? How was it that Zach's captors were still free? The only explanation he could think of was that it had taken Lenoir a while to realize he was missing. That would make sense; it wasn't as though they saw each other every day.

He decided to try sending Lenoir a message with his mind. Maybe if he thought hard enough, Lenoir would hear him somehow, or if he couldn't *hear*, exactly, he would somehow just *know*, like an instinct. Zach closed his eyes and thought so hard his face hurt.

A noise sounded above his head, and his heart leapt. But it was only his captors returning. He recognized their voices now. There were three of them, two men and a woman, all Adali. There had been more at first, but some of the voices had gone away and never come back. Sometimes they spoke Braelish, and sometimes they didn't. Even when they did, Zach didn't learn much. They argued a lot, the woman especially, and sometimes it became heated. They were arguing now.

"That's four, Ani. *Four*. Or have you not been keeping track?"

"I can count perfectly well," a woman's voice said angrily. "You're not the only one who can think."

"Oh, really? Then why am I the only one who sees what's happening here? Everyone who handled one of the corpses is dead. Do you think it's coincidence, Ani?"

"It may be," said the one called Ani. "We don't even know for sure what happened to the gravedigger. He may have fled the area. He was a coward, after all."

"Bah! You're a fool!"

"You are both fools," said a third voice. His accent was different from the others, much more pronounced. "Even if you are right, Kern, it is too late to turn back now. If we do not succeed, the whole clan is at risk. I would rather take my chances with vigilantes than lose everything."

"Vigilantes?" the other man echoed incredulously. "Is that what you think is going on? They found Raiyen with his throat stabbed in a hundred places and the life strangled out of him. We're no strangers to lynch mob justice. Have you ever seen such brutality?"

"You exaggerate," said Ani scornfully.

Zach's mind whirred as he listened. His captors were obviously scared, especially the man called Kern. It sounded as though one of them was dead, and maybe more. Zach didn't know what a "vigilante" was, but he knew plenty about lynch mobs. Every street urchin knew about those. They could just sort of *happen*, a group of passersby intervening to stop a thief or a vandal. The scarier kind was organized, brought together to catch a rapist or a murderer and make sure he got sorted. Mob justice wasn't uncommon in the Five Villages, especially in Kennian, and as far as Zach could tell, the hounds didn't worry about it too much. But he'd never heard of anything quite as ugly as what had happened to Raiyen.

The voices hushed abruptly as a new set of footsteps joined them. There were murmured greetings, and then an unfamiliar voice said, "Here you are. I came by earlier, but the house was empty. Where have you been?" Like Ani's and Kern's, this accent was softer, more like a normal Kennian accent. Zach decided that most of his captors were local, but one of them wasn't. Lenoir would have been proud of him for figuring that out.

"We went to find news about Leshni," Ani said. "They found him in an alley in Berryvine. You heard about that too?"

"I have. What of it?"

"That makes four," Kern said again.

"We suspect vigilantes."

"*You* suspect vigilantes," Kern hissed.

"You are too easily distracted," the newcomer said coolly. "Remember your purpose. If you succeed, your clan will be powerful, more so than many of the others. Keep that always in your mind, and you need not worry. The good of your clan is all that matters."

"Meaning that each of us is expendable," Kern said.

"Of course we are," the man with the heavy accent said. "The clan always comes first. Where are your values? Or have you been living amongst the city folk for so long that you forget who you are?"

"I was born here," Kern said. "What's the clan ever done for me? They don't even know I exist. What do I care if they're powerful?"

"It is not about power," the other man said. "Our people are suffering. This is a small price to pay to heal them."

"For you, maybe."

"You are free to leave at any time, Kern."

"And go where? I need the money." The floorboards above Zach's head sounded with footsteps, as though someone had started pacing. When Kern spoke again, he sounded calmer. "It's just . . . this is getting out of hand. You never said anything about hurting anyone. They were supposed to be dead already. And now these killings . . ."

"Enough," said the newcomer. "How much longer do you need? This is already taking far more time than you said it would."

"It has been more difficult than we anticipated," the

one with the heavy accent said. "We have failed twice, but we learned valuable lessons."

"You can manage without the other witchdoctor?"

"Raiyen's loss was a setback, but I do not think he truly had the stomach for this in any case. He served his purpose; I learned what I needed from him. We are close now. I just need to make a few adjustments."

"Then do it! The hounds are snooping around, and it's only a matter of time before they find us. Hurry your preparations, and inform me when you are ready to try again. I want to be there this time."

"As you wish."

The newcomer left, and the trio went back to arguing. Zach had stopped listening. He didn't want to hear any more about murder and vigilantes. He didn't want to think about what his captors were planning for him. Instead he clung to those few precious words the newcomer had spoken.

The hounds were coming. Lenoir was coming. Zach closed his eyes and waited.

Lenoir had never waited so impatiently for night to come. His leg bounced restlessly under the table, and his eyes strayed to the window every few minutes. He had not moved from the spot all day. The barmaid had gone from curious to nervous to disturbed. She had long since stopped coming over to refill his wine. It was for the best; he needed his wits about him. Finally, when he could stand it no more, he grabbed his coat and headed for the door, ignoring the look of relief on the barmaid's face. It was not yet sunset, but it was close enough. He had just enough time to make it to the main square in the market district. He was not sure why he had chosen the spot, but it seemed as good as any.

He sat on a bench on the west side of the square. His leg resumed its bouncing as he waited. The shadows were gathering, crawling out from beneath the buildings and across the square. It would not be long now. He watched the streetlamps being lit, each one casting a small circle of light onto the cobblestones below. He watched the merchants closing up their shops for the day. He looked out for Merden, but the soothsayer did not appear. Perhaps he was taking some time to recover from the previous night's excitement.

Darkness came, but the square did not empty right away. There were still street musicians, flower carts, and other traders whose wares were in demand in the evening. Romance was in fashion these days, and Kennian's young noblemen could often be found in the market district in the evening, looking for any advantage in their endless quest to impress young ladies. Lenoir wished them all away with no small measure of bitterness. Where such frivolities might once have provoked idle cynicism, they seemed positively perverse to him now.

An hour passed, perhaps more. Finally, the last of the evening merchants moved along. Lenoir was alone in the square. Shivering, he drew his scarf more tightly around his neck. He was grateful for the thick wool. Winter was nearly here. He experienced a brief pang as he realized he had seen his last spring.

He was daydreaming about Serles, her boulevards garlanded with new green leaves, when the attack came.

The scourge snapped around his neck, constricting immediately. Lenoir was jerked back against the bench. He clawed at the whip, but the barbs tore his flesh, preventing him from getting his fingers underneath. There was a powerful pull from behind, and he was dragged over the top of the bench. He hit the ground with his right shoulder, driving the air from his lungs. He could not draw breath to replace it; already, his vision was beginning to sparkle.

No! Not yet! This is not how it was supposed to be! Lenoir scrambled frantically, trying to loosen the scourge enough to allow him to speak. He had not counted upon the spirit ambushing him, not like this. It had never occurred to him that he would not have a chance to utter a single word before he died. As it was, he only remained conscious because of the scarf around his neck, for it provided a barrier between his flesh and the life-sapping touch of the scourge.

The scarf!

Lenoir yanked the knot free and pulled the scarf away from his neck, using the wool as leverage against the coils of the scourge. The barbs bit through, and for a moment he thought the scarf would tear. He pulled with a strength born of desperation, and finally the leather lost its grip on itself and the coils fell free. The air hummed as the green-eyed man drew the whip back to his side, preparing for another strike.

Lenoir gasped, filling his lungs with just enough air for a single word:

"Vincent!"

As before, the spirit hesitated, if only for a split second.

Lenoir swallowed another lungful of air. "Wait!" He held up his hand in a staying gesture, but the scourge lashed out and wrapped around his forearm. Lenoir expended his precious air in a scream. He scrabbled for his sword, but his left hand was clumsy, and the pain was so intense . . .

Forget the pain. You have only one chance.

"I can help you find them!" The words dissolved into more screaming.

And then a miracle happened. The pain stopped. The whip released him.

It was working.

"I can help you find them," Lenoir repeated, gasping. "All of them." The scourge remained still. The hope that flooded Lenoir's body gave him strength, and he lurched to his knees. The green-eyed man stood before him, head cocked, scourge dangling limply at his side. His fey gaze glinted inscrutably. He was waiting.

This was it, Lenoir's one chance. It was pure desperation. It was worse than that—it was suicide. But it was also Zach's only hope.

"We seek the same people, you and I," he rasped. "The corpse thieves. You have seen some of them through the eyes of the dead, and you have killed them. But there are more—those you have not seen. I am certain of it. And I can help you find them."

The spirit did not move. He regarded Lenoir with narrowed eyes, his face otherwise expressionless. Lenoir had no idea if his words were having the desired effect. He could not even be certain that the spirit understood.

"Vincent." He spoke the name deliberately, hoping to appeal to some vestige of this creature's former self. "Let me help you find them."

There was a long silence, punctuated only by the mad rhythm of Lenoir's heartbeat.

"Why?" The word issued forth like an icy wind from the depths of a crypt. Lenoir shuddered. It had not occurred to him that the spirit could speak, and he would have preferred to go to his grave without ever hearing that voice.

Collecting himself, he said, "Because I need to find them too. They have taken a boy I know, and they mean him harm."

"I have no care for the living," Vincent said, the inhumanity of his words matched by the dread chill of his voice. His face remained devoid of expression.

"That may be, but if I am right, the kidnappers, the ones who took the boy, are the same people as those behind the theft of the corpses. You have taken your revenge upon the men who actually did the deed, but what about those in whose name the deed was done? Should they who are truly responsible go unpunished?" He had practiced this speech a hundred times or more during his restless hours at the Courtier. It had sounded more convincing in his head.

"They will not go unpunished. I will find them."

"Only if you have seen them." Lenoir prayed that Merden's information was correct. Generation upon generation of oral tradition was not the most reliable of sources. "Those giving the orders are rarely the same as those who carry them out." This too was a gamble. Lenoir had no way of knowing how many culprits there were, let alone how many Vincent had seen.

The spirit was silent, his marble features betraying nothing of his thoughts—if he even had thoughts at all.

Lenoir licked his lips, trying to think clearly through the blood roaring in his ears. His fear was making him light-headed, but he had had many hours to prepare for this encounter. He thanked God for that. "When you . . . *saw* . . . the corpse thieves, did you also see a boy? Alive?"

The spirit did not reply immediately, and for a moment Lenoir feared that the conversation—and his life—had come to an end. Then Vincent said, "I saw no child."

Lenoir's heart sank, but in a way it was good news. "You see? That proves that you have not seen all of the corpse thieves, for some of them still hold the boy."

"According to you."

"True." Another wave of dizziness washed over him. This was the moment he dreaded most. It was time to make his offer. "But it will cost you nothing to accept my help. My life is forfeit—I know this. But if I die tonight, the boy dies too. All I ask is that you stay your hand for a brief time, long enough for me to find him. In return, I will find your corpse thieves, all of them. When I do, you can claim the vengeance that is your due—from the corpse thieves, and from me."

The spirit's absinthe eyes bored into Lenoir. His

youthful features, so chillingly beautiful, remained fixed as though in stone. "What is your care for the boy?"

The question caught Lenoir off guard. The spirit knew him for what he was. He had seen the corruption in Lenoir's soul; it was that corruption that had marked him for death. Why should such a man care what happened to a street urchin like Zach?

Lenoir dropped his gaze. "I don't know."

It was a lie.

"There is no redemption." The statement might as well have come from God Himself.

Lenoir shivered. "I know."

When he looked up again, something strange was happening. The uncanny light had dimmed in Vincent's eyes, as though the immortal soul trapped within had withdrawn someplace else entirely. Lenoir did not have long to wonder, however; almost immediately, the light returned in a blaze of green, and he felt the heat of the spirit's stare once more.

"It accepts your offer," Vincent said matter-of-factly.

Lenoir blinked. *"It?"*

Vincent ignored the question. "Take me to the corpse thieves."

Lenoir hesitated, stunned. *It actually worked.*

Only now could he admit to himself that he had not really expected to succeed. Yet here he was, on his knees in the market square, the green-eyed man standing expectantly before him. Vincent was letting him live. For now.

Clear your head, fool. There is work to be done. "I

cannot simply take you to them. I do not yet know where they are, and I need your help."

"What would you have of me?"

Lenoir stood, dusting himself off. He avoided looking at his arm; he did not wish to see what the scourge had done. Not that it made any difference—it was the same arm that was already scarred, and anyway, what did it matter how his flesh looked, when his life span was measured in hours?

"You need to tell me what you have seen," Lenoir said, surprised at how level he sounded. Perhaps he really had made peace with death. "You need to tell me everything."

CHAPTER 19

"There are two more," Vincent said, "and then I have done."

Lenoir nodded. They were seated on the bench where he had been waiting when Vincent attacked. There was something darkly amusing about it, sitting here conversing with an immortal spirit that had been sent from another plane to kill him. Passersby would notice little amiss unless Vincent looked directly at them, and even then, they would probably only wonder at the strange light of his gaze. His nature was not immediately obvious to the casual onlooker.

He was not exactly chatty. He expressed himself briefly, using few words and still less emotion. He answered Lenoir's questions, but not in much detail. Lenoir could not tell if he was being secretive, or if he had merely lost the gift of conversation. Or perhaps he had been like that even in life. Lenoir found himself wondering how long it had been since the spirit had spoken to anyone.

"How many corpses did they dig up?" Lenoir asked him.

"Two."

"Was it the same person who dug up both corpses?"

"No."

Lenoir's fear was beginning to settle, allowing more mundane emotions to break through. Like frustration. The spirit seemed intent on making it as difficult as possible for Lenoir to extract the information he needed. Was Vincent toying with him? If so, there was no hint of irony about him. The spirit sat perfectly straight, and for the most part spoke without inflection. He did not fidget or shift his weight. He seemed almost incapable of emotion. Almost. Lenoir recalled the reaction when he had called the spirit by name for the first time, the unmistakable shock. Vincent might show little emotion, but he was definitely capable of feeling it.

"Who dug up the first corpse?"

"I do not know his name."

Lenoir checked a sigh. "I was not asking for his name. What do you know of him?"

"He is dead. I killed him."

"So I had assumed, Vincent. But before that?"

"He was a gravedigger. From Brackensvale."

At last, he was getting something useful. "Did you see anyone else with the gravedigger?"

"Two others. Adali men. I killed them also."

Lenoir grunted thoughtfully. "I presume the gravedigger handed the corpse over to the Adali men." Vincent inclined his head almost imperceptibly. Taking the gesture for assent, Lenoir continued. "Did you see where they took the corpse?"

The spirit reflected on this. "What I saw will not be helpful to you. It was the inside of a shack, but I do not know where. The body was covered while the Adali transported it." It was the most complex thought he had expressed so far.

"I believe I know the place you are referring to. We found it some days later, by which time it had already been deserted. All that was left was a boy, and he had gone mad."

Vincent cocked his head. "Mad?"

"Yes." Lenoir shivered at the memory. "We found the boy tied to a chair, and when we released him, he attacked my sergeant. He was screaming and biting like a fiend. He was quite mad."

"I know this boy," said Vincent, surprising Lenoir. "He is not mad."

"Pardon?"

"The soul is gone now. He is alone."

Lenoir stared. "I . . . do not understand."

The absinthe eyes locked on him, sending a shudder down Lenoir's spine. "The soul they summoned, the one they tried to channel into the boy. It is gone. They did not succeed."

By the sword, Lenoir swore inwardly. Merden was right. The corpse thieves had been trying to replace the boy's soul with that of a dead child. "They succeeded at least partially," he said, more to himself than to Vincent. "The boy had two souls, it seems, and it drove him mad."

"For a time, but the spell did not last. The soul of the dead child returned to the spirit realm."

"How do you know?" Lenoir was so morbidly fascinated that he forgot even his dread.

"It is in my memories. The souls of the dead remember, and their memories are mine." The chill in Vincent's voice became icy, and the absinthe eyes narrowed to slits. "The dead should not have new memories. They should not be torn from their rest. It is a mortal sin."

Lenoir huddled deeper into his coat, but it gave him little comfort. The cold he felt did not come from without. "When I asked you earlier, you said you had not seen a child."

"That is so. But for a brief time, I saw through the eyes of a child. I saw you, though I did not recognize you at the time."

Of course. The boy Mika had been blindfolded when they found him in the abandoned farmhouse. He had probably not seen his captors, or anything else until Kody removed the blindfold. At that time, the soul of the dead child had been present in Mika's body, along with his own.

"Long has it been since I have seen through the eyes of the living," Vincent said distractedly. Untold years of emptiness echoed in his voice.

Lenoir returned to his original line of questioning. "The second corpse, did they take it to the same place?"

"Yes."

"What did they do with it?"

"Necromancy."

"They were trying to resurrect the dead children," Lenoir prompted, recalling Merden's theory.

"No."

Lenoir stared in surprise. "No? Then what were they doing?"

"The souls of the children whose bodies were taken have not been disturbed. Their flesh alone has been defiled."

What in the flaming below? Lenoir was thoroughly confused. "Then whose soul was channeled into Mika's body?"

Vincent seemed to consider his response before speaking. "The necromancers did not seek to reanimate the children whose bodies they took," he said, and Lenoir had the impression he was choosing his words carefully. "They only wished to find a suitable host body. It is another soul they seek to resurrect, a soul long dead. They failed to channel this soul into a dead body, so now they seek to use the living."

Lenoir felt sick. At the same time, he could not deny that he was captivated. One short week ago, he had been investigating (or, more accurately, Kody had been investigating) a set of bizarre, but ultimately harmless, crimes. Then, when Zach had been taken, Lenoir had assumed they were dealing with a run-of-the-mill predator—disturbing, certainly, but sadly commonplace. The reality of what was actually going on was unfathomable. Even Kody, who had seen a conspiracy that Lenoir himself had refused to acknowledge, would never have imagined something this dark and complex.

"Whose soul are they trying to resurrect?"

"I no longer recall his name."

"Was he from Kennian?"

"Yes."

"How long ago did he die?"

Vincent considered. "I have lost the ability to measure time as mortals do. But I think he would be a man now, perhaps twenty or twenty-five."

Assuming the boy had died at Zach's age, that would mean he passed away more than a decade ago. "What else can you tell me about him?"

"He was murdered."

Somehow Lenoir was not surprised. "Who murdered him?"

Vincent closed his eyes, as though remembering. "His father."

Something bumped Lenoir's memory, a thought brushing past too swiftly for him to recognize. He let it go; it would be back when it was ready. For now, he had to focus on the most direct route to Zach. "Let us leave that for the moment. You said you had seen two more corpse thieves. Do you know where they are?"

"Of course. I can feel when they are near."

Lenoir could not help himself; he had to ask. "Then why couldn't you find me, all those years ago?"

Vincent turned to look at him, and Lenoir knew immediately he had made a mistake. The terror returned in a surge so powerful that his stomach heaved.

He raised a shaky hand. "I am sorry I asked. It was foolish curiosity. I have no intention of trying to escape."

Vincent said nothing.

Lenoir stood unsteadily, his fear-soaked muscles barely able to carry him. "Let us go. We can interrogate your next . . . your mark." Somehow he did not think Vincent would think of the corpse thieves as "victims."

Vincent swept forward with liquid grace, Lenoir hurrying after. He did not know what Vincent considered "near," but he hoped they had some distance to travel, for he needed time to recover himself. He would not be an effective interrogator if he was still quivering when they arrived.

A light drizzle had begun to fall as Lenoir and Vincent quit the market district, and by the time they reached the Camp, it had become a full-blown downpour. It tortured the meager shanties that passed for dwellings, the construction of which could scarcely withstand the daily travails of gravity, let alone a storm. Rain clattered noisily against scraps of tin siding, soaked thatch and animal skins, gouged away muddy foundations. It pooled in every sag and hollow, running in rivulets from sunken rooftops. The haze of smoke that typically choked the narrow gaps between the tents and hovels began to dissolve as water leaked through, snuffing the cooking fires. Muddy pathways were swiftly becoming rivers of sludge, carrying refuse and excrement and anything else not tied down. In a few short minutes, the Camp had gone from depressing slum to perfect hell.

The stench of the place was almost more than Lenoir could take, and his stomach caught in his throat as he trailed Vincent between the hovels, doing his best to keep to high ground lest his shoes become steeped in something vile. He bowed his head against the rain, barely glancing at the scenes he passed—bedraggled men scrambling to cover holes in their shelters, bony dogs shivering in corners, thick brown water accumulating in puddles that threatened to flood nearby dwellings. Even so, he could not help registering the fact that nearly every face he saw was Adali. The Camp was one of the largest quarters of Kennian; Lenoir would not have guessed there were so many Adali squatters in the Five Villages. It made him realize how long it had been since he visited the slums. Like most hounds, he avoided the place at all costs. Though the Camp teemed with crime, nobody much cared if the slum dwellers were at one another's throats.

Even over the rain, Lenoir could hear coughing from inside many of the huts—from the smoke, or disease, or both. But he could also hear laughter. Children chattered and squealed, their small voices incongruously bright, like flowers pushing up through the muck. *Even here,* he thought, *life goes on. What have these people to look forward to? And yet they laugh. They have children. They strive. They do not wallow in despair and wait for death to claim them.* Caught in a sudden fit of self-loathing, he quickened his step, willing this errand to be over.

As for Vincent, the spirit was wholly undaunted by the rain, and seemed to take no notice of the mud that soaked his boots and trousers. His raven black hair was plastered against his skull, shining silver in the moonlight, but he made no effort to push it back off his face. He moved with purpose, his steps guided by some unknown sense. He seemed barely even to register his surroundings, relying on neither sight nor sound to orient him. Lenoir supposed that the only reason Vincent was on foot, instead of simply appearing in a shadow somewhere, was so his mortal companion could follow.

The spirit stopped in front of a nondescript hovel, turning to look wordlessly at Lenoir. Nodding, Lenoir ran a hand over this thinning hair and knocked on the door, a slab of rotting wood mounted on crude hinges of nails and wire loop. Vincent stepped back, melting into the shadows so completely that for a moment Lenoir wondered if he had vanished altogether.

A disheveled Adal answered the door. He eyed Lenoir suspiciously, glancing around to see if there were others nearby. "What?" he growled.

"Pardon me for disturbing you, sir, but I wonder if you might be willing to answer a few questions."

"What kind of questions? Who are you?" He had the high cheekbones and wide-spaced eyes of his people, and his brow was beaded with moisture. Rain or sweat? There was no way to tell.

"I am Inspector Lenoir of the Metropolitan Police." Lenoir spoke in a low voice, barely audible above the rain. It was doubtful that the neighbors were fond of hounds. "And I am soaked to the bone, so kindly let me in."

The look of terror that crossed the man's face was so obvious that Lenoir wondered how he survived in the slums. He was evidently not a hardened criminal. Lenoir doubted he could even hold his own in a card game. "What do you want?" the man repeated, his own voice lowered to a near whisper.

"You know perfectly well what I want." Lenoir was

not typically so direct, but with a man this cowardly, intimidation was the best tactic. "Let us go inside, and we can talk without involving my men."

"I don't see anybody else." The man looked over Lenoir's shoulder again.

"Of course not," Lenoir said impatiently. "It would make little sense for them to show themselves unless they are needed."

The man hesitated, but he stood aside for Lenoir to enter, closing the door behind him. *Definitely not a cardplayer,* Lenoir thought.

There was no fire in the hut, only a small oil lamp that scarcely cast enough light to see by. For the first time in a great many years, Lenoir was thankful for the dark.

"Vincent," he said calmly, "please show yourself. You will save us some time."

The man barely had time to look confused before Vincent appeared in a corner of the hut, his absinthe eyes flashing in the lamplight. The man started to scream, but Lenoir was ready, leaping forward and clamping his hand over the man's mouth.

"Silence!" he hissed. The man was much taller than he, and it took all his strength to keep the squirming wretch in check. "Do as you are told, and I will spare your life!"

Vincent, for his part, stood unmoving in the corner. That was well. The spirit's presence was terrifying enough; if he made any threatening moves, the man might break altogether. Lenoir needed him to be pliable, but coherent. It would do no good if he was literally scared witless.

When the man's screams had subsided to whimpers, Lenoir released him. "Sit," he commanded, and the man complied, plopping down onto a straw mat. He stared up at Lenoir with abject terror in his eyes. Lenoir knew that look. It was the look of a man marked for death. He himself had worn it only hours ago. Perhaps he wore it still.

"What is your name?"

"Kern."

Lenoir gestured behind him. "You know who this is, don't you, Kern? You have heard stories of him since you were a child, no?"

The man began to weep. Lenoir decided to back off the bellows, lest he stoke the fires too much. "I will spare your life if you cooperate. Do you understand?"

Kern was blubbering into his chest and seemed not to have heard. Lenoir leaned down and slapped him. "Do you understand?" The man nodded, snuffling. "Good. Now tell me, where is the boy?"

Kern sobbed loudly. "None of this was supposed to happen. There wasn't supposed to be any boy, at least not a living one! Just the bodies, they said. They never said anything about hurting anyone."

"Where is he?"

"I don't know!"

"Ridiculous. You and your friends have held him for days."

"Yes, it's true, but they moved him this morning. I don't know where, I swear!"

Lenoir dropped to his haunches and leaned in threateningly. With Vincent at his back, he felt powerful. He felt like Wrath itself. He was almost giddy with it. "Do you expect me to believe that?"

Kern began to sob again. Lenoir waited patiently until the spasm subsided. "The hounds were getting close," Kern said. "And the others were turning up dead. . . ." His gaze strayed to Vincent, and his eyelids began to flutter as though he might faint.

Lenoir swore under his breath. "Focus, Kern!"

The man nodded, obviously making an effort. "They said they were going to move him this morning. I would have gone with them, but I'm sick with fever."

Lenoir glanced at the man's brow. It was slick with moisture. He had noticed it before, but put it down to fear. He reached out and placed the back of his hand against Kern's forehead; sure enough, it was hot to the touch. "And you don't know where they took him?" he asked sternly. Kern shook his head. "Who is your leader, and where can I find him?"

"There were two, but one of them's dead."

"Raiyen."

Kern nodded miserably.

"And the other? Who is he?"

"His name is Los. He lives with the rest of the clan, in a camp near Berryvine. He's been staying in a shack not far from here, but he hasn't been back there in weeks. He was making preparations before, and now he stays with the boy."

Lenoir considered. It did not do him much good to learn the man's name, nor would it help to send watchmen to find out more about him. Lenoir was not looking to build a case against Los; what he needed was to find the man—and quickly.

"Who else are you working with?" Perhaps he would have more luck with another member of Kern's crew.

"All dead," Kern whimpered. "Just me and Ani left."

"Ani?"

From behind him, a chill voice spoke. "I know this woman. I have seen her."

Lenoir stood. They had gotten all they could from Kern, at least for now. He was bitterly disappointed at his luck. Kern's illness was the only reason he could not give them Zach's exact location. But perhaps this Ani would give them more. They needed to hurry.

"I never wanted to hurt the boy, I swear. Nothing is the way Raiyen said it would be. They tricked me!"

Lenoir ignored his feeble excuses. "That will be all for the moment. If I were you, I would stay in this hut and not leave, not even to move your bowels. Understand?"

Kern nodded mutely, and Lenoir turned to go.

Vincent stepped forward and snapped his wrist, sending his barbed scourge around Kern's neck.

"Wait!" Lenoir cried. "What are you doing?"

Vincent ignored him. Lenoir could only watch helplessly as the spirit choked the life out of the sickly coward called Kern.

When it was over, Lenoir turned and stalked out of the hut, only to find Vincent waiting for him outside. He whirled on the spirit, his anger flaring beyond the reaches of his fear. "Why did you do that? I gave him my word that we would spare his life!"

"You should not have."

"We might have needed him later!"

Vincent said nothing. He just stood there implacably as the rain pelted him, bouncing off his leather jerkin and streaming down the sides of his nose.

"You murdered him, when he might have been the only one who could lead us to Zach!"

"I had no choice."

"What do you mean, you had no choice? The fool was harmless!"

"He was marked. I had no choice."

Merden's words returned to Lenoir's mind: *It is said that he has no will of his own, at least none he can exert.*

"But you spared me," Lenoir pointed out, dimly aware that he did not sound appropriately grateful for it.

"You have not been spared."

Strictly speaking, that was true—Lenoir's sentence had not been commuted, only deferred. "But you could have waited, at least until we found Zach."

"Perhaps," the spirit allowed. "But it is done now." He turned and headed back the way they had come.

Lenoir could only follow.

CHAPTER 20

Ani was dead.

Her corpse lay in a heap in the middle of her apartment, the dark stain beneath her thick and cold. Vermin skittered along the floorboards, drawn to the smell of blood. The open gash in her throat was already moving with flies.

Some part of Lenoir had expected this, but that did nothing to dampen the despair that threatened to overwhelm him. This woman had been his only remaining lead, his best chance of finding Zach. She had also been Vincent's final target, the last of the corpse thieves whose faces he had seen through the eyes of the dead. Lenoir's time was nearly up, and he had nothing to show for it. He should have questioned Kern about motive when he had the chance, but he had been in such a hurry to find Zach . . .

Vincent stood in a corner of the room, carefully avoiding the thin blades of dawn that intruded through the shutters. He watched Lenoir silently, offering no comment on the scene. How long would he wait before

he concluded that Lenoir had nothing to offer him after all? Lenoir caught himself wishing for daylight and
a chance to escape. It was a fleeting thought, a survival
instinct, but he could not suppress it. He only hoped it
did not show on his face.

"Very well," he said aloud, "we must take the difficult route. What we cannot learn from this woman, we
must deduce for ourselves." His words were as much
for his own benefit as Vincent's. He could not allow
himself to be overcome with hopelessness. He had
once been the cleverest inspector in the finest police
department in the world. It was time he reminded himself why.

He talked himself through it. "This woman was obviously killed by her accomplices." In spite of what
Kern had said, he was convinced there were others besides Los, henchmen who were not part of the inner
circle like Kern and Ani. "They killed her because they
are worried about being discovered, which means
someone rattled their cage. Presumably, that someone
was Sergeant Kody." He paused. It was unlikely that
Kody had met anyone in the prison who had direct
knowledge of these crimes. "Kody must have learned
something that went to motive, and motive in turn led
him close enough to the perpetrators that they felt it
necessary to kill him and Sergeant Hardin. So—what
was the motive?"

Lenoir considered. Vincent had said that the corpse
thieves were trying to resurrect the soul of a boy long
dead, a boy who had been murdered approximately
ten years ago by his father. Here was a clue about mo-

tive, which Lenoir had brushed aside in favor of the more direct route of interrogation. It was time to reexamine the evidence.

He turned to the spirit, who still hovered silently in the shadows like a veiled threat. "Vincent, what can you tell me about the murdered boy? Was he Adali?"

Vincent cocked his head, remembering. "No."

"With the exception of the gravedigger, all the corpse thieves have been Adali. Assuming the rest of them are also Adali, we must conclude that whoever is trying to resurrect the boy is not a family member. Although they could be working for a family member, I suppose."

Lenoir recalled Merden's words about meddling with corpses. It was foolhardy to attempt such magic, because doing so invited retribution from beyond. *"Every Adal knows this,"* the soothsayer had said.

"If the corpse thieves are risking so much to resurrect this boy, they must be demanding a heavy price in return." An idea was forming in Lenoir's head. "Was the father a rich man?"

Vincent frowned. "I know nothing of that."

"Think," Lenoir pressed, too absorbed in his own thoughts to worry about angering the spirit. "Remember what you saw. Where did the boy live? What sort of clothing did his father wear?"

Vincent reflected on this. "Yes," he said eventually, "perhaps he was rich. His clothes were very fine, and he lived in a large estate."

Something rammed into place, like a ball and powder being loaded into the empty chamber of Lenoir's mind. "I know where we must go next."

Vincent glanced toward the window, its pane glowing softly with the growing dawn. "I cannot."

Lenoir cursed; then he almost laughed at the absurdity of it. For ten years, the spirit had been his only dread, his only terror. He had even avoided sleep, so fearful was he of encountering the spirit in his dreams. Now he was disappointed that Vincent could not accompany him. No one would admit having a hand in kidnapping a child, not without being put under considerable duress. The man Lenoir intended to see was powerful and would not be intimidated easily. Vincent's presence gave him leverage that he did not otherwise have. But he could not afford to wait until nightfall, for that would give the kidnappers a full day to proceed with their plans.

"I must go alone, then," Lenoir said. "We do not have the luxury of losing more time."

Lenoir reined his horse in at the gate, glancing at the flag snapping smartly in the breeze at the far end of the drive. Theoretically, the Duke of Warrick was in residence. Whether he would acquiesce to an interview was another matter. Belatedly, it occurred to Lenoir that he knew little of Braelish law in circumstances such as these, and specifically whether he had the authority to interrogate a man of such rank without express permission from the king. What would he do if the duke refused him entry? There was no time to pursue the matter through bureaucratic channels.

A guard emerged from the gatehouse. "Can I help you?"

"I am Inspector Nicolas Lenoir of the Metropolitan Police," he announced in what he hoped was an impressive manner. "I am here to see His Grace on a matter of official business."

The guard frowned. He looked Lenoir up and down before retreating to the gatehouse to confer with one of his fellows. He reappeared a moment later, the second guard in tow. "Wait here," he said. He slung himself onto a horse and cantered up the drive. Lenoir was left in the care of the second guard. He did not bother to dismount. Getting on and off a horse was simply too much work to undertake any more than was necessary.

He waited, his gaze drifting over the harsh lines of Castle Warrick. He had never seen it from so close a vantage before, and the proximity was not flattering. It was an irregular-shaped creature with a rib cage of towers, rugged flanks and tiny, suspicious eyes barely wide enough to permit the sight of an archer. It hunkered behind a stinking moat, a vestige of a bloodier age when noble residences were required to serve as fortresses against would-be invaders. The drive seemed somehow to lead *away* from the castle, rather than toward, and the iron gates bristled with spikes. Lenoir had never seen a less welcoming structure in all his life. *How fitting,* he thought dryly.

"You a friend of His Grace's?" the second guard asked, interrupting Lenoir's thoughts.

Lenoir shook his head, and the guard snickered to himself. Lenoir realized the question had been sarcastic. "Something is amusing?" he asked coldly.

The guard smirked. "If His Grace has any friends, I

don't know 'em. We haven't had a caller in weeks, and the last one was a messenger from the lord mayor." He dropped his voice. "The duke is not the most social of chaps, in case you haven't heard."

"I am surprised you feel at your ease to express such an opinion." Lenoir said it approvingly, in a manner designed to coax further offerings. The more he learned about his interview subject, the better.

"Have you ever met him?" the guard asked, as though that should explain it all.

"Once, at the inauguration of the new Metropolitan Police Station. We did not converse." The rare appearance had been quite an honor for the chief. Lenoir recalled with no small amusement the sight of his superior strutting and mincing like a parade pony, simultaneously proud and deferential. The guest of honor, meanwhile, had been perfectly indifferent to the chief's attentions. The duke had stood impassively while the lord mayor and the chief delivered their speeches, then retreated without so much as a farewell. His rudeness would have been remarked upon, had it been in any way remarkable for him.

"In that case," said the guard, "you probably know him as well as anyone."

"Surely you exaggerate."

"Not much. I've only met the man a handful of times myself. He never goes anywhere." The guard jerked his thumb in a vaguely southerly direction. "I used to work over at Kirring Manor. You know the place?"

Lenoir nodded.

"Never a quiet moment over there. Balls, banquets,

luncheons. When they wasn't coming, they was going—ballet and opera and God knows what else. *That's* how the highborn are supposed to live, you know?"

"Perhaps. But every man, no matter how ill-tempered, has friends, or at least business associates. You must have noticed people coming and going from here." *Adali, perhaps?*

"Like I said, not many." Dropping his voice conspiratorially, the guard added, "The duke's got something of a stink on him, you know. That whole business with his family and whatnot."

Lenoir did indeed know. The whole of the Five Villages knew. The Duke of Warrick was widely believed to have murdered his own wife in the heat of a jealous rage. So inflamed were his passions that he went on to murder his son, only to mourn the boy fiercely after the deed was done. Nothing had ever been proven, but the duke had hardly given the townsfolk reason to dismiss the tale. If anything, his reclusiveness, and his cold manner, only sealed his reputation as an antisocial creature capable of most anything. It was precisely those rumors that had drawn Lenoir to the duke's gates.

"Gossip," he said with an affected air of disdain. "I doubt His Grace had anything to do with his family's murder."

The guard shrugged again. "A scandal is a scandal."

"In my experience, a man as rich and powerful as the Duke of Warrick can get away with just about any scandal." In this remark, at least, Lenoir was absolutely sincere. In his judgment, it was not the duke's dark past that had earned him a permanent place in the annals of infamy. The discerning denizens of the Five Villages might be willing to overlook murder, but they could not countenance neglect.

"Yeah, he's rich all right," the guard said sourly. "And he certainly knows how to hold on to a copper."

Ah. There it is. The guard's loose tongue suddenly made a great deal more sense. "I take it you are not well compensated for your time?"

"You take it correctly, good sir." He paused and adopted a thoughtful look, as though something had only just occurred to him. "Say, you're a hound, right? You think I could get a job with you lot? What with my experience in the security business, and whatnot?"

Lenoir suppressed his smile. Did the man honestly think he was being subtle? Aloud, he simply said, "Perhaps."

He was spared further awkwardness by the return of the first guard, who gestured for Lenoir to be admitted. Lenoir dismounted, handed his horse over, and followed the first guard up the long drive.

He was ushered into the duke's study and told to wait. He stood at the center of the room, methodically taking in his surroundings. He could not have asked for a better location to conduct his interview. Parlors, sunrooms, and the like were designed for guests; they put forward a false face, one designed to impress. A study, however, was an intimate location, a place that revealed much about the host. This room was particularly eloquent. Though commodious, it was sparsely furnished, with only a few chairs, a desk, and a sideboard. A row of books marched in tidy ranks across a set of shelves near the fireplace. The hearth mantel was unadorned, the sort one might expect to find in a modest inn. And though the room was equipped with glass windows instead of shutters, they were small and practical, with none of the elaborate etching so often favored by the rich.

Virtually the only visible evidence of the duke's stature was the huge portrait hanging over the mantel, of a young boy of perhaps seven or eight. Dark, doelike eyes stared down at Lenoir, seeming to watch him. The boy had round cheeks full of youthful color, but he wore a somber expression; not a hint of a smile touched his full lips. He wore a bright blue doublet with a high collar, a style that had been popular about a decade ago. *The duke's son,* Lenoir decided. If he was right, the presence of the portrait was telling. *He misses the boy.* That much of the rumor, at least, appeared to be true. Lenoir stared at the canvas, unable to shake the eerie impression that the boy was staring back. *Watching through the eyes of the dead,* Lenoir thought, *just like Vincent.* He shuddered.

He let his gaze drop to a pair of sumptuously upholstered chairs facing the desk. Their soft velvet beckoned mockingly. He was tired—exhausted, really—but he supposed it would be impertinent to sit before being invited to do so. Not for the first time, he cursed the inane protocol of the noble classes. Impractical and hopelessly complicated, elite etiquette was a rigid cage disguised in lace, as fatuous and suffocating as a corset. Then again, he supposed that lowborn cretins such as he ought to be grateful that there was a code of conduct governing the interactions of the powerful and hyperambitious. Without it, the games of the nobility would almost certainly turn bloody.

The door opened abruptly, wrenching Lenoir back to the here and now, and the Duke of Warrick strode into the room. Lenoir was surprised at this prompt arrival; he had expected the duke to keep him waiting, as men of rank were wont to do. His bearing too was surprising, for instead of the affected, leisurely manner typical of his class, Warrick crossed the study with a purposeful gait, gesturing peremptorily at a chair before seating himself behind the desk. Lenoir paused, wondering if he should bow. Instead he settled for a brief incline of his head before taking the proffered chair.

"What can I do for you, Inspector?" Warrick asked without preamble.

Lenoir had never heard the man speak before, and he was struck by the cold gravel of Warrick's voice. It was entirely suited to a countenance seemingly carved from stone—the long nose chiseled in granite, the eyes chipped from slate. His angular features were framed in dark hair that reached nearly to his shoulders, a style far more pragmatic than fashionable. He sat straight and proud, yet he seemed restless, as though sitting was not a posture to his liking. Had Lenoir passed him on the street, he would never have known Warrick as a nobleman. He carried himself more like a general.

"Thank you for taking the time to see me, Your Grace," Lenoir said. "I know you must be busy."

"I doubt you know anything of my occupation, Inspector, but as it happens you are right. Busy enough that I have little time for empty formalities, so please come to the point."

Lenoir shifted under Warrick's piercing gaze. "I have some questions regarding the death of your son," he said as neutrally as he was able. Warrick arched an eyebrow, but that was the limit of his reaction. Lenoir pressed on. "I realize that it has been a long time, but certain . . . recent events . . . have brought the case to my attention."

Warrick regarded Lenoir silently, waiting for him to continue.

"I wish to emphasize that I am not here to open an investigation, or to reopen one, as the case may be. The events surrounding your son's death are not my concern."

The duke frowned. "You speak cryptically, Inspector."

"Forgive me, Your Grace. That is not my intention, but these are complicated matters, and not easy to explain. I shall attempt to be plain. A boy has been kidnapped, and I have reason to believe that he is the intended victim of Adali magic."

That got a reaction. Warrick snorted incredulously, and his mouth took a sardonic turn. "I am disappointed in our much-vaunted Metropolitan Police. Surely an inspector, at least, realizes that not all crimes are committed by Adali, the claims of the common man notwithstanding."

"Your skepticism is understandable, Your Grace,

but I assure you that I did not leap to this conclusion out of blind prejudice."

"Oh?" Warrick's dark eyebrows climbed a fraction. "You have irrefutable proof, do you?"

"Irrefutable? No. In more than twenty years of police work, I have rarely found evidence of that standard. Say rather that it is highly convincing." Lenoir sat back in his chair in what he hoped was a confident posture. The familiar rhythm of the conversation was soothing his unease, allowing him to settle into his role as interrogator.

Warrick grunted. "What has this to do with my son?"

Lenoir steeled himself inwardly. "The magic they are attempting is intended to resurrect a dead child, one who died approximately ten years ago. That coincides roughly with the time of your son's death, does it not?"

Something stirred behind Warrick's eyes, but Lenoir could not identify it. Was it outrage? Anticipation? Shock? "One has so many questions, Inspector." Warrick's voice had chilled several degrees. "I am not sure what you are attempting to imply, but I am even more interested in how exactly you came to this fascinating conclusion."

"I do not think it matters for the purposes of this discussion. Suffice it to say that my source is utterly credible. The kidnappers are attempting to use the body of a live child to host the soul of a dead one."

Warrick rolled his eyes. "Do not waste my time with supernatural nonsense. The bottom line is that you believe the kidnappers intend to harm the child, is that correct?"

"They do indeed. The ritual requires the boy's soul to be supplanted by that of another. If they succeed, the dead child will take over the boy's body."

The duke gave a hollow laugh. "Do not tell me that you actually believe in this magic?"

"Do you?"

Warrick's eyes narrowed dangerously. "Ahhh." The sound escaped his lips in a long, drawn-out breath. "I understand now. You believe this is all done at my behest, is that it?" A cold smile crept across his face. "I really must commend you, Inspector. Few of your fellow champions of the law have had the courage to accuse me of anything over the years, and none so creatively. I wonder, however, if you should have checked in with your superiors before coming here. Your chief—Reck, isn't it?—strikes me as a sensible man, far too sensible to have allowed you to come here on a fool's errand."

Normally, a warning such as this, from a man such as Warrick, would have given Lenoir pause. Indeed his entire approach to police work had been shaped by ruthless and powerful men. It was their impunity that had poisoned him, turned him into the cynical, pragmatic creature he had become. Their taint had driven him into the arms of the green-eyed man. But all that was past. He was immune now. A dead man could not be bought, could not be hurt. With nothing to gain and nothing to fear, *he* was the one with impunity.

"I am not concerned about the chief," Lenoir replied casually, "nor am I impressed by your bluster. Quite frankly, Your Grace, I am disappointed. I had sized you up as a different sort of man from those I am accustomed to dealing with. Thinly veiled threats are the weapon of the manipulative and the affected. I would have thought you more direct."

Warrick's expression darkened, and he leaned across the desk. "You are an excellent judge of character, Inspector. I have no need of veiled threats, for I can be very direct indeed. Therefore, I suggest you choose your next words carefully."

Lenoir swallowed hard, in spite of himself. But when he spoke, his voice was firm. "Tell me what you know, and I will ensure that you have nothing to fear from the Metropolitan Police." Vincent, of course, was another matter, but that was not Lenoir's concern. "Continue to withhold the truth, and I will find the boy anyway, and all those associated with this crime will be punished severely. I have no doubt that it will end with executions." *No doubt whatsoever.*

Warrick laughed softly, seemingly genuinely amused. "Do you really think you can intimidate me with the law?"

Lenoir returned his gaze implacably. "No, Your Grace, I do not." He stared into Warrick's eyes, letting the import of his words sink in.

The duke's smile waned, but it did not disappear altogether. He regarded Lenoir with a newly appraising look. "You are a hard man, Lenoir. You must be very good at your job."

"I used to be."

The duke frowned, but did not otherwise comment on the remark. "In any case, I know nothing of these matters. If a boy has been kidnapped, it was not done on my orders."

"Then you did not hire these Adali to restore your son to you?"

"Regrettably, there are few Adali of my acquaintance," Warrick replied dryly. "Nor do I believe in magic, Adali or otherwise. What civilized man does? I doubt this has anything to do with my son at all. It would make more sense for you to focus your efforts on the communities where such beliefs are common. Look into the deaths of local Adali children. God knows they lose a tragic number every year."

Lenoir considered the duke carefully. If he was lying, he was doing a credible job of it. That proved nothing, of course. "I do not think one needs to believe in magic to try something desperate. When we are desperate, we will try anything."

"It sounds as though you speak from experience, Inspector." Warrick's eyes bored into him.

Lenoir did not take the bait. It was time to bring this conversation to a head. "I am absolutely certain that whoever has taken the boy is attempting to resurrect your child." It was a lie, of course, and Warrick would probably see through it, but it was still worth trying. "As I told you, my source is credible. Unless you would have the blood of someone *else's* son on your hands, I suggest you tell me what you know."

He knew he had gone too far the moment he said it. Fury swept into Warrick's eyes like a possessing demon, and he sprang to his feet so suddenly that Lenoir half expected him to leap across the desk. As it was, Warrick retained just enough composure to remain frozen in place, shaking with rage. Lenoir would have stood up himself, but he shrank beneath the force of the duke's glare.

"Get out," Warrick said, his voice low and tremulous. Lenoir opened his mouth to reply, but Warrick cut him off, saying, "I swear before God, Inspector, if I have to tell you again, I will do so with a blade."

The words inspired no fear. Instead Lenoir's breast flooded with fury of his own. Not at the duke, but at himself, at his own stupidity. He had overplayed his hand, and he would get nothing further from Warrick. The miscalculation might very well cost Zach his life.

Lenoir stormed down the long drive, cursing violently. He had learned nothing, nothing at all that would help him find Zach. Whatever Warrick knew, he would never divulge it now. *A hard man*, the duke had called him, words spoken with grudging respect. Lenoir had overestimated how far that would get him.

He glanced at the sky. It was still early. He had until dark to think of something, anything, that would keep both him and Zach alive.

CHAPTER 21

For the first time in several days, Zach knew where he was. That should have been comforting, but it wasn't. If anything, it made him feel smaller, more forsaken, than ever before. That was because his captors had chosen the creepiest place in all of Kennian to stash him.

Zach had never much liked churches. When he was small, the nuns used to force him to attend prayers in the chapel at the orphanage, and every now and then he'd been dragged—literally—to weekend service at the larger of the two churches in the poor quarter. The nuns didn't make him go anymore, though. They had long since grown tired of the pranks, the outbursts, the embarrassments. Zach had succeeded in making such a nuisance of himself that his immortal soul was deemed not worth the trouble, and that was fine by him. It wasn't just that church was boring, though it was, or that its rituals were weird, though they were. Zach didn't like the way church made him *feel*. He didn't need to be told that it was wrong to steal, or to lie or cheat or any of the other things he did on a daily basis. God punished him for those things all the time, by making him go hungry, or letting him get beaten. The trouble was, God's punishments forced him to commit those sins again, which in turn made God punish him more. Zach had asked the priests how he was supposed to break this cycle, and they'd told him to pray.

He wondered if he should pray now. It had never worked for him before; he still went hungry, still got beaten. But maybe God would hear him better if he prayed in a church. Churches were supposed to be Houses of God, after all, though admittedly Zach wasn't sure about abandoned churches. He gazed up at the peeling frescoes and wondered if God was watching him through the sad eyes of the angels. If not God, maybe the angels themselves were watching, judging, already tallying the sum of his deeds so they would be ready with their verdict when he . . .

No, he told himself firmly, pushing the thought away. *It's just a building. And you won't be here for long.* It wasn't that hard to convince himself, since he was pretty sure he wasn't meant to die like this. He'd always figured that if he got it someday, it would be at the hands of some archcriminal he'd been chasing for months. That was how big-shot inspectors went down. They didn't get snuffed in churches for no reason at all.

His captors had brought him here last night, trussed up in a burlap sack like a kitten waiting to be drowned. He was surprised when dawn came and he could see where he was. He'd never been inside the abandoned cathedral, but every Kennian knew it. Zach had walked past it dozens of times, and had even tried unsuccessfully to break in once or twice, just to satisfy his curiosity. It was big and dark and deserted, which made sense, but it was also within the city walls, which didn't. It seemed awfully brave of his captors to bring him back into the city when the hounds were out looking for him. Then again, maybe they knew that the walls were too thick for anyone to hear him scream. He'd certainly tested that theory.

Zach had no idea why they'd moved him, but he liked to think it was because Lenoir was getting close. Not that whisking him away would help; Lenoir would track his captors down wherever they went. Zach imagined the inspector kicking open the ancient wooden doors of the cathedral, a pistol in each hand, his figure silhouetted against the sunlight. Pigeons would erupt from the rafters in fright as Lenoir strode boldly between the rotting pews, his eyes burning with righteous fire. Zach's kidnappers would try to flee, but Lenoir would bring them down with a puff of smoke from his flintlock. Over and over Zach pictured this scene, his imagination refining it a little each time. Maybe Lenoir would carry a saber instead of a pistol? No, the inspector was no swashbuckler—even Zach could see that. Besides, a pistol was better; it could drop a man from clear across the room, so the kidnappers wouldn't have a chance to escape.

That was assuming there would be anyone around when Lenoir arrived. Zach hadn't seen his captors since before dawn. For all he knew, they'd left the cathedral altogether.

His captors were planning something big for him, and soon. They probably meant to do to him what they'd done to the other boy, the one who'd screamed and screamed. Only this time, whatever had gone wrong was supposed to go right. Though no one said so, Zach knew instinctively that if it *didn't* go right, people would die, and he would probably be one of them. He had to get out of here before that happened. Lenoir was coming for him, but that didn't mean he had to sit around and wait, did it? If nothing else, it was probably a good idea to come up with an escape plan so he knew what to do when Lenoir started shooting.

Zach decided to map out his new location, as he'd done in the cellar and the farmhouse before it. Planting his heels and dragging his bottom, he inched his way out of the chapel and into the main body of the cathedral.

It was even spookier out here. Thin blades of light sliced between the boards covering the windows, casting the nave in ghostly relief. Wind moaned and wailed through unseen cracks, echoing eerily under the vaulted ceiling. Zach was uncomfortably aware of the space around him, of the empty gaze of stone generals peering out from the gloom, and he shivered against a chill that had little to do with the cold. He wondered if it was possible for churches to be haunted. He'd heard somewhere that the cathedral sat upon a vast web of catacombs, the walls of which were stuffed with corpses. It certainly seemed like the kind of place that would be haunted.

He dragged himself forward until he came to a sort

of dais, a short set of steps that led to a pulpit fringed with a wooden rail. It was from this spot, he supposed, that the high priest once lectured everyone about their wickedness. It had long since been stripped of anything valuable or fine, yet it still seemed to radiate judgment into the shadows beyond, a virtuous island in a sea of sin. Zach paused to rest against the stairs. He was surprised how tired he was. He was used to going without much food, after all. On the other hand, he *wasn't* used to being tied up and going without sleep for days on end.

A glint of metal caught his eye. It lay on the floor a few inches from his boot, lined up with the stairs. He shuffled closer. A metal cylinder about as big around as his fist was embedded in the floor, its top protruding about two inches from the tile. The rim was uneven, as though it had been filed down in a hurry. Something had once stood here—the Golden Sword, maybe?— that had been looted sometime in the past. Whoever took it hadn't bothered to make a clean cut. However much time had passed, the metal still looked sharp.

Zach's stomach did a little flip. Spinning on his bottom, he turned his back to the ring of metal, waving his fingers around until he located it. He shimmied back until he was almost sitting on top of it. Then he started to work at the ropes binding his wrists.

It didn't take long, and when the ropes finally came free, Zach yanked his arms apart in triumph. The pain took him by surprise, so sharp and sudden that he nearly cried out. His wrists screamed in protest at their prolonged imprisonment, and his shoulders burned and tingled. Gingerly, he rotated his aching joints until they moved more smoothly. Then he started in on the bonds tying his ankles.

That was harder. He couldn't get the leverage he needed against the metal ring, and his fingers were weak and uncertain. Eventually, though, he managed to get the knot free, and his legs came apart. Carefully, having learned from the experience of his arms, he tested his weight against his legs. Sure enough, he was wobbly, and he was grateful to have the stairs to lean against. But his legs had been less awkwardly situated than his arms, and after a few seconds, he was able to stand upright without much trouble.

"Maybe I won't have to wait for Lenoir after all," he whispered to himself, hearing the sound of his own voice for the first time in a very long time. How proud would the inspector be if Zach managed to get out of this all by himself?

He headed for the massive doors at the bottom of the cathedral. Shadows gathered around him as he drew farther away from the windows, and soon he couldn't see anything at all. He had to feel along the wood until he found a metal ring, which he hauled against with all his weight. The doors did not so much as rattle. Zach patted and groped, but he couldn't figure out where the two panels came together, much less how they were secured. He heaved against the ring again, but it was pointless. The doors stayed put.

There had to be another way out. He cast his mind back to the last time he was in a church, but it didn't help. The church in the poor district was much smaller and laid out differently, and anyway he hadn't exactly gone exploring. He had no idea where to look for another door. But there had to be one in a building of this size—he was sure of it. He just needed to find it.

He kept close to the walls, ducking through any archway or opening he could find. There were many, each one leading to a dead end, and it wasn't long before Zach started to get frustrated. How many separate nooks did a single place of worship need? Zach didn't know a chapel from a vestry, a library from a study, but this cathedral had them all, and none of them had an exit. The first fluttering of panic began to stir in his belly. He could feel the minutes hurtling by, a scary and unfamiliar sensation. Time had always felt like a vast desert stretching endlessly before him; now it slipped through his fingers like a fistful of sand. He started to consider the awful possibility that his captors might return before he could take advantage of his good fortune. He needed to find a way out, and he needed to do it *now*.

Finally, at the bottom of the south wing, Zach found a door. It wasn't much more than a slab of gloom in the shadows, and stood ajar, judging from the chill air that gusted from it. Zach leaned into it with his shoulder and was rewarded with a slight shudder. Gathering his weight, he threw himself against it, hard enough to drive the air from his lungs. With a loud bark, the door swung free, sending Zach stumbling into a short corridor. He could see sunlight at the far end. A swell of triumph fueled his limbs, and he dashed forward.

He emerged onto a covered walkway surrounding a

grassy courtyard overgrown with weeds. Vines sprawled across the pillars and choked the arcades, and moss erupted between flagstones caked in pigeon filth. A light rain drifted down from the sky, stringing watery jewels along the spokes of a large spiderweb. Zach had never seen this courtyard, and he knew with sinking certainty that it was enclosed by the cathedral walls.

But wait. . . . Zach closed his eyes, remembering the facade of the cathedral as best he could. It had been a long time since he'd been in this part of the city, even longer since he'd paid much attention to the abandoned relic in its midst. But he could swear he recalled a second, smaller door, just to the right of the main doors in the western facade. That would put it at the bottom of the walkway where he now stood. Taking a deep breath and praying as best he knew how, Zach ran to the far end.

Sure enough, the door was there, and his heart leapt. That is, until he saw the chains wrapped around an ancient, rusted lock and realized that the door might as well be made of solid stone.

A sob caught in Zach's throat, and he sank to his knees. He sat there, slumped in defeat, until a last spasm of defiance sent him hurtling against the door with a scream, his fists pounding painfully against the cold, unyielding wood. He beat the door until the pain became unbearable; then, his rage unspent, he seized a handful of vines and yanked. The stubborn plant didn't budge, just one more implacable surface in this prison of wood and stone.

Zach paused. He considered the vines more carefully.

Snatching up two fistfuls, he hauled against it with all his weight. Some of the thinner stalks snapped, but the bulk of it stayed put. Zach stepped out into the rain and peered up at the covered walkway. It looked flat on top, and was only a few feet shorter than the outer wall. If he could get up there, he could easily get to the top of the wall. Eying the vines again, Zach repeated his experiment with a thick batch growing along one of the pillars supporting the roof of the arcade. As before, it stayed anchored to the stone in spite of Zach's best efforts to tear it free. Untold years of growing wild against porous, decaying stone had left the roots strong. He tested it one last time, reaching as high as he could and letting himself dangle from the vine. Miraculously, it held.

Zach pulled off his boots, doing his best to avoid the stinging touch of the thistles crowding the edges of the walkway. He tied the laces together and stuffed his already-soaking socks inside. Then he flung his boots up onto the top of the walkway. Choosing the pillar with the thickest vine, he reached above his head and wound his fingers though the ropy plant. Cautiously, he cocked his left leg and grasped the vine with his toes. He pulled.

Roots snapped, and Zach's foot slipped, but he didn't fall. Choosing his next foothold more carefully, he found a thicker stalk to anchor his right foot to, and spread his toes wider to distribute his weight. He heaved himself up. Once again, the vine tore free, but not enough to let him fall. Slowly, his heart in his throat, Zach climbed. So long as he didn't move too sharply, or panic if he slipped a little, the vine would hold.

It took a long time to reach the top of the pillar, and Zach's arms ached so badly that he almost didn't have the strength to pull himself over the top. But he did, and he was so overjoyed that he lay on his back and giggled, heedless of the cold rain until he was almost soaked through. He pulled on his boots and heaved himself to the top of the wall surrounding the cloister.

Now he was presented with a new problem. The street was far below, too far for him to jump. The vines didn't reach the other side of the wall, and there were no footholds he could see. He couldn't climb, and none of the nearby buildings were close enough to jump to. He needed help.

Zach crouched on the wall, scanning the street for signs of life. For a long time, he saw no one, which wasn't surprising for this part of town, especially when the weather was foul. Eventually, though, a youth appeared at the far end of the road.

"Hey!" Zach called, his voice croaking from disuse. "Hey, you!"

The youth paused. "What?"

"I need a ladder!"

The youth gave him an incredulous look. "Does it look like I've got a ladder?" He walked away.

"Durian's balls!" Zach swore. He'd started to shiver, and water streamed from his plastered hair. He waited. A long time passed before someone else came along. This time, it was a woman, and she had a pushcart. It was full of straw. Zach flicked his eyes skyward and said a prayer of thanks.

"Hey, miss!" The woman didn't seem to hear him, so

he tried again, waving his arms frantically over his head. "Miss!"

The woman looked his way. She stopped. "What're you doing up there, stupid child? Break your neck, you will!"

Zach adopted his most pitiful voice. "I'm stuck! Please, miss, let me jump into that cart!"

"Not bloody likely. That'll break your neck for sure! Besides, I've just been mucking stalls. It's full of horse shit!"

"Please!" Zach's voice cracked in desperation. "I'll be fine, I swear! I need to get down right now!"

The woman hesitated, and for a moment Zach feared she would refuse. But then she shrugged and wheeled her load over to the wall, positioning it as close as she could. "You're a stupid boy," she called, "but be it on your head."

Zach bit his lip. Now that he was looking straight down at it, the cart didn't look like such a soft landing. A big pile of wet straw was certainly better than stone, but it was hardly goose down. It didn't smell very nice either. But Zach had no choice. If he stayed where he was, his captors would find him and he would die for sure. Swallowing hard, his pulse hammering in his ears, Zach eased himself over the side of the wall and jumped.

He landed in a painful heap, momentarily too stunned to move. His right foot had missed the straw and struck the edge of the cart, and when he shifted, pain arced up his calf and into his thigh. It was probably broken. Still, it could have been worse. Zach sat up and rubbed his head, and was pleased to find himself otherwise intact.

He hopped off the cart, careful not to put weight on his bad foot. "Thanks," he mumbled to the woman.

"How'd you get up there, anyway?" She squinted at him through dirt-fringed eyes.

"Long story."

The woman grunted. "Well, you got what you deserved, I suppose, 'cause now you smell like horse shit." So saying, she wheeled her cart away, leaving Zach standing in the rain.

He paused to orient himself before heading off in the direction of the police station. It would take him a while to get there, especially with his sore foot, but it seemed like the quickest way to find Lenoir. He hobbled down the street, tired and a little dizzy, but hopeful enough to keep his step lively and determined.

The streets were quiet, even several blocks away from the cathedral. The weather had driven everyone indoors. Zach saw no one until he rounded a corner and walked right into someone coming the opposite way. He hit the ground hard, crying out as his bad foot was wrenched beneath him. It was raining hard now, and water streamed into his eyes. He could only vaguely see the tall man who reached down to help him stand.

Zach was pulled to his feet, and found himself gazing up at a tall Adali man with hard eyes. He had never seen the man before, but Zach knew him all the same.

A small, helpless sound escaped his throat, and he slumped as though someone had reached inside and pulled his skeleton right out of his skin.

"Come now, boy," the man said in a voice so familiar that it set Zach's body to trembling. "Let us get you back where you belong."

CHAPTER 22

Lenoir nestled deeper into the collar of his coat. The sky hunkered low over the buildings, shedding its watery burden in relentless sheets. Lenoir's thinning hair was flattened against his skull, and he cursed himself for being without a hat. *That's what you get for being an uncivilized brute,* he thought wryly. He needed to find someplace warm and dry, someplace he could think things through. He turned his horse toward the nearest haven he could think of.

"My word, Nicolas!" Zera exclaimed when he appeared at the top of the stairs. "You look half-drowned!" Turning to a servant, she called, "Brandy! And towels, quickly!"

Lenoir planted himself in front of the fireplace. Steam immediately began to curl off his overcoat. Zera hovered, her eyebrows stitched together in displeasure as she stared at the puddle accumulating at Lenoir's feet.

"My apologies," he muttered. "Would you prefer I stand on a carpet?"

"I certainly would *not*. I would never get it dry in this weather." She took his coat, shook it out, and handed it to a servant. "Why in God's name did you let yourself get this wet, anyway? Where have you been?"

Judging the second question more important than the first, he said, "At Castle Warrick."

Zera could not have looked more shocked if he had suddenly sprouted horns. "Castle Warrick! Whatever for? I thought you were in fear of your life, Nicolas! What happened to all that business about a vengeful spirit? For that matter, what about the boy you were supposed to be finding?" There was something disapproving about her tone, as though she had caught him gallivanting about instead of seeing to his duty. Even as she berated him, however, she dragged a chair to the hearth so he could sit. Being a proper hostess was utterly ingrained in her.

"Thank you," he sighed, sinking gratefully into the chair. It was the least splendid of her furnishings, he noticed. He could hardly blame her. "It was my business with the boy that brought me to the duke," he explained as he propped his boots near the fire.

Zera gave him a wary look as she slipped into one of the winged chairs flanking the hearth. "That doesn't make sense."

Lenoir grunted. "The duke expressed a similar view." He paused to accept his brandy from the servant. He took a long sip, rolling the sweet fire on his tongue before he continued. "It is probably too much to explain. Suffice it to say that I think the duke's tragedy plays a role in all this. I think someone is trying to help the duke replace his lost son."

Zera let out a humorless laugh. "Replace his son? Don't be absurd! We are talking about a child, not a pet. One cannot simply *replace* a dead boy."

"I know how it sounds." He took another sip of his brandy. "Tell me, Zera, have you ever heard of necromancy?"

She stiffened, the color fleeing her lips. Anger flashed briefly in her eyes before she mastered herself. "Would you ask me that if I were not Adali?" she asked coldly.

"Probably not. I mean no offense by it. I thought it was the quickest way of explaining my theory."

"Your theory involves black magic?" she sneered. Lenoir had never seen her so waspish, but then, he had never waved her race in front of her before either. He had not realized her anxiety ran quite so deep. It was as though she considered her place in society to be nothing more than a fragile illusion, a spell that might break at any moment.

"My theory involves people who believe in black magic. And perhaps even some who don't. For myself, I scarcely know what to believe anymore. After all, I have spoken with a spirit from beyond."

If possible, Zera's lips became even paler, parting with terrible awe. "*Spoke* with it? My God, Nicolas! Never mind the duke—what happened with the green-eyed man?"

Lenoir hardly knew where to begin. "I knew I

couldn't escape him, so I decided to make a deal with him."

She gaped at him, aghast. "Are you mad? You would strike a bargain with a demon?"

"A demon?" Lenoir echoed thoughtfully. "Perhaps. Or perhaps he is an avenging angel. It does not really matter, does it? Either way, my life is forfeit." He was surprised at how calmly he spoke the words. "I had nothing to lose by offering myself to the green-eyed man. So that is what I did. I offered to help him hunt down those he wishes to punish, in exchange for his help in finding Zach. And he agreed, if you can believe it."

Zera sprang from her chair, her eyes glazed with fear. She began to pace in front of the hearth. Lenoir was touched by her concern. There were few people in the world who cared whether he lived or died. "You offered to help him hunt down those he wishes to punish," she repeated slowly. Her gaze turned on him, and it was accusing. "You offered to hunt down people just like you."

Lenoir blinked. He had not really thought of it in that light. Even if he had, however, it would not have changed his decision. "Perhaps people like me deserve their fates."

"How wonderfully convenient your fatalism is," she snapped. "It excuses your actions as well as your inaction. It lets you condemn others even as you wallow in your own self-pity." She resumed her pacing. "Why didn't you flee, Nicolas? Why not leave this place behind, just as you did Serles?"

"There is nowhere I could go that he would not find

me." Lenoir paused, shrugging. "I have accepted this, Zera. I am at peace with it. All I want is to find Zach before my time comes."

She folded her arms tightly over her chest, as though shielding herself. "And the spirit will help you do that?"

"He has already led me to two of the kidnappers. Neither of them had the boy, but we were close." *So close, but we still left empty-handed.* Lenoir stared down into the amber liquid in his glass, fighting to suppress a sudden wave of hopelessness. He had come here to think through his next move, but he was no closer to deciding what to do when darkness came.

"Where will you go next?" Zera asked, as though reading his thoughts.

He gave a despondent little shake of his head. "I don't know. The spirit will return at dark, and I will have to report on my meeting with the duke. If the spirit is not satisfied that I have made any progress, our deal will expire, I think."

He looked up at Zera. She was standing over him, scowling. "I still don't see what Warrick has to do with anything."

"If the rumors about the duke are true, he murdered his family in a fit of passion, only to bitterly regret it later on. What if someone offered him the chance to restore his son to him?"

"Rumors. Is that what you are reduced to now?"

"It is only a hunch," he admitted. "But I have grown to trust my hunches. Every good inspector does. Sometimes, to connect the dots, we must make a leap of faith."

"A leap of faith?" Zera arched a finely sculpted eyebrow. "That doesn't sound much like you, Nicolas."

"Perhaps not anymore, but it was once very like me. And it was like Kody too, which is why he drew a connection between the corpse thieves and the kidnappers before anyone else did. He was smarter than I gave him credit for. He saw the pattern, though we had no idea what to make of it at the time." Lenoir realized belatedly that he was already referring to Kody in the past tense. *How quick you are to give up hope, Lenoir.*

"And you know what to make of this so-called pattern now?"

Lenoir downed the last of his brandy. He had scarcely swallowed before the servant appeared to whisk his empty glass away. Not for the first time, he marveled at the efficiency of Zera's domestic staff. They were always hovering somewhere nearby, unseen, waiting for a subtle signal to appear. "As I said before, I am convinced that necromancy is involved. The kidnappers were trying to restore a dead child to life. They failed, but now they are attempting something similar. If I'm right, they are trying to channel the soul of the dead boy into a live host. That's what they wanted with Zach and that other boy, the one who went mad."

Zera threw herself into her chair. She stared at Lenoir, her eyes smoldering with something unreadable. "You are listening to yourself, aren't you? Bringing the dead back to life?"

"I have stopped worrying about how crazy it all

seems. The evidence is compelling, and in any case, I have no competing theory."

"What evidence?" Zera scoffed.

She's right, he admitted inwardly. What he had found did not really qualify as evidence. It was hearsay and speculation, and though it came from multiple sources, that did not necessarily mean it was accurate. He had no doubt that if he had been talking to the chief, instead of Zera, the reaction would have been even more skeptical. Yet for all that, he did not doubt himself. Perhaps that was because his theory had been corroborated by Vincent. Perhaps perversely, Lenoir considered the word of a supernatural creature to be beyond doubt.

"I am convinced of my theory," he said simply.

Zera's eyes narrowed. "Suppose you're right about the necromancy. What makes you so sure it has anything to do with Warrick? His son died, what—ten years ago?"

"That is the thinnest part of my hypothesis. But it fits with the details provided by Vincent."

"Who?"

"The green-eyed man."

She let out a sharp, incredulous breath. "You're on a first-name basis with a demon?"

Lenoir smiled wryly. "I suppose I am, but I would not say that we are friends. In any case, he has explained much that I did not understand, things that I would never have figured out on my own."

Zera shook her head, her mouth hanging slightly open. She had been completely robbed of her customary poise. "I'm sorry, Nicolas, but I'm still having a difficult time with this. It seems like every time I see you, you bring a story more incredible than the last. How exactly is it that this . . . *creature* . . . helps you, anyway?"

"He communes with the dead. You must have heard the stories of him—he occupies an important place in Adali myth, I'm told. He has provided me with quite a lot of useful information. One particularly important fact is that the boy the kidnappers are attempting to resurrect has been dead for a long time. He was murdered by his father, who was a wealthy man. In other words, it all fits."

Zera regarded him thoughtfully. "All right, supposing the duke really was willing to try dark magic to bring his son back to life—how would he go about finding someone to do it? It's not as though he could just march into an Adali camp and start asking around, is it? Even if he had a servant he trusted with such an outrageous task, the Adali would throw him out on his ear the minute he so much as hinted at magic."

"Especially the Asis clan."

Zera snorted softly, her mouth curling into a smirk. "My, my, Nicolas. I am impressed. You really have learned a lot, haven't you?"

Under other circumstances, Lenoir might have been annoyed at her apparent surprise. Today, however, he was too preoccupied for pride. "Perhaps Warrick didn't approach the kidnappers at all. Perhaps *they* approached *him*."

"And how would they do that? I doubt the Duke of

Warrick would simply open his gates to a random Adal."

Now it was Lenoir's turn to snort. "Indeed I think we can rule that out. Perhaps they wrote him a letter."

"That is no less ridiculous. Do you honestly think the duke would have responded to an unsolicited message promising to restore his dead son through dark magic?"

She had a point. Lenoir tapped his knee in thought.

"Then there is the question of *why* anyone would risk himself to help the duke," she continued. "There's always money, I suppose, but the proscription against dark magic is strong amongst my people. It's hard to imagine how much money would have to be on offer to make it worthwhile. Especially since, as you're no doubt aware, coin is only used for trading with southerners. As soon as the clan headed back north, the value of that money would plummet."

Lenoir had never heard Zera refer to the Adali as *her people* before. Perhaps it was not so surprising; she had been raised among them, after all. Their ways had once been hers, even if that was virtually impossible to imagine now.

"The circumstances of the death do sound similar, but then again, I suppose Warrick is hardly the first highborn man to strike down his son. Why, that was a favorite political tactic barely a hundred years ago."

"The objections you raise are perfectly reasonable," said Lenoir.

"But?"

Lenoir shrugged. "But a man in my business is skeptical of coincidences. Assuming that another wealthy man in the Five Villages murdered his son many years ago, who would be in a better position than Warrick to reward those who were willing to risk everything? You said yourself that the payment would have to be extraordinary. Warrick is the most powerful man in the Five Villages. He has much more than gold to offer." An idea began to swim up from the depths of his mind, moving slowly toward the light.

Zera clucked her tongue impatiently. "Come, now. You know his political clout is useless to an Adal."

"Yes." Lenoir was barely listening now. His gaze grew unfocused, turning within. The idea bumped gently against the frozen surface of his consciousness, its outlines tantalizingly visible. *It's so close. What am I missing?*

"Warrick has absolutely nothing to offer a bunch of half-starved nomads who are too afraid even to go home," Zera concluded.

The ice broke. The idea surfaced.

"You're wrong," said Lenoir, his gaze snapping into focus.

She regarded him coldly. "Is that so?"

"Land."

"I beg your pardon?"

How could it have taken him so long to see it? "The duchy covers hundreds of thousands of acres. The Asis clan is struggling to survive because they don't have access to pasture to graze their cattle. Something to do with their status amongst the other clans. If they had title over some of the duke's lands, or at least permission to graze there, it would change everything for them."

Zera was shaking her head vigorously. "No, no. The Adali are nomadic, Nicolas. You know that. They don't own land, and they never stay in one place for long."

"The Asis do. They are always within a few miles of Berryvine. That's because they have no access to decent migration routes. Their whole way of life has been compromised. But having their own land would fix that forever."

Zera rolled her eyes and leaned back in her chair. "Honestly, Nicolas, now you're grasping. What you say is possible, it's true, but there are a dozen other explanations that are just as likely. You are desperate to save the boy, so you're seeing what you want to see."

Lenoir was baffled. It was so obvious to him now that he was amazed that he had not worked it out before. Yet Zera was determined to discard his theory entirely. "How can you ignore the connection?" he asked incredulously.

She gave a dismissive wave. "Because it's imaginary, a product of your own construction. Whether it's a constellation or merely stars depends on who is looking."

Lenoir paused. He regarded Zera in silence. Had he ever used that phrase in her presence? He had been drunk too many times in these apartments to be sure, but it seemed highly unlikely. He had mocked Kody mercilessly every time the sergeant trotted it out. To the best of his knowledge, he had never used it himself.

He was certain Zera had never met Kody. They had spoken of the sergeant only a few days ago, and Zera had not known who he was. "That is an interesting analogy," he said carefully.

She gave him a quizzical look. "About the stars? It's a common saying. Have you never heard it?" She smiled warmly, the elegant hostess once again.

It was that shift in her expression, so effortless, yet so incongruous in the moment, that betrayed her.

Only a few minutes before, Lenoir had referred to Kody in the past tense. Zera had not picked up on that. Zera picked up on everything.

As though in answer to his thoughts, her smile turned suddenly sad. "What a pity, Nicolas. We get along so well."

A blow landed heavily against the back of Lenoir's head. Pain erupted in his skull, and he tumbled out of his chair. He looked up to find a servant standing over him with a fireplace poker. It came down in a humming arc, and Lenoir rolled aside, the heavy iron slamming into the floorboards where his head had been. He hooked the man's ankles with his foot and swept his feet out from under him. The servant came down hard. Lenoir managed to wrest the poker free, simultaneously driving his knee into the other man's groin. He struck a blow across the servant's face with the poker, and the man went still.

Zera backed away toward the windows. Her eyes blazed with defiance, and she made a sharp movement with her hand. Lenoir realized that he had misread her gesture moments before. She hadn't been dismissing his argument; she had been calling reinforcements. *You blind fool,* he cursed himself inwardly.

He dared a glance around the room, looking for any hint of movement. Whomever Zera had signaled to was concealed somewhere nearby. He held the poker at the ready, his mind frantically trying to gauge the distance to the stairs.

"Did you kill them?" he cried, surprised at his own anger.

"Who? Your hounds?" She sneered. "What do you care? I thought you despised them."

"Hardin did not deserve to die. Kody does not deserve to die."

"Deserve?" She laughed bitterly. "I never thought to hear such naïveté from you, Nicolas."

The creak of a floorboard alerted Lenoir to movement behind him, and he spun, leading with the poker. The weapon crashed against the side of a man's face, caving in his cheekbone and sending a spray of blood across the creamy velvet upholstery of a nearby chair. The man slumped to the floor.

"A pity about the chair," Lenoir said. The comment was rewarded with a shriek and a glass projectile thrown at his head. He ducked as the delicate ornament shattered into a thousand tinkling shards behind him.

Footsteps thundered overhead and on the stairs. Lenoir had no idea how many men might be in these apartments; he was not even sure how many floors there were. He needed to get out. Casting a final glance at Zera to make sure she was staying put, he turned and headed down the stairs.

He met only one servant on his way out, heading the

opposite direction on the stairs. Lenoir grabbed the handrails with both hands and swung his boots into the man's face, sending him tumbling back down to the marble landing. He was still moving when Lenoir got to the bottom of the stairs, but not quickly enough to be a threat. Lenoir ran past him and out the door onto the high street. He swung himself onto his horse with the vigor of a man of twenty. Then, with one final look at the place that had been a haven for him for so long, he galloped off into the rain.

CHAPTER 23

Lenoir did not exactly *decide* to ride to the hospital; he simply steered his horse there, without conscious thought. He needed a familiar face, and Bran Kody was just about the last person left in the Five Villages that Lenoir had spent any significant time with over the past few years. Pathetic, certainly, but a fact nonetheless, and so Lenoir made his way to Mindale Hospital, the only clinic in Kennian that the Metropolitan Police trusted to care for their own. If Kody was still alive, he would be here. It was probably too much to hope that the sergeant might be awake, but Lenoir could accept that. He had always found Kody's company to be much more agreeable when the sergeant did not speak.

Lenoir was shown to a cramped little room at the end of a long, foul-smelling corridor. He found the physician bent over Kody's cot, checking the patient's pulse. Lenoir waited in the corridor.

"He's alive," the physician said as he quit the room.

Lenoir waited for him to elaborate, but he did not. "How is he? Will he recover?"

The physician shrugged. "Anyone's guess. The stomach wound is all right, but the head wound—that's another matter. He'll either wake up, or he won't." So saying, he took his leave, his footsteps echoing along the barren walls.

Lenoir entered the room hesitantly. He found a stool jammed in the narrow space between the wall and the pallet on which the sergeant lay, and he perched on the edge of it, folding his fingers awkwardly in his lap. As his gaze took in the length of Kody's prostrate form, something suspiciously like guilt tugged at the bottom of his stomach.

The sergeant's features were cast in harsh relief, brushed in lamplight and chiseled out of shadow. Combined with the pallor of his skin, it gave him a ghoulish look, like a man hovering somewhere between life and death—which, Lenoir supposed, was exactly what he was. He was too tall for the pallet, his feet hanging over the edge in a position that would surely have been uncomfortable if he were awake. Lenoir rose from the stool and propped it under Kody's feet. Bereft of any place to sit, he slumped against the wall.

How sentimental you have become, Lenoir. A week ago, you would not have bothered to visit this man at all. Now you fret over his circulation.

He was not really sure why he had come. To pass the time, he supposed, until darkness fell. It was better than being alone. Kody was alone too; his parents no longer lived in Kennian, and his fellow hounds were out scouring the streets for his attacker. Lenoir could have pointed them in the right direction, but Zera would certainly have fled by the time they arrived, and he could not risk unleashing hordes of incompetent hounds on his crime scene. They would only destroy whatever clues might remain. Better to wait for Vincent, who was more useful than any backup the Metropolitan Police Department had to offer.

He would not have long to wait. The afternoon was waning fast. The days were growing short, and darkness would drop swiftly from the sky like a hawk diving for its prey. He should be looking forward to dusk, to Vincent's arrival. In spite of his miserable failure with the duke, he had tangible progress to report. He should be thrilled to have stumbled across such an important lead. It was providence itself, a life preserver in a heaving sea, thrown to his grasping arms in the final moments before drowning. But he could not find it in himself to be grateful for it. Instead he felt more alone than ever before.

"Why should I care, Kody?" he asked aloud. "What was she to me, or I to her?"

The man on the bed did not stir.

"I confided little in her, and she still less in me. I was just another patron in her salon." Yet they had been kindred spirits, if not exactly friends, keen students of human nature who perceived the world around them with uncommon clarity. They saw the hidden gears and levers that powered the machine of society. Even more significantly, they understood each other, a rare and precious bond for two people who were not accustomed to being understood. Close or not, Zera had known Lenoir better than anyone else in the Five Villages. That she should be involved in the only crime he had cared about in a decade was a bitter twist of fate.

"How blind I have become. As bad as every other slob in the kennel, unable to follow his own logic to its necessary conclusion. Instead I sit in perfect ignorance until the perpetrator herself spells it out for me." He shook his head in disgust. "Of course a man like Warrick has no connections in the Adali community. Even if the idea was his own, how could he have found someone willing to admit they practiced *khekra*? He would need a proxy, someone with connections in that world."

Kody's handsome features were stern, even in repose. His eyebrows sat heavily over his eyelids, and his mouth turned down slightly at the edges, giving it a disapproving cast.

"Yes," said Lenoir quietly, "I am blind. Whatever the scenario—they came to him, or he to them—there is simply no way it plays out without a go-between. Someone the duke already knows, someone well placed in Kennian society. Who else could it have been?" Zera alone had a foot in both worlds; in this, she was certainly unique. If Lenoir had not been such a fool, he would have seen that.

In fact, the more he thought about it, the more likely it seemed that the whole enterprise was Zera's doing. Lady Zera had long been in the business of giving people what they wanted. Lenoir had often admired her almost uncanny ability to home in on secret desires and find a way to satisfy them. She knew how to connect people, how to manipulate them, putting them together as easily as she would a child's jigsaw puzzle.

She knew how to make sure that powerful people were in her debt. Powerful people like the Duke of Warrick.

"Of course she would want the duke in her pocket. An Adal trying to make her way in the big city. So vulnerable. Always just one rumor away from disaster. The duke could free her from that forever." Lenoir understood the cutthroat world of "polite society" too well to consider such designs trivial; he knew them for the matter of survival they truly were.

It was all so obvious, yet Lenoir had failed to see any of it until he was quite literally beaten over the head with it. Years of apathy and inaction had dulled his edge. He had already paid for his sins with his own life, though the debt had yet to be collected. He accepted that. What he could not accept was that Zach might be forced to pay the same toll.

Lenoir leaned over the bed. "Can you hear me?" If so, Kody made no sign. Even his eyeballs were perfectly still beneath the lids. It was just as well, really. If Kody knew how incompetent his supervisor had become, he might conclude that Lenoir was responsible for his state. And he would be right.

Shadows pooled along the floorboards like water in the hull of a slowly sinking ship. The corridor grew dark as weakening shafts of sunlight were slowly strangled by the shutters. Lenoir watched Kody in silence, the passage of time marked by the steady rise and fall of the sergeant's chest.

Lenoir would have sworn that he *felt* it when Vincent arrived, for the touch of darkness raised the hairs on his arms.

The voice spoke behind him, smooth and cold as a pebble. "Did you find the corpse thieves?"

Lenoir did not turn around. "No. But I found something else."

"I seek nothing else."

Lenoir sighed. "I know what you seek, Vincent. And we are very close to finding it. Now that it is dark, I need your help."

The spirit rounded the bed, coming to stand before Lenoir. His absinthe eyes glimmered eagerly in the growing dark. "Tell me."

Lenoir grabbed his coat and stood. "We can talk on the way."

The streetlamps cast softly glowing cones onto the flagstones of the high street. Vincent remained outside their reach, whether by choice or necessity, Lenoir could not tell. They stood before the sandstone facade of Lady Zera's apartments. The windows were dark.

"She most likely left this place right after I did." Lenoir had been reconciled to this fact from the moment he fled the scene, but it still caused his guts to twist over. If he had lost her, he had lost Zach.

"There are people inside," said Vincent.

Lenoir exhaled slowly, savoring the taste of his relief. "How do you know?"

"I smell their blood."

Lenoir shuddered. "You have many gifts, Vincent," he said darkly as he started up the steps. The doors were locked, but that proved to be no obstacle. Vincent simply vanished, and a moment later, the latch opened and the door swung wide. Lenoir stepped into the gloom. The foyer seemed small and close, its familiar outlines suffused in shadow. All was silent. It occurred to him that whoever was in the apartments was almost certainly waiting for him, and they probably assumed he would return with reinforcements. "We should expect resistance," he said, drawing his pistols from under his coat.

The spirit turned his uncanny gaze on Lenoir, and though his face remained expressionless, he somehow exuded an unmistakable air of disdain. He was not concerned about resistance.

Lenoir led the way to the second floor, moving cautiously. A stair creaked beneath his weight; he stopped, listening intently, but there was no movement. He continued on. The second floor spread out before him, illuminated only by the pale glow of streetlamps struggling through thick windows. Zera's sumptuous furnishings were little more than misshapen lumps of shadow. Lenoir scanned the darkness, tracking his pistols from right to left. He took a step, and glass crunched beneath his boot—the remains of the ornament Zera had thrown at him. She had not bothered to tidy up. She was long gone, presumably. Whoever was still in this house had been left behind to deal with the hounds they assumed were coming. So much the better; it left him with someone to interrogate.

"Can you see in this blackness?" Lenoir whispered.

"Of course."

"Is there anyone here?"

Vincent moved through the room, his boots silent

against the plush carpet, his eerie gaze sweeping systematically over the dark shapes of furniture. Lenoir could not suppress a shiver as he watched the spirit prowl. It felt like a nightmare, as though he were concealed behind the sofa, huddled in terror, watching himself from outside his own body as the spirit hunted him. The feeling of being stalked was so visceral that when Vincent looked over and met his eye, Lenoir felt momentarily faint.

"There is blood on the carpet," Vincent said quietly, "but it is long since dried. There is no one in this room."

"There are three rooms on this floor," Lenoir whispered back.

The spirit vanished. Lenoir moved away from the stairs, positioning himself so that his back was against the wall, his pistols trained on the stairway leading down from above. The weapons shimmied slightly, revealing the unsteadiness of his hands. He should have taken a glass of wine before he came. He licked his lips, waiting.

Vincent reappeared, his report consisting of a short shake of his head. Lenoir flicked the barrel of his pistol at the stairs and cocked his chin. Vincent understood; he went first. Lenoir followed a few steps behind, one pistol pointed over the rail to cover the first floor as they ascended. His mind told him that Vincent had searched the room thoroughly, but it was impossible to shake the instinct to protect his flank.

The crack of a rifle shattered the silence. Lenoir started so badly that he nearly lost his balance, and he dropped one of his pistols as he grabbed the rail to prevent himself from falling. Vincent was tossed against the wall with the force of the bullet. For a moment, everything was still. Then the spirit righted himself and continued up the stairs, moving with the same fluid grace as before. He turned left at the top stair and disappeared from Lenoir's view.

A second rifle shot sounded, followed by the hissing pops of flintlock weapons. The handrail exploded into splinters, and a painting plunged from the wall. Lenoir crouched with his arms over his head, his thumb cocking the hammer of his own flintlock even though it was pointed uselessly at the ceiling.

There was a pause, silence. Lenoir glanced up, but all he could see was smoke. It drifted and curled at the top of the stairs, as languid as an opium cloud, lending a strange aura of serenity to the scene. Then someone shouted—a strangled, horrified cry—and the air hummed with the sound of a whip. The floor shuddered beneath something heavy—a body going down, Lenoir guessed. At least one set of footsteps pounded up the stairs above his head. Then more shouting, cursing, and inevitably, screaming. Lenoir sat frozen on the stairs, unable to move, unwilling to bear witness to the horror taking place a few feet away. His scars seemed to itch and squirm, and a cold sweat broke out on his brow. He could hear someone thrashing just above, boots thumping and scraping against the floor.

Vincent would wade through them easily, one by one, driven not by rage or bloodlust, but by whatever power animated his long-dead limbs, whispered in his long-dead ears. He would not stop until Lenoir was the only mortal alive in these apartments.

He will kill them all, and I will never find Zach. The thought came to him suddenly, with perfect clarity, and it was like oil applied to a rusted hinge. Lenoir's knees unlocked. His head came up. His lungs drew air, slowly, unsteadily, until he was ready. He crested the stairs.

He was no longer worried about gunfire. Zera's men had spent every barrel on Vincent, and there was no time to reload. Lenoir's was the only pistol left in the equation, on this floor at least. He leveled it over what was left of the handrail and surveyed the scene.

Vincent was stooped over a body at the far end of the room, unwinding the coils of his scourge. He glanced only briefly at Lenoir, but he did not seem to be wounded. He had obviously been hit multiple times; his clothing was in tatters, his white skin glowing through the bullet holes like a galaxy of stars on a moonless night. Yet whatever injuries he had incurred were already gone. Lenoir recalled how quickly Vincent's flesh had regenerated that day in the street, when the sunlight had melted the tissue from his bones. The screams of Zera's men echoed anew in Lenoir's mind, a sound of incomparable terror as they watched their bullets tear ineffectually through Vincent's flesh. Had there been blood, he wondered? Driving the thought away, he surveyed the rest of the room.

Another body was draped over the back of a chair near the bay window, a pistol beneath each hand. It was too dark to be sure, but it looked as though the man had been shot, probably by one of his own. There was a third man lying prone near Vincent, partially concealed by a sofa. A rifle lay on the floor nearby. This had been the sharpshooter, the man who had taken the first shot. From the way Vincent's body had moved, Lenoir guessed that the ball had taken him in the shoulder, but the spirit had seemed to feel no pain. Certainly he was not feeling any now, neither in his limbs nor in his soul, for he surveyed the scene with his usual dispassion, coiling his cursed whip around his arm.

"There are five more of them," Vincent said. "They fled up the stairs."

"We need to leave at least one of them alive," Lenoir said sternly. "Do you think you can control yourself?"

Something like irritation flashed through the spirit's eyes, and Lenoir wilted a little. "I cannot stay my hand against those who have defiled the dead. But I can delay their execution. You know this to be so; otherwise, you would not be standing here."

Only a supreme effort prevented Lenoir from showing his dread in the face of this reminder of his impending execution. "Good," he said as evenly as he was able, "because we need to question them regarding the whereabouts of their leaders." This time, he did not bother to mention Zach, instead focusing on what Vincent wanted. He hoped it would be enough to persuade the spirit to exercise some restraint.

Lenoir fetched the flintlock he had dropped on the stairs, and they headed up to the third floor, Vincent leading as before. This time Lenoir anticipated the shots, dropping to a crouch as soon as they sounded. Even as they rang out, a heavy set of footsteps took the stairs to the fourth floor. *Coward,* Lenoir thought, even though he knew he would do the same. *Where will he go, anyway?* The only way out was in the opposite direction. Or was it? It occurred to Lenoir that the man might be able to escape onto the roof, and from there to a neighboring building. The town houses were built close enough together that even Lenoir would not have much trouble jumping between them, provided they were roughly the same height. The thought brought a lurch of panic, for Vincent might consider the man who fled to be the token survivor, the only one he intended to leave alive. *If the survivor escaped, they would be right back where I started.*

Lenoir waited until the last of the shots died away before charging up the remaining few steps. Smoke obscured his view, but he could hear what sounded like swords being drawn. There was movement in the haze, and someone lunged at him. Lenoir squeezed the trigger without thinking. His gun went off with a flash and a puff of smoke, and the man grunted, dropping his sword and clutching his chest. His momentum carried him into Lenoir even as his knees started to give way. Lenoir flung the dying man aside, leaving him to tumble down the stairs.

Cursing, Lenoir pointed the barrel of his weapon at the ceiling. The last thing he needed was to pick off targets of his own; Vincent did not require any assistance in that department. Yet if he stayed where he was, he would be forced to defend himself, and he was not skilled enough with a gun to be sure of merely wounding. Better to go after the coward, he decided.

He spun around the rail and headed up, leaving Vincent to deal with the chaos below.

He paused on the landing, gazing up into the gloom. The stairs ended just ahead; this was the top floor. It was only now, as he planted his back against the wall, that it occurred to Lenoir that he might be walking into another ambush, or that some of the men below might follow him up. He could hear nothing over the shouts on the third floor, and could see little for the veil of smoke that continued to drift up the stairs. Vincent was occupied below. Lenoir was on his own.

You are dead anyway, he told himself firmly. *You do this for Zach.* Thus armored, he crept to the top of the stairs.

It was a bedroom, presumably Zera's. It looked to be the only room on this floor, and had sloping walls that suggested an angled roof. That was well; it would make it more difficult for the coward to escape that way, especially if the adjoining buildings were of the same design. Lenoir glanced toward the windows, a pair of which divided the wall opposite him into three sections. Dark curtains concealed the view of the street, making it impossible to tell whether the windows were open or closed. There was no chill, but that proved little; the windows might only have been opened moments before. The stillness of the curtains was similarly unreliable, for the plush material obviously weighed a great deal. It was safest to assume that the coward remained in this room and had not yet escaped onto the roof.

The hearth lay dark against the far wall. A dressing table sat between the windows, with a massive bed opposite. The most likely place to conceal oneself, Lenoir concluded, was behind the bed. He leveled his pistols at what he judged to be chest height. Then he called out, "I will not hurt you."

A flurry of movement and a telltale *click* alerted him to the impending shot, and he dropped to the floor. Splinters and dust showered him from the wall above. Instinctively, he squeezed off a shot of his own, but fortunately he missed by a wide margin. The coward ducked behind the bed again.

"This is unwise, my friend," Lenoir called. "You have at most one shot left, assuming your weapon is double-barreled like mine. I have two. Even if you somehow manage to kill me, I have an ally, one who cannot be harmed by your pistol. But you know that already."

He waited. There was no sound.

"Do you hear that? It is quiet below us. That can mean only thing: your friends are dead. You are the last one alive. I would very much like to keep you that way, but I have little control over the creature I came with." A stifled sob sounded from the other side of the bed. Lenoir knew that terror only too well. He almost felt sorry for the man. But he kept his voice carefully devoid of pity as he said, "He will be here soon. If he sees that you are cooperating with me, he may stay his hand. Otherwise . . ." He let the word hang in the air, malignant and oppressive.

"Keep it away from me." Spoken in little more than

a whisper, the plea barely had enough strength to cross the room.

"I will do what I can." It was the truth, and the most he could promise, but it still felt like a lie. "Put your weapon on the floor and kick it toward the windows where I can see it."

For a moment, there was only silence. Then something heavy sounded against the floor, and a flintlock skittered out from behind the foot of the bed. It came to rest near the far window, spinning lazily over itself. It was a single-barreled weapon. Lenoir was sure he had seen only one gun. He prayed he was right.

"Now stand up slowly and keep your hands where I can see them."

The man stood. His arms stuck out at his sides, as rigid as boards, and Lenoir could see that he was shaking. He wore a sword belt, but the scabbard was empty. Lenoir gestured with his pistol. "Where is your blade?"

"I—I don't know," the man stammered. "I don't remember." Lenoir might not have believed him, but at that moment a dark stain spread across the front of his trousers. In his fear, the poor wretch had wet himself.

"Who are you?" Lenoir asked, deciding to start off easy. He was young, perhaps twenty-five, with long blond hair and wiry limbs. Lenoir thought he looked familiar. "You work for Zera."

The man's gaze flicked briefly to his gun, as though he were reconsidering his surrender. Lenoir doubted he would go for it, but he kept his pistol trained on the man's chest all the same. "Yes," the man said finally.

"Where is she now? Is she with Los?"

The man's eyes widened almost imperceptibly before he averted his gaze, staring down at his boots in a pathetic attempt not to give anything away.

"Where are they?" Lenoir demanded. The man continued to stare at his boots. Lenoir sighed. "We have been through this, my friend. It is in your best interests to answer my questions." More silence.

"My turn," said a familiar voice, and Vincent stepped out of the shadows.

The man shrieked and leapt for his gun. Lenoir dove for the cover of the stairwell. The gun went off. For a moment, everything was still. Then came a moan unlike anything Lenoir had ever heard, a sound of pure despair that froze his blood.

Lenoir straightened. The young man was on his knees, his head bowed in resignation. Vincent stood over him.

"Don't kill him!"

The spirit turned, and Lenoir had to bite his lip to keep from crying out. There was a hole the size of a cherry just above Vincent's right eye. It had already begun to close; in a few seconds, it would be gone. "I am not a fool, mortal," the spirit said disdainfully, seemingly oblivious to the ghastly wound. "If I intended to kill him, he would already be dead." Vincent turned back to the young man, who had begun to sob quietly. "What do you mean to do with him?"

"Ordinarily, I would hang him off the balcony by his ankles." Actually, Lenoir had only done that once, and it had proven to be more trouble than it was worth. But it sounded good. "But since you are here, I don't think we need to bother with that."

He crossed the room and knelt in front of the young man. Grabbing a fistful of straw-colored hair, he jerked the man's head back so that he was looking into Lenoir's eyes. "I want to show you something."

Releasing the man's hair, he pulled back his sleeve to reveal the hideous scar on his forearm. He slapped the wretch's forehead to make sure he was looking. "See this? Do you know what this is?" The man shook his head frantically. "No? Have you never seen a cadaver, my friend? This is dead flesh. Necrotic, it is called. The flesh of a corpse. Do you know how I got this?"

The man's face crumpled, tears and mucus and saliva streaming forth as though someone were wringing out a wet cloth.

"I got it from this creature beside me, this spirit of vengeance. You saw what he has done to your friends."

"Keep it away from me," the man pleaded again, his eyes screwed shut.

"Tell me where they are."

"They *told* us not to get involved with her. They *said* this would happen!"

"Who?"

"The others. My cousin and me, we needed the money. But the others she tried to hire, they said no. They said it was bad business."

"You should have listened," Lenoir said gravely. "Now tell me what I want to know."

"Spare my life! Spare me, and I'll tell you anything!"

It would have been so easy to lie. Lenoir had done it thousands of times before, with little enough justification. Surely even God Himself could not blame Lenoir for lying now. Yet he could not bring himself to do it. Instead he looked up at Vincent and said, "The arm."

He moved aside as Vincent unhooked the whip from his belt. The man scrambled to his feet and tried to flee. Lenoir did not even bother trying to stop him. The scourge caught his arm as he ran past, and the scream it tore from his throat forced Lenoir to shut his eyes.

Lenoir counted to five. It might have been longer, for he could barely concentrate over the screaming. Panic thrummed in his nerves, and he struggled against an almost overwhelming urge to flee. His instincts surged against his willpower like a raging river threatening to breach a dam, but he held his ground.

"Stop."

He forced himself to open his eyes. To his relief, Vincent obeyed immediately, giving his wrist an expert twist to dislodge the scourge. The young man lay on the floor, limp and shuddering. The flesh on his arm was black. Blood oozed from the puncture wounds, dark and strangely thick. The man's eyes rolled back slightly, and for a moment Lenoir feared he would pass out. Instead he lurched suddenly and vomited.

"I know how you feel," said Lenoir, but in spite of the words, there was no sympathy in his voice. "It is a curious sensation, is it not? The body scarcely knows how to process it, the mind still less. The barbs are like the fangs of a venomous snake, only instead of pouring poison into your veins, they suck the life force from you. Or so I imagine—who knows what effect that cursed weapon truly has? It is better, I think, to have the whip around one's neck. That way, you die before you are forced to feel your flesh rotting, before you are forced to smell your own blood congealing. I for one do not wish to savor my death. When it comes, I want it to overwhelm me, not sneak up on me like some miserable thief." He found himself staring at Vincent as he spoke these words. As usual, the spirit merely returned his gaze impassively.

He returned his attention to the young man at his feet. "What about you, friend? How do you want to die?"

The man looked up at Lenoir with haunted eyes. "I want to die old, in my bed."

"Alas, that seems unlikely. But at least you can die with a clean soul." He paused, feeling Vincent's gaze on him.

"A clean soul," the spirit echoed, his voice cool and biting like a winter wind. His uncanny eyes seemed to flare momentarily.

"Tell me where Los is," Lenoir repeated, gently this time.

He could always tell when a man was broken. Sometimes it was the posture—a bowed spine, or slumped shoulders. Sometimes it was the voice, weighed down by resignation and despair. Mostly, though, it was the eyes that gave it away, and this time was no exception. The young man looked up at him dully, all traces of defiance wiped away. All that was left was a flat surface in which Lenoir saw nothing but his own reflection.

"He's in the cathedral," the man said. "The abandoned cathedral at the far end of town."

Relief crashed over Lenoir in a dizzying wave. "And the boy—is he there as well?"

"For now, but he'll be gone by tomorrow, one way or another."

Lenoir frowned. "What do you mean, one way or another?"

"Lady Zera said tonight is the night. If they get it right, the boy won't be himself anymore. If they get it wrong . . ." He did not finish, but he did not have to. Lenoir was already heading for the stairs.

"Do you know where the cathedral is?" Vincent called after him.

"I do."

"What do you want me to do with this one?"

Lenoir paused on the stairs. "Do you have a choice, Vincent?" He spoke in a voice so low it was all but inaudible, even to him. Somehow he knew the spirit could hear him.

"No."

"Then do not ask me."

Lenoir hurried down the stairs and out into the night. He did not wait for Vincent. He knew there was no need.

CHAPTER 24

It had stopped raining. A sharp wind nudged the clouds aside, leaving the moon stark and hard-edged amid a scatter of stars. Standing water pooled along the street, shivering liquid silver under the glare of the moon. The cathedral seemed to rear up from the water like a kraken, vast and dark and disfigured. Lenoir wondered that it should look so sinister to him now. He had taken little enough notice of the place before. It was not a particularly grand building, dating from a period known more for pragmatism than aesthetics. Perhaps that explained why it had been left to hibernate, forgotten and forsaken, for over a century.

He found it strange that Los had chosen this place for a hideout. Lenoir could scarcely imagine a more conspicuous location for criminal activity, or one so supremely inappropriate for performing witchcraft. He knew little of Adali religion, but they were generally considered believers, practicing a hybrid form of worship that blended their native traditions with the Hirradic faith of their southern neighbors. It surprised

Lenoir that Los and his followers would risk God's wrath by bringing heathen witchcraft to His very house. Then again, Los was risking a great deal already. Perhaps conscription into the armies of the damned was just one more item on the list.

Lenoir scanned the grim structure uneasily, wondering how many enemies it sheltered. Would it be possible to gain entry without alerting the kidnappers to his presence? Stealth had never been his gift.

"Do you have a plan?"

The voice in his ear made Lenoir jump. Cursing under his breath, he turned to the spirit. "Our first priority must be the boy. We do not know what they might have done to him, and we do not dare kill his kidnappers until we are sure he is safe, in body and mind."

"That is an objective, not a plan."

Lenoir scowled, but he knew the spirit was right. "It would be ideal if we could find the boy without being discovered."

Vincent considered the cathedral. "He is in the crypts, belowground."

"How do you know?"

"I saw him."

Lenoir opened his mouth to seek an explanation, but decided he did not want to know. Instead he asked, "Is he well? Are the kidnappers with him?"

"He lives. His captors are with him."

"How many?"

"I saw five, plus the boy."

Lenoir could scarcely control his impatience. He had found Zach at last. All he had to do was separate the boy from his captors and the day would be won. "Assuming the kidnappers are all together, it should be safe to enter through the front door."

Vincent disappeared, and Lenoir headed for the main doors. He waited for several agonizing minutes before there was any sign of movement. Thumps and scrapes sounded softly from the other side, as from a great distance. The doors were obviously massive in girth as well as height, and Vincent seemed to be having difficulty opening them. Eventually, however, there came a great, cavernous creak, and one side of the door drew inward. Absinthe eyes flashed in the gloom.

"The nave is empty," Vincent said, "and I do not smell anyone nearby. They are all in the crypts."

Lenoir shuddered. Perhaps the location was not so inappropriate after all. Over the course of centuries, an unknown number of Kennians had been entombed in the network of catacombs beneath the cathedral. It made a grim kind of sense that Los would surround himself with the dead while attempting to call forth one of their own.

"The entrance is at the base of the tower," Vincent said, "through the vestry." Seeing Lenoir's surprise, he added, "I have been here before, more than once."

"Lead on, then."

It proved difficult to follow, for it was almost pitch-black inside. Lenoir sensed, rather than saw, the vastness of the room around him, seeming to stretch in all directions. He caught only glimpses of Vincent, for the spirit's hair and clothing were as black as their surroundings; only the occasional flash of his eyes marked his location. Lenoir kept to the center of the aisle, or so he judged, his fingers groping the shadows for potential obstacles. The last thing he needed was to shatter his knees against the invisible pews.

"This way," Vincent called softly, and Lenoir turned awkwardly to his right. The door to the vestry was unlocked, and he moved through it to a room that was, impossibly, even darker. "The stairway is here." Vincent spoke in a whisper now. "Above us is the tower. Below is the way to the crypts."

Following the sound of Vincent's voice, Lenoir found a door that stood ajar. He nudged it aside. A faint glow from somewhere below sketched the outline of stone steps leading down. Lenoir could just make out another set of stairs leading up from his right, curling in a tight spiral to ascend the tower.

He headed down, moving as silently as he could. He could sense Vincent behind him. Cold, damp air seeped from the bowels of the cathedral, clinging to his skin like a wet rag. It carried a faintly metallic smell, and beneath that, the scent of paraffin.

The stairs curved gently as they descended, eventually disgorging him into a well-lit room of rough and ancient-looking construction. A thick stone wall with several archways divided the room into two naves, each of them containing a barrel-vaulted sanctuary. There had once been some kind of adornment in the sanctuaries—frescoes of Durian, Lenoir guessed, or perhaps the Generals of the Host—but the paint had long since worn away, leaving only scraps of color. The lower half of the wall was built from huge slabs of unremarkable gray stone, but the archways had been lined with fine red brick. Cassiterian, Lenoir judged, salvaged from whatever temple had once stood on these foundations. He knew little of architecture, but the crypt clearly dated from the early classic period. *Still, it is younger than Vincent,* he thought, and he could not suppress a giddy laugh.

At the far end of the room, a set of steps descended into a long hallway. "Where does that go?" Lenoir whispered.

"It leads to the dead," said Vincent, "and also to the living."

The tunnel reeked of paraffin from the torches that lined the walls at irregular intervals. The smoke stung Lenoir's eyes as he scanned the area for places to hide. There were none; if one of the kidnappers should appear, he would spot the intruders immediately. There was not even enough shadow for Vincent to move instantly from one place to the next. Like Lenoir, he would have to walk.

Lenoir blinked. He spun suddenly, looking at Vincent; the spirit returned his gaze impassively. *So much for* that *question,* Lenoir thought. Vincent was unharmed by the torches. Sunlight alone, it seemed, was his enemy.

A pair of recessed archways appeared in the walls about fifty paces ahead, and as Lenoir approached, he saw that they were packed with skulls. Row upon row of them had been stacked together in neat lines, completely filling the recess. Glancing farther down the hall, Lenoir noticed several more such archways lining the corridor. He was reminded of the catacombs beneath his beloved Serles, where the skulls and leg bones of millions of Arrènais formed the brick and mortar of a vast necropolis beneath the bustling streets. He wondered, as he had so often in Serles, who these people were, how they had come to be here. Was it a privilege, or a punishment? And where were the rest of their remains?

Vincent paused at the first archway, his gaze drifting over the skulls, lingering on one or two as though they were especially significant. He whispered something in a language Lenoir did not recognize. Could the spirit identify these bones as individuals? Did he know their names, and the lives they had led? *"I saw him,"* Vincent had said earlier. Now Lenoir understood. Vincent had seen Zach and the kidnappers pass down this hallway. He had watched them through the eyes of these very skulls. Feeling a sudden chill, Lenoir gathered his coat more tightly around him and pressed on.

The hallway seemed to go on forever. Torchlight seethed and flared along the walls, contrasting eerily with the perfect stillness of the dead. The skulls watched Lenoir's progress from their archways, empty eye sockets seeming to follow as he passed. He could feel Vincent's presence just behind him. The sensation of being watched pressed in on him from either side. The corridor felt cramped and impossibly crowded. Lenoir began to sweat, in spite of the cold.

A pair of torches ahead signaled the end of the hallway. They flanked a single closed door. Lenoir glanced over his shoulder at Vincent. "What will we find on the other side of that door?"

"It is another room like the one we entered from, only much larger."

"Are there any more skulls inside?" Lenoir was slowly becoming more accustomed to using Vincent's supernatural gifts to their advantage.

But the spirit shook his head. "Once, but no longer. I cannot see into that room."

Lenoir approached the door cautiously, bending his head against it to listen. The torches rustled and snapped overhead, but he heard nothing else. "Is there anything beyond this room?" he whispered.

"Yes, but I know little of those halls. These catacombs have known many uses."

Lenoir thought. "Can you travel to the other side of this door?"

Again, Vincent shook his head. "It is not dark enough for me to travel that way."

"Well, then," Lenoir sighed, "ready your weapon, Vincent." He drew one of his pistols, cocked it, and grabbed the cold iron handle of the door. Closing his eyes and uttering a silent prayer, he swung the door open.

Vincent swept past, as swift and silent as the shadow of a hawk. Cursing, Lenoir dove in after him, gun raised, his eyes raking his surroundings. He had only a fraction of a second to take it in: the huddle of bodies in the far corner, heads turning, eyes wide with shock. The air seemed to go out of the room in a single, collectively drawn breath. Then everyone started shouting.

Vincent's whip had already found someone's throat. The man was yanked forward with the force of it, his scream strangled off by the grip of the scourge. The others scattered. Lenoir hesitated, frozen with indecision as he tried to spot Zach amid the chaos. The kidnappers were flowing out of the room like cockroaches fleeing the light, darting beneath archways to disappear into the tunnels beyond. Lenoir could not see the boy. But he did glimpse a familiar face, a pair of beautiful, fierce eyes glaring hatefully at him from the depths of a hood. *Zera.* He pointed his gun at her, but she only sneered and fled the room. Without thinking, Lenoir went after her.

The torchlight from the room behind barely managed to penetrate the tunnel, and soon Lenoir was moving through darkness. He blinked furiously in a vain effort to hasten the adjustment of his eyes, straining to hear the sound of Zera's retreating footsteps. She had been on the opposite side of the room, and had a few seconds' head start. If she knew her way around these tunnels, she would have even more of an advantage. Lenoir tried not to think about it as he charged blindly ahead.

What are you doing here, Zera? And yet somehow, Lenoir was not surprised, even though it made little objective sense. Some part of him even admired her for it, however grudgingly. *How headstrong you are, and how foolish. You should have left this city behind. But you just had to be here, didn't you, to witness your triumph firsthand?* Lenoir had seen it in her eyes as they faced off in the salon, a burning defiance that would not be cowed, no matter the danger. *You are not afraid of me. Even now, you think you will win. You will not let it go. And so neither will I.*

A wall reared up unexpectedly in the dark, so close that Lenoir nearly crashed into it. The tunnel had come to a dead end. He must have run past a branching corridor somewhere. Cursing, he retraced his steps at a trot. He had not gone far when he felt a breath of cold air on his cheek, and he reached out, his fingers grasping the corner of an archway. A faint dripping sound drifted through the darkness. Lenoir passed under the arch and kept moving.

After a few minutes, the outline of the tunnel began to glow faintly. Lenoir came to a room that joined two corridors. Torchlight from the far corridor revealed several rows of what appeared to be wine casks. There were at least two dozen of them, their arched backs clustered together like a herd of beasts grazing silently in the shadows.

He started across the room. Suddenly, he glimpsed movement to his left, and he whipped around just in time to see someone leveling a crossbow at him. Lenoir ducked as the bolt whizzed overhead, shattering against the stone wall at the far end of the room. He could hear his attacker reloading, and he crouched, but it was too dark to see between the barrels. Keeping low, Lenoir moved back one row, away from the lit corridor. He wanted to keep as much of the room between himself and the light as possible, giving him the visual advantage. Any move his attacker made would be backlit, whereas Lenoir would be lost in shadow.

He gulped in air, trying to bring his labored breathing under control. It sounded horribly loud to his ears; he was sure it would give away his position. *It serves you right,* he thought bitterly. He had let himself get too out of shape, and now even a short burst of running was enough to tax his lungs. He tried to listen past his own breathing, straining for any sign of his attacker. If the man got the drop on Lenoir, it would be over. Crossbows were deadly accurate at short range, and unlike flintlocks, they gave no warning of an imminent shot.

Lenoir had seen enough of his attacker to be sure it was not Zera. Every second he wasted in this room let her slip farther from his grasp. He could not afford to crouch here, waiting for the other man to make the next move. Reaching into his pocket, Lenoir drew out his watch. It was an expensive piece, one of the last mementos he had of Serles. He ran his thumb over it regretfully, feeling the familiar texture of the engraved back. Then, readying his pistol, he threw it.

The watch landed near the door with a forlorn clatter. A shadow moved to Lenoir's left. He fired. The shadow staggered and flailed, knocking over one of the casks. Under cover of the noise, Lenoir charged. The man was lying prone, grasping for his fallen crossbow, when Lenoir appeared from behind a cask and unloaded the second barrel of his pistol. The man jerked and went still. Lenoir dropped the spent flintlock into his coat pocket and drew his other gun. Two shots left, and no time to reload. He would need to spend them wisely. Sparing a sad glance at the innards of his shattered watch, Lenoir passed through the door at the far end of the room and into the lit tunnel beyond.

To his right, the tunnel only extended a few feet before coming to an abrupt end, like an unfinished thought. To his left, it disappeared in a distant haze of paraffin smoke. Lenoir judged that it ran roughly parallel to the tunnel from which he had come, probably leading back to the large room with its many arched passageways. He took off at a run, feeling more confident now that he could see his surroundings.

He had guessed correctly: the tunnel ended at the room where Lenoir had first come upon the kidnappers. It was empty now, save for the corpse of the man Vincent had slain. Lenoir paused. He could continue to search these corridors aimlessly, but it would take time, and it would be dangerous. Besides, he doubted that whoever had Zach would stay here, not with Vincent prowling around in the dark. It would make more sense to flee the cathedral altogether. So decided, he made his way back down the corridor lined with skulls. The dead watched him pass, their secrets unspoken, at least to him.

When he reached the bottom of the stairs leading to the vestry, he hesitated, wondering if he should grab a torch. The cathedral was a great cavern of black, with too many places to hide. He had no wish to blunder blindly about. Yet the torch would mark his position like a beacon; he would be an easy target, especially for a pistol or bow.

He heard a faint noise, something he would have missed entirely had he still been moving. It sounded like the scuffle of a shoe, and it was coming from somewhere above.

Lenoir took the stairs as quickly as he dared. The

light faded as he ascended, until it was all but gone. He stopped at the top of the stairs, listening. A rustle sounded from above, so subtle that he almost thought he had imagined it.

The tower.

Lenoir crouched at the bottom of the spiral stairs. He breathed deeply, trying to keep his panting quiet, and the drafts of air brought a familiar scent to his nose. It tickled his memory; for a moment he could not place it. *Lilac? No—jasmine.* Then he remembered: Zera always smelled faintly of jasmine. Cocking the hammer of his pistol, he started up the stairs.

Suddenly, the walls reverberated with a sound that made Lenoir's heart lurch. It poured down the narrow stairwell like a deluge of cold water, drenching him in horror. The screams were wild and inarticulate, the terror of a mind driven past reason. Lenoir knew that voice, knew it as laughter and questions and tall tales. It was thin and high-pitched, the voice of a child.

Lenoir took the stairs two at a time.

CHAPTER 25

The screams continued, horribly amplified by the tight stairwell, ringing in Lenoir's ears until he thought he would go mad. He scrabbled his way up the stairs, using both hands now, clawing at the stone walls with fingers that were raw and bleeding. It was the only way to keep his balance, for the steps were shallow and steep, the stone worn smooth with time. He was grateful for the dark, for it spared him from vertigo. One misstep would send him tumbling down, and he would almost certainly break his neck.

The screaming stopped as abruptly as it had begun. Lenoir would not have thought anything could be worse than that sound, but the silence was more ominous still. He tried to quicken his pace, but his legs burned, and his breath came in wheezing gulps. Still the stairs coiled relentlessly above him, reaching into folds of blackness. He had never paid much attention to the tower from the outside, but he recalled that it was visible for several miles around. He had no idea how far he had climbed, or how many stairs remained. *It does not matter. You must continue.*

From above, Lenoir heard what he thought sounded like glass breaking. He ignored it and pressed on, hoping it was a sign that Zach was still struggling. Gradually, the smell of paraffin filled his nose, growing stronger as he ascended. He slowed warily. A moment later, his step sounded with a wet *splat*. Orange light flared suddenly from above. Lenoir leapt back just as the stairs burst into flames, a carpet of fire rushing down the steps with a roar. His boot took light. It burned hungrily, but he managed to tamp the flames down enough to kick it off.

He swore viciously, shielding his eyes from the stinging black smoke. He had managed to avoid being roasted, but it would be a long time before the paraffin burned itself out. The flames were not high, but they were hot, and he dared not risk getting any of the paraffin on himself, especially now that he only had one boot. This was not going to be easy.

He fished the spent flintlock out of his coat pocket and holstered it along with its mate. Pressing himself flat against the outer wall, he craned his neck, trying to see as far up as he could. It did not look as though the fire covered too many steps. He would have to risk it. Taking a deep, steadying breath, he flung his coat down over the flames. He managed to stretch it over three steps, but it was not enough; the fire continued to burn above him. There was nothing for it; Lenoir gritted his teeth and ran through the flames.

It took only a few seconds, but it felt like an eternity. The sole of Lenoir's left foot burned instantly in the hot oil, and he could not suppress a scream as he brought his weight down on it. He crossed over the last of the paraffin-soaked steps and peeled off his flaming sock, lifting a thick layer of skin along with it. He bit his lip to prevent another scream and permitted himself a few seconds perched on the stairs, his head swimming with the pain. He tore off the sleeve of his shirt, pausing to steel himself before wrapping his foot in the fabric. He would not be able to put his full weight on it, but he was at least ambulatory.

You can slow me down, Zera, but you cannot stop me. I am coming for the boy. Perhaps it was the pain, but he felt lighter somehow, as though something more than skin had burned away. He had walked through fire and emerged—not purged, not purified, but *whole*, and his blood sang with the triumph of it. Gingerly, he got to his feet. By the light of the flames, he could see that the stairwell ended not far above. He pushed himself up the remaining stairs.

Night swept through the crack of the open door. Lenoir smelled rain. He paused at the threshold, pistol readied. He could hear nothing.

"It's over, Zera," he called. She knew he was there, anyway.

"You're right, Nicolas," her voice drifted through the dark. "And yet you continue to pursue me, when you must realize that it will get you killed. What do you care for this boy, anyway?"

"I don't really know," Lenoir answered, peering through the crack in the door. Dawn was breaking over the horizon, but there was not enough light to see by.

Zera's voice seemed to come from straight ahead, possibly from behind the bell cote, but he could not be sure. He needed to keep her talking.

"Of all the boys in the Five Villages," she said, "my fool associates had to pick up your pet. But even so—what is he to you, really? Little more than a trained monkey. And yet here you are, about to die for him. It is not like you, Nicolas. You are usually far more pragmatic."

"Zach," Lenoir called, "are you all right?"

"He can't hear you," Zera returned coolly. "He is well past the reach of this world."

Zach's screams seemed to echo anew in Lenoir's brain. He shoved his way through the door. It was a reckless move, and he paid the price. Someone tackled him to the floor, driving the air from his lungs and pinning him beneath an enormous weight. Lenoir's gun went off as it hit the floor. His attacker grabbed his wrist and twisted, wrenching the flintlock free and knocking it aside. Lenoir found himself staring up into the bloodshot gaze of the largest Adal he had ever seen. The man's hands closed around his throat.

"Hurry, Los," Zera called. "It's almost daybreak."

Lenoir was amazed at how cold the woman was. Earlier, in the salon, she had at least seemed regretful that they had been pitted against each other. Now, within sight of her goal, she cared no more for him than if he were a perfect stranger. *How little we can truly know another person,* he thought. Even someone like him, who made it his business to read people, had been completely taken in.

Focus, you fool!

His mind had already begun to wander as he was

deprived of air; he struggled to stay alert. He pictured the boy: that was his anchor. He fumbled for the gun holstered at his waist. It was empty, but he doubted he would be able to get a shot off anyway. He had something else in mind.

Los did not realize what Lenoir was doing until it was too late. The Adal released Lenoir's throat to grab at his hand, allowing him to gulp down a precious lungful of air before slamming the butt of his pistol into the side of Los's head. The Adal reeled, and Lenoir rolled out from under him, coughing and gasping. He gazed frantically about for the other pistol. Los was reaching for it too. Lenoir grabbed the other man by the cuff of his trousers, and they struggled. The Adal was stronger by far, but Lenoir still had his empty flintlock. He managed to get another good blow in to the side of Los's face before twisting away, his fingers grazing the hilt of his other gun.

He was just about to grab it when Zera kicked the pistol out of his reach. Lenoir snarled in frustration and grabbed her ankle instead, bringing her down. Los landed a solid punch against Lenoir's temple, and his vision flared. Another like that and he would be out cold. In desperation, he brought his knee up under the Adal's groin and found his mark.

Throwing Los off him, Lenoir scrambled on all fours to reach his loaded pistol. He got there just in time, spinning and firing just as Los leapt at him. The ball caught the Adal in the neck; Los was dead before he fell, collapsing on top of Lenoir in an inert heap. Lenoir lay still for a moment, catching his breath. As the dead man's blood spread across his chest, so too did the realization of what he had done. Los was the witchdoctor. Whatever he had done to Zach, he was in no position to undo it now. For all Lenoir knew, Los was the only man in the world who knew whether Zach's condition could be reversed.

But Lenoir could not dwell on that now, for there was a more pressing matter to attend to. He rolled the dead man off him and stood awkwardly, his injured foot making him unsteady. He did not see Zera right away; she must be somewhere on the opposite side of the bell cote.

He rounded the wooden frame and stopped dead, the barrel of his pistol lowering a fraction. "You would not dare," he whispered in horror.

Zera's eyes sparkled madly. "Wouldn't I?"

Zach lay unconscious on the parapet, his hair ruffling serenely in the wind. He was inches from the edge. Zera had the collar of his shirt twisted in her fist; the barest move of her arm would shove him over the side. The fall was two hundred feet at least.

Lenoir leveled his pistol. "Let him go."

"I don't think you really want me to do that," she returned smoothly, her voice a dark mockery of the cajoling tone she used at the salon.

"You know what I mean. Get away from him, or I will shoot."

Zera only smiled. "You seem to be forgetting, my dear Nicolas, that you are empty."

He *had* forgotten, or he might have been able to bluff his way through. But the dismay showed on his face, and her smile only widened.

"Don't worry, Nicolas. I have a solution." She paused

to let that sink in. Behind her, dawn slashed the belly of the sky, a bloody red pooling on the floor of the horizon. It was a dawn Lenoir had not really expected to see, yet he felt no joy in looking upon it. Indeed, he resented its intrusion, for it stripped him of his only ally. Vincent could not come to him now. He was on his own.

"What is your solution?" he growled.

"You want the boy returned to you unharmed, yes? I am willing to do that, provided that you allow me safe passage out of Kennian. You will turn around and go back down those stairs. You will leave the cathedral and take the west road back to the center of town. I will watch your progress from here. When I judge you are far enough away, I will leave the boy here in the tower and disappear. You will never see me again. Is that simple enough?"

Lenoir considered. His gut burned in protest at the idea of letting Zera go. She should be made to pay for what she had done. Yet his mind told him it was the only way. He had no doubt Zera would make good on her threat. He could see it in her eyes, that look of an animal cornered, of a creature that will do anything to survive.

"If I let you go, how do I know you will not simply kill the boy anyway?"

"Why would I do that? I'm not a monster, Nicolas, in spite of what you may think. I am prepared to make sacrifices for what I want, but I take no pleasure it. I have nothing against the boy."

"And what of his condition? How can I be sure he will recover?"

She shrugged. "I have no idea. I'm no witchdoctor. You'll have to figure that out on your own, whether you let me go or not."

Lenoir hesitated a few moments longer, but deep down, he knew he had already made his choice. She was right and they both knew it. Besides, Vincent would track her down eventually. Like him, Zera was marked for death.

"Very well," he said, "I agree to your terms. I will leave you here with the boy and head in the direction of the station. You can watch me for as many blocks as it pleases you. I will return in three-quarters of an hour, by which time I expect you to be gone, and the boy to be alone in the tower, unharmed."

"That is acceptable," Zera said.

"No," said another voice, "it is not."

Zera hissed in anger and surprise as Vincent stepped around the bell cote. Startled, Lenoir looked immediately to the horizon. Dawn had already cast a thin blanket of light over the city. The only shadow remaining at the top of the tower was formed by the lee of the bell cote. Vincent's left side was exposed. Looking back at him, Lenoir saw that his flesh had begun to turn an angry red; tiny tendrils of smoke rose from the surface of his skin. If the spirit felt any pain, however, he gave no sign. He stared at Zera, his absinthe eyes seeming to pin her in place like a stunned rabbit. "She cannot go free," he said.

Fear clutched Lenoir's heart in a cold fist as he realized what Vincent intended. "We must do as she asks," he said, unconsciously raising his hand in a warding gesture. "The boy is in danger."

"The boy is not my concern. This woman has sinned against the dead. She must be punished."

"Her punishment can wait!" Lenoir's voice was shrill with desperation.

"I have only moments left." Emphasizing his words, the skin on his left hand opened and began to burn away. "By the time night returns, she will be gone."

"She cannot escape you!"

Vincent turned his gleaming gaze on Lenoir. "You did."

Lenoir could hear Zera's terrified breathing from where he stood, a near-hysterical sound that rose in pitch with every successive breath. Any second now, she would bolt. Vincent would stop her. But by then it would be too late. She would push Zach before she ran, hoping the move would buy her a few seconds' distraction. Lenoir saw it all as clearly as if he were watching a play he had seen before.

"Please," he said, his voice scarcely audible even to his own ears. "Just let me save the boy."

For the barest of seconds, the stained glass of Vincent's eyes cracked. Lenoir saw the humanity behind, a frail and tortured thing that peered out like a prisoner longing to be free. "My will is not my own," the spirit whispered, and the voice seemed to come from somewhere behind those eyes, instead of the cold, hollow depths of his chest.

Then, as suddenly as it had appeared, the crack in Vincent's gaze was gone, the smooth, imperturbable surface restored. He turned away, stepping fully into the sunlight.

His flesh withered and peeled back in coils of smoke. Raw muscle appeared, only to blacken and char, revealing the white bone beneath. Lenoir's stomach heaved, but he could not bring himself to look away. Like Zera, he was pinned to the spot.

Zera swooned as though she might faint, but she retained enough presence of mind to jerk her arm, threatening Zach. Lenoir thought he saw Vincent's step lurch, his stride momentarily broken, but he continued forward. Lenoir was helpless to stop him, and too far away to prevent Zera from doing what he knew she would. Still, he moved, his limbs feeling heavy and foreign as the world itself seemed to slow.

With a hateful shriek, Zera pushed Zach from the parapet. It happened so fast that all Lenoir saw was a flutter of clothing disappearing over the edge. He threw himself at Zera, roaring in fury as he drove her to the floor. He did not care if he was in Vincent's way. He did not care if the spirit killed them both. He drove his fist into Zera's face, again and again.

A scream snapped him out of his blind rage. It was Zach's voice, and it was coming from just over the parapet. Lenoir scrambled to his feet, staggering at the sight that greeted him.

A charred and bloodied Vincent was hauling back on his whip like a fisherman with a huge catch, dragging something unseen over the parapet. His blackened flesh was kindled into flame, burning away what remained of his muscle. In moments, he would lose the ability even to move. Lenoir lunged at the parapet. Zach was dangling by his arm, the scourge wrapped tightly around his wrist. The boy was screaming as his flesh died in the grasp of the accursed weapon. Reaching down as far as he could, Lenoir grabbed Zach's forearm and heaved.

They tumbled over the top together. Lenoir heard the air hum as the whip came free and found a new target, and then his ears were filled with Zera's screams. He twisted his head to see what remained of Vincent drop to his knees, his bare bones cracking against the stone. Only scraps of flesh hung from him now, but he no longer needed any. The scourge did its work without his help, squeezing the life from Zera's throat in seconds. Then, as Lenoir watched, Vincent disintegrated into a pile of ash. The scourge flashed once with a faint green light and vanished, leaving Zera's blackened throat behind. Moments later, even the ash was gone, borne on the wind to God-knew-where.

Lenoir rolled Zach gently onto his back. The boy's skin was deathly pale, but his eyelids fluttered. Suddenly, his body lurched, and he began to choke. Lenoir just managed to get him onto his side before he vomited. Instinctively, the boy's arm curled up to his stomach, as though he could protect it from the pain he remembered, or the morbid sensation that had replaced it. He opened his eyes and gasped.

"It's all right, Zach," Lenoir said gently. "You are safe now."

The boy's eyes fixed on him. There was no recognition there, only lingering terror. Lenoir's heart sank. He had seen that look before, in the eyes of the boy Mika, whose experience left his mind violently shattered.

"You are safe, Zach," he repeated, more firmly this time.

Slowly, Zach's gaze came into focus. Fear gave way to confusion, then relief. He tried to speak, but succeeded only in choking again. Lenoir helped the boy to sit until the coughing fit subsided.

"Where is he?" Zach gasped.

Lenoir hesitated. "Who?" He hoped Zach had no memory of Vincent. The boy had gone through enough without having a sight such as that to haunt him for the rest of his days.

"The other boy."

Lenoir shivered. "You saw him?"

Zach paused, confusion returning to his eyes. "Sure I did. He was here. I mean . . ." He trailed off uncertainly.

"It does not matter. What matters is that you are safe, and we can go home."

"Home," the orphan repeated absently, as though testing a foreign word. Lenoir kicked himself inwardly for his thoughtlessness. But Zach had other things on his mind; he looked down at his arm, hefting it awkwardly as though it did not quite belong to him. "My wrist feels funny." He took in the sight of his blackened flesh with surprising equanimity. Perhaps all his fear was spent.

Lenoir sighed. "Yes. That will never go away, I'm afraid, but you will get used to it. And yours is a small wound, hardly noticeable. It will not greatly affect your life."

Zach nodded, accepting this appraisal without comment. He looked around, seeming to take in his surroundings for the first time. His gaze came to rest on Zera. "Who's that?"

Lenoir looked over. She lay on her stomach, her

face turned toward them, eyes fixed on some distant plane. Lenoir wondered whether she could see Vincent. He wondered whether Vincent was looking out at them through her eyes. He shivered again. "That is Lady Zera," he said, surprised at the tinge of regret in his voice.

"She's dead."

"Yes, she is."

"I guess I don't need to work for her anymore, huh?" Zach looked up at him, and for the first time, Lenoir saw something like the familiar boyish curiosity blooming in his eyes. He could not help smiling.

"No, I don't suppose you do."

"I'm hungry."

Lenoir got to his feet, extending his hand to help the boy. "Well, then, we should get you something to eat. But first, I think we had better find a place to wash up."

They headed for the stairs, Lenoir limping on his injured foot, Zach wobbling on shaky legs. "Is it too early for steak?" Zach asked.

"I don't think so."

Lenoir held the door open. Zach paused on his way under Lenoir's arm, looking up at him severely. "You took a really long time, you know."

"I know," Lenoir said softly. "I am sorry, Zach."

The boy shrugged. "You can make it up to me later."

Lenoir forced a smile. He could never make it up to Zach, not if he had a hundred years, let alone the single day that remained to him. But for the next few hours at least, he was damn well going to try. He could not think of a better way to spend his last day alive.

CHAPTER 26

"This place is small," Zach said, scanning Lenoir's apartment with an air of faint surprise.

"It is," Lenoir agreed, "though it is surely more comfortable than your quarters at the orphanage."

"Not much," Zach said with the brutal honesty of the young. "You really live here?"

"You thought it would be grander, perhaps?"

The boy shrugged. "I guess so, yeah. I mean, you're an *inspector*." He pronounced the word almost reverently.

"Indeed. A poor public servant, alas." Lenoir gave a mock bow. "I do not wish to blunt your ambition, Zach, but it is not so very glamorous being a hound. The truth is, we hounds occupy a modest rung on the social ladder. I suspect there are talented whores who earn more than I do."

"A good whore does pretty well, from what I've seen."

Lenoir regarded him with rueful affection. A child in one breath, a seasoned adult in the next. Perhaps that was what drew him to the boy—that compelling mix of innocence and experience. Living proof that it was possible to live among the poison without becoming fatally ill, that one could see the world for what it truly was, yet still work toward something better. "Would you prefer to sleep at the orphanage?" he asked.

Zach shook his head. "I won't get any sleep there. The sisters will ask me a million questions, and the other kids too."

"So I thought. Rest here, then. Later on, you can go down to the station and give your statement."

Zach looked up at him. "What do you mean, *I* can go down? You'll come with me, right?"

Lenoir pasted on a smile. "Yes, of course. Now rest."

The boy was fast asleep within minutes. He was exhausted, but otherwise appeared none the worse for his ordeal—except, of course, for the scar on his wrist. Lenoir found he did not have it in him to explain the nature of the injury, or how Zach came to have it. Lenoir had not spoken of it again since they quit the tower, and Zach had not asked. The boy seemed to accept the scar as a relatively benign consequence of his captivity, and considering what had almost happened to him, Lenoir could not disagree.

He left Zach in peace and headed for the station. He would send one of the watchmen to the orphanage to tell the nuns that Zach was safe. He had debated going himself, but he needed to use these last few hours to file his report, for there would never be another opportunity, and he did not want the details of the case to die with him. Not that there would be much for the Metropolitan Police to follow up—there were no arrests to be made, at least not with the evidence on hand, and anyone whose involvement could be proven had already received judgment. But Kody's family, and Hardin's, deserved to know what had happened to their sons.

The station was nearly deserted. The hounds were still swarming the streets in search of Hardin's killer. Lenoir found the chief in his office, poring over a stack of recently penned reports, his leathery face pulled into a forbidding scowl.

"Where in the flaming prisons of the below have you been?" Reck said as he looked up from his papers. "I was beginning to think you got the same treatment as Hardin!"

Lenoir sat. He had not been invited to, but he did not think he could stay on his feet for much longer without passing out. He had never been so exhausted in all his life. "I told you I was tracking down the kidnappers."

"That was two days ago!"

Lenoir snorted incredulously. "Two days," he whispered in amazement.

"Is something funny, Inspector?"

Lenoir rubbed his eyes, the lids feeling like rasps against the bloodshot orbs. "No, Chief. It's just that I can hardly believe it has only been two days. So much has happened."

Mollified, the chief sat back in his chair, arms folded. "So let's hear it."

"I know who attacked Kody and Hardin," Lenoir said without preamble. "At least, I know who ordered it done, and where it took place."

Reck grunted. "I'm relieved to hear it, because we're getting nowhere out there." He gestured dismissively at the pile of papers on his desk. "Fifty reports, and the best information we have is that Kody bought a meat pie across the street. The rest of it we already knew. He talked to Izar before he left, but he didn't say where he was going, or why. Izar is in a state, as you can imagine. Thought he should have seen it coming, and other such guilt-ridden nonsense."

"Ridiculous. It would have been nearly impossible for anyone to reconstruct Kody's lead based on what he learned at the prison, even if the prisoners cooperated fully."

"Which they manifestly did not. Stedman, idiot that he is, started off the interview by telling the prisoner that Hardin was dead. Guess how eager she was to talk after that." Reck shook his head in disgust. "If I thought I could get by with only three inspectors, I would just fire him and get it over with."

You had better hold off on that, Lenoir thought wryly. Aloud, he said, "I suspect what Kody learned at the prison went to motive, which he was able to piece together in conjunction with information we found in Berryvine."

"Well?" The chief spread his hands impatiently. "Don't keep me in suspense. Who do I have to round up?"

"No one. Hardin's killer is already dead. Her name was Zera, known as Lady Zera by those in her social circle."

Reck's eyebrows rose. "Lady Zera? Well, that certainly explains a lot, like why we were called to the scene of a shoot-up at her place last night. Do I have you to thank for that little massacre?"

Lenoir shifted uncomfortably. "I was there, although I only killed one man myself."

"We found two killed by gunfire. The rest were strangled with some sort of barbed rope. Looks like the barbs were poisoned too." The chief narrowed his eyes, scrutinizing Lenoir intently.

"Zera had powerful enemies," said Lenoir, choosing his words carefully. "I stayed out of their way, so long as they were working in my interests. *Our* interests."

The chief frowned. "Let's come back to that in a minute. You want to explain to me why we got word of the incident from a neighbor, and not you? Why didn't you wait for backup before you confronted her? You're too seasoned an officer to be pulling greenhorn crap like that, Lenoir."

I had backup, Chief. Better backup than any hound. "I was in a hurry. A boy's life was at stake."

Reck seemed to accept that. "You knew this Zera, didn't you? Seems to me you've been seen at her salon once or twice in the past." He paused to let that sink in. Lenoir wondered how long the chief had been waiting to spring that little warning on him.

"I knew her well," Lenoir said. There was no point in denying it.

"Why would she want Kody and Hardin dead?"

"I don't know the full story, but she obviously believed they knew something that could connect her to the kidnappings, so she wanted them disposed of."

Reck rubbed his chin thoughtfully. "I wonder how Kody figured it out."

"I'm not sure he did. He might only have sought her

out as a source of information about the Adali. We might never know for certain."

"Wouldn't that be a kick in the ass?" Reck said sourly. "Death by coincidence."

"Kody is dead, then?"

"He's the same. I was talking about Hardin."

Lenoir nodded. "Anyway, I would be surprised if Kody actually knew much about what the kidnappers intended."

"Which is what, exactly? And how was Lady Zera involved?"

"I believe that a small group of Adali was in the process of procuring a very significant favor for someone powerful, in exchange for major land concessions to their clan. Zera was the liaison."

The chief shook his head blankly. "I don't get it. What does that have to do with kidnapping children?"

Lenoir sighed and passed a hand over his eyes again. "I will explain everything, I promise. I came here to file a full report. Better for you to read that. The story is . . . complicated."

To his immense relief, the chief only grunted and said, "Sounds like it."

"I had better get started," Lenoir said, rising. "Have you sent word to Kody's family?"

Reck inclined his head briefly. "They came in on the stagecoach last night. The mother isn't taking it well."

"They never do." Pausing at the door on his way out, Lenoir said, "It has been a privilege to work with you, Chief."

Reck eyed him suspiciously. "Going somewhere, Inspector?"

Lenoir gave a thin smile. "I was only thinking that it has been a very long couple of days."

"That it has," Reck said quietly. "That it has."

Lenoir scanned the cramped lines of his handwriting, reading over the report one last time. He had not bothered to use a scribe. He told himself that was because he needed time to sort through his thoughts, but the truth was that he wanted to be alone while he recorded the depressing history of his investigation. It was so easy now to connect the dots, to trace the constellation among the stars. He spared himself nothing in the retelling, and he was sure that the chief, in reading the report, would shake his head in disgust at Lenoir's incompetence.

Lady Zera's frequent questions surrounding the investigation should have betrayed an unusual interest in the case, Lenoir read. *I should have noticed these signs, but my judgment was clouded by my personal relationship with the accused.* Dipping his quill in ink, he added a note in the margins: *I was also quick to dismiss coincidences that Sergeant Kody remarked upon.* If Kody died, Lenoir wanted it known that the sergeant had not been as blind as his supervisor.

In other details, he was more economical. While he could not avoid mentioning *khekra*, and the intention of Los and his cronies to use Zach in their magic, he did not go into particulars. Let his colleagues get that information from Merden, if they chose to interview him. Spelling it out in his report would make him sound insane, or at least backward and superstitious. That might damage the credibility of everything else in the report, and Lenoir did not want to provide any excuse for the case to remain open. He owed that much to Kody and Hardin. On the matter of *khekra*, therefore, he confined himself to the bare minimum, saying only, *It is a common belief among the Adali that magic can produce curses or windfalls, and such spells often go for a steep price. I have concluded that Los and his follow- ers intended his magic to result in something of great value to the Duke of Warrick, in exchange for which they hoped to secure grazing rights to His Grace's lands.*

Lenoir's eyes paused on the next line. *While the mo- tive is clear, there is no tangible evidence of any contact between the kidnappers and the Duke of Warrick.* He read the words aloud, and they stuck in his throat.

"What did you know, you bastard?" he whispered at the page. He was not sure what he himself believed. It was possible the kidnappers had not yet approached Warrick with their plan, intending to contact him only once they had succeeded. Or Warrick might have been in on it from the start. In the end, what did it matter? Lenoir had no proof. Carelessly accusing Warrick would cause the Metropolitan Police no end of grief, and for what? Even if he was guilty, the odds of him being held to account were virtually nil.

Dipping his quill again, Lenoir underlined the words *tangible evidence*. He was confident that Lendon Reck would understand him perfectly.

No amount of editing, however, would address the most glaring flaw in the report, which was the absence of any mention of Vincent. Nor was it simply a lie of omission; to account for the shoot-up at Zera's, Lenoir had been obliged to fabricate something. His report described an unknown Adal, implied to be a member of the Asis clan, who pursued the kidnappers and picked them off one by one.

If my information is correct, the report said, *the man called Raiyen was exiled from the Asis clan for performing* khekra, *which was forbidden among them. It is my belief that Raiyen's designs were in part intended as an act of atonement, a way of regaining his status within the clan. He reached out to his kinsman and fellow witchdoctor, Los, to assist him in the enterprise. However, if their actions were not sanctioned by the clan elders, the clan could well have taken the law into their own hands, as Adali are frequently known to do, preferring their own traditional justice to the more formal mechanisms here in the Five Villages.*

With any luck, the deaths at Zera's apartments, as well as those at the cathedral, would be explained as an act of vigilante justice. The Metropolitan Police would make some effort to track down the culprit, but the Asis clan would claim to know nothing about it. And they would be telling the truth. It was an unavoidable loose end, but Lenoir was reasonably confident that it would not be enough to prevent the case from being closed.

He gazed at the finalized report for a long moment. Absurd as it was, it felt as if his entire life were on those sheets of parchment. It was the last record he would leave behind.

It was shortly before dusk when Lenoir left the police station. For some reason, he found himself heading for the market square, the place where he had first spoken to Vincent. It seemed like the most appropriate place to meet the spirit again, for the last time.

Lenoir sat on a bench and watched the evening routine unfold. He felt much calmer than he had two nights before, when last he sat here waiting for Vincent to appear. There was no longer anything to fear. It was not that he welcomed death—he would happily have deferred it indefinitely—but he could face it now, serene in the knowledge that Zach was safe. Lenoir had done what he set out to do. *"There is no redemption,"* Vincent had said, but he was wrong. Lenoir had reclaimed something of himself in these, his last hours of life. He was no longer filled with self-loathing. His apathy had given way, if not to peace, then at least to acceptance.

He might have dozed off, for darkness seemed to come upon the square suddenly. Lenoir felt eyes on him, and he twisted in his seat to find Vincent watching him from the shadows. In spite of his resignation, he could not help the spasm of fear that jolted his limbs. Would Vincent speak to him, or simply attack without warning? Belatedly, Lenoir wondered if the market square had been a poor choice of venue after all. *At least my death will cause a spectacle,* he thought wryly. It would be nice to be remembered for *something*.

Vincent sat down on the bench beside Lenoir. He said nothing at first, his uncanny gaze sweeping over the square. He watched the flower merchants and the street musicians, the young couples and the stray dogs, his expression utterly inscrutable. Lenoir would have given anything to hear his thoughts.

"The boy lives?" Vincent asked finally.

"He does, thanks to you."

"I have never used my weapon on a child before. I was not certain he would survive, even for a short time."

There was another stretch of silence. Lenoir said, "You went for Zach instead of Zera. I was . . . surprised."

Vincent looked at him. "As was I."

"Oh?" Lenoir cocked his head. "You were surprised that . . . *it* . . . commanded you to save the boy?"

"It did not."

Lenoir looked at him blankly. "I don't understand."

"It commanded me to kill the woman. The boy . . . that was my own choice." If Lenoir had failed to understand the significance of these words, the look in Vincent's eyes would have driven it home. His gaze burned with emotion—genuine, human emotion—intense and complex and utterly unexpected. There was confusion, excitement, and even a little fear. There was also something more difficult to identify. Pride, perhaps?

"Your *choice*?" Lenoir echoed in disbelief.

"Yes." Vincent's voice was low and intent, as though he were relating a powerful secret.

"You defied it?"

"Not exactly. But I chose."

"I thought you said that your will was not your own?"

"I chose," Vincent repeated, as though to himself. "I decided to act, and it worked. It has never worked before. I stopped trying centuries ago."

"Well," said Lenoir, for lack of anything better.

Vincent looked back out over the square. Lenoir

waited. When several minutes had passed in silence, Lenoir said, "Should we go somewhere else to do this? Can you make it quick?" His voice betrayed him at the last moment, choking off the final word. He just wanted to get it over with.

Vincent shook his head, and for a moment, Lenoir thought it was in response to his question. Then Vincent said, "It no longer seeks your death."

Lenoir stared, certain he had misheard. "What did you say?"

"You are no longer marked." He did not elaborate. His expression was once again inscrutable, his eyes reflecting the world around them without offering a hint of what lay behind.

Lenoir looked into the face that had haunted his nightmares for a decade, and for the first time, he found nothing to fear. Neither did he find anything to celebrate. He was so stunned, so drained, that he could not even rejoice. All he could do was nod, indicating that he understood. That seemed to be enough; Vincent stood.

"Will I see you again?" Lenoir heard himself ask.

Vincent's lip quirked into something just short of a smile. "Let us hope not."

Lenoir started to thank him, but the spirit was already gone. Lenoir sat dazed for a moment. Then he began to shake. He felt weak, as though his bones were melting, leaving only a sack of flesh. He slid onto his side, lying down on the bench, his breathing sounding thickly in his ears, as if he were underwater. He closed his eyes against the harsh glare of the streetlamps. He slept until morning.

Epilogue

Kody, idiot that he was, was trying to stand.

"Just take it easy, Sergeant," the physician said worriedly, reaching out to grab Kody by the arm. "You've been in that bed for a week. Your muscles aren't going to be—"

Kody's knees buckled, forcing Izar to lunge in and catch him. Lenoir did not bother trying to help; there were too many people around the bed as it was. "Don't be a fool," he said irritably. "Hardin's family will understand."

"I'm going," Kody repeated firmly, leaning against the wall as he tested his balance. "I just need a minute."

"You need rest," the physician said, "and plenty of it."

Kody scowled at him. "Didn't you just finish saying that I've been in bed for a week?"

"This is a waste of time," Izar put in with his customary brusqueness. "If Kody says he's going, he's going, so let's get on with it."

"You don't miss a fellow hound's funeral," Kody

said. "It's just not done. Even my parents are going. They're with Hardin's folks right now."

Lenoir rolled his eyes, but Izar was right—there was no point in arguing. Such sentiments were rife in the force. Brothers in arms, or some such drivel.

"You will return to the clinic, though, won't you?" the physician asked, fixing Kody with a stern look.

"What for?"

"Observation. There might be brain damage. Or the wound in your stomach could become infected."

Kody gave an impatient wave. "I know how to look out for gangrene."

"The brain damage may be harder to detect," Lenoir said wryly. "But you have my word, sir, that I will keep an eye on him." He jerked his head over his shoulder, indicating that they should go.

When their carriage pulled up outside the church, Lenoir saw that Kody was right: the entire Metropolitan Police force was there. Even Crears and a couple of the other constables from the outer villages had turned up. Combined with relatives and friends, the little church turned out to be inadequate for the numbers, and many were left to gather in the courtyard, awaiting the burial. Surveying the crowd, Lenoir could not help wondering how many of these same colleagues would have turned up for his own funeral. Even the legendary solidarity among hounds would probably not have been enough to inspire much of a turnout. Hardin might not have been terribly competent, but he had been well liked. Lenoir, on the other hand, had few friends, and no family. He was forced to acknowledge that his death, so narrowly avoided, would have gone largely unlamented.

He hovered awkwardly at the back of the church. There was a place reserved for him up front, along with the chief and the other inspectors, but he did not want to sit among Hardin's family and close friends. He did not belong there; he had barely known the man. Instead he posted himself near the doors, watching the proceedings at a distance.

The priest droned on, as priests do. Lenoir's thoughts were elsewhere, and he did not realize until halfway through the ceremony that Kody was standing right beside him. The sergeant stood rigidly tall, his features set in grim lines. He barely seemed to register what the priest was saying. Perhaps his thoughts were elsewhere too.

"Why were you not seated with the others?" Lenoir asked after the ceremony had ended and they were heading for the courtyard.

Kody glanced at him out of the corner of his eye. "No reason."

Lenoir snorted. "It would have been difficult for you to stand for so long, in your condition. You would not have put yourself through that without a reason."

"What do you want me to say?" Kody growled. "That I feel guilty? Well, I do. Satisfied?"

Lenoir stopped. "Not remotely, Sergeant, for that is a foolish sentiment. You are not responsible for what happened to Hardin."

"Of course I am," Kody said in a heated whisper. "I'm the one who dragged him out there without proper backup."

"He was supposed to *be* your backup."

But Kody was not really listening. "I led him straight into the wolf's den. He didn't even know what he was getting involved in."

"Sergeant, if anyone is responsible for Hardin's death, it is I." Unlike Kody, Lenoir did not trouble to lower his voice. What did he care if someone overheard? It was the truth, spelled out in indelible ink on a sheaf of parchment in Reck's office. "The apothecary told us everything we needed to know. I should have put it together. I *would* have put it together, had I really bothered trying. So if you want to be angry with someone, be angry with me."

Kody's lips pressed into a thin line, and Lenoir could read his thoughts as clearly as if he had spoken. He *was* angry. Bitterly so. But as always, his discipline won out, and he said nothing.

Lenoir nodded. "Good. And while we are clearing the air, Kody, let me say this: the next time you charge off without informing your inspector where you are going, it will be your last day on the force." He paused, adding more gently, "I should not like to have to listen to that priest drone on about *you*."

Kody blinked, taken aback. He opened his mouth as if he would say something, but then closed it again. Rather than stand there while the sergeant cast about for some soppy reply, Lenoir moved off in search of the chief.

People were scattered throughout the courtyard in groups of twos and threes, swapping stories about the deceased, or, if they had not known him well, making generic conversation about the state of criminality in the city. The hounds seemed particularly disposed to this line of thinking, the general consensus being that Kennian was going to the dogs. *Just as well*, Lenoir thought dryly. *Otherwise, you slobs would have to find real work.*

He spied Izar brooding alone near the outer wall, and made his way over. "Why do you not mix with the others?" Lenoir asked.

"You know why, Inspector," Izar said, and Lenoir supposed that was true.

"They will not hold it against you."

Izar shrugged. "Some of them will, but I don't give a damn about that." He looked down at Lenoir, his gaze smoldering with resentment. "It's not them I blame."

Lenoir understood. "Not everyone involved was Adali."

"Most of them were."

"Every race has its bad apples."

"Not every race is judged by them."

There was a stretch of silence. Then Lenoir said, "For what it is worth, Sergeant, I don't think this case proved anything, except that desperate people will do anything to survive. Their methods might have been unusual, but we have seen far worse, and there was certainly nothing uniquely Adali about their motivations. The basic human formula is the same."

Izar made no reply. Lenoir left the sergeant alone.

"Inspector," someone called. Lenoir turned, and it was a struggle to keep the dismay from his face. Kody's father was making his way over.

They had never met, but there was no mistaking him. Jess Kody was every bit as physically imposing as his son, with the same purposeful stride and quietly stubborn set to his jaw. His eyes lacked the fire of the sergeant's gaze, but that might just have been age.

"Sir," Lenoir said awkwardly, holding out his hand. "I am pleased to meet you."

Kody shook his hand and nodded. For a moment, he did not say anything else; he just stood there, staring. Lenoir shifted uncomfortably. After what seemed like an eternity, Jess Kody cleared his throat and said, "I just wanted to thank you."

Lenoir's eyebrows flew up. "Thank me?"

"For everything you're doing for my son."

Instinctively, Lenoir glanced over to where Bran Kody was standing with Hardin's family. The sergeant was looking over at his father, an expression of mild panic on his face, but he obviously did not dare to extract himself from the bereaved parents.

Lenoir had no idea what to say. He could not think of a single thing he had ever done for Bran Kody. His confusion must have shown, for Jess added, "I know he's young to have made sergeant, and he has you to thank for that."

"He has himself to thank. He is young, yes, but he is competent. He earned his place. I merely recommended him for promotion."

Kody nodded. "Bran says you taught him everything he knows. He says you were the best." Lenoir noted the past tense, and was surprised to discover that it bothered him. "He was so excited when he got assigned to you," Kody's father continued relentlessly. "A few years with you, he said, and he'd make inspector. Anyway, with everything that's happened with Sergeant Hardin and all . . ." He glanced back over his shoulder at Hardin's family. "Just makes me realize how proud we are of Bran."

"And so you should be," said a new voice, and Lendon Reck appeared at Lenoir's side. He gripped Jess Kody's hand in a firm handshake. "A fine hound, your son. Wish I had a hundred like him."

Lenoir could have kissed the chief. He wanted nothing more than to end this conversation, to slink away unseen and not have to listen to sugary fantasies about how he was a mentor. He had never been a mentor, to Kody or anyone else.

"Kody is tough as nails," Reck said. "Look at him, up and about after everything that's happened. Gotta admire a hound like that. He'll have my job someday."

Jess Kody was trying not to look pleased. "Anyways," he said gruffly, "I just wanted to say how grateful his mother and I are that he's working with such good people."

"And we're grateful to you," said Reck, "for raising the kind of man who makes such a fine contribution to this city."

And I would be grateful to you both if you ceased this inane prattle before I vomit. Lenoir kept his expression carefully blank, lest it betray his thoughts. He could not help wondering how many times the chief had made this speech, to how many proud fathers. But it was new to Jess Kody, and he appreciated it. He gave

Lenoir and the chief a final handshake before returning to his family and the Hardins.

Lenoir let out a long breath. "I'm glad you came
when you did."

"I could tell you were about ten seconds away from
saying something stupid." Reck fixed him with a stern
expression. "By the sword, you look awful. It's been
almost a week. Have you even slept?"

"Not much," Lenoir admitted. He would have thought
his body would be accustomed to going without sleep by
now, but without the distraction of Lady Zera's salon, the
hours felt longer, heavier. It was not that he avoided sleep,
not anymore. He was no longer plagued by nightmares.
But in their place was a vague anxiety that he could not
identify, a constant buzz in his brain that kept him awake
through the night. He felt restless. Adrift. For years, he
had coasted through life without bothering to make
choices, for he knew them to be meaningless. It was like
window-shopping, looking through thick panes of glass at
things he could never have. Now the glass was gone. Row
upon row of possibilities was laid out before him, and it
was subtly terrifying.

He had made one choice, however, and it felt like a
first step. If he could take a second step, and another
after that, he would find his way eventually. And this
time, he knew where he wanted to go. It was a path he
had abandoned a long time ago, thinking it an illusion.
But he had been wrong. It had been there all this time,
waiting for him.

"I have the warrant," he told Reck, holding up the
sheet of parchment.

Reck grunted and took it from him. He scanned the page with a frown. "This is damn stupid. You know that."

"Feine had a man beaten nearly to death."

"A lovers' squabble. Hardly a menace to society. Anyway, you already made it clear that we're onto him. He'll think twice next time. That should be enough."

"Are you ordering me to drop it?"

"I should. You're going to cause yourself a world of shit, and me too. What exactly are you trying to prove, anyway?"

"Nothing."

"Right. And while we're on the subject of fool's errands, I read your report. Subtlety isn't your strong suit, Lenoir. You practically accused the Duke of Warrick outright."

"Indeed? I seem to recall saying there was no evidence against him. Not yet, at any rate."

Reck stepped forward until his nose was an inch from Lenoir's, and he dropped his voice to a low growl. "I don't know what's gotten into you, but I've got enough crusaders in my kennel, Inspector. If I hear you've been harassing Warrick, it'll be your job."

Lenoir met his gaze unflinchingly. "Are you afraid of him, Chief?"

"Damn right, and so should you be. He could shut down the entire force. I've got a whole city to worry about. If that means I have to leave the high and mighty to their business, then that's how it's got to be."

"For the greater good?" Lenoir asked wryly.

"Something like that, smart-ass."

"And if I were to turn up irrefutable evidence against Warrick?"

Reck shook his head and swore under his breath. "Maybe that blow to your head was worse than you thought. Do I have to spell it out for you? Even if I let you bring him in, no magistrate in this country would prosecute him."

"Perhaps." Lenoir paused, shrugging. "But we are arguing over nothing, Chief. I have no evidence against Warrick in this case, and I doubt I ever will."

Reck was no fool. He narrowed his eyes. *"In this case?"*

Lenoir only smiled. "As for this"—he held up the warrant—"I will deal with it first thing tomorrow."

Reck sighed resignedly. "Take Innes, and maybe Izar too. In case His Lordship resists."

"He will not. It would be unseemly. He will be haughty and disdainful all the way to his cell, I think."

"Still, make sure you have enough backup. I've had enough of burying hounds for a while."

Lenoir nodded. He looked back down at the warrant, unable to suppress a smirk. *Lord Alvin Feine*, it read. *Attempted murder.* It would never stick, of course, but Lenoir was confident he had enough for severe battery. The attempted murder charge was a bluff, designed to rattle His Lordship's cage. And if it sent a message to the rest of the nobility, well—that was a nice bonus.

The crowd began to move out of the courtyard, heading for the cemetery around back. Lenoir followed, but his mind was already elsewhere. He hoped

the burial would not take too long, for there was one
more thing he needed to do.

Lenoir drew his horse up outside the forbidding gate
of Castle Warrick. He glanced up at the sky. A dark
belly of clouds was gathering, threatening snow. He
hoped his errand would be through before the storm
broke, for he had no desire to ride all the way across
town in the wet. Of course, his errand might be through
before it began; there was a good chance he would not
be admitted to the duke's sight at all. Perhaps that
would not even be such a bad thing. He risked the
chief's wrath by being here. If he were turned away,
through no fault of his own—surely the mere attempt
would be enough to satisfy his conscience? Then again,
perhaps not. Lenoir scarcely knew what to expect of
his own conscience anymore. They had been strangers
for so long.

A single guard manned the gatehouse—the same
man Lenoir had met on his previous visit. *The would-be
hound,* he recalled. It gave him an idea.

"Afternoon, Inspector," the guard called as he
stepped out onto the drive. "Is His Grace expecting
you?"

"I sincerely doubt it. And I would appreciate it if
you could show me in without announcing me."

The guard's eyebrows flew up, and he gave a nervous little titter. "It, uh, doesn't quite work like that,
Inspector. His Grace always insists on his visitors being
announced."

"I'm sure. But these are exceptional circumstances."

He leaned down over his horse's neck. Taking the cue, the guard approached warily, on the pretext of taking Lenoir's bridle. "Make this happen, and I can promise you a position at the Metropolitan Police." As a clerk, most likely, but Lenoir did not feel compelled to go into details.

The guard eyed him skeptically. "Yeah? How do I know you'll follow through? Because if I do what you ask, I'll be needing a new job, right enough."

"I can only offer you my word. Whether that is enough for you depends on how badly you want to be a hound."

The guard hesitated. He glanced back at the manor. "All right," he said in a low voice, "but if this doesn't work, I'll still hold you to that promise."

"Fair enough." Lenoir dismounted.

The guard showed him to the same study as before, murmuring into the ear of the butler as they walked. The servant frowned, but before he could object, the guard beat a hasty retreat. The butler muttered to himself and left.

Lenoir waited. A few minutes later, he heard a familiar voice on the other side of the door.

"What do you mean, you don't know who he is? This is absurd!"

"I'm sorry, Your Grace. He wouldn't give his name."

"Then why in the flaming below did you let him in?"

"It wasn't . . . that is, I didn't . . . Let me just fetch the guard. . . ."

"Durian's blood! I don't have time for this!"

The door burst open, and the Duke of Warrick

charged in. He drew up short when he saw Lenoir, his eyes narrowing in fury. "You."

"Good afternoon, Your Grace. I am terribly sorry for the subterfuge, but I thought it unlikely that you would admit me."

"You were clever enough to realize that, but not clever enough to realize that I'd just have you thrown out?"

Lenoir glanced at the butler, who hovered uncertainly behind Warrick. At a word, he would fetch the guards. Lenoir had to be quick. "I will spare you the trouble, Your Grace. What I have to say will only take a moment. You need not even respond, if you do not wish."

Warrick snorted incredulously. "Why, thank you." He made a peremptory gesture with his hand, and the butler disappeared. "You have nerve, Inspector, I will give you that."

I have faced far worse than you, Your Grace. Aloud, Lenoir said, "Lady Zera is dead."

"Indeed?" Warrick replied blandly. Either he already knew or he genuinely did not care. Perhaps both.

"So are her followers. Her designs are undone."

Warrick flicked an impatient glance at the ceiling. "Your moment is almost up, Inspector. What has this to do with me?"

"We both know the answer to that. You agreed to provide Los's clan with a significant parcel of land, in exchange for his efforts to resurrect your dead son. Zera was the go-between. Whether she came to you first, or the other way around, it does not matter."

Warrick folded his arms, regarding Lenoir with a

bored look. "You came here merely to repeat your absurd allegations? You waste my time and your own."

"I came here to tell you that I *know*." Lenoir paused, wrestling with the anger that threatened to spill over into his voice. "I know you conspired with Zera, and I strongly suspect you have other designs that are every bit as shadowy. The signs are everywhere, for anyone who cares to see them. Your business dealings are highly profitable, yet invisible. No friends, no business associates, yet you protest how busy you are. Anyone who has met you can see you are not a man of leisure, but no one can say how you occupy your time. It is all highly suspicious, Your Grace."

"And yet you are the only one to remark upon it."

"I doubt that. Perhaps I am just the only one who is making an issue of it."

"And where does that leave you, I wonder?" Warrick asked, his eyes glittering dangerously.

Lenoir shrugged. "I cannot prove anything, as you well know, but the moment I can . . ."

Warrick laughed. It was a harsh, gravelly sound, as though his throat were unaccustomed to it. "Is that meant to be a threat?"

"Certainly not. I am in no position to threaten you. But you are not as untouchable as you believe, and one day, I intend to prove it."

Warrick's smile did not waver. "How very heroic. It reminds me of the time my young son informed me that he wanted to be a dragon slayer when he grew up. Let me tell you what I told him, Inspector: be very careful you don't get burned."

Lenoir inclined his head gravely. "That sounds like good advice, Your Grace."

Warrick picked up a small bell and rang for the butler. The servant appeared almost immediately; Lenoir hoped for his sake he had not overheard anything. "I bid you good afternoon, Inspector," Warrick said, "and the very best of luck in your quest."

Lenoir followed the butler out of the manor and down the drive, ignoring the sharp looks the man directed his way. It had begun to snow. Thin, hard beads of ice pelted Lenoir from above, freezing the thinly covered crown of his head. A dark sky hunkered just above the rooftops, settling in for a siege. It would be a long, cold ride.

Lenoir turned up his collar and thanked God he had a good coat.

ABOUT THE AUTHOR

E. L. Tettensor likes her stories the way she likes her chocolate: dark, exotic, and with a hint of bitterness. She has visited fifty countries on five continents, and brought a little something back from each of them to press inside the pages of her books. She lives with her husband in Brooklyn, New York.